A
Harlem
Wedding

A
Harlem
Wedding

A Novel

Tiffany L. Warren

WILLIAM MORROW
An Imprint of HarperCollinsPublishers

For Yolande, who was always worthy

A
Harlem
Wedding

PART I

Chapter One

April 1920
Brooklyn, New York

Papa says the only way for colored people to have equality is to agitate for it. Today his agitation includes my senior promenade at the Brooklyn Girls' High School. Since it concerns me, it would be nice if Papa cared about my wishes on these matters.

He. Does. Not.

I have no desire to protest about those white girls banning us from their little old dance. I'm perfectly fine with having our own private celebration, and I told Papa as much when I mentioned that the white students had voted on whether we'd be allowed to attend.

By an overwhelming majority it had been decided that us colored girls would be excluded from the dance. This surprised me, but maybe it shouldn't have, especially since we'd been denied a vote. Papa said we'd been disenfranchised.

As usual, when it comes to the color line, I could fall out in the middle of the floor, scream or cry bloody murder, and it would make no difference at all to Papa. He and his cronies were going to write their letters. This time to the principal, the superintendent, the mayor, God, and everybody else.

Now, Papa is fully energized after a dinner of roast beef and vegetables as he paces in front of the dining room table where Mama sits quietly. His trudging back and forth makes my insides tumble and my head pound, so I stay a safe distance away on the living room sofa. I wish I hadn't had that second slice of cake as now the entire meal rests too heavily in my stomach.

"I will have Miss Fauset get the addresses of all the families with colored girls graduating," Papa barks in his typical, all-business, gruff way of speaking. "So that I can assure we are all aligned in this conflict."

Mama looks up from the letter she's been reading all evening, perhaps annoyed at Papa's interruption, but if she is I cannot tell by her expression. Mama's serene smile is fixed upon her stunningly gorgeous face.

No matter what chaos Papa causes or chicanery I find myself embroiled in, Mama's smile hardly ever changes. It could be that her stoicism is the mark of a dutiful wife and mother. Or it could have something to do with the nerve pills she takes that she doesn't think I know about.

Besides, I don't know why Papa's discussing this with Mama anyway. He's decided the task of finding the parents' addresses is for Miss Jessie Fauset, his literary editor at *The Crisis*, not Mama. Because he's lumped this affair into the oppression-of-the-people bucket, and Miss Fauset handles these kinds of things for Papa. The struggle things.

"Are you sure the other parents want to make such a big fuss about this, Will?" Mama asks, wringing her hands, already getting worked up about it.

I can see the lines of frustration on Papa's forehead as he furrows his brow, even though I think Mama's question makes plenty good sense. I know for certain that my best friend Margaret's parents aren't agitators. Her father runs a successful business and has both black and tan customers. He may not want to lose any money to one of Papa's protests.

"If they don't then they must be made to understand what's happening here," Papa says, his tone matching the exasperation on his face. "We cannot stand for any discrimination against our daughters. They have toiled at their studies as diligently as the white scholars and have paid their school fees."

I wish I could sink into the couch cushions and disappear. I may or may not have toiled very much. But it isn't my fault. I never wanted to go to the Brooklyn Girls' High School in the first place. I wanted to finish my classes in England at the Bedales School.

But Papa had given me a grand lecture about how I hadn't applied myself, because no great talent had emerged from that investment in my education. If you ask me, my extraction from Bedales had more to do with how much it cost for me and Mama to live abroad while he stayed here in Brooklyn than it had to do with any lack of unique gifts on my part.

At any rate, when Papa snatched me away from my friends at Bedales, I did not have quite the number of classes I needed to graduate. Papa had waged a war at my enrollment into the Brooklyn Girls' High School to ensure that I wasn't left behind while my friends went off to college.

Poor Mr. Felter, our principal, probably still hasn't recovered from that initial encounter with Papa. And now he's embroiled in another battle.

"I will get the addresses tomorrow, Papa," I say to save Mama from more of Papa's explaining. And to rescue Miss Fauset from this task that doesn't have anything to do with *The Crisis*.

Papa turns to look at me as if he's only now remembered I'm here. He gives me the beginning of a grin that doesn't fully bloom. That's enough, I suppose. He's rarely pleased enough to give a full smile. I will take this over his ranting.

"Very good, Yolande. I am glad you see the importance of this."

"Yes, Papa. I do."

I don't dare admit I'd rather we have a separate senior promenade for the colored girls. The senior committee chose the Hotel Margaret (not named after my friend, ha) and everyone knows they don't want us there anyway. So, why can't we just go to Harlem and dance all night?

"Mr. Felter is determined to shirk his responsibility to you and the rest of the colored students by saying the promenade is a private social event where he has no jurisdiction," Papa continues sermonizing. "He has drawn the color line before, and he must be stopped."

But next year I won't even be at this school, and this will be a fading memory. I wish I was attending Columbia or New York University, but Papa has arranged for me to attend Fisk University, his alma mater. So that's decided. No one will remember me at the Brooklyn Girls' High School. And if by chance I am remembered, I do not want it to be for Papa's fight with Mr. Felter.

But I don't say any of this, because for now, Papa is pleased with my initiative and support of the struggle. I settle for this tiny approval, since there is nothing I can do to stop this effort anyhow. The train has left the station, so Mr. Felter may as well get off the tracks unless he wants to be run right over.

"What infuriates me most," Papa says as he finally sits at the table, signaling the end of the speech (for now), "is that I am certain it's not the girls they're concerned about having at the promenade. It's their escorts. And I will not allow these valiant and gifted young men, who have been hand-selected by careful mothers, to be treated like they'd rape and pillage their precious ivory-skinned daughters."

Mama glances at me, her lips curving into a wry smile. Her expression tells me Papa doesn't know our secret, and I am glad about that. He might be disappointed to know that I do not currently have an escort to the senior promenade. George Cuffee was my intended date, but he's attending some unimportant family function out of town. Well, as far as I'm concerned, it's unimportant, but George disagrees. Abandoning me at the last minute is unforgivable, especially since I have not yet found a replacement, and the dance is less than two weeks away.

Mama says she and her friends will find a suitable escort, but I don't know if I believe them. George is the only decent boy who wanted to ask me. The rest of them are all terrified of Papa.

"Yolande, are you still sleeping over with Margaret tomorrow night?" Mama asks timidly, knowing exactly how Papa feels about me spending the night outside our home.

"Yes. We're going to shop for new shoes to wear with our promenade dresses. And stockings too."

"And you will be home Sunday morning, before they attend church as a family?" Papa asks.

The plan had been for me to go with them because there are plenty of potential escorts at the Welmons' AME church. Since I go to school with all girls and hardly ever attend a church service, it is difficult for any boy to be in my company long enough to find me interesting.

"I think it'll be fine just this one time, Will," Mama says, coming to the rescue (thank goodness). "Many of our friends attend that same church."

"I do not care what many people do," Papa says as his fist comes crashing down onto the table.

"But Papa, I love going places with Margaret and Anna. They are the closest thing I have to sisters." My voice is whiny, but I can't help it. Papa is making a beggar out of me. "Won't you make an exception this one time?"

"It would do Yolande some good to socialize with her friends. And the Welmons' daughters are good girls."

Papa's lips become a thin, tight line. He never likes being defied, but on the rare occasion when Mama and I stand in unity, we are a great team.

"Very well. I suppose it can't hurt. She is almost an adult and should be able to distinguish between fact and fable."

I give Papa a gracious and adoring gaze and feel fortunate that he cannot read my thoughts. If he could he'd know that I care little about fact or fable when it comes to church. Papa needn't worry about that at all. I'm going to that church for the boys.

* * *

IT ALWAYS FEELS strange sitting with the Welmon family on their church pew. They attend Mother AME Zion Church in Harlem and when I visit, I squeeze between Margaret and Anna, to Anna's irritation. Mostly because Margaret and I whisper the entire service while Anna tries to look cute.

We are an interesting trio, Margaret, Anna, and I. Margaret is tall, lean, and elegant with her mother's lighter-than-a-paper-bag skin tone and pretty features. Her height and slim shape make her look much older than eighteen years, and those huge almond-shaped eyes intrigue all the boys.

Anna is slim like Margaret, but she and I are closer to the same height. Both sisters have those beautiful eyes, but Anna is dark, like her father.

And then, there's me. I have my own assets, and I am smart enough to leverage them once the boys realize they don't have a chance with Margaret and happen to look my way. Like the women in my father's family, I have a round face with sleepy eyelids, and fair skin. My curves and cushion are in all the right places, so I've been told, but I'd be fine if there was a little less cushion.

Since my family doesn't attend church services, I have learned by watching Margaret how to have the appropriate responses when the minister is preaching. I clap at the opportune times and even throw in an *amen* or two. At least they don't go to one of those shouting churches where people fall out in the aisles when they feel touched by the spirit. I visited one of those with another friend and while I was highly entertained, I was also a little frightened. What if that spirit jumped on me?

Papa had insisted I didn't need to worry about that, because most of the folk being touched by the spirit had just worked themselves into an emotional frenzy. But I'm not certain that he has all the answers on this subject. I was there, and it looked real to me.

Margaret nudges me in the ribs with her pointy elbow and I stifle a yelp. Then Anna nudges me for almost yelping.

"There's Charles," Margaret whispers.

I glance in the direction she's pointing, and there is Charles Waters, looking debonair and rich. And he is both. His family has more money than they can even spend. Mama says it will be a coup if Margaret gets a marriage proposal out of him, because his mother has other plans for her son. But I don't tell Margaret this nugget. Besides, who's thinking about marriage right now except our mothers?

"Who's that sitting next to him?" I whisper back.

The young man, whom I've never seen before, is very handsome even from across the sanctuary. He's got a pretty, toothy smile and perfect eyebrows. I have a thing about a boy's eyebrows, especially when they take time to groom them.

"That must be his musician cousin visiting from out of town."

"Musician? He can't be much older than we are," I say, trying to get a better look at the boy's features without obviously staring.

Anna glares at me and Margaret, but Margaret just rolls her eyes at her older sister. I don't roll anything, because Anna's sharp elbows are poised to nudge me again for being too noisy during the sermon.

We quiet down and pretend to listen although now I'm excited to get to the benediction. During the spring, their congregation usually leaves for lunch or dinner and comes back for an evening service. While we're on the break, the young people try to get away to go have a bite to eat at the Y, and maybe even walk around Harlem, feeling fine in our church clothes. No matter what, I get to spend the entire day in Harlem with the Welmons until we all take the streetcar back to Brooklyn in the evening.

As soon as the preacher says amen, Margaret pulls a tube of lipstick out of her purse and hands it to me after slathering a layer of red all over her pouty lips.

"Am I not stunning?" she asks as she toots her pout in my direction.

I look down at the tube in my hands. "You are perfectly divine, but do you have one that's less red? A pink perhaps?"

"Oh, does Papa's little girl want a sweet candy pink?" Margaret teases. "Let me see."

She digs around in her purse and produces another, less harlot-like shade. This one I accept and dab a tiny amount on my lips instead of the slathering that Margaret put on hers.

"Now we're both gorgeous," Margaret says with a shimmy that I don't think is quite appropriate for church. "Let's go find Charles."

Old sour Anna stands in Margaret's path as we try to exit the pew. She takes one look at Margaret's lipstick and shakes her head. "Where are you two going?"

"Move Anna," Margaret says. "You know where we're going."

"Mmm-hmm. It's the Lord's day, so make sure you're not up to no good. You too, Yolande," Anna fusses, sounding like somebody's mama. Just not mine.

Margaret gives Anna a rude shove on the top of her shoulder, and she moves out of our path. Finally, away from the watchful eyes of Anna and Mr. Welmon, we make a beeline for Charles and his grinning companion.

"Wouldn't it be grand if we had cousins escorting us to the promenade?" Margaret says wistfully as we move through the groups of chatting churchgoers.

"Yes, but I thought he was only visiting." I'm not going to get my hopes up on a migrant colored boy.

Charles's eyes light up when he sees Margaret crossing the room. I love how obsessed he seems to be with her, like he can't get enough of looking at her. Papa never looks at Mama like he just wants to eat her up, and they've been married forever. I wonder if he ever did. Does getting married to someone change that? I hope not. I think I want someone to gaze at me like that always.

When we make it over to where the boys are standing, Margaret gives Charles's hand a chaste squeeze and then steps back so that no one can say we're being fast. We don't need anyone insisting that we have any extra chaperones.

Up close, Charles's companion is even more handsome, and so tall. He towers right over me, and I don't mind it one bit. His eyes widen at my coquettish smile, and then he bashfully looks away. I was hoping he'd be a smooth charmer like Charles.

"Are you going to introduce us to your cousin?" Margaret asks.

Charles looks confused for a second. "Oh, this isn't my cousin, this is Jimmie Lunceford. He's in my cousin's band. Jimmie this is my girl, Margaret Welmon, and her friend Yolande Du Bois."

Margaret beams, probably at being properly titled *my girl* by Charles. Jimmie struggles to maintain eye contact with me, but he does give us a smile. My, he has pretty teeth. I bet he doesn't eat sweets or have any cavities at all.

"Pleased to meet you both," Jimmie says.

"The pleasure is all mine," I say, easing closer so Jimmie knows I mean it.

"Would y'all like to go have lunch at the Y before second service?" Margaret asks. "It's so nice outside. We can probably get an ice cream too."

It tickles me how Margaret never waits for Charles to ask her out to any amusement. She lets him know what's going to happen and he falls right in line.

But this time, Charles exchanges a fidgety glance with Jimmie. Is he going to turn down Margaret's request for lunch? I hope not, because I'm hungry too. Whether or not the boys are buying, I need to eat before being forced to sit through more church.

"You know I'd love to go," Charles explains, his hand lightly touching Margaret's now angrily folded arms, "but I'm going with my cousin Andy and Jimmie. Their band came all the way from Denver, and they're making a phonograph recording at the Columbia Graphophone Company."

I feel my eyes stretch wide, while Margaret keeps pouting. "That sounds like fun," I say. "Will you be playing an instrument, Jimmie? Or do you sing? What kind of music is it?"

"I play a whole slew of instruments, but today I'm going to be playing the alto saxophone," Jimmie says.

Jimmie's shyness just melts right away, as he seems to stand even taller with his square shoulders and muscled arms. I can hardly breathe, he's so handsome, but I manage to maintain my composure.

"It's jazz music," Charles says, now trying to get back in the conversation with someone, because Margaret has all but turned her back to him.

"Well, come on then, Yolande," Margaret says in a huff, not at all impressed by this talk of instruments and jazz. "Maybe we can find our own lunch. Perhaps George will buy us sandwiches."

George W. Cuffee. I don't want to go to lunch with him, after he's left me without an escort to the promenade. I cannot cut him off completely, though, because Papa thinks he's a fine young man.

If only Papa hadn't launched into his battle formation. Then, I wouldn't need an escort at all. But Papa takes every fight to the bitter end, because he's a leader of the colored people from America to Liberia, especially the brilliant ones he's dubbed the Talented Tenth.

Well, maybe he isn't the leader of everyone, but that's sure what it feels like. It's why the old ladies in the neighborhood snitch about my every move. I can't blow a bubble without Papa hearing it pop.

Before I realize what's happening, the room starts spinning, and I stumble to the left a few steps. Thank goodness for Jimmie Lunceford and his strong arms. He catches me right before I tumble into the back of the pews.

"Are you all right, Miss Yolande?" Jimmie asks. "It is a little hot in here, do you need to sit down?"

"No, I'm quite all right, thank you." I'm not all right, though, I'm starving, and the anxiety of Papa and the promenade just about overwhelmed me in the moment. But I smooth the wrinkles from the front of my dress and beam at Jimmie. He deserves it, for saving me and all.

"Maybe they can go with us, Charles," Jimmie says, his hand still touching my elbow, and steadying me. "There's room for spectators to listen to the band while we record."

For some reason, Charles seems annoyed at this suggestion. Perhaps he doesn't want us tagging along. Maybe he's not as mesmerized with Margaret as I thought.

"I wish they could, but they need to be back for church this evening. We might not make it in time," Charles says.

"Where is the recording taking place?" Margaret asks. "Maybe we can catch part of it and then leave early."

Charles sucks in a sharp breath and shakes his head. "Way down in lower Manhattan at the Woolworth Building. There won't be time to find lunch, get all the way there, listen, and come back."

Margaret lifts an eyebrow at Charles. "Do you have another girl meeting you at the recording?" she asks. Charles's mounting protests must have made her suspicious.

Jimmie and I exchange glances, and I wonder if he's thinking what I'm thinking. Now I wish Margaret and Charles weren't here so that we could get properly acquainted.

"There's no other girl, Margaret. I just don't want you to get in any trouble right before the senior promenade. What if your father makes you stay home as punishment?"

Now, this is funny. The way our mothers have painstakingly planned and purchased dresses, and given us money for shoes, hairpins, and what have you, there is no colored father in Brooklyn who would dare impose such a punishment. Not even my papa. The wrath of their wives would be too great.

"You let me worry about how my father will or won't punish me," Margaret says with a sass in her tone. "I think I'd quite like to hear a jazz recording."

"And it doesn't start until two o'clock, so we have time to get a sandwich if we hurry," Jimmie says. "I think Miss Yolande might need something to eat."

Charles let out a defeated sigh. "Okay, Margaret, you two can come, but when Mr. Welmon and Dr. Du Bois start roaring, don't say I didn't warn you."

"We'll worry about that later," Margaret says, her excitement returning. "Let's go."

"What will we tell your mother when we don't make it back to church?" I ask, now feeling just a twinge of worry. Mr. Welmon doesn't roar like Papa. The promenade might not be canceled, but I am not in the mood for one of his speeches about decorum, and the great woman I should be growing into.

"You know what?" Margaret says, with her nonexistent bosom poked as far forward as she can muster. "I am just going to tell her that we're going out with Charles for dinner, and that we will be back before church is over. Wait here."

We all watch Margaret disappear into the crowd of milling congregants. I turn to Jimmie to spark a conversation and surprisingly he's already gazing at me. That makes my heart race, because the only other boy I've ever caught staring at me is George.

"So, Jimmie, are you attending college in Denver while you travel with the band? Did you have to take time away from your studies?" I ask, simply marveling that he's here in Harlem, because Denver seems like another country, it's so far away.

Charles covers his face with his hand, but I can tell he's snickering while Jimmie looks good and nervous.

"I mean, it's okay if you're not in college," I say, thinking maybe he's embarrassed about that. "It's not for everyone, although you can't tell my papa that. Every issue of *The Crisis* is full of talk about graduations and the colored colleges."

"Your father is *that* Dr. Du Bois? From *The Crisis*?" Jimmie asks, his eyes wide as saucers. "My father reads that magazine religiously. He saves every copy."

"Yep, that's her papa," Charles says, clutching his side trying to hold in his laughter. "Are you gonna tell her, Jimmie?"

"Tell me what?"

"Oh." Jimmie stares at the ground bashfully. "He just wants me to tell you that I'm only a sophomore in high school."

"You must be joking," I say, unable to believe this. "Only a sophomore, but here making a record with a real jazz band?"

Jimmie's head pops up, now with a look of pride on his face. "I'm only seventeen, but I'm good enough to be in the George Morrison Jazz Orchestra. We were supposed to be going to Europe after this recording, but instead we've booked six weeks at the Carlton Terrace."

"I am impressed, Jimmie. That is amazing." He must play exceptionally well to be allowed in a traveling band at this young age. "Doesn't your mother fret over you? I don't think my mama would let me go to the end of our street at seventeen."

"She does, but she trusts Mr. Morrison to keep a close eye on me, and I don't get up to mischief anyhow."

"You're a good boy, Jimmie?" I ask, teasing with a flirtatious wink. "Can't I convince you otherwise?"

"Maybe," Jimmie says, blushing again.

Charles rolls his eyes at our flirting just as an irritated-looking Margaret rejoins our group, with Anna in tow.

"All right, I'm ready to go," Margaret says. "My mother is making me bring *her* along."

Jimmie's face is full of questions. "This is Margaret's older sister, Anna," I explain. "She does go out with us sometimes."

"Correct. Because you two can't be trusted," Anna declares with a motherly glare over the top of her eyeglasses. "Now what are we getting into? Are we really going to dinner?"

"You've muscled your way into our afternoon." Margaret's scowl is deep, and her cheeks are fiery red. "But you don't get to ask questions. You just follow along and keep quiet."

My stomach lets out an anxious growl and instinctively I touch my tummy. This tickles Charles and Jimmie, so I'm not sure if I should feel embarrassed, but I do.

"Let's get Miss Yolande some lunch. Please," Jimmie says as he offers his arm for me to grab. "Hold on to me so you don't go stumbling again. Just until we find you a sandwich."

I feel a different kind of swooning when I wrap my arm in Jimmie's. A different kind of warmth, and a different kind of hunger.

And Jimmie . . . well, he sure seems ready to feed me.

Chapter Two

April 1920
Manhattan, New York

I don't know what I was expecting when Jimmie said we could watch while his jazz orchestra made a recording at the Columbia Graphophone Company, but it certainly wasn't being sequestered in a tiny room behind glass. There's hardly any space to move around at all, and there aren't even enough chairs for all of us. Charles stands while Margaret, Anna, and I take turns sitting in the two hard wooden seats.

"I thought it would be more glamorous than this," I say as I give up my chair to Anna and stand close to the glass.

I wave and smile at Jimmie, not wanting him to know anything feels less than perfect. He was so excited to invite us here, and he's just so handsome holding his saxophone with all those grown-up musicians.

"Move over some so I can see," Anna fusses.

"You hear with your ears Anna," I respond just as saucily. "You don't need to see anything or anyone."

"Well, I certainly don't want to stare at your juicy behind the whole time," Anna snaps.

I give my juicy behind a wiggle just for Anna's viewing pleasure. Margaret and Charles crack up laughing at this, but Anna huffs and puffs.

"You could've stayed at church," Margaret tells her, "but you tagged along trying to be nosy. So just hush."

"They can't hear us," Anna says. "That's what their band leader said. The glass is soundproof."

"Well, I want to hear *them*," I quip as I wave at Jimmie again. He smiles and winks at me, so he must not be able to tell we're snapping at one another.

The band sits in a half circle with the band leader, Mr. Morrison, in the center holding a violin and a bow. He must play and direct them at the same time. And there's a young woman on the piano behind the band. Right in the front of the room, near the glass window, is a small recording machine atop a wooden table.

Mr. Morrison's right hand rises, and all the musicians sit at attention. "Everybody ready to hit it?" he asks them. "We're going to do three takes, but we only need to get to three if the first two aren't good."

"Boy, I sure hope they get it done in one take," Anna says. "I'm ready to go."

"Hush," Margaret hisses.

"Instruments up," Mr. Morrison says as he brings his violin to his chin and lifts his bow into the air. "Let's help Jimmie impress the young lady, huh?"

It tickles me to see Jimmie blush and glance at his feet. He's so bashful and it's the cutest thing ever. But it's only for a moment, because in a flash the music starts.

Something seems to come alive in Jimmie when the music begins. He doesn't look or play like a seventeen-year-old kid. Plus, he keeps glancing across the room at me, like he's playing just for my pleasure. My goodness, I think I can feel it in my soul—like we're connected.

I bob my head and dip my shoulders in time to the music and that seems to spur him on. His fingers fly like crazy, and he inches to the edge of his seat. The more I move, the more *he* moves, so I dance and dance until it feels like we're the only ones in the room.

Then, the song is over, and Mr. Morrison turns to us and takes a bow.

"We should let Jimmie have a young lady visit every time, huh?" Mr. Morrison asks the band, making Jimmie blush again. "You gave us something extra today, son."

I just clap and cheer. If that something extra was because of little ole me, I'll come to every one of his recordings.

* * *

ON THE STREETCAR ride back to Harlem, the excitement of the day starts to wane as I ponder my dilemma. I still don't have an escort for my promenade. I peek at Charles and Margaret, practically joined at the hip, and imagine myself alone with no date. Maybe we should've gone back to church this evening where there were some potential escorts instead of running off on an adventure.

And poor Jimmie. His knee bounces like crazy. I hope I'm not making him uncomfortable with my silence, especially since he's shown me such a perfectly good time today.

"You nervous?" I ask as I drag my gaze away from Margaret and Charles to look up into Jimmie's handsome face.

"Uh, no. Why do you ask that?"

I grin as I point at his knee, still bouncing.

He looks down at it like he hadn't even noticed. "Maybe a little," he says, before forcing his knee to quit.

"Why?"

"Well, you were talking before, and now you're quiet. I thought maybe I did something. Or didn't do something."

"Oh no. You're great," I say scooting closer to him. "This might be the best day I've had all year."

He shudders when I let my hand glide over his knee before resting it in the crook of his arm. I feel his pulse race and his breaths get shallow. This might be more than nerves, and I am pleased at the effect I'm having on him. He studies my face, like he's trying to remember this moment.

"This is the best day I've ever had," Jimmie manages between ragged breaths.

"Ever?"

He looks away, like if he doesn't, he might explode. Then his knee starts bouncing. And he forces it to stop. Again.

"Yes."

"Even better than a birthday party with your favorite cake?" I ask as I gently take his face and turn it back toward me. I don't want him to look away.

He only nods his response.

"Even better than your first time kissing a girl?" I ask.

His eyes widen, and then I wonder if he's ever kissed a girl. He's so handsome that I'm sure some pretty girl must have pulled him behind the bushes and stolen a kiss even if he hadn't gotten up the nerve.

"Yeah," he says, finding his voice, now heavy and full of longing. "Even better than that."

"Then today was worth it, even though I'm still in a pickle."

"Is that why you've been quiet?" he asks, taking my hand from his face and putting it in my lap.

"Mmm-hmm."

"What kind of pickle?"

"I was supposed to be visiting church with Margaret to find an escort to the senior promenade."

"Oh. You're not there every Sunday, then?" His poor knee starts bouncing again.

"No. We live all the way in Brooklyn, but Papa doesn't care too much for church services anyway," I explain.

"I can't believe there aren't any boys at your school to escort you. Pretty as you are."

"You think I'm pretty?"

"You are."

Now, for the first time today, I feel shy and look away from Jimmie's searching eyes. "Even if all the boys thought the way you do, there aren't any at my school. I go to an all-girls high school."

"Well, when is the promenade?"

"In ten days, I'm afraid."

"I'll still be here in ten days. I can escort you if you want."

"Would you really? But you'd have to get a new suit. Everyone else will be wearing new things."

"I have money," Jimmie declares proudly.

"But won't your sweetheart back in Denver be jealous?" I ask the question that's been bothering me. "I would be."

"I don't have a sweetheart back in Denver."

I burst into a flurry of giggles as I pull Jimmie close, not caring one bit about sour-faced Anna. This is just too good to be true. I was worried for nothing.

"Well, then that's all settled. You can be my escort. I'd like that."

"All right."

"But you must meet my papa first. Will you come to our home for dinner this week?"

Jimmie's eyes dance with delight. "Of course. I'd love to meet the famous Dr. Du Bois."

I only hope that after our dinner, Jimmie still looks this way, and that he still wants to take me to the promenade. That he continues to think I'm pretty and doesn't become aware of all my flaws.

Because I cannot promise that dinner with Papa will be delightful.

Chapter Three

April 1920
Brooklyn, New York

I thought it would be nice to have fresh flowers for our dinner this evening, to lift everyone's mood. And by everyone, I mean Papa. So, I went to the market earlier and got a nice bouquet of tulips and daisies. They're bright and exude friendliness, but I can't quite get the flowers to look the way I imagined them. I've rearranged them multiple times to no avail. One of the tulips keeps drooping over to one side, making the entire bunch look lopsided.

"What's this all about?" Papa mumbles as he trudges through the dining room, flipping through the pages of the latest issue of *The Crisis*.

"Didn't Mama tell you?" I ask, knowing full well she didn't. We wanted it to be a surprise, but now with his gruff mood, I'm reconsidering. "We're having a dinner guest."

"She did not tell me we were having company. Since you're so concerned with this centerpiece, I'm assuming it's your guest," Papa says as he sits at the head of the table and folds the magazine shut.

"It's a new friend. His name is James Lunceford, and he's going to escort me to the senior promenade."

Papa takes a moment, strokes the bottom of his goatee—thinking. Then he frowns.

"I don't know any Luncefords," he says.

"He's not from Brooklyn. He's from Denver, so that's why you don't know him."

Papa shakes his head. "Denver? Out of the question."

"Papa, why don't you meet him first, before you say no? I met him at church."

Papa lifts one skeptical eyebrow. "And what does that indicate?"

"Oh, nothing I suppose, but he's very nice. I'd just like you to get to know him before you write him off."

He smirks and folds his arms across his midsection. "What, pray tell, happened to George?"

"He abandoned me at the last moment and left me with no escort to the promenade. He has to go to an out-of-town family function."

"And this young man is the replacement?"

Papa's question is a loaded one. George has been circling around the subject of serious courtship. Of course, I have college in front of me, so marriage is a long way off, but in Papa's opinion (Mama's too) it doesn't hurt to have proper suitors lined up for the inevitable.

"He's certainly replacing George as my promenade escort, Papa." I keep my eyes fixed on the bouquet of flowers.

Papa makes a grunting sound. "Don't you think George might be hurt to know his sweetie found another young man to escort her to the promenade, when she could have simply had a nice evening with her friends?"

My hands fall away from the vase as I meet Papa's gaze with an incredulous look.

"That's not fair, Papa. That's not fair at all." My voice trembles and hitches with anger and frustration. "George and I are only friends. And he's more your friend than he is mine."

"Don't get hysterical, Yolande," Papa snaps. "I was only thinking of George's feelings."

"Well, you should be thinking of my feelings on the most important day of my life."

Papa roars with laughter. "Your senior promenade? There will be more critical days. Like your wedding, for one. This will pale in comparison to that day."

"Papa . . ."

"You know how important it is for gifted colored people to marry each other and bring more gifted progeny into the world. It is the only way to elevate the race," Papa says in his sermonizing voice.

I take slow, even breaths so as not to show my irritation. I know Papa's teachings and philosophies. The Talented Tenth is what we are. In his mind, only a small percentage of Negroes are worth anything, and we need to stick together, marry each other, and have children until there are enough of us to provide colored doctors, lawyers, engineers, dentists, writers, and artists for all of America. I guess the other 90 percent can just sit around and drink moonshine as far as Papa is concerned.

Papa wants me to find a gifted man to marry so we can multiply our gifts. But shouldn't I be aware of said gifts . . . if they exist? Papa had enrolled me in that fancy school in England, to try and discover my gifts. Then he pulled me right out of there, just when I was starting to like it, because *he* said I hadn't done anything exceptional with my time there.

"Who says George is gifted at anything?" I ask.

"That is a fair point," Papa concedes. "However, I think I have convinced him to explore university life, when he wasn't at all interested in it before."

I squeeze my eyes shut. Why would Papa be convincing George about anything? Isn't that for George's father and mother to do?

"He'll be attending Fisk in the fall right alongside you, my dear," Papa says cheerily.

"Splendid." My tone is pointedly unenthusiastic.

"I thought you'd be happy to have your friend coming along with you." Papa's smirk tells me he knows the opposite is true. "Now you don't have to be distracted with the attentions of other young men. You'll be able to concentrate on your studies, which are sure to require all your attention."

Mama walks into the dining room from the kitchen, smoothing the front of her dress. She gives me a concerned glance, so I suppose I look rather frantic. Papa and his meddling can sometimes make me feel that way. I don't want George with me at Fisk, smothering me and reporting back to Papa my every move.

"Is everything all right?" Mama asks. Her words are for me, but she looks at Papa when she says them.

"You didn't mention we were having a dinner guest," Papa snips.

Mama effortlessly rearranges the flowers so that they sit up perfectly in the vase. "No, I did not. He is Yolande's guest and she wanted him to be a surprise."

"You both know I hate surprises." Papa lets out a long and irritated-sounding sigh.

And now his nostrils flare as there is a firm knock on the door.

"Well, he's here now," Mama says. "Please be cordial, Will."

"I don't need to be instructed on how to behave in my own home, Nina," Papa barks.

Mama purses her lips and ignores Papa's flaring nostrils as she strides over to answer the door. But I'm worried now. Papa was already annoyed, and now Mama's got him all primed to be insufferable.

"Papa, please be nice."

He only grunts in response as he rises from the table and Mama walks over with Jimmie and Mr. Morrison. Thank goodness Jimmie had enough sense to not come alone. When Papa sees that Jimmie has come with reinforcements, he cocks his head to one side with interest.

He looks Jimmie up and down, sizing him up, although even at his young age, Jimmie's more than a few inches taller than Papa.

"And who does *this* young man belong to?" Papa booms, his voice sounding way too loud for the dining room, the noise ricocheting from the walls.

Both Mr. Morrison and Jimmie take a few steps toward Papa, but Jimmie stands tall with his shoulders squared, looking Papa right in the eyes as he extends his right hand to shake. "I'm James Lunceford, Dr. Du Bois, from Denver, Colorado. I belong to the good Lord, and my parents James R. and Ida Lunceford."

Papa narrows his eyes incredulously, like he's never seen a boy like Jimmie before. Most of the time when he huffs and puffs, the boys just wither and float away like autumn leaves in the park. But Jimmie stares right at Papa, his smile never fading.

Papa glares down at Jimmie's extended hand, and then slowly looks back up at him again. Then, he takes Jimmie's hand and shakes it hard, like he's trying to rattle Jimmie, but Jimmie stays planted and doesn't lose his balance. Guess he's strong with all his sports playing and whatnot. Papa doesn't seem pleased at all, even though Jimmie is being friendly as can be.

"James, from Denver," Papa says as Mama eases to his side, "how do you find yourself in Brooklyn, New York?"

"Well—" Jimmie opens his mouth to reply, but thankfully Mama bursts in.

"I have heard wonderful things about Denver," she says pleasantly. "It's beautiful there isn't it?"

"Yes, ma'am, Mrs. Du Bois." Jimmie turns his attention to Mama and this time his friendly expression is reciprocated.

"Aren't you handsome?" Mama gushes.

"Thank you, ma'am," Jimmie says, blushing but still keeping his chin up like a man. I beam at him proudly. Take that, Papa.

Mr. Morrison, probably thinking Jimmie has suffered enough, holds his hand out for Papa to shake. Papa doesn't try to intimidate Mr. Morrison, though. Papa shakes Mr. Morrison's hand firmly yet respectfully. One grown man to another.

"He's a member of my band," Mr. Morrison says. "The George Morrison Jazz Orchestra, and we're here on a six-week engagement at the Carlton Terrace."

"A jazz musician. So, no college?" Papa asks.

"Not yet, sir, I—"

Papa now locks gazes with me, in one action dismissing Jimmie. "Yolande, make sure to never neglect your education for something like jazz music."

"Yes, Papa, but Jimmie is still in high school. He's not old enough for college," I say.

"He's seventeen years old," Mr. Morrison says, his brows now furrowed, irritated probably by Papa's dig at jazz music.

"Seventeen and already traveling with a jazz band?" Papa asks, now reassessing Jimmie. "Must be some band."

My eyes dart nervously between Papa and Mr. Morrison. Papa's question mocks, and Mr. Morrison does not seem to be the kind of man who enjoys being mocked.

"It is a very impressive band," Mr. Morrison says loudly. "Although, since I'm their leader I am indeed biased. Jimmie here is something of a prodigy. He plays seven instruments and can read music. One day I'll be playing in his band."

"Add an education to that, and you may just be able to keep a roof over your head," Papa says matter-of-factly.

"Wouldn't you two gentlemen like to get your hands washed for dinner? The chicken is ready to come out of the oven," Mama says, thankfully rescuing us from this abysmal dialogue. "It's right this way."

I glare at Papa as Mama leads them to the water closet. He gives me the most innocent of looks back, like he hasn't done anything wrong. Completely insufferable.

"Papa, *please*," I whisper.

One corner of Papa's mouth lifts into a grin. Or is that a sneer? I cannot tell the difference. I hope it's the former and he's going to give Jimmie some grace, for my sake.

When they return, Mama rushes into the kitchen, with me at her heels so that I can help her bring the meal to the table. It's a simple one. Roasted chicken, mashed potatoes, green beans, and fresh rolls bought at the bakery, but buttered only a few moments ago. My contribution to the meal is lemonade, and Mama baked a butter cake, my favorite one of her desserts. She's so much better at baking than cooking, but she does well with chicken dishes. Roasted or fried.

"Everything looks and smells wonderful, Mrs. Du Bois," Jimmie says enthusiastically. "I haven't had too many home-cooked meals since we've been here."

"Thank you, James. I do hope you enjoy it."

"I'm sure I will," Jimmie replies. "I can't wait to write to my parents about tonight. My father reads *The Crisis*, so he's going to be thrilled."

"Does he now? What line of work is your father in, son?" Papa asks.

This is the first moment I see Jimmie's confidence waver. Perhaps he didn't think he'd have to defend his father's employment or educational background, and maybe I should have warned him of the interrogation. I just hoped by surprising Papa, the questions would be kept to a minimum, but clearly, I was wrong.

"At the moment, he performs maintenance on an office building in downtown Denver," Jimmie explains after glancing at Mr. Morrison. "We sold our farm in Oklahoma City to move to Denver a few years ago."

"So, he's a janitor?" Papa asks as he passes the platter of chicken.

"Yes sir," Jimmie says.

Mr. Morrison clears his throat and casts an irritated glare in Papa's direction. "James R. Lunceford is a solid family man, who is raising two well-mannered and brilliant young men," he says. "He directs the choir at several AME churches in the community as well, and his wife plays the organ. They are a lovely family, Dr. Du Bois."

"Oh, I am not suggesting otherwise," Papa says. "I am only curious, you see."

Papa doesn't seem to want to tangle with Mr. Morrison, and I am so glad Jimmie had the sense to bring him along.

"You seem to have good manners, James," Papa continues. "So, I shouldn't have to tell you how to treat a young lady on an evening out, correct?"

"No sir. My mother and father taught me well."

"I am sure they have," Mama says, beaming at Jimmie. "You seem very mature for seventeen."

"He is," Mr. Morrison says. "I never have a moment's trouble out of him out here on the road. He is a joy."

"Have I passed your test, Dr. Du Bois?" Jimmie asks directly. He takes a bite of food and chews it slowly.

Papa sets his fork down and stares at Jimmie. And Jimmie stares right back. Both of them chew and chew on Mama's chicken; neither cracks a smile, blinks, or looks away.

"There is no test," Papa says. "It's only the senior promenade. One night is inconsequential."

Jimmie swallows his food as the light seems to disappear from his eyes.

And I understand why. Papa's response is clear. Jimmie is approved for one night only. The senior promenade, and nothing further.

Chapter Four

April 1920
Brooklyn, New York

The night of the senior promenade is supposed to be about us seniors. We should be hearing how proud everyone is of our accomplishments. And compliments from the mothers and fathers on our beautiful dresses, spiffy suits, and shiny shoes. But *this* senior promenade is not for the colored graduates of the Brooklyn Girls' High School.

This evening does not belong to us at all. It belongs to Papa, the Talented Tenth, and the movement.

From the moment we arrived at the Welmons' brownstone, the meeting place for all the colored girls and their escorts, Papa has held center stage. You would think he was ten feet tall the way all the other fathers stand by silently while he speaks, and Papa is the shortest among them.

"This is a victory for us tonight," Papa boasts. "Even a thing as trivial as a senior promenade is an opportunity for us to take a stand. We mustn't allow a single indignity. Every time they draw the color line, we must band together to erase it. Else our children, and our children's children will continue to feel the scourge of discrimination."

Mama and Miss Fauset gaze proudly at Papa as he sermonizes. His two biggest fans sit side by side on Mrs. Welmon's lovely blue velvet sofa, sipping too-sweet punch from crystal cups. Pretty Miss Fauset has a chic short haircut, button nose, heart-shaped mouth, and fashionable dress. Mama looks so much older sitting next to Miss Fauset, though she is quite elegant in her custom-made dress.

But while they are not alike, Mama and Miss Fauset have the same goal. They both support Papa while he steals our moment to shine.

At least Jimmie is here, and he hasn't left my side. I am the center of *his* attention. Since his parents are back home in Denver, he brought Mr. Morrison, Andy, and Mary along to see him off to the promenade.

"I am biased," Jimmie whispers so as not to interrupt Papa's speech, "but I think you have the prettiest dress of all the girls here."

Well, of course my mama, *the* Mrs. Nina Gomer Du Bois, wasn't going to let me go to the senior promenade looking any kind of way. She bought the fabric months ago. Pure cream silk, fit for a debutante ball or a wedding, and handstitched Italian lace for the bodice, hem, sleeves, *and* gloves. And let us not forget about the silk stockings and brand-new ivory pumps.

I love the way my dress flares out at the bottom and is cinched at the waist, since my waist is the only thing on me that's tiny. My bosom is looking quite fetching, if I do say so myself. The wide skirt hides the pudginess around my stomach. That is nobody's business anyway, especially not Jimmie's.

"My mother hired a dressmaker because we didn't like anything we saw in the stores."

"Must be nice." Jimmie chuckles. "My suit came right from Blumstein's."

I think Jimmie could wrap himself up in a tattered blanket and still look good. His navy-blue store-bought suit and cream-colored bow tie fit him to a tee, and the pink rose boutonniere on his lapel matches the beautiful corsage he placed on my wrist.

"Did Mr. Morrison help you pick it out?" I whisper back, wishing Papa would finish up so that we can have real conversations.

"No. Andy and Mary took me shopping for everything. But Mr. Morrison helped me trim my mustache."

I squint to find the mustache on Jimmie's face, but there's only a tiny shadow. The shadow does look symmetrical, so I suppose it qualifies as a mustache.

"It looks very nice, and so does your suit."

I have seen more than one of the other girls from my class cut a look at Jimmie out of the corner of her eye. Especially the ones their mamas hooked up with distant cousins or leftover boys from the church.

"We must get a photograph of all the young people dressed up," Mama announces. I catch Mama wink at Mrs. Welmon as if they'd planned this very distraction in case Papa got too full of himself.

Papa squeezes Mama's hand then turns to the rest of the group. "Come everyone, let's go outside while the sun is still shining, and get a nice photograph of all the young people together. We'll make sure to feature them in *The Crisis*."

Mr. Welmon grabs his Kodak Brownie camera and the stand and moves to the front door. The entire group of promenade attendees and their parents follow, leaving their too-sweet punch and plates of snacks on the tables for Mrs. Welmon to clean up later.

"Your papa doesn't seem to be paying us any attention tonight," Jimmie whispers as we hang back to allow the parents to go outside first.

"Well, he gets this way anytime he has an audience," I whisper back, enjoying the closeness and the yummy scent of whatever cologne Jimmie has splashed on himself.

"I thought it was because he doesn't like me much."

"Why do you think that?"

Jimmie chuckles. "Yolande. Your papa's questions felt like a mathematics exam that I didn't have time to study for."

"Oh. Papa does that to every boy, and it scares most of them."

"Well, I'm not scared, but I want him to like me."

"Get into Columbia University or Harvard. Then he'll love you to pieces."

"I think I'd like to go to Morehouse. Where are you going to attend?"

"Papa has decided I am going to Fisk. His alma mater."

"Is that what you want?"

"Well—"

"What are you two whispering about?" Margaret asks as she wedges herself between our bodies and links her arm in mine. Charles sidles up next to Jimmie.

"It's none of your concern," I tease. "Give me back my escort."

"You're hogging each other," Margaret complains. "Don't I get to have my best friend at all tonight? You haven't even complimented me on my dress. Yours is quite fetching."

The tulle skirt on Margaret's pink dress swishes as she walks, and while the length would probably reach mid-calf on my short legs, it comes just past Margaret's knee. The ballerina pink plus Margaret's long legs make her look like a dancer.

"My dear Margaret, tonight your dress is second to none," I say.

"Well, it might be second to one, but I'm supposed to be complimenting you, am I right?"

"'My dear Margaret'?" Jimmie chuckles. "Are you writing her a letter?"

"Well, I do write her letters. Every day."

"And I her," Margaret adds. "Sometimes you think of things late at night that just can't wait until morning."

"That's silly," Charles says. "And a waste of postage. Won't you see each other at school?"

Charles nudges Jimmie, looking for a conspirator, but Jimmie seems curious about our letter writing.

"During the week, we hand deliver the letters, of course," I say to Jimmie and not Charles.

"I like that," Jimmie says. "When you go away to college, and I'm back in Denver, I'm going to write you."

"What if she doesn't want your letters?" Charles asks, poking Jimmie in the ribs with his pointy elbow.

"She will."

I scoot past Margaret and wrap my arm in Jimmie's once again.

"I *might* be interested in your letters, Jimmie. We'll see."

He bites his bottom lip hungrily and for a second, he seems much more mature. Like he's not too worried about me playing hard to get. I believe he's used to winning every game he sets out to play.

* * *

FINALLY, AFTER ESCAPING our parents' endless number of photographs, and sitting through a painfully long dinner, we arrive at the Hotel Margaret at a little past nine o'clock. The promenade started more than an hour and a half ago. I feel ready to burst from excitement at the spectacle of it all.

The parents had pooled resources and rented two black limousines for all seven couples and Mr. and Mrs. Welmon, who volunteered to be our chaperones. Of course, Margaret is annoyed at her parents being in attendance, and who could blame her? I would be mortified if Papa and Mama had tagged along.

At the entrance of the hotel is a crowd of reporters. Thanks to Papa, this dance has become big news for the movement and the entire city of Brooklyn. The colored journalists are here to report a victory, and the white ones probably want to see if any madness will ensue because of our presence.

The hotel is the tallest building in Brooklyn, ten stories with pyramid-like points on the very top. It is bathed in the moonlight that also illuminates the East River, and there is a chilly nip in the nighttime air. It seems as if the stars are shining brighter tonight, like even the constellations know it's a special occasion. If I could imprint the entire image on a postcard, I would slide it in my scrapbook for safekeeping. I want to remember it all.

"Who are all these people?" Margaret asks, hesitating to step out of the limo when the driver opens the door.

"Looks like reporters," the driver says. "I've got another group to pick up from a dance up in Harlem, so you all need to get on to your promenade."

"Is it safe?" Margaret leans down to me and whispers as we proceed to the door, clutching our escorts' arms.

I shrug and pull closer to Jimmie, not that he'd be much protection if it wasn't safe. Anytime there's a horde of white men standing anywhere, blocking a path, there is a potential for disaster. Which is why some of our fathers followed behind our processional in their cars. Not my Papa, however. He had letters to write and business to attend to. He had agitated the hornets in their nest, and feeling his work was done, has moved on to another crusade.

Margaret's concerns were for naught, however, because the crowd parts to let us through the hotel's entrance without incident. There are a few flashing lights from the cameras, but that is all.

"Do you think our picture will be in the paper?" Jimmie whispers as we cross the threshold and step into the grand lobby.

"Maybe the colored newspapers," I whisper back.

In the hotel's lobby there are lovely spring floral arrangements, enveloping the entire space with their fragrance. Above our heads is an enormous and impressive glass chandelier that catches the light and reflects it as it sparkles onto the shiny marble floor.

Our principal, Mr. Felter, and Mrs. Younger, the senior class advisor and promenade planner, stand at the entrance to the ballroom. While Mrs. Younger greets us with a welcoming smile, Mr. Felter's grim expression tells me that he'd rather not have to deal with any of this, or any of us.

He had sent several letters to Papa trying to put his foot down and ban our entry, but Papa hadn't let Mr. Felter's disapproval stop him. He'd gone all the way to the superintendent of the Brooklyn schools and the mayor. Now, we're the ones faced with the defeated Mr. Felter. Maybe Papa *should* be here, so that Mr. Felter can direct his anger at the right person.

Jimmie greets Mr. Felter, but Mr. Felter glares at him. With my arm wrapped in Jimmie's, I can feel him tense. I feel nervous too. It is one thing when an older colored man, like Papa, gives a young colored man a rough time. It is dangerous when there's venom coming from a white man.

"Girls," Mr. Felter says as we stop at the ballroom's entrance, "we don't want any trouble here tonight. So, ensure that your *Negro* escorts do not approach any of your classmates, to dance or otherwise."

Mr. Welmon clears his throat and steps to the front of our group. He gives Mr. Felter a once-over and shakes his head.

"These young men are not concerned with any of the other girls. They have their own dates." Mr. Welmon's voice is loud and commanding. It is comforting to have him here with us.

"Be sure of it," Mr. Felter says in an ominous tone as he strides away.

Mrs. Younger opens her arms and beckons us forward. "Please come inside," she says. "Enjoy the evening. There are wonderful treats and punch, and the music is hopping. You must get out on the dance floor and have a good time."

I choose to focus on Mrs. Younger's warmth and not Mr. Felter's chilly disposition as we enter the ballroom. But it is evident that we are not welcomed by all. Silence descends upon the promenade as soon as the other attendees notice our arrival. There are two tables put together for us and they are slightly separated from the rest of the attendees.

Papa would roar at this. But Mr. Welmon whispers to us to ignore the obvious slight, sit at our tables, and to stay together. The boys are not to leave our sides for an instant.

I try to ignore the dirty looks being shot in our direction by the white boys and some of our classmates. Without our knowledge or participation, the senior class had taken a second vote. Most of the girls agreed that we should be included, but now some of them look like they wish they'd voted differently.

"Why would we be going after their dates when we've got the prettiest ones here?" Jimmie asks Charles.

"We wouldn't, but they sure are scared about that," Charles says.

"I think they're afraid of those reporters taking a photograph of one of our escorts and one of their girls," I say, as I give a sidelong glance to a group staring at us from another table. "Imagine if that showed up in tomorrow's newspaper. I don't think they want that to be the headline."

"Mr. Felter's head would explode," Margaret says. "Let's go over to the refreshment table and see what they have."

The four of us rise and, all around the ballroom, other couples turn in their seats and strain their necks to see what we're doing. Then, they move out of our way at the table like we're diseased. Even though they've been going to school with us the whole time, eating lunch with us in the same cafeteria, and sitting in the same class-rooms.

I try to ignore them as Jimmie and I select tiny sandwiches, cook-ies, and cakes to place on our plates. Then, we take pre-poured cups of punch and proceed back to our table. The whole time there are dozens of sets of eyes glaring at us.

"Don't pay them any mind," Jimmie says with a mouth full after taking a huge chomp of his turkey sandwich. "It's worse than this in Denver."

"I'm trying not to, but I don't know when they got it in their minds to hate us. We've been just fine this whole time. And now because we ask to be treated fairly, they're offended."

"They're fine with us as long as we're not equal," Margaret says while daintily sipping her punch and stealing glances at our classmates.

"You got that right," Charles adds with an angrier, unsafe tone to his voice. "They're only happy when they have one up on us."

"We sound just like Papa and his NAACP friends," I say, it suddenly occurring to me that we're having a *movement* conversation at our senior promenade.

Margaret shakes her head. "No. Your papa says that if we show ourselves to be as gifted and as talented as they are, they will accept us."

"Respect us, perhaps, but it seems they'll never accept us," Jimmie counters, sounding older than his seventeen years.

We all sound older than what we are. Struggle is an aging thing, I guess.

"Would you like to dance?" Jimmie asks, after finishing his punch. "This is my kind of song."

The band, who had stopped playing when we entered the ballroom, has now resumed. I move my shoulders in sync to the upbeat swing number. Even though my new shoes pinch my toes, I do want to dance with Jimmie. I'd like to feel his strong arms around me, and a chaste dance is the only way I'll get that tonight.

"Let's dance then," I say. Jimmie jumps up and pulls out my chair and extends his hand to help me stand. He didn't lie to Papa. His parents had taught him how to treat a young lady.

"Margaret and Charles, are you two coming?" Jimmie asks. "Don't leave us on the dance floor all by ourselves."

The thing is, we wouldn't be alone, because there are quite a few of the white couples shimmying on the floor. But we would be the only colored couple, so we'd feel alone even if we weren't.

Margaret nudges Charles and he scrambles to his feet. "A dance sounds nice," she says. "We might as well make the most of this, right?"

"You only get one senior promenade," I say.

On our way to the dance floor, one of the newspaper reporters makes a beeline straight for us. Thinking only of what Mama might do, I affix pleasantness on my face as he approaches. Jimmie takes my hand as if he doesn't see the reporter, but the man seems insistent on getting his story, whatever that's supposed to be.

"Are you the daughter of Dr. William Du Bois?" the reporter asks in a booming voice that competes with the band.

I nod as I bounce my shoulders in time to the music. Jimmie follows my lead and rocks from side to side. The reporter looks silly standing there while we dance, especially when Charles and Margaret start on the other side of him.

"How are you and your friends enjoying the senior promenade?" the reporter asks.

If Papa was being queried this way, he would make sure to mention the struggle we endured to get to this moment. The letters he wrote and the important men that he petitioned. He would make sure the reporter had a triumphant quote claiming our victory.

And maybe this reporter thinks I am like Papa, the way he's almost salivating for my response.

"We're having a fine time," I reply. "A mighty fine time."

Jimmie takes one of my hands and twirls me in a circle. The reporter skulks away, perhaps disappointed that I didn't give him something newsworthy. But a nineteen-year-old girl enjoying her senior promenade with a perfectly handsome seventeen-year-old boy shouldn't be newsworthy.

I think it's quite the natural order of things.

Chapter Five

May 1920
Harlem, New York

I agreed to lunch with Miss Fauset today to talk about my submission for *The Brownies' Book*—an essay on African geography. She offered to take the streetcar to Brooklyn, to meet me at our home, but I convinced her that I'd been craving a ham sandwich from the Harlem Y lunch counter.

Of course, I don't care about a sandwich, ham or otherwise. My only desire is to see Jimmie. He's rooming with the rest of the band at the Y, but Papa has been making contact difficult ever since the senior promenade. He's filled my time with tasks and assignments and has not allowed me to spend the night over with Margaret, where the Welmons keep a less watchful eye on our movements.

Honestly, the only reason I care about getting published in *The Brownies' Book* is that I know it will satisfy Papa. It'll be proof that I can be as gifted as the other children he and Miss Fauset choose to showcase in the book's pages. He's convinced that deep inside of me is some sort of writing or drawing prodigy. I do enjoy making pretty illustrations of objects like flowers and bowls of fruit, and I am quite good, but I don't know about writing stories or poetry. Still, writing is Miss Fauset's specialty, and if anyone can make a writer out of little old me, she can.

I push my sandwich around on the plate, because for once, I'm not hungry. I'm just anxious to get through this lunch, so I can disappear for a few hours and make up a good excuse as to why it took me so long to get back home from Harlem. But by the time anyone is alarmed by my absence, I'll already be home and tucked away in bed.

"Tell me, Yolande, what did you think of your submission?" Miss Fauset asks. "I'd like to hear how you measure your own writing."

I shrug. She's supposed to be the expert at these things, not me. I wouldn't know what to think about it.

"I think . . . that it took a good deal of time to write it, and that I also had to listen to Papa bore me with talk of the Pan African World Congress just because I asked him how to spell Abyssinia."

Miss Fauset seems amused by this, even though I am not joking. Papa seizes any opportunity to bore me with facts that disappear right into the ether as soon as he's finished. It's not that I don't want to remember. It's just that there are so many things I must know. How can one person hold on to all of it?

"What is your opinion?" I ask, almost sounding miffed, but not quite. "Aren't you the one who decides what does and doesn't get into *The Brownies' Book*?"

"In most cases. But there are times when your father takes liberties."

This doesn't surprise me at all. Papa always offers his unsolicited opinion. Mama and I will be talking about the simplest of things—my new dresses, perhaps—and Papa will give his two cents on who's the best seamstress, and what are the best fabrics, what's in style and what's not. Margaret's father couldn't care less about her dresses. I think most fathers probably don't care at all, let alone feel the need to lecture on the topic.

But Papa frets over everything I do, down to the smallest detail. Mama and I are extensions of himself, so we must present ourselves as such. People pay him a good amount of money to speak at their events and fundraisers, so we must all look like perfection whether we're with him or on our own.

"Well, I may never live up to his standards," I admit. This is true in writing and in everything. "I'd have better odds sending my story to the *New York Tribune*. Did you see where they quoted me?"

"Of course I saw. Your father strutted around the office like a peacock, carrying that article around all day, forcing everyone to read it." She laughs like she vividly remembers Papa strutting. It must have been a sight.

"Papa bragged about me at work?" I am sure my face cannot hide my surprise.

"He sure did. And said you were a little agitator. That it's in your blood."

But I wasn't trying to stir up any controversy. I'd simply told the truth. We were having a fine time, even though those white people had done everything in their power to ruin our evening.

I might not agree with Papa's viewpoint on what I said to the reporter, but I don't dare voice that to Miss Fauset. She would undoubtedly tell him. Nothing said in her hearing is safe from Papa. Sometimes I think she shares too many things with him. Even Mama doesn't divulge everything. She says a woman must always have her secrets. Perhaps Mama should tutor Miss Fauset in the ways of dealing with men.

"Did you truly enjoy yourself at the dance?"

"It was perhaps the best night I've ever had."

Miss Fauset's eyes shine with delight then narrow suspiciously. "Did that have anything to do with your dashing escort?"

I cannot contain my smile. Thinking of Jimmie makes the joy burst right out of me like the insides of a corn kernel when you hold it to the heat.

"It had everything to do with him, Miss Fauset. I do believe we were the handsomest couple at the dance."

She chuckles. "Would the rest of the couples agree with that?"

"Oh, probably not, because I'm not tall and lovely like Margaret."

Maybe I shouldn't have said this, because now Miss Fauset's expression has changed. She was tickled before, and now she's giving me that *dear dear* pity look mothers give to their homely daughters.

"You are quite lovely, Yolande, and your dress was beautiful."

"It *was* beautiful, wasn't it?"

"I don't believe you shared how you met this young man."

Now I'm narrowing *my* eyes suspiciously. "Are you spying on me for Papa?"

Miss Fauset lets out a deep sigh. "Maybe . . . ," she says.

"Then I am done talking about Jimmie."

"Oh, Yolande. Your papa just wants to make sure you're safe."

"Safe? Jimmie has exceptional manners. He may, in fact, have better manners than I do. He goes to church, you know?"

"Is that where you met him?" she prods.

"Miss Fauset. Please."

"Well . . . I don't know if your mother talks to you about these things—"

"What things?"

Miss Fauset stares off into the distance like she's deep in thought on what to say.

"The things that could happen between a handsome young man and a lovely young woman." She groans heavily like she just told me the biggest secret ever whispered. "And . . . the consequences of those things," she adds.

"My mother does not talk to me about those things."

Miss Fauset shakes her head wearily, as if she had known this would be the case. Again, I think Miss Fauset is extending pity and compassion where it isn't needed.

"But Papa tells me everything," I hurriedly add, so that Miss Fauset can stop looking so frustrated. "He's told me about the dangers of boys since the time I got my monthly visitor."

"Mon dieu!" Her eyes grow large with shock and awe. She exclaims in French because she can't help it.

She speaks French all the time, like all the other affluent Harlem Negroes. It lets everyone know they've spent summers in Paris, or sometimes even years abroad. I'm not fluent, although I can throw a phrase around here or there. It doesn't matter to Miss Fauset, though. She's going to speak her French, and you either pick up what she means from context or ask her to interpret. But if you ask for the interpretation, she gives you a look of pity like she wishes everyone would just elevate their mind with a little education.

"I just cannot imagine receiving that kind of instruction from a father," Miss Fauset continues, "and I was very close to mine."

"I'd much rather Papa with those types of conversations. He gets right to the point. No wringing hands. There's much more angst when discussing certain topics with Mama."

"Well, even if your father explained, he cannot possibly know what it feels like to be a young woman spending time with a very handsome boy she likes."

I pretend to be enlightened. I am nineteen. It's not like I've never kissed a boy before, and I am waiting for Jimmie to lose some of his manners and do just that. But maybe I *should* be listening, because Jimmie is different than every other boy I've ever known.

"Things can just get carried away, very quickly," Miss Fauset says with a grave expression on her face, "and before you know it, your college dreams are over and you're living in the spare room of your handsome boyfriend's parents' house. Forced to be married and a mother too soon."

In Jimmie's parents' house in Denver? A baby? That sounds terrifying.

"You don't have to worry, and neither does Papa," I say, shaking my head for good measure. "Besides, Jimmie is a good boy."

"And you?"

"I am a young woman on her way to Fisk University in a few months, who is clearly not about to be immortalized in print. The editor of *The Brownies' Book* has been very evasive on the topic of my submission."

Miss Fauset's shoulders shake with mirth. She seems to enjoy my wittiness more than she does my writing.

"Ah, oui, ma chérie. Your story."

"Oui."

She clears her throat. Several times. "I think it is a solid first effort."

Why would she take me to lunch to give me bad news? She could have just written me a note and sent it by Papa if she didn't want to waste postage.

"I wrote and rewrote that story so many times. I honestly don't think I can look at it anymore."

I chomp my sandwich now because I'm done talking about it. A solid first effort when I've worked so hard means I don't have what it takes to be published, and I am fine with that. I have other things to do. This is Papa's dream anyway. Not mine.

"Well, it isn't really a story, is it?" Miss Fauset asks, determined, it seems, to engage me in a discussion about this.

I finish chewing and wipe my mouth with the napkin before responding. "I sure thought it was."

"It reads more like a school homework assignment. Albeit a very well-researched one."

Now I'm confused. Yes, there are certainly all kinds of well-researched facts in my story. That was the whole point, I thought. To educate the little brown children about our ancestors in Africa. That is what Papa instructed me to do, and now Miss Fauset is saying something different.

"What would make it a story?" I ask, now curious even though I don't want to be.

She leans forward, now, her eyes bright, like she enjoys this. "Well, first, your reader needs to feel something. What do you want the readers to feel?"

I think about all the little children reading my story in *The Brownies' Book* and then going to find Ethiopia and Abyssinia on the map. And knowing that their beautiful brown skin comes from that land across the Atlantic Ocean.

"I want them to be amazed," I say.

"Well, then, you must inject amazement into your characters' actions. The boy in your story's eyes should light up as he's learning. His heart should race. Maybe he can't find words to describe his joy at learning."

I close my eyes and imagine this, and I can almost see the little boy running to look at a map and his fat cheeks shining with glee. I can see the little girl in my mind too, but I don't know if I put those images on the pages.

"You're making me feel excited about the story right now," I admit.

"Wonderful, now you know how to fix it."

But she's wrong. I don't know *how* to fix it, just that it needs to be fixed. I don't know if I even want to be a writer, just that it makes Papa happy when I try.

"I don't know about that, Miss Fauset. I think sometimes you and Papa overestimate what I'm capable of accomplishing."

"You're not giving yourself enough credit. You underestimate yourself."

"I'm not going to promise I'll have time to inject anything in that story before I leave for summer holiday."

Miss Fauset clears her throat and lifts her eyebrow. "You could if you'd spend more time editing and less time sneaking around Harlem with your friend."

"I beg your pardon, but . . ."

Miss Fauset motions to the window with her head just as Jimmie walks past the Y. I feel my cheeks burn hot, as I try to think of an explanation.

"He's been pacing in front of that window for almost our entire time here," Miss Fauset says. "Perhaps we should've invited him to join us for lunch."

"Oh no, that won't be necessary. He's just waiting for me to finish so he can walk me back to the streetcar."

Miss Fauset's eyes seem to sparkle with amusement at my mild stretching of the truth. He will be walking me to the streetcar. At some point. I didn't say it was going to be right away.

"Please don't tell Papa."

Miss Fauset opens her mouth to protest, but I grab both her hands.

"Please," I beg. "Papa doesn't understand, and we're not doing anything wrong."

"Only if you promise you'll be home in a few hours."

"I will. I promise."

I am planning to tell Papa I stayed at the West 135th Street library working on edits to my story, and that time had escaped me. It won't be a lie. I will stop in the library for a moment to say hello to the librarians. And the time will escape me, I'm sure, while I'm with Jimmie.

"Also remember that there will be plenty of boys at Fisk to look at," Miss Fauset says, "and enjoy."

I lift my eyebrows at this. Enjoy? Do tell, Miss Fauset.

"I'm only thinking of Jimmie, but Papa has convinced George Cuffee to attend Fisk next year."

"Well, Jimmie is still in high school," Miss Fauset says. "It might be nice to get reacquainted with George. You two were having a good time all spring until Jimmie came along."

"No, until George abandoned me right before my senior prom-enade. And Jimmie is almost grown, Miss Fauset."

"Trust me, this summer love will be forgotten by Christmas."

Jimmie stops his pacing as if he heard Miss Fauset's pessimistic words. Our eyes meet and I wave at him. His face lights up, and he gives me an enthusiastic wave back.

When I turn to look at Miss Fauset again to say my goodbyes, she has a worried expression on her face.

"He's only one boy, ma chérie," she says. "One of many you will meet. Give yourself a chance to find out what kind of woman you'll become."

I give Miss Fauset a wide-eyed nod that I hope makes her think I agree with her advice. But she isn't one I'd listen to about men. She is content to give all her time to *The Crisis* and Papa's taskings great and small.

What can she tell me about matters of the heart?

Chapter Six

May 1920
Harlem, New York

Summer is here. I should be thinking about my upcoming holiday, shopping for my Fisk wardrobe, and all the fun I'll have being away from Papa. But the only thing on my mind is how Jimmie's six-week engagement at the Carlton Terrace is almost over. Soon he'll be back in Denver with all the cute girls who are just getting up the nerve to flirt. And now I've taught him how to respond.

Today, he clutches my hand as we saunter up Lenox Avenue eating ice cream cones. Today he's still sweet and all mine.

"I'm so glad you're here, Yolande. I didn't think you'd be able to get out after your papa scolded you the other day," Jimmie says as he licks the side of his custard.

"Well, usually when he gets going and it's too much, I can't take it," I explain. "I fainted and Mama came to the rescue like she always does with a cold cloth."

Papa had gone into a complete tizzy because Margaret and I came home much later than we'd intended, and we obviously hadn't been at the cinema. It's overwhelming when he does that. I'm of age after all. I should be able to stay out and enjoy a warm spring night with my friends.

"You fainted? Right in the middle of his speech?" Jimmie asks.

"Yes. He can be insufferable sometimes."

"Well, was he angry about me?"

I chuckle. "No, silly. He didn't know I was with you."

Jimmie's hand slides out of mine. "I hate that you can't tell him about us. What's so bad about me?"

Papa's made it clear to me what he finds distasteful about Jimmie. Jimmie is a gifted jazz musician, and Papa doesn't think that jazz music has any value when it comes to the movement—case closed. But I don't want to talk about things we can't do anything about.

"Nothing, Jimmie."

"But you're here anyway," Jimmie says with a hopeful smile. "So, you must not care too much about what he says."

"Oh, I care what Papa says, but I can't get enough of being here with you in Harlem."

Jimmie laughs as his ice cream starts to drip. "Is it me or is it Harlem?"

I point to his cone. "You're dripping, Jimmie. But it's both. I begged Mama to let me come so I could say goodbye."

Goodbye. We both knew the moment would come, but I wish the summer could last forever.

"Can we just say, until the next time we meet?" Jimmie asks. "I am never saying goodbye to you."

"Of course, silly. I just said that for Mama. With her, the more dramatic, the better. Me seeing you today had to seem like a life-or-death matter."

"Well, you didn't stretch the truth. I would've died if I didn't get to see you again. I just might die on the way home."

Then, I remember that I brought something for Jimmie. I let go of his hand, reach into my little pocketbook, and pull out an envelope. He takes the pretty ivory stationery from my hand, trying not to stain it with ice cream.

"Here, let me take your cone. I don't want you to spoil it," I say as I take the treat from Jimmie's hand without waiting for him to object.

He carefully slides the envelope open, taking care not to rip the delicate paper. Inside is a sheet folded in half. On one side is a drawing of a boy and girl. The boy holds a saxophone to his lips and the girl wears gloves and bracelets, one arm extended in the air as if she's dancing. Both their eyes are closed, and there are musical notes drawn coming from the mouth of the saxophone.

"This is us," Jimmie says, just as tickled as he wants to be.

"Open it. It's a birthday card. I will be on summer holiday by the time your birthday comes, and you'll be on your way home, but we can't not celebrate."

"You remembered."

"Of course I did. Now open it."

On the inside of the card is a poem, written carefully in swirly, curly script. I took time with this, because I hope Jimmie will cherish it forever. There's also a photograph of us on the night of the senior promenade.

"Don't we look good in our fancy clothes," he says. "My mother is going to love this picture."

"That's exactly what my mama said. She wanted your mother to have it for the memories."

"Well, it's my picture, not hers. So, she'll have to enjoy it and then give it back to me."

I cackle. "I didn't know boys kept scrapbooks."

"Well, I never have before, but now I have a picture I'd like to save. And a birthday card."

"Oh, read the poem. I'd like to hear how it sounds in your voice."

Jimmie stares at me long and hard, like my words do something to him. And I'd like to etch that innocent expression into my memory and hold onto it forever.

One spring I met a boy named Jimmie,
Who plays the sax like no one can.
And during that fine spring in Harlem,
That boy became a fine man.
From your forever friend,
Yolande.

Tears fill Jimmie's eyes, but he tries to hide them as he carefully folds the card and photograph back into the envelope. I just smile and hand him back his ice cream. With my handkerchief I swipe away one tear that trickles down his cheek before he has the chance to blink it back. My sweet Jimmie.

"Are you going to carry a torch for me while you're at Fisk?" he asks, his voice cracking, even though I can tell he's trying to make it sound confident. "Lots of big men on campus will be waiting to whisk you away."

"They won't play the saxophone like you, though, Jimmie."

I don't mention that George Cuffee is going to Fisk too, because why would I ruin this precious moment?

"My teacher back home says music is the language of the soul," Jimmie says.

"If that is true, your soul loves talking to mine. And mine loves listening. I'd love to speak too, but I don't play any instruments. I'm not gifted at anything, I'm afraid."

"But you *are* gifted! I think everyone's soul must speak a different way. Your drawing touched me and so did your poem."

"Yes, but that's only 'cause you're sweet on me, Jimmie. I am simply ordinary. I have come to terms with that."

Jimmie stops walking. "You are not ordinary, Yolande. Don't say that about yourself."

"You've seen my mother," I say. "She could be a beauty queen. Perfect in every way, even after having babies."

"Babies? I thought you were an only child."

"Yes, my brother Burghardt was born before me and died as a baby. Now, Papa is left with me as his sole heir."

"And you make him proud."

"Maybe I will, someday, if I discover I'm brilliant at something he deems important."

"You'll show him when you go to Fisk," Jimmie says with confidence I do not share. "I'm sure of it. You'll make your mark."

I step in close to Jimmie, stand on my tiptoes, and kiss the corner of his mouth. I don't care that we're out in the open on the street, or that anyone might report back to Papa.

"Yolande. Your papa."

Then, before he can stop me, I snatch Jimmie's hand and start running. Right up Lenox Avenue. Past the shops, restaurants, and juice joints. We push through a group of poets standing in front of the library looking wise. The air smells like Harlem, full of pleasant and rank scents commingled. It's the fragrance of summertime and freedom. Of our love.

"Come on!" I squeal, as Jimmie resists, like he's not sure about this adventure, but of course he keeps following me.

Finally, we're here. In front of Lafayette Theatre on 7th Avenue and 131st Street. I have to catch my breath with my hands on my knees now, huffing and puffing. "We're here," I say between breaths.

"Where? The theatre?"

I point up to the elm tree we're standing under. "No. The Tree of Hope. Sometimes we call it the Wishing Tree. You and the band were supposed to touch it before you did your engagement at the Carlton Terrace for good luck."

"Oh, well our engagement is over now. Whatever magic is in the tree didn't get on us."

"But you can touch it now. Maybe the good luck will follow you back to Denver."

He takes my hand so that we touch the tree together.

"But I'm not a performer," I say, blinking up at Jimmie, confused. "I don't think it has any magic for me."

"We are magic," Jimmie explains. "So, I'm adding them together. The magic of the tree and the magic of us."

Through Jimmie's loving touch, I swear I can feel it. The magic surging from the tree and between us.

And then, without any thought or concern of what gossip Papa's minions may bring him, I pull Jimmie close to me and place a soft kiss on his lips. Because that's the way magic is sealed, isn't it?

PART II

Chapter Seven

July 1921
Harlem, New York

Miss Fauset's office at *The Crisis* isn't as warm and inviting as her Harlem brownstone. The brownstone always smells of baking bread or cakes. No, Miss Fauset's office is all-business, like Papa's. Dark, expensive cherry-wood furniture, papers, and books. Few personal effects. No artwork on the walls or vases of flowers. Nothing to spruce up the place. It even smells like the lemon-pine furniture polish the cleaners use.

"Yolande," Miss Fauset calls out as I step across the threshold. "Have a seat. I'll be right with you. I have one more letter to open, and then I'll be ready."

I sit at a round table on the opposite side of Miss Fauset's desk instead of in front of the desk. I don't want to feel like one of her employees.

"Mon dieu!" Miss Fauset exclaims as she finally turns her attention to me. "These men cannot follow simple instructions and yet somehow they are leading organizations, cities, and even entire countries."

"That's because they're men."

Miss Fauset frowns as she walks from around her desk to join me at the table, holding what I assume are the edited pages of my story. "Do you think that makes them more fit to lead? Them being men?"

"No, I don't. But they do, and they're always choosing each other to be in charge."

"You're exactly right about that." She laughs as she sits down next to me.

Miss Fauset hands me the pages. I can already see they are covered with red pencil marks. I feel the confidence fly right out of me.

"Well, didn't you like it at all?" I ask, not meaning to sound so wounded.

"I did, ma chère. I enjoyed it immensely. I can tell that what you transcribed here was a fond memory for you."

"It was. We marched behind the football players in a parade and then we won the home game! Whooped Tuskegee and sent them packing."

Miss Fauset tosses her head back as she laughs, and I notice the single strand of elegant pearls that she wears. She is ever so chic and sophisticated. After I graduate from college, I wonder what it might be like to live as she does. With a career and my own apartment. Well, Miss Fauset's mother lives with her, but maybe I could have my own.

"Because I went away to college, Yolande, I could almost create a picture in my mind of this parade. But what about our readers?"

"The children who read *The Brownies' Book*?"

"Yes. You must give them all five senses. What did it smell like?"

"Smell like? Miss Fauset! It smelled like outside."

"Be specific, Yolande. Nashville. In the fall. What did you smell?"

I close my eyes and remember. The ground was damp, and leaves had fallen from the trees. It smelled earthy.

"There was the scent of fallen leaves and moist earth. There was excitement in the air, because we were ready to do battle."

Miss Fauset squeals. "Yes, Yolande! That's exactly what I mean. Now, sounds."

What sounds were in that memory? "The only sounds you could hear were the *rat-tat-tat* of the band's drumline, the swishing of our big round skirts, and the hundreds of feet falling in step behind the team. Fisk's football team's own little personal army."

"Do you see how easy that was?" Miss Fauset asks. "If you do the same through the rest of the selection, I think we can publish you in the August *Brownies' Book*."

My eyes become saucers. "Do you mean this? Will Papa object?"

"He gives me full editorial authority over *The Brownies' Book* now. I think he will be happy you are ready to publish alongside others of my students."

"Papa will be so proud."

"Well, what about you? Aren't you proud of yourself?"

I consider this for a long moment. I suppose I am happy to have received Miss Fauset's approval, but there isn't any unbridled feeling of joy at this accomplishment. Perhaps I don't care all that much about writing.

But now, I wonder. What is the thing that might make me proud?

"What makes you proud, Miss Fauset? *The Crisis*?" I turn the question back to her. It can't be that boring magazine, but the way she's grinning I think it might be.

"Yes, *The Crisis*. So much of it has my touch on it." Miss Fauset beams. "Especially the literary aspects of it. I am very proud of that work. It's in every well-to-do colored person's home in the country."

"But the magazine is Papa's and the NAACP's. Don't you have anything all your own to be proud of?"

"My work teaching young writers fulfills me, even as I work on my own novel. One day it will be published."

"Papa will help if you ask him."

She only smiles. I wonder if she doesn't want Papa's help, but that would be silly. He's a man of influence. It doesn't make sense to not ask him to open the door.

Unless she knows more than one man of influence. The way she quickly finishes and sends me on my way this Friday afternoon makes me imagine she's meeting a fine man for dinner. Maybe he's whisking her away somewhere private. Perhaps she's bold enough to entertain at her home, though I doubt it.

But I am quite envious that she might decide to do any of these things and have no one to question her or dictate otherwise. No papa, because hers has passed away, and no bossy husband. She has real freedom.

"So, Yolande, you have your work to do. We will reconvene in a week. You are now on deadline."

"Deadline?" I ask, tickled by these marching orders. "Oh my. Like a true writer."

"Because that's what you are. Now, unfortunately, I must answer more of your papa's letters. We are preparing for the Pan African World Congress in a little more than a month's time."

"I know. I begged Papa to let me go. He wouldn't."

"You wouldn't enjoy yourself, trust me. Your father can be very testy at these events. He gets agitated at the slightest offense."

I roll my eyes, quite familiar with that version of Papa. "Why do you tolerate him, Miss Fauset?"

"You'd be surprised, Yolande. He rarely turns his anger toward me. I can often calm him when his other associates cannot."

That is a nugget of information that may come in useful someday. Who knows when I may need an ally against Papa.

Chapter Eight

August 1921
Harlem, New York

I do not like to admit that Miss Fauset was right about this, but although my feelings for Jimmie haven't faded one bit, writing regular letters during my freshman year at Fisk was almost impossible. I had my hands full trying to pass classes, and I didn't have much time for homework or rest, much less letter writing.

Of course, having George at Fisk further complicates things. To think he wasn't even planning on going to university at all, until Papa made it clear he wouldn't give his blessing unless George was an educated man. Suddenly, George decided he wanted to be a teacher, so Papa took him under his wing. And since Papa approves of George, I am expected to take his advances seriously as well.

We spent my entire freshman year acting like an item on campus, and everyone seems to think we make a rather chic and handsome couple at that. But Dr. McKenzie's rules are so strict on us freshman girls that we may as well be in prison. So, there was no chance of too many dates.

It's been a very chaste courtship, thanks to George's fear of Papa and my lingering feelings for Jimmie. We don't hold hands or kiss or anything like that. But George tells people that we're an item, and I don't correct him. It's easier to just go along to get along.

I'm thinking of Jimmie now because he's sent me the most beautiful card, telling me that he's decided to come to Fisk after he graduates. I feel awful because I didn't send him anything for his birthday. Now, I must find some kind of gift, and quickly.

But it'll have to be after we're done entertaining. George has scored himself a treasured invitation to dinner. Mama enjoys entertaining in our new Harlem apartment, so we've had guests for dinner all summer long.

I fold Jimmie's card and place it in the scrapbook in my bedroom before joining them at the dinner table. Papa and George are already having their "man" conversation.

"Dr. Du Bois, Harlem is where all the up-and-coming Negroes live now. You were smart to move," George says. He glances at me as I take the seat across from him, but only for a second, before he's back to the real object of his affection.

"Well, I'm neither up nor coming," Papa responds with a dry snort. "I'd like to think if there's a destination, then I've already arrived there. I just met with a group of businessmen about starting a colored bank here, because we need to circulate our money within our community."

"Oh, indeed. I didn't mean to assume otherwise, sir. You are a giant among men. And the way you love writing and artistic pursuits . . . something's happening in Harlem."

Papa considers this flattery. "Well, my literary editor Miss Fauset also lives here. And so does my business partner Augustus Dill. Harlem has become a central location for the movement."

"I was perfectly fine in Brooklyn," Mama says as she passes a platter of pork chops around the dinner table. "There is a great deal of ruckus that happens in Harlem."

"And Yolande?" Papa asks, brushing off Mama's concerns with an irritated grunt. "Does the ruckus bother you?"

"I am in favor of ruckus and shenanigans," I say, giving Mama an apologetic glance, "but I understand Mama's reasons for being against it."

"I want to take you dancing," George says with his chest stuck out like he thinks he's the bee's knees. "Let you experience Negro Harlem."

I almost tell him I know all about Negro Harlem and dancing in clubs. My Jimmie had a six-week engagement at the Carlton Terrace!

And now he's going to be with us at Fisk after he graduates.

"I joined a club at Fisk, Papa," I say, changing the subject for Mama's sake, and mine. If I think too long on Jimmie, I may just burst into tears.

"A club? I hope it isn't one that will interfere with your studies."

"No. It's the Decagynians."

I watch Papa's face and wait for his eyes to light up. I knew he would approve of this, and I had been waiting for the perfect moment to share.

"The women's literary society. Excellent."

"I'm quite enjoying it. We read poetry and novels and then come together to discuss them. We've been reading a good deal of Shakespeare, but I want to read Negro poets as well."

"Indeed. Well, it's no wonder your writing has improved so much. Miss Fauset has shared your latest piece for *The Brownies' Book*, 'Retrospection,' and I almost didn't believe you were the author."

"Papa!"

"It was that good, Yolande. Please receive that as praise and not criticism. Having Miss Fauset mentor you was a wonderful idea."

Mama abruptly stands. "Would anyone like more lemonade?"

"No, Nina, I'm fine." Papa gives Mama an odd look before she quickly exits, not waiting to see if George or I need lemonade.

"As I was saying," Papa continues, "I may ask Miss Fauset to introduce you to some of her young writers. Perhaps they will inspire more of this kind of art from you."

"Young male writers?" George asks with a scowl.

Papa seems amused by this. "Tell me you aren't concerned about a bit of competition, George. I thought you wanted to be an Alpha man."

"Oh, sir, I do. If only they allowed a chapter at Fisk, I'd already be making myself known to my potential big brothers."

Papa shakes his head in frustration. "I have entreated the alumni about Dr. McKenzie and these draconian rules. Why are young Negro men not able to form fraternities like they are on white campuses? And young Negro women sororities? He seeks to make Fisk a plantation where he is massa."

Oh, no. Papa is sliding away from the dinner table and to the front lines of a movement. Come back, Papa. I do not wish to go there tonight. We were talking about my lovely story.

"I think I will run for office in the Decagynians next year, Papa."

It's too late. He has that far-and-away look in his eyes. His rallying-the-troops look. His letter-writing look.

"Yolande, remind me of this, and do not allow me to forget. When I return home from the Pan African World Congress, I am going to write Dr. McKenzie about fraternities and sororities on campus."

"Yes, Papa. I will."

George is sitting there looking just satisfied with himself and I wish he'd go home, since he's not here to see me anyway—he's courting Papa. I was so close to having a real conversation with Papa about my writing. I'm about to be published in *The Brownies' Book*, and that's big news for me.

But it seems that neither Papa nor George is interested in having further conversation with me tonight about my interests. So, I'll just go and write Jimmie all about it. I am sure he'll be very proud.

My Jimmie is coming to Fisk.

Chapter Nine

Ah, I am so glad to be back at Jubilee Hall. My roommate Minnie has beaten me here, and she has captured the bed next to the window. Even though I like to gaze out at the people crossing the Jubilee Hall lawn, the window is drafty and last year I caught a terrible winter cold. So, it's probably best that my bed is on the wall on the other side of the room. I lie on my back staring at the ceiling, watching a spider creep into the corner.

"There are some nice new kids," Minnie says as she spreads her hand knitted quilt across her bed. "Did you get to meet them?"

Minnie's so tiny that she can't reach all four corners of the bed from one side, so she keeps walking around the bed to straighten the quilt. Her hair is pulled into a cute, curly side ponytail that next to her dark brown skin makes her look like a colored doll.

"I only met one girl . . . what was her name?" I bite my lip trying to remember. "The one with the gigantic, tragic hair."

Minnie bursts into laughter. "That was Chrystal Tulli. She's from Memphis."

"Oh well that explains it. The hair, I mean." I roll over onto my side and grimace. "Wait, that sounds awful. I mean, she's a pretty enough girl. She's got those big ole doe eyes all the boys seem to really like. She can't help it if it's so hot in Memphis they don't know how to do a proper press and comb."

Minnie holds her side like she's going to fall clean apart from laughing so hard. "Yolande, that doesn't make it any better."

"Well, I doubt if that hair will improve much here in Nashville. It's just as hot here as it is in Memphis. She's gonna have that big ole bouffant either way, I suppose."

"I hear she's a dancer."

I shrug. "Enough about her, what about John Washington?"

Minnie swoons. "He's back and just as handsome if not more."

"Maybe this year, you'll talk to him."

"Yes, and then we can all go over to Pearly's Diner for double dates."

Pearly's is one of the few places the boys and girls can sneak away to and fraternize. It's owned by a Black church mother in Nashville, and they watch over us like we're their own young people. Any Fisk student is welcome, and if they're struggling to pay tuition or a laundry bill, Miss Pearly will give them a job waiting tables.

"What if I'm not interested in double dates?" I ask while swinging my legs off the side of the bed. My little spider friend marches down the wall and onto the floor. I'm glad he decided not to stay on the ceiling. I don't want to smoosh him, but he needs to exit the premises posthaste.

Minnie stares at me, confused. "But why wouldn't you want to have double dates? Aren't you and George still an item? I thought you'd get serious over the summer holiday."

"George and I are my papa's doing. Do you know he convinced George to attend Fisk?"

"Oh my. That explains his grades."

This makes me laugh. George struggles in just about every subject, but especially anything requiring him to write an essay. I help him with those the best I can, but I am not much of a tutor, I'm afraid.

"Is there anyone else you're sweet on?"

I think about Jimmie's letter over the summer and the belated birthday card I sent him back. We didn't correspond further, but maybe that was because I mentioned George. I *had* to. I couldn't lie to Jimmie. Maybe it was the wish we made at the Wishing Tree that forced the truth from me.

"There was someone, but that's probably over now."

"Then, you might as well hang on to George," Minnie says with a shrug as she plops onto her bed. "He's handsome, and your folks like him."

"Well, I need to like him too, and I don't know that we're a match."

I wonder if my honesty has scared Jimmie off from attending Fisk now. Maybe I shouldn't have told him since I am feeling tired of George and Papa's courtship anyway. And I'll be happy to see Jimmie again. I haven't stopped thinking about him since I got his letter.

"Tell me what you're not saying, Yolande," Minnie implores with a look of concern on her face.

"Only that the other boy who I was quite fond of says he's enrolling at Fisk next year."

"That means you have a whole year to break things off with George. Unless you'd just like to have him all year, so you won't be lonely, and let him down gently over the summer."

I stare at my sweet and savage friend in disbelief. "Minnie, you'd do such a thing?"

"No, but a boy sure would."

"I suppose you're right, but this is much more complicated than that. My papa will want to know why I've set George aside and there will be hell to pay if there's not a good reason."

"Well, if you're supposed to be with this other boy, things will work themselves out in the end, won't they?" Minnie asks.

I think of the wish Jimmie and I made by the Wishing Tree and wonder if there was really any magic in that kiss. If there was, is it powerful enough to get me out of this pickle with George?

Chapter Ten

September 1922
Harlem, New York

Turns out I didn't need the Wishing Tree magic to get George out of Nashville. I only needed to wait for him to get his spring grade report. Three failing grades in English, algebra (his second try), and sociology helped him decide to choose a different path of education.

Against Papa's advice, he's withdrawn from Fisk and has decided to learn a trade. He wants to become a cobbler and open a shop in Harlem. A perfectly fine idea if you ask me.

But now he's furious with me.

"You don't think I'll be able to provide for you now?" George rants, completely unprovoked. "Don't worry, Yolande. I'll make enough to keep you in expensive dresses, and you won't miss your weekly trip to the beauty parlor."

George's tone is so nasty and mean, you'd never think that just a few moments ago he was asking if I'd like to look at furniture for the apartment we're going to have when we get married.

All I said was he might be putting the cart before the horse, and that maybe he should see how much cobbling pays before he starts shopping. I think that's logical. I don't know why he's so angry about it.

"Obviously, I've upset you somehow," I say as I stand to leave the Y. George is rather loud, and people are turning to look at us. "And I'm not feeling well today. I'm having some tummy pain, so I cannot take this aggression for absolutely no reason."

I can only imagine the gossip that will be shared at dinner tables tonight, but George doesn't seem to care about that.

"For no reason? There's plenty reason. And you wouldn't have tummy pain if you'd stop eating any- and everything."

"That was uncalled for, George. You're being very rude and unkind."

"You're just like your father!" he blurts, and now almost everyone in here is staring at us. Some, I'm sure to see if I need rescuing, because George sounds like a maniac.

"Papa has nothing to do with this." My voice rises to match George's now. May as well. Everyone is watching anyway.

"He does. He's the one who spoiled you and made it impossible for anyone else to live up to those expectations."

George no longer sounds angry. Just defeated.

I turn to leave the Y cafeteria just before the river of hot tears rushes down my face. George might consider me spoiled, but no one asked him to come chasing after me or courting my papa's favor.

All those faces staring at me as I ran out of the café . . . I've never been more embarrassed in my life.

* * *

UNTIL TODAY.

I don't know how far my scream could be heard when I read the announcement in the *Amsterdam News*, but now Mama is fanning me, because I feel faint, and Margaret is reading the newspaper. A few moments ago, we were shopping for dresses to go in my trunk to take back to Fisk, and now my life might as well be over. I'll never be able to show my face at the Fisk Alumni Labor Day picnic now, and that's my favorite summer activity. Everyone there will be whispering about this.

"What on earth did you read?" Mama asks me as she leads me over to the library wall, so that the sturdy brick can support my weight.

"It was a-a-a we-w . . . ," I stammer, trying to get the words out, but failing miserably.

"A wedding announcement, Mrs. Du Bois," Margaret says. She's reading the newspaper I'd let fall to the ground. "I cannot believe him, Yolande. I am so sorry."

"Well, who on earth is it?" Mama asks impatiently.

"'Mr. George W. Cuffee,'" Margaret reads as I squeeze my eyes shut, "'and Miss Angela Whetstone of Brooklyn, New York, to wed in the early winter.'"

"Now you just wait a minute here," Mama says, stamping her foot angrily. "When did you and George break things off?"

"I didn't know we had officially! Mama, I don't care about that part! Angela can have him. Why would he announce it that way when all of Harlem still thinks we're an item?" I wail as tears streak down my face. "Why would he want to humiliate me that way?"

"Yolande, don't go into hysterics about this," Margaret fusses. "You are over him anyway. We've talked about this."

"Oh hush, Margaret. If Charles had done something like this—"

"Then I would know that he already had that girl waiting in the wings, and I would hold my head up high, because they are both scoundrels," Margaret says emphatically. "Don't you shed one tear over him. Not one."

"You *know* the tears aren't over him," I say as fresh ones trickle down my face.

"Everyone will think they are."

Mama takes the paper from Margaret's hands so she can read it herself. She stamps her foot again.

"Oh, he's going to feel my wrath on this. Imagine trying to launch a business with no customers."

Margaret gasps. "You wouldn't," she says.

"I would, and I have done much worse."

Mama turns to look at me, maybe for an *amen*, but I'm in no condition to agree or disagree. I'm fading fast. Not quite fainting, but it
feels like the blood is draining out of my head, torso, arms and, as it
travels downward, I'm falling, sliding down the outside wall of the
West 135th Street library.

Everyone is going to know George did this to me. And everyone
in Harlem is going to have one big, hearty, laugh—

Chapter Eleven

October 1922
Harlem, New York

What is the meaning of this, Yolande?" Papa says in my bedroom in as gruff a voice as he dares to muster while I'm still recovering from the surgery on my appendix. And even though he barely raises his voice, Mama glares at him from her bedside vigil.

"It's a telegram, Papa," I say, stating the obvious. I know he is asking why and how I am receiving a birthday greeting from Jimmie.

I look down at Jimmie's words. *Accept my sincere greetings on your birthday. Jimmie.*

He's at Fisk now and the thought of that makes me want to rise right from my sick bed and get on that train to Nashville. I am almost well enough to travel, but classes have started without me, and the girls are already, I'm sure, swarming over Jimmie. When I passed out in the street after reading George's wedding announcement, they discovered at the hospital that my appendix had burst and needed to be removed. That's why I'm still home and not back at school. I suppose I'm glad it happened while I was home and not in Nashville.

I wonder how much he's grown in these two years. Let me stop thinking, before I give myself a fever and Mama calls the doctor.

Papa puts both hands on his hips and turns his attention to Mama. "The young hooligan from the senior promenade. Jimmie."

"He's not a hooligan, Papa. And he goes to Fisk now."

Mama's face lights up as she beams at Papa. "Oh, isn't that wonderful,

Will. He chose your alma mater. You must have made a fine impression on him."

"You did, Papa."

Papa gives me a frustrated glance from the corner of his eye and then looks back at Mama. "And so, he can't wait for you to get to campus, he must pester you while you're trying to get well?" he asks.

"Will!" Mama says. "How is she being pestered? I think this is very sweet of him to remember her birthday. None of her other school friends have sent greetings yet."

"He always sends a card, Papa. Unlike George, who you thought was the cat's meow. I bet George didn't know it was my birthday. Or my favorite color, or my favorite food."

"Silly and trivial things," Papa says.

"But I bet he knew every one of those things about you. I think he was more excited about the idea of you as his father-in-law than me as his wife."

"You are not equipped to be anyone's wife at the present, Yolande. And after what happened with George, the last thing you need to be concerned about at Fisk is a boy. You had a difficult time last year. If you want to graduate you need to buckle down on your studies."

Well, what happened with George was that he was two-timing me with Angela Whetstone. And honestly, aside from being the laughingstock of everyone and embarrassed all over Harlem, I couldn't care less about George marrying someone else.

More than anything, I was upset that Papa blamed me for George's loss of interest in me. He didn't blame George's wandering eye. Somehow it was all my fault, and my tears were my own to wipe away. He had letters to write.

Anyway, I'm feeling much better now that I know Jimmie made it to campus and is waiting for me. I wish I could've been there to greet him . . . and to let those hungry hyenas know that I have first dibs on him.

"Chemistry was not my fault, Papa," I say, hoping to take Papa's attention away from Jimmie, George, and all things boys. "And Miss Callinge simply hates me. I cannot help that either."

"You will get a tutor for chemistry, and study harder. As for the dean of women, it is unfortunate that you inherit both my friends and my enemies. However, no daughter of mine will beg for someone's favor. If the woman has decided not to like you for no good reason, there is nothing that can be done. Treat her as if she does not exist."

That's easy enough for Papa to say. He doesn't have to get permission from that old battle axe to do any old thing. But I'm determined this year that even if the dean of women doesn't care for me, she's not going to stop me from having my best year yet at Fisk.

"All right, Papa. I will."

"I also am asking you to steer clear of Jimmie."

"Papa!"

Papa raises his hand to stop my protest. "I know you're of age to choose your own companions. I am just warning you of that kind of boy."

"You don't know him!"

Papa's face is red with fury, so Mama intervenes. She stands and strokes Papa's arm. He looks down at Mama's hand like it's a foreign thing. He calms a little, but not much.

"Will," Mama pleads, "let them have their fun. We had fun when we were their age."

"That is precisely what I am concerned about. Thank heavens Yolande has a very competent chaperone. Miss Nellie would never let her get up to mischief," Papa says with confidence.

I try not to smirk when I think about what Papa doesn't know about Miss Nellie. We learned freshman year that once she falls asleep, a whole team of horses could trot right through her room and she wouldn't even break a snore. She can hardly keep her eyes open past nine o'clock, so as long as we stay awake longer than she does and someone keeps watch, we can have all kinds of fun.

The bigger concern is the white administrators, who are ready to expel girls for any reason. We're all of age, so we should be able to entertain the opposite sex if we aren't doing anything lewd and are in at a reasonable hour. But the curfews are ridiculous, especially for the girls. The only way around them is to have a job or some approved activity off campus, like at church or a volunteer organization. We've learned ways to circumvent the rules, although some girls still get sent home when they've done something dumb like getting caught laid up with a boy. The boys get sent home too, but less frequently than the girls.

Luckily, because of Papa's influence, I am usually not a target of the administrators. They would never hear the end of it if they tried to expel me. I suppose that is protection, but it also makes the other girls jealous sometimes. But there are many things that make the other girls envious of me . . .

Like just last year someone said I was stuck up because Charlotte DeBerry and I rode to Nashville in a private car on the train with a drawing room. That wasn't about being stuck up or privileged. It was only because I catch every germ and bug, and Papa didn't want me to be sick when I got to school.

No one understands these things. They only assume that I'm some little rich girl. Sure, I arrive to campus with a trunk full of dresses, while some girls only have two to their name, but I don't flaunt these things. Papa works hard and spoils me, even though there are times when money is not always as abundant as it seems. But appearances must be kept so I have my allowance. I share with my friends, and I never brag because that is just tacky.

Being blessed with more is something that I don't take for granted. I also know what it means to struggle. Okay, that's not true. I don't intimately know what it is to struggle, but I have heard what it's like and I want no part of it.

"Papa, I will obey the rules and Miss Nellie. And Jimmie is a good boy."

"No matter," Papa says with a shrug of his shoulders. "I encourage you to pursue your gifts instead of boys."

"Well, first my gifts will need to present themselves." I say this only partially in jest.

"Your drawing has greatly improved, and Miss Fauset says that the pieces you sent her over the summer are even better than the ones we published in *The Brownies' Book* last year. You may see some of your articles in *The Crisis* soon."

I search Papa's face for any signs that he might be exaggerating, but he appears to be sincere with his praise. I believed it was a grand stretch finally convincing Papa to put my work in *The Brownies' Book* not once, but twice. Never did I imagine being invited to submit to *The Crisis*.

Papa is obsessed with all the young writers in Harlem, and he likes to entice them into submitting their poetry and stories to *The Crisis* with various contests and prize money. He'd pay them all if he could. Then Miss Fauset collects them to her bosom like some mother duck gathering her ducklings, trying to make them all go to her church and have teas at her apartment and the 135th Street library. Or is it the other way around? Maybe Miss Fauset collects them and then Papa entices them. Either way, they both are enamored with anyone who scribbles a word down and calls it a poem.

Not that the writers aren't talented. It's only Papa's obsession with them that is strange, not their vocation. I am equally impressed by Jimmie and his musical instruments. That is a gift if I ever saw one. I don't understand why Papa dismisses Jimmie's gift the way he does.

"You're going to get her too excited, Will," Mama fusses. "I need her to rest, so the doctor will give her a clean bill of health."

"I feel good now, Mama. I want to get the final fittings done for my winter dresses this week."

"You're not in any pain? Just yesterday you didn't want to get out of bed," Papa says suspiciously.

"I am in a tiny bit of pain, but I mustn't let too much of the quarter get away from me. I want to graduate on time, without spending the entire summer taking classes."

"A tiny bit of pain?" Mama asks. "You were moaning and groaning loud enough to be heard outside."

"I feel much better now, Mama. Can we just go take care of my dresses? And maybe down to Blumstein's to pick up a few things for fall. I need a new brassiere and undergarments."

Mama and Papa exchange skeptical glances, but I don't care if they think my healing is miraculous. Thinking about seeing Jimmie again has put me in the best of spirits, and if that has cured my body then they should be rejoicing.

Chapter Twelve

Mama was too protective to let me travel to Nashville alone, no matter how many times I tried to convince her that I'm capable of getting myself on and off a train. Mama wouldn't hear of it, and Papa had unfortunately agreed with her. Sometimes, I think Papa is just elated to have both of us out of his hair for a while.

The train conductor walks down the center aisle, looking entirely too bright-eyed and bushy-tailed for it to be seven o'clock in the morning.

"We'll arrive at the Nashville station in twenty minutes," the conductor announces. "Please make sure to gather your valuables, and do not leave anything behind."

"Miss Nellie will be at the station?" Mama asks. "It will be good to see her again."

"Yes, Mama."

I don't mention Jimmie because there's no need to set her to worrying about that yet. Jimmie's response to my letter about my arrival was ambiguous, so I'm unsure if he's coming to meet me at the station. I don't know if I'd blame him if he didn't come, but telling him about George was the right thing to do, I'm sure of it.

"Look," Mama says. "We're at our station. Gather your books there, Yolande." Mama points and I gather.

As the train comes to a stop, people begin to push out of their seats in a very disorderly fashion. Mama and I press into the aisle too, as I stand on tiptoes to see out the window.

When we finally exit the train, at first, I don't see anyone I know, not even Miss Nellie. The platform is so crowded.

"I didn't expect there to be so many people out and about this early on a Sunday morning," Mama says with exasperation in her tone. "Quickly, let's get over to the unloading area before someone makes off with one of our bags."

How can Mama be so weary and disgruntled when she slept soundly the entire way here? But any irritation that I might have felt fades as soon as I see Jimmie waiting with Miss Nellie for our bags to be removed from the train.

Jimmie's here, looking like he stepped right out of my dreams! Taller, even more handsome than before, and that shadow of a mustache has grown all the way in, though he still has it neatly trimmed.

"Jimmie!" I wave enthusiastically when he looks over at Mama and me.

"Yolande, calm down," Mama warns. "You are not completely healed."

I may not have my full strength, but I ignore Mama's fussing as I pull away from her and race with arms outstretched toward Jimmie.

When Jimmie reaches me, he gently lifts me into his arms and spins me. His smile is so wide that it erases any discomfort I felt from the lifting. He quickly swipes his eyes to catch his happy tears, but I don't try to hide mine.

"I almost thought I wasn't going to see you again," Jimmie says. "I mean, when you weren't on campus at the start of the year."

"Well, I made it." I resist touching Jimmie's arms and chest, though both look deliciously chiseled in his dress shirt and tie. "You're all grown up now, huh?"

"Sure am. Let me get your stuff, so I can load Miss Nellie's car. Do you know she let me drive?"

I follow Jimmie as he jogs over to the baggage. "She did?"

"Yep. She says I drive better than she does."

I point at a large black trunk with a blue ribbon tied on the top. "That's mine."

"It looks heavy," Jimmie says with a chuckle.

"It's not too heavy. I managed it when we got on the train in New York," I say. "It's just clothing."

Jimmie retrieves my trunk and lifts it like it's no heavier than a feather and walks it over to Miss Nellie's car, while I find our suitcases. Mama reaches the baggage area, and she greets Miss Nellie. Both women stare at me with knowing grins on their faces.

"When James offered to drive me to the train station this morning, I thought he was simply being kind to an older lady," Miss Nellie says.

Mama laughs as I look away, unable to meet their gazes. "Yolande also did not mention to me that her senior promenade date would be coming to collect her."

"Her promenade date? Oh, so there is history?" Miss Nellie asks, her tone full of amusement. They're both smiling at Jimmie as he gathers all three of our suitcases at once.

Jimmie seems to be enjoying this teasing way more than I am. "Hello, Mrs. Du Bois," Jimmie says. "It's wonderful to see you again."

"The pleasure is all mine, James," Mama says. "And Yolande's."

My cheeks get warm, as Miss Nellie and Mama burst into laughter. Jimmie beams at them and hauls the luggage as we follow closely behind.

"He has certainly grown, hasn't he?" Mama whispers as we approach the automobile. "Even more handsome than I remember."

Jimmie helps Mama and Miss Nellie climb into the backseat and then helps me into the passenger seat to ride beside him. It would be a perfect day if it wasn't so hot. My hair is going to be a puffy and tragic mess by the time we make it to campus.

"Will you mind if my teammates carry your things upstairs at Jubilee Hall?" Jimmie asks me after he cranks the automobile up and climbs into the driver's seat.

"No, but where will you be?"

"James leads the choir at Ebenezer AME Church," Miss Nellie says. "He'll be late if he hauls your bags and trunk up six flights of stairs."

Jimmie peeks sheepishly at me out of the corner of his eye. "You aren't angry, are you?"

"How can I be angry about you going to church?"

He shrugs. "I don't know. Do you want to go too? What about you, Mrs. Du Bois? I'd love for you to hear me play the organ."

"I'd love to hear you play, James," Mama says, "but I am starting to feel unwell. I think it's from the long train ride. I'll probably be fine after a good nap and a cup of tea."

The last place I'm trying to go after sitting on a long train ride is a hot, stuffy church. And Ebenezer's pastor is long-winded too. But I'm not ready to be separated from Jimmie after having been apart from him for more than two years. He's looking so fine that I never want to leave his side again.

"Of course I want to go to church. Minnie can make sure my trunk gets put away, and I can hang my dresses later."

The way Jimmie beams at me, I know that's the right answer.

"Good. I want to spend the whole day looking at you," Jimmie says.

"Shouldn't you be thinking about God in church?" Miss Nellie asks.

"I will be," Jimmie quips. "I'll be thinking about how God healed Yolande so that she could come back to school."

"Her healing was quite miraculous," Mama says. "She got your birthday telegram and was all better the next day."

"Mama!"

"Well, you were. Miss Nellie, I hope you'll help keep an eye on what she's eating. She can only maintain her good health if she eats well."

"I will help too, Mrs. Du Bois," Jimmie says. "I know she likes sweets, but I'll help keep her healthy."

"You'll do no such thing," I fuss at Jimmie. "I'll eat what I want."

"Thank you, James," Mama says, ignoring my declaration. "We'll need all the help we can get. As you can see, she's rather stubborn."

As we approach the campus the familiar landscape comes into view. The green, wide-open fields surrounding the Fisk campus give our school a remote feel, but up ahead in the distance, I can see the majestic Jubilee Hall. My home away from home.

"Was the football team victorious over Morehouse?" I ask.

"Yes, we won twenty-one to seven. And I scored a touchdown."

I clap excitedly. "I knew you'd win. Congratulations!"

"I believe there's going to be a parade later this evening. Are you going to carry a banner with my name on it?"

"I may carry a banner that says Fisk football," I say. "I'm not sure if I should carry a banner with your name yet. What if there's some other girl on campus carrying the same banner? I'll feel right silly, won't I?"

Jimmie's eyes widen and he shakes his head. "There's no one else carrying a banner for me."

"Humph."

That's not what my roommate, Minnie, says. But I'm not going to hold it against him if other girls are interested in him. It's not his fault my appendix decided to rupture right before the term started and I wasn't on hand to let everyone know he was spoken for. As long as he knows that any other random flirtations are over now. I'm here, and obviously our reunion was meant to happen. Hopefully, we can skip right over the carcass of the relationship I never really wanted with George.

That's buried in Harlem and the obituary was printed in the *Amsterdam News*.

Chapter Thirteen

The church service was long and tedious as most church services are, but the thing that really exasperated me was seeing Chrystal Tulli of the tragic hair gazing at Jimmie from the choir loft the entire service. Now, we're at one of Ebenezer's frequent picnics that they host when the weather is nice. Right behind the church, under the oak trees, they set up tables and chairs and make good ole Memphis-style barbecue.

As Miss Nellie and I sit at a picnic table sipping lemonade waiting on Jimmie to finish talking to the musicians so he and I can go together for some barbecue, we watch Chrystal cross the lawn, making a beeline for Jimmie. With two plates in her hands.

I just know she didn't make my Jimmie a plate! She saw us come in together. She saw him show me to my seat. But I will just sit and wait. One thing Mama taught me, and my situation with George reinforced, is to never, ever compete for a boy. Because when you do, you end up embarrassed.

"Well, she's sure marking her territory, isn't she?" Miss Nellie says.

Jimmie glances over at our table, nervous as can be, before he directs Chrystal to give one of her prepared plates to one of the musicians. I bite down on my bottom lip to hold in my laughter, but Miss Nellie hollers.

"Oh, he's a smart one," she says.

He dashes over to our table, grinning like he's proud of himself. But I'm wondering why Chrystal got such nerve in the first place. Was he flirting with her before I got back to campus?

"Do you all mind if I sit?" he asks Miss Nellie as he approaches. I roll my eyes, pretending to be annoyed.

"Of course you can sit here with Yolande," Miss Nellie says, "but I'm going to help the other ladies set up the dessert table. Aren't you going to get something to eat?"

"Why don't you eat the plate Chrystal made for you?" I ask.

Miss Nellie chuckles as she leaves me and Jimmie alone at the picnic table. My stomach growls and so does Jimmie's. We're both starving for some of that barbecue, so any major discussion will need to wait.

"Well, why didn't you?" I ask.

Jimmie's smile is slow and sure. "I don't want anyone to think Chrystal is my sweetie, 'cause I'm only sweet on you."

"I sure couldn't tell." It's hard for me to maintain a scowl when he's this handsome. "You and Chrystal were making eyes at each other the entire service."

"I would've much rather it was you in the loft, but you're not in the choir. Why don't you join? We could always use another member."

"I'm not much of a singer, Jimmie. I leave that to the girls in the Harmonia Club."

Jimmie takes my hand and gently pulls me to my feet. "You don't have to be all that great for the choir. You can let the best singers sing loud, and you can just blend."

As we start walking toward the barbecue line, I can feel curious eyes on us. Let them take us in and get used to this. I hope this erases the memory of George from everyone's mind.

"You just want to have an excuse to see me off campus on the practice nights."

"You got me there," Jimmie admits. "I didn't think there would be so many rules here. I have more rules here than I have at home."

"I hate that we won't have any classes together," I say. "I've already taken most of the classes you have this year. But what if, next term, I take a music class as an elective?"

"You'd do that just to have a class with me?"

"You're not the only one sweet on somebody, you know."

"Well, why didn't you run to make me a lunch plate like Chrystal, then?" Jimmie asks, rubbing his rock-hard midsection, just like an old potbellied uncle would. "A man is starving after all that playing."

I toss my head back and laugh. "Is that the kind of thing you like, Jimmie?"

"A girl running to make me a plate? No, not particularly."

"Well, good. Because I might do it, if I feel like it, but other times, I might not. And you would have to be fine with it either way."

"I'd be mighty fine with it."

"Plus, all those cackling old hens can't wait to have something to report back to my papa."

Jimmie looks around the picnic area and seems to notice for the first time that more than one group of ladies is staring at us.

"Your papa has friends here? At Ebenezer?" he asks. "I thought he wasn't much for church."

"He has friends in Nashville and at Fisk," I explain. "When I go home for the holidays, he loves to give me a report on what he thinks he knows about my activities. But he doesn't know everything."

"Wait. What doesn't he know about?" Jimmie asks with a worried frown.

"Jimmie, you're so jealous."

I get nervous when Jimmie stops in his tracks, right before we get to the line for the barbecue.

"Shouldn't I be? You wrote to me about a guy you were dating, Yolande," he says quietly, so that only I can hear. "I don't know how I'm not supposed to be jealous."

I take a deep breath, and exhale. "All right. Let's talk about that."

"I don't want to. It's over and done now, right?"

"It's over. It's done."

"Well, I don't need to know the details. I do need to eat though. I was so tempted to take that plate from Chrystal, 'cause I could eat a horse right now."

But I do want to tell him about George, and that it was more Papa's doing than mine. I just don't want to do it now, out in the open. This cannot be a sore spot between us.

"Well, I'm glad we're getting our food together. I don't want to hear Papa's complaints. He'll say he sent me to Fisk to get an education, not to make supper plates for mannish boys."

"Am I mannish?" he asks in a way that answers the question in the affirmative.

"Papa thinks so."

"What do you think?"

I let my eyelashes flutter flirtatiously before I give him a coquettish wink. "I like mannish, so I don't want anything to change."

The women's auxiliary ladies serve the food in the barbecue line, and they look perplexed to see us walk up together. I'm sure one of them showed extra special attention and love to the plate that was prepared for Jimmie at Chrystal's request. But now here he is in line, seeking another plate with a different young lady. Whoever had wagered on Chrystal winning Jimmie's heart by way of smoked ribs and potato salad was mistaken.

"You hungry, young man?" Sister Brown asks while cutting her eyes at me. "You sure played well this morning."

"Thank you, ma'am," Jimmie says politely. "And yes, I'm starving. I think I could eat the whole pig."

I laugh as Sister Brown starts loading up his plate with food. "I think that's what I'll call you. Piggie. Piggie Lunceford."

Jimmie leans down toward me until his forehead touches mine. He smiles when I make an oinking sound, like the biggest, greediest pig on the farm.

"You can call me whatever you want," he says, then plants a chaste kiss on my forehead.

I gaze lovingly up at him and then look at Sister Brown. "He's a mess, isn't he?" I ask.

"Mmm-hmm. He sure is. I didn't know you had gotten back to Nashville, Yolande." Sister Brown hands Jimmie his plate and starts making another one for me with much smaller portions. "How are you feeling? Miss Nellie told us you had taken ill at the end of the summer."

"Much better now. It was my appendix. Just decided to go bad right after the big Labor Day picnic. I didn't even get to attend the Fisk alumni ball. That is my favorite summer party."

"Oh, it was your appendix? I thought it had something to do with that other business."

My face tightens. "No indeed. Do you mind if I have another tiny scoop of potato salad. It's my favorite."

"Are you sure, dear?" Sister Brown's face does something that looks like a smile but really isn't. "You know we ladies have to keep watch over our figures."

I blink rapidly trying to hold back tears. I don't know if Sister Brown is intentionally being unkind, so maybe her advice comes from a friendly place, but it sure sounds mean.

"Yolande looks fine to me," Jimmie says. "Better than fine. She could eat the whole bowl of potato salad and still look mighty fine."

Sister Brown gives her smile-not-smile again and plops another scoop of potato salad on my plate. I snatch the plate from her and we walk back to the picnic table.

"Big ugly heffa," I mumble under my breath.

"I'll admit, that did seem rude of her," Jimmie says. "But I think she might be rooting for Chrystal."

"I'm sure she is. Chrystal's people are from around here, and they don't care for me. I don't care for them either. I only attend church here because Fisk makes us go."

"Oh."

"But now that you direct the choir, I have a better reason."

"Yep. They can just get used to looking at Piggie and Yolande."

I set my heavy plate on the table and grin at Jimmie, I mean, Piggie. "They just better."

In the pit of my stomach, I feel a tangle of knots that Sister Brown brought up *that other business*. Why would she have mentioned the thing that happened with George? That salacious bit of gossip had made its way all the way from the streets of Harlem to the country parlors of the Nashville church ladies.

And she brought it up in front of Jimmie! No. Her advice hadn't been friendly at all.

Chrystal had her sights set on Jimmie, and clearly, she had accomplices.

Chapter Fourteen

October 1922
Nashville, Tennessee

I can barely get the door to our room closed before I start to tell Minnie everything that happened at church, but she flies right over to me and almost knocks me off my feet with a hug.

"Yolande, I am so glad you're finally here. I was terribly lonely."

I untangle myself as I notice my trunk turned on its side. I imagine my things being crumpled and rush over to turn it right side up.

"Oh, I'm sorry. Those boys came barging in here and I didn't know how you wanted your things situated."

"It's fine," I lie. It's not fine. "Lonely? But why? Margaret Pennybacker and Miranda are here. And Ellen and Jocelyn Johson are right next door. The entire Decagynian Club."

"There are a few new girls that show some promise. And the club is the club. We haven't made any major decisions really."

"What? We have got to start planning for the spring pageant. We're already behind if no one's done anything."

"Well, everyone was waiting for you."

"Why in the world would you be waiting for me? Who is this year's president? You didn't say in your letter."

When Minnie doesn't respond, I turn from straightening my belongings to look at her. She refuses to meet my gaze then her shoulders slump as she sighs.

"Who is it? Chrystal? Minnie, we had plans for this year. I told you exactly who to nominate."

Our friend Frieda is a senior and the only acceptable choice in my absence. That is the only way we'll be able to commandeer the pageant from Chrystal and the Harmonia Club girls who think they should be in charge just because they can sing. The lead writer of the pageant always takes direction from the president of the Decagynian Club because we are the literati. But if a singer gets control of our president seat, the pageant will be nothing more than a concert with no literary merit whatsoever.

I slam the lid of my trunk shut and join Minnie on the edge of her bed. This term is not starting well at all.

"Chrystal Tulli isn't the president," Minnie says in a quiet voice.

"Oh? Then Frieda won?"

Minnie shakes her head. "You won."

"I won? What? How can that be? I wasn't here for the election."

Minnie nervously wrings her hands. "I tried to nominate Frieda, but she wouldn't accept. She says she has too many classes to take if she wants to graduate." Minnie can hardly breathe she's talking so fast. "Then, I panicked when Amanda nominated Chrystal, and no one seemed to mind it or want to offer another name."

"Oh, my goodness."

"And then, I just blurted out your name."

"You couldn't have blurted your own name?"

Minnie squeezes her eyes shut and shakes her head. "No. Why would I do that? But Chrystal laughed and called you Hospital Bed Yolande, and then a lot of the girls turned on her and said that wasn't very thoughtful of her."

The nerve of that country bumpkin! While it's true we're not friends, we also weren't enemies.

"It was downright hateful," I say. "And not very much in the spirit of sisterhood."

"Well, anyway," Minnie continued, "the club decided that you could be the president when you got here. Anne Fisher is the vice president and Frances Warren was voted in as the secretary. I think that it really speaks to your influence with the girls that they elected you in your absence. You should feel honored."

"I appreciate the honor, but I don't know if I want the job either."

I suppose Papa will be delighted to hear about this. His daughter, the president of the women's literary society at his alma mater? He will brag about it, I'm sure. Our photo will undoubtedly find its way onto the pages of *The Crisis* this spring.

But what if I'm terrible at it? Papa's friends at Fisk and the alumni who stay involved will tell him if the spring pageant is a failure. If it is, I will never hear the end of it.

"Oh, but everyone except Chrystal and Amanda believe in you," Minnie says. "Think about the fun we'll have planning everything. You'll get to say who can sing any solos, and you can choose anyone other than Chrystal."

I feel myself getting angry again thinking about Chrystal at Ebenezer, making googly eyes at Jimmie from the front row of the choir.

"She's after Jimmie. She was practically throwing herself at him right in front of everyone. Singing a church hymn like she was Mamie Smith in a nightclub."

Minnie waves her hand in the air and cackles. "But Jimmie's not thinking about her. I saw him keep her at arm's length at the rally the other night. She tried to corner him, but he ducked and dodged and ran right out of there."

It makes me feel good to know that Jimmie had rejected her right in front of everyone. Sometimes I think pretty girls like Chrystal are just appalled when boys like Jimmie choose plain and plump girls like me.

"She had the audacity to fix him a plate at the church picnic."

"A plate? In front of everyone?"

I don't even need to explain the severity of this infraction.

"But did he eat it?" Minnie asks, probably worried for Jimmie's life.

"He knew better than to do that."

Minnie laughs again.

"Well, I'll have to make her pay for that hospital bed joke," I say, and mean it.

"Don't do something too terrible. We need her to sing for the pageant. Our best singers graduated."

"I know the perfect way to keep her in the pageant and eat her heart out at the same time."

I can't tell Minnie what I intend to do just yet. I must have a conversation with someone else first before my plan goes into action.

Chapter Fifteen

November 1922
Nashville, Tennessee

I couldn't care less about singing in a church choir, but now that I know Chrystal is after Jimmie, there's no way I wouldn't join Ebenezer's. The best part is that practice falls during campus dining hours, so because of that, we all have permission to have dinner at Pearly's Diner immediately following rehearsal. If only Dr. McKenzie knew that Miss Pearly's son, Jerome, looks the other way while the young people mingle because we're spending our parents' hard-earned money in their restaurant.

Jerome is especially fond of the Fisk sports teams because they bring in even more traffic after the games. So, Jimmie and I have our own favorite booth in the corner. We use it after the games and on choir rehearsal night.

"Do you want a patty melt?" Jimmie asks me as I snuggle in as close as I can without looking indecent. Our thighs touch under the table, and we hold hands. "A milkshake?"

"Mmm-hmm. That sounds delicious, but I probably shouldn't have either of those. A plain turkey sandwich and tomato soup is better. With a glass of water."

"That's no fun at all."

"I know. But I haven't been feeling well, and I promised I would follow my papa's meal plan until I am fully better."

"And I promised your mother I'd help you stay healthy. Do you think you rushed back to school before you were ready?"

I smile at him. "If I did, it was for a good reason."

Jimmie blushes and looks away from my gaze, reminding me of how shy he was when we first met.

"I have a favor to ask of you on behalf of the Decagynians," I say sweetly.

"I'll do it."

I laugh. "But I haven't told you what it is yet."

"Tell me."

"I'm hoping you'll help me with the music for our spring pageant."

He brings my hand to his lips and places a sweet kiss on the back of it. "Of course. Yes. What do you have in mind? Will there be singing? Do you want me to play? Do you want a band?"

"Yes, all those things. What do you think about playing music while the girls recite poetry?"

"During the recitation?"

"Mmm-hmm!"

He tilts his head to one side like he's imagining what that might sound like. "I like that idea. We'll have to tinker with it some, to make sure the music doesn't overtake the recitations."

"But it's a good idea?"

"Yes, I can almost see it happening in my head. Will you be reciting a poem?"

"Only if you'll play for me."

"Of course. Do you think I'd let anyone else play for my girl?"

Minnie slides in our booth across from us, interrupting our moment.

"You two act as if this isn't a public establishment," Minnie says as she points at our intertwined fingers.

"Who is coming here on a Thursday night except us?" I ask. "Everybody's home eating dinner and getting ready for work or school in the morning."

"Who knows?" Minnie asks with a shrug. "Miss Nellie might find herself in the mood for rhubarb pie."

"Does she often get pie cravings?" Jimmie asks, now worried.

Oh, my goodness. Now she's got him on edge. "Minnie worries too much, just like you, Jimmie. We're of age, and we're at a diner, not a speakeasy."

"That is true," Minnie says, "but you're practically sitting in his lap."

"I am not."

Minnie shrugs again. "I'm just telling you what my little eyes spied."

I put a small space between myself and Jimmie. "Better?" I ask.

"Barely," Minnie says, then she laughs. "I'm just teasing, but Chrystal and Amanda keep saying things, so you best be careful."

"What kinds of things?" Jimmie asks, leaning forward protectively, but I pat his hand, calming him.

"Only that you're a good boy, Jimmie, and Yolande doesn't care one bit about Jesus anyway," Minnie says with a laugh. "They're waiting for you to choose a proper Christian girl as a companion."

"Old jealous cows," I say as I throw a napkin at Minnie. "But they're wrong on both counts."

"Jimmie's not a good boy?" Minnie asks.

"Nope, he's a grown man, can't you tell? What's wrong with them that they can't see that?"

Jimmie grins. "But I am a good man."

"And you are mine," I declare.

My declaration could be heard across the diner, and that's the entire point, because these girls are about to get on my last good nerve. Chrystal stares over at us, lifts one of her bushy eyebrows, and smiles. Is that supposed to be a warning?

Chapter Sixteen

November 1922
Nashville, Tennessee

Mama does not look well as we stand on the train platform awaiting her train back to New York. She has overstayed her time in Nashville, and I'm ready for her to go her merry way. She's hovering, and I'm feeling hovered over.

Besides, Papa needs her at home. There's no telling what mischief he'll get up to if left unattended, although Miss Fauset won't let him stray too far from home. Thank goodness that when Mama's here taking care of me someone is there to take care of Papa.

"I left Miss Nellie the menus your papa had the doctor prepare. She is to inform the kitchen staff of your dietary needs."

"We don't need to make such a fuss. I can eat what everyone else does."

"Eating what everyone else did is what landed you in that hospital bed, Yolande."

Hospital bed, Yolande. Hearing those words put together that way makes me groan and is more reason I don't want to seem different to the rest of the girls.

"Healthy food is already being prepared. I don't want them to go to any trouble on account of me."

"Well, they should. If it wasn't for your father highlighting this university in the pages of *The Crisis*, their enrollment numbers wouldn't be up. They should be treating you like something special here. You are the daughter of their most notable alumnus."

This is why the dean of women hates me. Mama and Papa expect to have the royal treatment for themselves, and for me. I don't want any special treatment. It makes the other girls even more jealous, and makes the administrators look for alternative ways to make me suffer when they don't feel comfortable punishing me outright.

"Also, Yolande," Mama says, her tone turning very serious, "I want you to be very careful concerning Jimmie."

"Mama . . ."

"No, you listen to me. That young man has the kind of looks and charisma that can talk you right out of your undergarments."

I try not to giggle, but I do hope he does exactly that.

"And he is way too young and too poor to make an honest woman out of you."

Yes. Yes, Mama. That is why God made rubber, and then men made prophylactics. So that we don't make a baby.

"Mama, Jimmie is such a church boy and a square. You're worrying for nothing."

"Well, then maybe it isn't Jimmie I should be worried about."

"You know I would never do anything to dishonor you or Papa. You don't need to worry about me or Jimmie."

Mama grins. "I can't wait to tell your father you're the president of the Decagynian Society. He's going to be so tickled."

"I hope he can make it down for the spring pageant. It's going to be spectacular."

"I'm sure he will try. If you write him in advance, he will put it on his schedule."

Yes, Papa must see the pageant. And when he does, he will see why I love Jimmie so, and why I found my way back to him.

Chapter Seventeen

November 1922
Nashville, Tennessee

Sneaking off campus on a Friday night takes planning, coordination, and allies. The first thing you need is a cover story in case someone does a bed check. That's easy for me. I'm always sick with some sort of stomach ailment, and Minnie knows to say that my dinner must not have agreed with me. Miss Nellie believes this without question, because it is often true. I can't count the number of times I've sat in the water closet feeling miserable after eating an extra bowl of ice cream, or a second slice of cake.

Second, you need transportation. Luckily, Jimmie's friends on the football team were more than willing to help me sneak out to meet him. Once I successfully escaped the sleeping Miss Nellie and changed into my traveling outfit (a boy's shirt, hat, and slacks) I had someone waiting to pick me up on the corner to drive me to the Andrew Jackson Hotel.

It took a bit of cajoling and promising to get John a date with Minnie, but since he was a janitor at the hotel, he was able to sneak me into the band's practice room where Jimmie was going to be at the end of the night. It was a big effort to pull off the surprise.

Poor Jimmie looks so worn out after playing all evening with the band, but John said that no matter how tired he was, he always takes time to practice his saxophone before going back to campus.

He doesn't even notice that John and I have crept into the room as he plays a haunting and forlorn-sounding tune.

"That was beautiful, Jimmie."

He turns around and looks rather stunned to see me with John at my side.

"Yolande, what are you doing here?" he asks, his voice full of alarm as he puts down his saxophone and rushes over. "It's after curfew. You're going to get in trouble. And what are you wearing?"

I laugh as I snatch off the baseball cap and twirl, showing off my baggy dungarees and button-down shirt.

"Jimmie, you worry too much. Miss Nellie is asleep, and Minnie is keeping watch."

"But how did you get off campus?" he asks, still sounding nervous.

"I've been sneaking off campus since freshman year," I say with a giggle. "I had a ride. Aren't you happy to see me?"

"Of course I am, but I don't want you to get expelled."

"It's cool, man. No one saw her, except a couple of the housekeepers," John says. "I brought her in the staff entrance."

"Thank you. I appreciate it," Jimmie says to his friend.

John slaps Jimmie on the back. "Think nothing of it. You'll return the favor at some point, brother."

They both laugh as John leaves and closes the door, leaving me and Jimmie alone, finally. I stride across the room to where Jimmie left his saxophone and run my fingers over the instrument. Then, I look back at Jimmie and wonder what he's waiting for.

"Come here, silly," I say, beckoning him over. "Play some more. That's why I'm here, you know. I want to hear you play for me."

"I don't always play with the band on Friday nights, so how did you know to come?"

"I overheard Captain Bragg's girl saying you and John were at the hotel tonight, so she was sneaking off to meet him somewhere."

"Is everyone sneaking to meet everyone?"

I giggle as I pick up the saxophone to finger the keys. "We're young and over eighteen. What did they think we would do? They should just let us keep each other's company anyway."

When Jimmie doesn't respond I gaze up at him. He has a strange look on his face. Maybe he doesn't like me playing with his saxophone. I hope I'm not breaking anything.

"What's wrong?" I ask.

"Nothing."

I hold the saxophone out to him. "Then play for me. What you were playing before."

The tips of our fingers touch as he takes the instrument from my hands. "I think I'd like to play something else. Something I composed for you while we were apart."

"You wrote a song for me?"

He holds the saxophone to his lips and begins to play. The melody starts off low and deep, kind of like the sound thunder makes when it comes across the field at the start of a storm. Sad and melancholy, searching for a place to strike, but finding none. And then, the notes quickly climb and cascade back down before settling into a long trill that sounds like a wail.

Then, when it seems like he held the trill for an impossible length of time, he starts his ascent again. The notes are now shorter and lilting. The sound is uplifting and hopeful.

As he gets to the end of the serenade it is high-pitched and less sensual, but upbeat and sounds joyous. And toward the end the notes come back down to a calm and middle-toned hum.

"I love it," I say as he removes the saxophone from his mouth, letting me know he's finished. "But tell me how you came up with all that. You are so creative. How do you remember the notes?"

"It's a head composition," he explains. "Part of it came to me in a dream, and then I built on it."

"A dream? You were dreaming of me? I am flattered, Jimmie."

I lightly kiss the tips of his fingers still touching the saxophone and then spin over to the sofa where I plop down. He watches me with awe in his eyes.

"How do you know no one's ever dreamed of you?" Jimmie asks as he sets the saxophone down and tentatively moves closer to me. Seeming unsure as to whether or not he should sit next to me on the sofa, he chooses the chair instead. "You don't know what people are dreaming about."

"That's true. I've never had anyone tell me they've dreamt about me, though. You're the first."

"I dreamed about you the whole time we were apart."

I kick off my shoes and pull my feet onto the couch, making my body into a tight ball. "What kinds of dreams? I hope they weren't the naughty kind. I am a good girl, Jimmie."

This breaks the tension in the room, because finally he laughs. "You've snuck here after curfew dressed like a boy, but you're a good girl."

I wink at him, even though I know what he's getting at. "The best."

"It makes me wonder what kinds of shenanigans you were getting into before I got here," Jimmie says in a huff. "You seem to know all the tricks."

"You're going to hurt my feelings." I cross my arms and pout. "I came all the way here, risking life and limb to spend time with you and you're insulting me now."

"I'm sorry, I didn't mean to hurt your feelings," Jimmie says. "I'm sure glad you came."

I knew it was going to come to this, and we should have this conversation now, and get it out in the open.

"That's more like it. But to answer your suspicions, I didn't get up to *those* kinds of shenanigans at all. Us girls would sneak out past Miss Nellie, though, if we wanted to see a late-night movie or even go dancing. Once, we even went all the way to Memphis to a club. That was big fun."

"Memphis? How'd you get away with that one?"

"We almost didn't get away with it, I'll say that much. We stayed over at a girl's family's house because we were going to church with them in the morning. It happened to be Chrystal Tulli's people's church."

"Oh boy."

"Exactly. We could barely keep our eyes open, so they knew we'd been out partying. Everybody in that church talked bad about us, I'm sure, but nobody had any proof of our mischief."

Jimmie shakes his head. "At least you made it to church."

"Yes, but I had to keep pinching Minnie because she snores when she sleeps, and she kept nodding off."

"And you're sure it was just you girls? You didn't meet up with any fellas at the club?"

I narrow my eyes at him. "Okay, spit it out. You want to know about George, right?"

"The song I composed," he says, "did you hear how it started out kind of sad?"

"Yes, I heard that. It worried me that you said it was about me, and it sounded all kinds of sorrowful. I was glad it got happier at the end."

"Well, it started that way because I was sad when you wrote to me that you were seeing somebody. I couldn't stop thinking about it. The only way I got through it was by playing my saxophone and dreaming about you."

I bite my bottom lip and look away from his tear-rimmed eyes for a moment. Now there are tears in my eyes too. And when I look up at him and he sees my distress, in one fluid motion, he's on the sofa, next to me, comforting me.

"I almost didn't want to tell you about it at all," I say, as a tear travels down my cheek. "It was all Papa's doing anyway."

"Slow down. What was your papa's doing?" He's taken my hand and is gently stroking it, making me feel loved.

"The whole thing with George. Remember he was supposed to be my date to the senior promenade, but he canceled on me, and then you came along."

"Yes, I remember."

"Well, he and Papa were the ones who had the love affair," I explain breathlessly, the words rushing out of me. "Papa convinced him to enroll at Fisk, even though he had no plans of attending university. He withdrew at the end of last year. His grades were terrible."

"I see."

Jimmie stops stroking my hand.

"Then, over the summer he decided to be a cobbler and open his own shop. But Papa mostly loves how industrious he is, and how he takes every bit of his advice without hesitation or argument."

"Still?"

I shrug. "Being my sworn enemy has never been a reason for Papa to end a relationship with anyone."

"So, you loved him?" Jimmie drops my hand into my lap. "Because it's hard to become someone's enemy unless you once cared for them."

"Jimmie, are you listening to me? I didn't love him. Papa did."

"Then, how did you become enemies?"

How do I explain this without Jimmie thinking that I was in love with George? I was furious about the engagement and wedding announcement, but only because of the embarrassment of it all, not because I was heartbroken. But will Jimmie believe that? From the look of his flared nostrils and furrowed brow, I just don't know.

"Papa would invite him over for dinner, and on outings with the family. He let George drive his car. It was like one day it was the three of us, me, Mama, and Papa, and then the next day we were a foursome."

"And you forgot about our wish under the Wishing Tree."

I take Jimmie's hands and squeeze them. "Never. But everyone told me that *you* would forget about it. That you'd realize how handsome you are, and you wouldn't settle for one girl all the way across the country when you'd have girls clamoring for you in Denver."

Jimmie brings my hand up to his lips, kisses each finger, then holds my hand to his heart. "I never looked at another girl. The girl I escorted to my school's senior promenade was my mother's best friend's daughter, Eugenia. She's as homely as the day is long, but we've known each other since we were little kids."

"I bet she was happy to go with you."

"Eugenia was doing me a favor. Keeping me from having to ask anyone else. Everyone thought it was strange that I wasn't out chasing girls. Even my mother."

"Your mother wanted you to be a skirt chaser?"

"She didn't want me this hung up on you. Dreaming about you and writing songs and things."

"Well, I understand what she means, Jimmie. If I was your mama, I would've felt the same way."

"But you came back to me, so our wish magic is still working."

"Things didn't work out with me and George. Maybe George could tell my heart wasn't in it or maybe he realized he'd been courting Papa and not me. But I didn't know things were over between us until I read the announcement of his engagement to another young lady in the newspaper."

"Oh my. That's embarrassing. What did your papa say?"

"He wasn't even in town, but he blamed me. Of course it was something I'd done. Couldn't have been his precious future son-in-law. The future father of his talented grandchildren."

"Why didn't you just tell your papa you didn't want George?" Jimmie asks. "Wouldn't he have heard your concerns? Does he want you married to someone you don't love?"

"He wants me married to someone who will make a good husband. I don't know if love has anything to do with it. But Jimmie, if only I had known you'd truly be waiting for me, I would've fought him. I'm sorry for not believing in you. But after a while, you didn't seem real."

He pulls my face to his and places a tender kiss on my lips. I shudder. "Does this seem real?"

"Mmm-hmm. But I need another one to be sure, and you need to wrap your arms around me too. That'll really seal it."

I turn my body so that we're facing each other on the sofa, and he quickly pulls me in close. He cradles the back of my head with his hand and now kisses me more deeply than he did the first time. My fingertips stretch across the expanse of his shoulders and I climb into his lap, straddling him now, feeling lucky that I'm wearing dungarees and not a dress. Because if the only thing stopping us was the thin fabric of my panties, we'd be in trouble.

Breathlessly, we separate, before we get to the point where we can't stop ourselves. One of my hands has migrated to the base of Jimmie's neck and is massaging him there, and his hand is on my lower back where it feels like fire, and dangerous.

"I'm not used to this Yolande," Jimmie says, his voice heavy and thick with desire.

"Well, me either, but it feels so good, Jimmie, I don't wanna stop."

He untangles our limbs and lifts me out of his lap and back onto the sofa. "I don't want to get you in any trouble, Yolande. A man is supposed to be a gentleman about these things."

"I trust you."

"Well, I don't trust me," he says. "That's why I stopped kissing you."

We sit for a few minutes, side by side, no sound except our heavy breathing and our beating hearts.

"Jimmie," I whisper as I lightly graze his fingertips with mine.

"Yes?" he whispers back.

"Do you forgive me for George? I don't want that to hang between us, because I did not love him."

He sits quietly for a long moment, holding my hand. Breathing. Staring straight ahead. I'd pay anything to know what he's thinking.

"I forgive you."

I exhale, relief filling my body as I squeeze the hand that's holding mine and release the flood of tears I've held back all night since hearing Jimmie's sad song. I hope that he means it; that this loving feeling lasts. And that our Wishing Tree magic counts for something. It brought him back to me, so it must not be done with us yet.

Chapter Eighteen

November 1922
Nashville, Tennessee

As the girls from the Decagynian Society file into the Jubilee Hall meeting room, they each give curious glances at Jimmie, who greets everyone on arrival. He's so polite and friendly, while they're all wondering what he's even doing at our meeting.

"The Decagynian Society is a girls club," Amanda says. "So, no matter how much certain members . . . even the president . . . might enjoy spending time around you, Piggie Lunceford, you have got to go. Back down the hill to the boys' dormitory for you."

"You wait a minute, Amanda," I snap. "Don't you think I got permission for him to be here? He's here for a purpose, and not just because he's my boyfriend."

The *b* in *boyfriend* had an extra bite to it for Amanda and Chrystal, who didn't say anything, but stood there behind her friend, clearly in support of Amanda's attack.

"I will wait for everyone to arrive before I make my announcement, but have a seat and get comfortable," I say as more girls enter the room.

Minnie passes out cucumber sandwiches. And later there will be cake that I purchased out of my own allowance. It would've been better if Mama had time to bake and ship me one of hers, but she said she needed more than a few days' notice. I'll have to remember to ask her earlier next time.

When the last girl has arrived and Minnie has gotten her seated and fed, I signal to Jimmie so that he can join me in the front of the room. Now is the time for my announcement.

"All right, everyone. I think you all know Jimmie Lunceford. Most of you know he plays football, but did you also know he is a skilled musician?"

Chrystal rolls her eyes at my introduction of Jimmie. Of course she knows he's a musician.

"Jimmie is going to be the musical director of this year's spring pageant. Like every year, there will be singing, but since we are a literary society, this year there will also be poetry readings accompanied by jazz music."

"Poetry readings?" Amanda says. "Excuse me for saying this, Yolande, but that sounds quite boring."

"It won't be boring with jazz music accompanying the readings," I explain. "And Jimmie is the best. He is going to bring an entire band. I heard him play in Harlem while he was still in high school."

I feel my eye twitch, but I am not going to allow either of them to get the best of me. I am the president, and I'm in charge.

"Jazz music?" Chrystal asks. "Does Miss Nellie know about this?"

"I think some folks get the wrong idea about jazz," Jimmie says. "And what we'll play will go with the mood of the poetry. If it's a happy piece, we'll play an upbeat tune that people can bounce to, but if it's serious, I'll play something slow and melancholy. I promise, it's going to be fantastic. They'll be talking about this pageant for years."

"We'll really have to come up with something grand to outdo ourselves next year," I add, feeling grateful for Jimmie's explanation. The girls hung on to his every word, and how could they not with that beautiful face?

"I'm excited," Minnie says. "I'm going to look for a poem to recite."

"Might I suggest you look in the pages of *The Crisis*?" I ask. "Every month, some of the most talented colored poets are highlighted. It would be a credit to our race if we, the Decagynian Society, turned our attention to literature created by us and for us."

"Yes, everyone," Amanda says, "make sure you subscribe to *The Crisis*, Dr. Du Bois's magazine. Get those subscriptions up, so that Yolande can keep wearing pretty dresses."

I laugh even though I'm sure Amanda means to rattle me.

"Well, *The Crisis* is the NAACP's publication, and not my papa's. I would hope your families already subscribe."

"Mine doesn't," Chrystal says. "My father says the NAACP was started by white people and is concerned with the advancement of white folk more than anything else."

I am not about to enter a debate with anyone on the merits of my papa's work, and Chrystal knows it. She would say anything to embarrass me.

"What the NAACP does or doesn't do has no bearing on the Decagynian Society or our pageant," I say. "So, if no one has any questions about our theme this year, which is Poetic Interludes, let's break into committees."

"I'd like to lead the costume committee," Minnie volunteers. "Everyone knows I'm great with the sewing machine."

"Excellent. Thank you, Minnie," Anne, our vice president says, thankfully taking over for me because I am on the verge of rage. "Frances, take Minnie's name down. We'll also have a decorations committee, music committee, and poetry selection committee. Yolande and I will have oversight on all of them."

I ease down into the chair next to Jimmie, and he places a calming arm around my shoulders. The assuring squeeze he gives me soothes my nerves and communicates to the girls that we are a team. Their jabs can't hurt me as long as he's by my side.

"That went well," Jimmie whispers.

"You're joking, right?" I whisper back.

He nods. "I feel like this is partially my fault."

"Because you chose me and not her?" I shake my head. "No, it isn't that. Not entirely. She's disliked me since last year. But us being an item certainly hasn't helped."

"Everyone knows we're an item, but I don't mind it, because it keeps all the guys away from you," Jimmie says proudly. He pulls me closer, which makes me glance over at the door to the meeting room.

The last thing we need is Miss Nellie bursting in, seeing me and Jimmie snuggled close like this. So, I put space between us.

"We have to be careful."

"Of what? I'm usually the nervous one."

"I know, but it can't even look like we're doing anything wrong. The administrators are just itching to expel girls for the tiniest of things, and you're only allowed here for a purely scholastic reason. Not to socialize."

"You're right." He stands. "I'm going to get back to my dormitory. But I think the girls are excited about the idea. It's going to be good, and your papa will be proud."

"If he even hears anything about it."

"You hope he will," Jimmie says, shuffling from one leg to the other. "That's why you told the girls to pick poems from the magazine, right?"

"Papa and Miss Fauset publish the best Negro poets in the country, so it only makes sense."

"I am sure he does." Jimmie's skeptical tone doesn't match his words.

"Would it be wrong for me to make my papa proud?" I ask. "Because I will be happy if he is."

Jimmie leans in as if he is going to kiss me, but I lean back and shake my head. He remembers where we are—Jubilee Hall—and he waves a respectful goodbye greeting instead.

"Will you be in the library tomorrow to visit after classes?" he asks.

"Yes, will you wait for me?"

He grins, and sheepishly nods as he half runs and half skips down the main corridor of Jubilee Hall and out the door into the late afternoon. I wish I had plans to sneak out tonight to Pearly's or to the Andrew Jackson Hotel to spend more time with him.

Unfortunately, tonight, Jimmie will have to settle for his dreams.

* * *

I HATE NEEDING to use the toilet in the middle of the night, but the giant root beer I drank after the Decagynian meeting is determined to keep me awake. I glance over to see if Minnie is stirring even the slightest amount, because if she is I'll ask her to walk to the end of the hall with me.

She isn't stirring at all. In fact, her snoring could wake the dead, as my mama says.

So, I shimmy from under my thin blanket and slide my feet into my slippers. I'll have to trek down the long, dark hall all alone.

I am not overdramatizing either. The hallway is too long and there's a dim lamp every fifty feet or so. Luckily, I walk up and down this hall daily, so I'm used to it, but it still feels infinite when one must use the toilet. I've even counted the steps. There are 177 steps between our dormitory and the toilet.

Sometimes, when we're up at night, Miss Nellie's lamp comes on and she pokes her head out into the hallway to see if we're up to any mischief. But as hard as she sleeps, any girl who makes enough noise to wake Miss Nellie if they're sneaking out deserves to be caught. She doesn't open her door tonight though, and I would welcome her lamp casting a brighter glow onto the dark wooden planks beneath my feet.

It's at step 114 that I hear the giggling. I recognize the unmistakable husky and throaty-sounding laugh that belongs to Chrystal. I know Amanda's voice too, and a couple of other girls'. But Chrystal's voice is the loudest. Whatever they're laughing at, she finds it highly amusing.

"Can you believe we're going to be reciting poetry for the pageant?" Amanda asks. I stop in my tracks when I hear this question.

"It's a silly idea, but what do you expect?" Chrystal asks. "It's Yolande. The president no one wanted in the first place."

"Lots of people voted for her," another voice says. That's Joanne, I believe. "So maybe they did want her to be president."

"No one wanted it to be said that they didn't vote for her," Amanda says. "She's such a bully, the way she struts around here like she's some kind of princess."

My jaw drops. I don't strut around anywhere acting like anything. They are such jealous cows.

"Well, I think it's nice that she got Piggie Lunceford to play music at the pageant," Joanne says. "He's really good."

"His name is Jimmie, *not* Piggie. That nickname is just the stupidest thing I ever heard," Chrystal says. "I refuse to call him that."

"Everyone calls him that now," Amanda says.

I cover my mouth with my hand to keep from laughing and cross my legs at the ankles. I have to pee, but I want to hear the rest of this.

"We don't call him that, Amanda," Chrystal says. "And when they're done and over, he won't want anyone calling him that either."

"You don't think it'll last long?" Amanda asks. "They seem thick as thieves if you ask me."

"But Yolande is so homely. A waste of light skin," Chrystal says. "Jimmie will be done with her by the end of the year."

I might not have a dancer's body, long hair, or a sharp thin nose, but I'm far from homely. I'm so furious I want to kick Chrystal and Amanda's door in and let them know I've heard every word they've said. They're not even trying to whisper. I wonder if they know their voices carry out into the hall. It makes me wonder about things I've said behind what I thought was a closed Jubilee Hall door.

"What does he see in her anyway?" Amanda asks.

"Same thing they all see. She's rich and everybody in the world knows her daddy. Marry a girl like that, a man never has to worry about keeping food on the table and a roof over her head."

"I don't think Piggie is the lazy type," Joanne says. "Maybe he just likes her."

"Stop. Calling. Him. That."

Chrystal sounds furious, but even though I want to hear her unleash even more fury on Joanne, I can't hold it anymore and must run to the water closet.

Once inside and behind the closed and locked door, I sit on the cold porcelain and curse the hot tears that fall from my eyes onto my lap. Most of the time I can ignore girls like Chrystal and their vicious taunts about my looks. But that one, *she's a waste of light skin,* always cuts especially deep. Especially coming from girls like Chrystal, who are pretty in every way but that. Like she thinks that the only reason Jimmie prefers me is because I've got a lighter complexion than she does.

But she doesn't know what she's talking about. Jimmie won't be done with me by the end of the year or ever. So maybe a homely light-skinned princess is exactly the thing he likes.

Chapter Nineteen

Tonight is pageant night and never have I felt more nervous. Everyone's white dress is immaculate, even the tragically clumsy Amanda, who seems to attract mud fingerprints and chocolate smudges. Everyone's hair is pin curled to perfection. Chrystal's required a whole box of pins to tame that Memphis monstrosity, but it has been subdued. Each poem has been memorized, practiced, and regurgitated. The songs harmonized. Jimmie's band warmed and tuned.

Then, why am I so anxious?

Because Papa and Miss Fauset have ambushed us all with their presence. Papa has a meeting in Georgia and Fisk is on the way. Apparently since he is so proud of me and the Decagynians—he placed our club photograph in the April edition of *The Crisis*—he wanted to see the pageant in person.

Now, none of what we've planned feels good enough. Gifted enough. Worthy enough. I am now reconsidering every poem and musical selection. I am certainly wishing Papa wouldn't have to stare at Jimmie on stage all night. The only thing that would've made it bearable would be if Mama was here with him instead of Miss Fauset. She is not an acceptable exchange for Mama, not when it comes to protecting me from Papa.

Backstage at the Jubilee Hall auditorium, I nervously check everyone's props as Jimmie and the band arrive.

"You're late," I snap at Jimmie. "Is this everyone?"

I realize I've spoken much too harshly when I see Chrystal's face ease into a knowing smirk. She's always lurking in the shadows waiting for me to commit some terrible sin when it comes to Jimmie. Waiting to point out that not only am I a waste of light skin, but that I'm also a terrible person.

When I turn to face Jimmie, he looks hurt but also concerned. "This is everyone. Is everything all right?"

I shake my head once to the right and once to the left. And right when everything goes blurry and I start to lose my balance, Jimmie scoops me right up into his arms. He leads me away from everyone and to an open seat where I can breathe and hopefully gather myself. I can't fall apart now. Not with Papa here to witness it.

"Tell me what's wrong," Jimmie says as he rubs my hands in his, making me feel calmer already.

"Papa is here."

"At Fisk? For the pageant?"

I cannot stop the flood of tears. "Yes. With Miss Fauset. As a surprise."

Immediately, Jimmie wipes tears from my face. First with his hand, and then with the handkerchief he pulls from his pocket. "He will be proud of you. Why aren't you glad?"

"Because what if it isn't good enough? What if he hates it?"

"You chose these poems from ones he selected for *The Crisis*."

But I chose to set them to music. Jazz music with Jimmie as the band leader. Jimmie hadn't seen how furious Papa was to learn Jimmie was at Fisk.

"I know, but I am just worried."

Jimmie slides his forefinger under my chin, tilts it upward, then covers my mouth with a slow, soft kiss. The kind that warms your center and sends a tingle to the tip of your toes.

"I will be proud of you. Won't that be enough?"

He kisses me again, and I forget the question I'm supposed to be answering, and the reason he asked me in the first place.

* * *

PAPA SITS IN the front row, like the guest of honor, even though he didn't tell anyone he was coming. And Miss Fauset sits to his right looking young enough to be my sister. Jimmie has been trying, all night, to get his attention, but it's as if Papa's purposely not paying him any mind.

Even still, the pageant is going swimmingly, as Jimmie said it would. The only slight hiccup was Chrystal Tulli taking a tumble as she walked to the front to sing her song. During the break she insisted Minnie tripped her, but she did not. Chrystal was just embarrassed that she saw me and Minnie snickering together in a corner. She made such a big to-do about falling though, and Jimmie helped her up, like a true gentleman.

Now, we're in the second half of the show, and it's my turn to recite my poem. This is supposed to be the highlight of the pageant, but I'm so nervous, I'm afraid I'm going to do worse than Chrystal.

I walk slowly to center stage, swishing my white ruffled dress for dramatic effect. I feel that I need these little extras because I'm not singing like the Harmonias, even though Jimmie insisted I don't.

My stomach is in knots, but I lock eyes with Miss Fauset, who gives me an encouraging smile and a wink. Papa's expression is without emotion. His feelings about this are of course predicated on my talent. Am I gifted enough for him to claim? We will see.

"Hello. My name is Yolande Du Bois, and I am this year's president of the Decagynian Society," I say with confidence I do not feel. "The poem I selected appeared in the June 1921 edition of *The Crisis* magazine. It's called 'The Negro Speaks of Rivers,' by a young Harlem poet named Langston Hughes."

I give Jimmie the cue to begin his composition, which is full of slow drums and wind instruments. He said he wanted it to sound like the rushing current of a river. The entire composition is less than a minute and it is meant to be played quietly, almost to a whisper, so as not to compete with the poem's words.

I wait for my place, where Jimmie's band takes a break in the music. Then, I lift my arms to the sky like we practiced.

"'I've known rivers,'" my voice booms into the audience. "'I've known rivers ancient as the world and older than the flow of human blood in human veins.'"

I watch Papa's face transform with pride as I recite Langston Hughes's profound words that carry us colored folk from the shores of rivers in Africa to the rivers here in America. I chose this poem specifically because of Papa's deep connection to Africa and how he insists we shouldn't let anyone in this country get away with believing our history began on slave ships or plantations.

With my last word, Jimmie's clarinet player does a breathy trill, and the snare drum makes a *hushhhhhh* sound. There is silence until I take a curtsy and bow. Then, Papa leaps to his feet and gives me a standing ovation. Miss Fauset joins him, and I peek back at Jimmie. He's standing too.

But it's Papa approval that I cherish most, because it is so rare and . . . fleeting.

Chapter Twenty

My palms are damp with sweat as I watch Papa and Miss Fauset approach the front of the auditorium where the pageant cast is waiting to greet our attendees. Jimmie and I stand side by side, our bodies as close as they can be without touching. The two directors of the show, in the center of the line, and receiving our congratulations. Neither of us seems to be able to focus on our well-wishers as we watch Papa advance. He isn't smiling, but then he isn't scowling either. Miss Fauset's facial expression is neutral.

"Are you sure this was a good idea?" Jimmie whispers. "Did you tell him I was doing the music in the pageant? Did he know I was here at all?"

"He knows you're here at Fisk and he knows we're friends," I say. "Don't worry. Before I left home, he told me I was of age and able to choose my own companions. He should be happy I have someone down here like you who looks after me."

I smile at Jimmie, trying to calm him down, but I can't tell if it helps or not. I don't want him to be nervous about Papa, so before he and Miss Fauset make it to the front of the line, I break away from Jimmie and run over to greet them. I give Papa a warm hug that cracks his stern expression for a moment as he embraces me back.

"Well done, Yolande," Papa says. "I am especially fond of that Langston Hughes poem you selected. He is going to be famous one day."

Miss Fauset hugs me too. "And we will be able to say we published him in *The Crisis*."

"Come, Papa. Jimmie wants to say hello too." As I pull Papa's arm, I feel slight resistance, but I ignore it. He's going to talk to Jimmie whether he wants to or not.

But Jimmie doesn't wait on the receiving line. He's walking toward us and meets us halfway. He extends his hand for Papa to shake, and I nervously think of the first time he did that and Papa's disrespectful response. But this time, he gives Jimmie a hearty handshake.

"Welcome home, Dr. Du Bois," Jimmie says cheerily. "To your alma mater, I mean."

"Thank you, James. I hope you are getting settled in well here at Fisk." Papa doesn't sound friendly as he says this, but at least he is polite. That must count for something.

To show that we're a united front, I leave Papa's side and stand close to Jimmie, linking my arm through his. Papa's nostrils flare and the corners of his mouth twitch, but he keeps looking at Jimmie.

"He's a sociology major like you were, Papa," I brag before beaming up at Jimmie.

Papa clears his throat and glances quickly at me and then at the place where my arm and Jimmie's arm connect. It seems to annoy him. "I see. It's good that you are supplementing your music with a strong education. That is wise."

"I intend to follow in your footsteps," Jimmie says. "I'd like to be an educator as well."

"Well, Yolande speaks highly of you. It was good seeing you again, James." Again, Papa says polite words, but without warmth or friendliness. "We're going to have lunch tomorrow, Yolande, but now Miss Fauset and I have a late meeting with an alumnus."

"The pageant was fantastic," Miss Fauset says. "We are so proud of you. I can't wait to write an article about it for *The Crisis*."

"Yes, and when Yolande comes home for the summer, you must introduce her to Langston if you haven't already. He will be *very* pleased to hear about a Harlem socialite reciting his poem," Papa says with a suggestive chuckle. "Have you met him yet?"

I shake my head as I feel Jimmie's body stiffen and his jaw tense. Papa must notice too, because there's a mischievous gleam in his eyes, and I don't like it.

Papa grins and looks at Miss Fauset. "Then, Miss Fauset will have to arrange a private meeting," he says.

Papa reaches for me, perhaps for a goodbye hug, but I can't move. I stay at Jimmie's side, because Papa knows exactly what he's doing. It's terrible.

"I am happy to hear that Yolande speaks highly of me, sir, since I have every intention of marrying your daughter one day," Jimmie blurts out.

My ears ring. I'm completely unprepared for this announcement in front of the entire student body. Of course, I knew Jimmie had these thoughts, but I didn't think he'd say it now! I don't know how Papa will respond, but it sure doesn't look like he's about to congratulate us.

"Marry her, you say?" Papa closes his eyes and drops his arm to his side, as if the weariness from his travel has suddenly overtaken him. When he opens his eyes again, his gaze pierces my soul. "Are you asking my permission?"

Jimmie clears his throat. "A man, I believe, states his intentions. I am, indeed. I'm asking for your blessing."

"Intentions. Well, son, how do you intend to care for Yolande? She has a taste for the finer things, you know."

"I know what she likes."

Oh, my goodness. *I know what she likes?* What in the world is he trying to do? Get me locked away in a tower with Miss Nellie on the other side?

"You have a long way to go before you can provide for a wife. Focus on your studies, son, and you may one day become a fine man," Papa says in a voice that is too stern, too forceful, and too loud.

People have stopped their conversations and have turned their attention to ours. Just like when George was yelling at me at the café. Must I always be the center of some public spectacle?

"Your daughter already believes I am a fine man," Jimmie counters, unable to let Papa have the last word.

Now Papa has clearly had enough. The lines in his forehead are deeply creased with his angry frown. "This music you play, James. I'm not taking that too seriously."

"But haven't you started a record company, Papa?" I ask, trying to help Jimmie save face.

"Yes. Black Swan Records. I do see the merits of music when it is used to advance the movement. I don't care much for boogie-woogie jazz music. It just sets folks to dancing, drinking, and carousing. It doesn't do anything for our legacy as colored folk."

"Music will be my legacy, sir," Jimmie says. "It is art, just like writing, painting, or anything else. It is art."

"Some music is art. Not jazz," Papa says, doubling down. "We must disagree on that point."

"I wholeheartedly disagree."

"And I appreciate you standing here. Toe-to-toe, like a real man, and saying exactly what is on your mind. That is an admirable trait." Papa smirks as he says this, but this I believe. No one stands up to him, but Jimmie has. He must respect that.

"Thank you, sir," Jimmie says respectfully. He never once raised his voice at Papa, even though Papa certainly earned it.

"I see why my daughter admires you. But now, if I am to keep to my schedule, we must go."

Now, I do leave Jimmie's side to hug Papa goodbye, and then Miss Fauset. Jimmie offers Papa his hand to shake once more, but he either doesn't see it, or ignores it. I cannot be sure. Miss Fauset, however, does give Jimmie a warm embrace.

"Bravo, young man," she says before quickly pulling away and following Papa, who is rapidly departing.

I don't know if Jimmie has accomplished anything except pushing Papa further away. I wish he had spoken to me first before making his grand announcement. Because no matter what Papa thinks or believes about jazz, or about us, I already love Jimmie. He's good enough for me, and when we're done with our schooling, I would love to consider being his wife. But that is a long way from today, and it leaves too much time for Papa to meddle and interfere.

Perhaps there is a better way to set Jimmie's mind at ease than by earning Papa's approval—an impossible feat.

Chapter Twenty-One

Are you sure you still want to do this?" Minnie asks as I pack a nightgown and a few toiletries into my overnight bag.

It occurs to me with Papa in Nashville that this is a somewhat dangerous plot. Perhaps I should change course and meet up with Jimmie another night. However, things have already been set in motion, and it is tonight that Jimmie works at the Andrew Jackson Hotel. And, because we've done so well at the pageant, Miss Nellie is not apt to be watching us girls so closely.

"Won't people just assume I am with my papa if I'm missing?" I ask.

"They probably will, but do you want to take that chance?" Minnie asks, wringing her hands as if she's the one taking the risk instead of me. "Won't your papa be furious if he finds out you're sneaking off with Jimmie in a hotel room?"

"You worry too much," I say to Minnie. "Just keep watch. Make sure Miss Nellie stays away from our room and things should be just fine. You know John will cover for us at the hotel. We won't be there all night, and I'll be back before anyone wakes."

"Are you excited? Have you been alone with a boy in a bedroom before?"

"Not a bedroom."

"I wish I had a boy like Jimmie who would pull off a caper like this. Lucas is too scared to sneak a kiss at the movies."

"Jimmie doesn't know anything about this. He's too much of a gentleman."

Minnie scoots to the edge of her bed. "You planned this? How scandalous, Yolande."

"I don't know that we'll go all the way, silly."

"But far enough. I don't know. Maybe you shouldn't do it. What if Jimmie can't stop himself once you get him all worked up?"

"I told you Jimmie is a gentleman, Minnie. He'll do what I ask. Always."

It is time for us to go a little further anyway. The kiss under the Wishing Tree was for children. This will be a new, grown-up promise. Of the things to come once we're husband and wife.

* * *

JOHN RATTLES THE keys in the dim hallway outside the practice room, and Jimmie looks up from sweeping the band's root beer bottle caps and other debris. He peers into the hallway and sees us. It only takes a moment for him to recognize me in my sneaking-off-campus disguise.

"You are crazy," Jimmie says in a loud whisper as he rushes over. "Your papa is in town."

"I just have a better cover story then," I say as I throw my arms around his neck and cover his face with kisses.

He quickly peels me off him. "Someone might see," he says.

John laughs. "You think folks don't know what goes on?"

"I suppose they do."

John shakes his key ring and starts walking toward the staircase that goes to the guest rooms. "Come on anyway, lovebirds. Let's get y'all behind a closed door."

I start to follow John, and Jimmie gently grabs my arm. "Wait, John, what are you doing? Yolande and I can hang out here. We don't need a room."

"Yes, we do," I say in a voice barely above a whisper.

Jimmie spins around to look at me. "We do?"

His expression is full of questions, but I give him a reassuring nod. Doesn't every young man dream of this moment with his sweetie? I wonder if he's afraid. I am.

But since Jimmie's not moving, I reach for his hand as we follow John. And then, we seem to fly up the two flights of stairs.

At the door of the room, John quickly and silently turns the correct key from his key ring and opens the door. I lift my foot to walk inside, but Jimmie shocks me by sweeping my legs from under me and cradling me in his arms.

"Jimmie," I gasp. "What are you doing, silly?"

"Carrying you over the threshold," he whispers in my ear. "In case."

I throw my arms around his neck and kiss him deeply, inviting him to do whatever he means by "in case." I feel him stumble. Maybe the kiss made him weak, because he's a strong boy and lifting me is nothing.

But he finds his footing, crosses the room, and gently sits me on the bed, with me planting soft kisses on his face the entire way.

"Don't move," he says. "I'll be right back."

Jimmie rushes over to John, and they're whispering. I see John take a square package out of his pocket and hand it to Jimmie.

While they're talking, I quickly shimmy out of my boy's clothes and drape them neatly over the chair. Then, I nestle into the sheets in only my brassiere and panties.

When Jimmie returns, his eyes feast on my body. On every curve of my bare skin.

"You know, Chrystal says I'm a waste of light skin," I say in a sultry-sounding voice that I didn't know I had. "What do you think, Jimmie? Is my skin a waste?"

He opens his mouth, but nothing comes out. Then, he just moves across the room.

"Nothing about you is a waste," he says as he sits at the foot of the bed as if he's nervous about coming closer. "But what is happening, Yolande?"

Is my nearly nude body not invitation enough?

"We can just cuddle if you want. I can even put my clothes back on."

"N-no. I mean, if you want to, it's perfectly all right."

I give him a throaty, grown woman, sexy laugh. "Come here, silly. I want you to touch me, else I wouldn't be here."

With these words, something primal and urgent seems to break loose in Jimmy. He rushes forward and into my waiting arms.

His kisses are sweet, but my hands tremble nervously as I fumble with his buttons, so he helps me with that task. As he disrobes, we never stop kissing so that our bodies don't have to come unglued.

In moments, it seems, Jimmie's clothes are discarded like mine and our limbs are intertwined. We're hardly breathing on account of our kissing, but I don't think we need much air.

Miss Fauset's advice lingers in my mind, and a brief image of me rocking a baby in a Denver living room flashes. But it doesn't make me stop kissing Jimmie, nor does it make me reconsider coming here tonight and guiding his hand to the warm place between my thighs. Jimmie seems hesitant though, like he thinks he may hurt me.

"I'm ready," I whisper breathlessly, encouraging him to proceed.

"O-okay."

He fumbles with the prophylactic in the square package that he received from John, but I wait patiently. Once he has it on, I pull Jimmie on top of me. Heat radiates from both our bodies, and when he enters me, it feels like a million jolts.

It's overwhelming. It's amazing. I bet this is exactly what those people feel like in church when they say the spirit gets all over them, because I feel like I've been transported to heaven. I could stay here with Jimmie all night and for all eternity.

How could this be a sin?

Chapter Twenty-Two

May 1923
Nashville, Tennessee

Yolande, why did you not warn me that boy was going to practically ask for your hand?"

I should have known he was going to light into me as soon as I got in the car. This short drive to lunch is going to feel like an eternity. I wish the driver couldn't hear our discussion, but Papa doesn't care about embarrassing me.

"Papa, he didn't. He's just a kid. He knows he must graduate and find work."

"He needs to do more than find work. He needs to find his purpose and determine what he will do to sustain a household before he thinks about a wife."

"All right, Papa."

"There is nothing more sickening or more tragic than two people who tether themselves together without any idea how they will sustain themselves. How they will find food, clothing, and shelter. All because of a sex attraction."

"Papa!"

The driver widens his eyes but pretends not to be listening. I hate when Papa decides to give me one of his spontaneous lectures in front of strangers.

And speaking of adult subjects. Can Papa tell? Can he see it on me? Do I look different somehow, now that Jimmie and I have gone all the way? I don't feel different. Only a little sore . . . instinctively

I squeeze my thighs together as if my secret place is snitching
on me.

"Hear me well, Yolande. That kind of young man will have you
squandering any natural intellect you have."

"He is brilliant and gifted."

Papa shakes his head furiously as he pulls a note from his folder.
The script on the front is Miss Fauset's handwriting. I recognize it
from her letters to me. Thank goodness, something from *The Crisis*
or the movement for him to rave about to distract him from Jimmie.
Surprisingly, Papa doesn't rave. Whatever Miss Fauset has written
in her note makes him smile. He slowly places the page back in the
envelope, but instead of tucking it in his folder he puts the note in his
inside jacket pocket.

"Will she be joining us for lunch?" I ask.

"Who?"

"Miss Fauset," I say as I point to his jacket pocket.

Papa scowls. "No, she won't be joining us. She had business to
attend to, and then we're going to be on our way to Atlanta later
this afternoon. You may not get to see her until you're home for the
summer."

"Oh no. Well, do tell her I am so glad she was able to see the
pageant."

"Yes . . . the pageant."

"Did you tell a fib when you said you enjoyed it, Papa?"

He sighs. "I could have done without Jimmie and his jazz music,
but you already know that. It cheapened the poetry, in my opinion.
You allowed him to ruin your moment in the spotlight."

"The music was my idea, Papa. Jimmie played at my request."

Papa folds his arms across his chest and grunts. "Then you cheapened your own moment. No matter. The audience seemed to enjoy it,
and Miss Fauset will write a favorable article in *The Crisis*."

I refuse to let the tears fall as the driver delivers us to Papa's friends Dr. and Mrs. Beauregard. The Beauregards attended Fisk with Papa, and I happen to enjoy their company. Sometimes, I have Sunday dinner or tea with them even when Papa isn't visiting.

"Please fix your face, Yolande," Papa whispers as we wait for Mrs. Beauregard to come to the door. "You're scowling."

"You just said the pageant was cheap and ruined."

Papa's nostrils flare. "I said it was my opinion. You must learn to receive feedback, Yolande."

"Well, you didn't have to say it so mean."

Papa opens his mouth to speak, but the door opens and instead he smiles at Mrs. Beauregard.

"Diana," Papa says warmly, "I cannot believe it has been over a year since we've seen each other."

"And it is all your fault. At least we have Yolande," Mrs. Beauregard says, as she hugs me first before giving Papa a sisterly embrace. "Come on inside."

My stomach growls at the aromas tumbling out through the door. The other reason I love visiting the Beauregards is Mrs. Beauregard's cooking. This smells like chicken and dumplings and homemade apple pie. I wish Jimmie had been able to come along. Maybe Mrs. Beauregard will make me a plate to take back to Jubilee Hall, and then I can share it with Jimmie.

Mrs. Beauregard shows us to the sink to wash our hands, which I am sure Papa appreciates as he is so averse to germs, and then we go directly to the dining room where Dr. Beauregard is already waiting for us. He stands when we enter and claps Papa heartily on the back. Dr. Beauregard is tall and robust, but friendly as can be.

"Yolande, it is always so wonderful to have you at our table. We especially love it when you visit without your father. You can come anytime." Mrs. Beauregard's face shines in my direction as she speaks, and I smile my thanks. I try to shift my mood, but after Papa's tongue lashing in the car on the way over, I am finding it difficult to keep from bursting into tears as we sit down.

"Thank you for the open invitation. The food in the dining hall does get monotonous at times. It's good to know I have places to visit for a change of pace." I hope this sounds witty and light, because I feel quite the opposite of that.

Papa places his fork on his plate. "The food in the dining hall," Papa says, "is nutritious. You must watch everything you consume, due to your proclivity for illness."

"Don't discourage her," Dr. Beauregard says. "Maybe she'll bring that young man she's seeing. Piggie Lunceford. Oh, I'd like to shake his hand."

Mrs. Beauregard laughs. "Thomas is just pleased at the way Piggie helped Fisk trounce Tuskegee in the final seconds of the game."

"They thought they were going to get a victory in our house. Piggie showed them!"

Papa looks at me with a pained expression on his face. "Piggie?"

"Yes. Jimmie is an athlete, Papa. He eats a lot of food. Everyone calls him that." Of course, I don't mention the part where I gave him the nickname.

"He's a fine young man," Mrs. Beauregard says, perhaps seeing my discomfort and wishing to rescue me. "I've never heard anything untoward about him and your daughter."

"That is a relief since I am not taking him very seriously," Papa says.

I stare at my plate and hope no one sees the tears pool in my eyes. He's already said these things to Jimmie. Why must Papa disparage him to the Beauregards, who seem to think highly of him?

"Yolande is a talented artist, and this young man seeks to make a living as a jazz musician. He says he's going to be an educator, but that his legacy will be jazz music. So, what does that tell you?"

"I see your concern," Dr. Beauregard says, although he doesn't particularly sound like he agrees.

Mrs. Beauregard gives my hand a reassuring squeeze. "Enlighten me," she says. "What would be the concern there?"

"How would they expect to make a living when his jazz music gigs dry up? It's the popular thing now. It won't last. Will she be able to wear these fine dresses she loves on a church musician's salary? How will my grandchildren eat?"

"Oh, there are many ways for a college-educated man to make money," Mrs. Beauregard says blithely. "Sometimes daughters have to defy their fathers when it comes to the man they love."

I look up at Mrs. Beauregard just as she winks at her husband. He blushes and grins.

"Well, Yolande knows I have her best interests at heart," Papa says. "At any rate, both she and Mr. Lunceford have their degrees to procure before they think of their futures. He is only a freshman."

"A freshman? Well, he's a big strapping lad, isn't he?" Dr. Beauregard asks.

Papa clears his throat. "Yes. Strapping, indeed."

I wonder if this is supposed to mean that matters are closed when it comes to Jimmie. I cannot bear to think of breaking things off with him. That is simply not possible. Not after what we've shared. When I am apart from him, I count the moments until we are together again. I wake up with his name on my lips, and his face is in my dreams. I cannot close this matter. It is open whether I wish it to be or not.

"What can we do when young people are determined to be in love, W.E.B.?" Mrs. Beauregard asks.

"We cannot do much, of that I am sure, but I can remove my daughter from *this* temptation," Papa says. "There are perfectly good colleges in New York. There is a Negro college in Washington, D.C. She will make the right choice for her future, or Nina and I will help her, you see?"

Mrs. Beauregard gives me a look of pity. But I don't think she truly knows how heavy this burden is that I carry. The responsibility of being Papa's heir. I must be proof of his Talented Tenth philosophy. I believe he has become obsessed with who I marry because he has lost faith that I am exceptional. Perhaps if I am joined with a man he deems worthy, whatever exceptional part of him I do carry may be passed on to his grandchildren, and there may be a chance at the glory he lost when my brother Burghardt died.

Papa got me as a consolation prize after the first child perished, and sometimes I think he wonders what he would have if our birth orders had been different. If I had been the lost child and Burghardt had come in my place.

The ghost of my brother's unrealized potential haunts me . . . and Papa . . . always.

Chapter Twenty-Three

May 1923
Nashville, Tennessee

My head throbs after dining with Papa and the Beauregards. Papa is determined to disparage Jimmie to anyone who'll listen. And I do believe his threat to pull me from Fisk and make me attend college somewhere else is real. He'll do it. To keep me from Jimmie . . . he would.

I burrow my head under my pillow to block the afternoon sun that's streaming through our window. I want to shut my eyes and not talk to anyone until Papa's left town and taken his threats with him. Not even Jimmie, though the memories of his touch echo through my mind and consume every thought not stolen by Papa's warnings.

And of course, because I want to push the world away, someone is knocking on my bedroom door.

"Go away!" I shout from under the pillow.

"But, Yolande." It's Margaret Pennybacker from next door. "Miss Fauset is downstairs for you."

After the abysmal lunch with Papa, I almost don't want to see Miss Fauset, but maybe she can help me convince him that he's wrong about Jimmie.

She seems so pleasant as she waits for me at the bottom of the stairs, so I put on my bravest smile. "Bonjour, Mademoiselle Fauset," I say, because I know she'll be proud of me for speaking her favorite language.

"Bonjour, ma chérie," she says, hugging me.

When I pull away from her, she tilts her head to one side to regard my eyes, puffy and red from crying, and my tear-streaked face.

"Yolande, what's wrong?" she asks.

I take Miss Fauset's hand and lead her to the private parlor where girls entertain guests for tea. I close the door behind us, and plop down onto one of the armchairs.

"Papa refuses to treat me like an adult."

"Yolande . . ."

"It's bad enough that he's sent me to this college that's like a prison. We have curfews like we're children . . ."

"Well, maybe that's not a bad thing."

"We're of age."

"C'est vrai, mais vous n'êtes pas intelligents."

I shake my head at the insult. "It's not nice to call us stupid even if you say it in French. Besides, Jimmie and I are not dumb. We are in love . . . and Papa is impossible."

"Did something else happen at lunch? I knew I should have tried to make it, but I couldn't get out of that meeting."

"He just won't hear any reason about Jimmie! Miss Fauset, we love each other."

"Love? I see . . ."

I don't like the look on Miss Fauset's face. Her incredulous pity is as infuriating as Papa's disregard.

"Jimmie's going to have his own band and tour like Mr. Morrison. He wants to play in Paris too," I say, my voice panicked and desperate to convince her.

"Musicians don't make a lot of money most of the time."

"Oh, I know, but I am trying not to think about that. And surely Papa will help us."

Miss Fauset is quiet for a long moment, but I need her to say what's on her mind.

"Yolande, a woman cannot get married and imagine herself still being taken care of by her papa."

Of course what she says is true, but when Jimmie talks about going on the road with the band and sleeping on buses and eating chicken sandwiches out of greasy brown paper bags, it sounds exciting. Still, I don't want to consider sleeping on the bus because we can't afford a room or the sandwich being the only meal we've eaten in days.

"I just can't imagine not being with him."

"Well, imagine yourself living pillar to post. For love."

"Papa doesn't believe I love Jimmie. He thinks it's only a sex attraction."

"Did he use those words?" Miss Fauset asks, shaking her head, probably at Papa's frankness.

"Yes, but he doesn't understand. Haven't you ever been in love, Miss Fauset? You must know how it is."

She gets a faraway look in her eyes, like she's thinking of her love right now. "I have." Her voice comes out barely above a whisper.

Perhaps I should not have asked this question. Miss Fauset is not married and, according to Mama's gossip, she hasn't any potential suitors anywhere in Harlem. Maybe she is not the one I should be asking about love.

"Wouldn't you do whatever it took to be with your love? Or would you try to escape it?"

"Love is strange . . . and messy," she says after another deep sigh.

"What would you do if you were me? Would you listen to Papa? Or your heart?"

"The Bible, in the book of Jeremiah, says the heart is deceitful above all things, and desperately wicked. Who can know it?"

A Bible verse. She's giving me a Bible verse. "What does that mean?"

"It means that your heart may lead you down a dangerous path. Why not let your reason catch up with your heart? Then, test what your heart desires against what reason decides and then, if they align, proceed."

"What if they do not align? What if my heart and reason choose differently?"

"Be smart, Yolande. But mostly, remember you aren't in any hurry. Jimmie is not old enough or independent enough to entertain marriage. If your love is true, it will endure."

"It is true."

"Then, allow him to mature and prove himself. When he can provide a suitable life for you, your papa will not be able to protest."

"But what if Jimmie is offended by this? I believe in him now; I know he will make a life for me."

Miss Fauset smiles. "Well, in the Bible, Jacob worked fourteen years before he was finally able to marry Rachel, the woman he truly loved."

Another Bible reference. She must know these are somewhat lost on me.

"I hope Jimmie doesn't have to work fourteen years. I don't want to wait that long."

She takes my hand and squeezes it. "I don't think you will. He seems very determined. I didn't think he'd make it past that first summer, yet here he is at Fisk. He's already shocked me once."

"He will surprise Papa too. It will just take some time."

"But, Yolande, I do want to caution you. The things your papa says about a sex attraction, they are not entirely untrue. It is hard sometimes to tell the difference between true love and the things we feel when the attraction is so strong."

There couldn't be anything more perfect than what I feel about Jimmie. There isn't anything more perfect.

"What do you mean, Miss Fauset?"

"Have you and Jimmie ever had a disagreement? Has he ever been angry with you?"

I wring my hands nervously as I recall when Jimmie and I talked about George. He was heartbroken and disappointed, but not angry.

"No, I can't say that he has. I hurt him once, and he forgave me, but there was no anger."

"You can't know if you love a person until you have seen every version of them. He needs to see every version of you as well, ma chère."

"Is that what happened with your love? The one you thought of when I asked the question?"

Miss Fauset sighs. "Yes. He got angry with me about something, and I saw a side of him that opened my eyes. It changed everything."

"And where is he now? Your love. Did it not endure?"

Miss Fauset squeezes my hand and blinks rapidly. I can tell she's trying to hold back tears, and that scares me mightily. How could a woman like Miss Fauset, so beautiful and sophisticated, be this befuddled when it comes to love?

"Love is strange and messy, Yolande," she says again. "Bonne chance."

Good luck. That doesn't make me feel confident at all. In fact, I feel even more terrified than before. Perhaps I should've stayed in my room.

Chapter Twenty-Four

May 1923
Nashville, Tennessee

I am pensive as I share a bowl of ice cream with Jimmie at Pearly's. We're an hour away from curfew but the place is mostly empty. The ice cream has melted into a soupy mess. I guess neither of us feels like dessert after Papa and Miss Fauset's visit.

But we only have a week and a half before it's time to go home for the summer, and we're in this strange murky place. We've taken a huge step forward in our relationship by sharing the physical love that should help bind us, but now I am on unsure footing.

"Do you have something on your mind?" Jimmie asks, breaking the heavy silence.

"I wonder what you're going to do all summer," I say, although I wasn't wondering this at all. I only want to prevent silence from befalling us again. "Will you go to be with your family in Ohio? Or to Mr. Morrison in Denver?"

"I will go where there's work. Wherever there's a gig, that's where I'll be."

"You don't know for sure?"

"Not yet. Sometimes Mr. Morrison finds out about things at the last minute, and we all pull together and make it happen."

"That's sounds nerve-wracking."

"It's exciting."

"Not if it's time to pay rent."

Jimmie bursts into laughter. "I'm sorry. But do you pay rent?"

"You're laughing at me?" I cannot figure out what's funny.

"I didn't mean to. It's just that I've never ever seen you worried about money. You pick up your letters from the mailroom with your five dollars inside and you spend it until it's gone."

"It's for me to use," I say, feeling confused and somewhat attacked. "I don't understand why you think I should save it."

"I don't think you should save it. But why are you worried about how Mr. Morrison's band members pay their rent?"

"Because one of Mr. Morrison's band members told my papa he's marrying me. And that member got me a lecture."

"Your father doesn't think I'd be able to take care of you?"

I stare at him, unblinking, hoping that my long pause tells him exactly what Papa thinks.

"I don't think he's decided about you or what he thinks you'll become," I finally offer. "He says you may become a fine man one day."

"Then why are you so sad? You've been down since he and Miss Fauset left yesterday."

"I'm sad because Papa didn't approve of my idea for the pageant. And he told me so on the way to our lunch with his friends."

"But everyone else loved it. The pageant was a success. I heard even Miss Callinge and Dr. McKenzie had good things to say about you and your leadership."

Jimmie doesn't understand how Papa can make storm clouds form over any joyful moment. With one gruff word or even just a disapproving look, any bliss I might be feeling evaporates.

"I think he's helping me see the entire picture, Jimmie, when I'm only looking at the beautiful parts."

"I don't see any flaws with the pageant, you, or . . . us. You are perfect. We are perfection."

I reach across the table and squeeze Jimmie's hands. "But I am not perfect, Jimmie. This ice cream we're eating is going to give me a terrible stomachache tonight, and I know it. But I'm eating it anyway."

"What is the problem with that? We all eat things that aren't good for us."

"But we don't all end up in the hospital because of it."

"So, I'll help you make healthy choices with your food," Jimmie jokes, pulling the bowl of ice cream away from me.

"But what if something happens and I need to go into the hospital? Will we even be able to afford medical treatment?"

"Why do you think I won't be able to make money? I'm getting my education. Same as you. Same as your father."

Jimmie's voice sounds desperate now, and I don't want him to feel this way. I am just worried that we are too young to know what's best. Miss Fauset's words—pillar to post—kept me awake all night. I don't want to live that way.

"Yolande, come out and say what you're thinking. Do you want things to be over between us?"

"No, Jimmie. I love you."

"Then why are you giving me a list of doubts?"

"Because we are so young, Jimmie. Especially . . . you." There, I've come out with my truth. "There is time to prove that we can forge an amazing partnership."

"Partnership?"

"Papa believes that there must be something other than attraction and love to sustain a marriage."

"Do your parents love each other?" he asks.

I am not sure how to answer this question. My parents have a solid marriage, I believe. Papa takes care of the finances, business things, the properties, so Mama never has to give any attention to any of that. She takes care of me, and Papa can leave it all in her capable hands. They don't seem to share what Jimmie and I have, or what I've seen with other couples like the Beauregards. But I can't say that they don't love each other.

"They have been together since they were young. Mama is younger than Papa. I do not see in them what we have, but perhaps they had it in the beginning."

"How are they now? Do they sneak kisses when they think you aren't looking, or do you sometimes hear laughter coming from behind their closed bedroom door?" Jimmie asks. "Do they take little trips together and come back with jokes only they share? Do they listen to their favorite music together or go to shows?"

"Papa isn't that kind of man. He hardly ever laughs. Mama and I go on summer holidays together, and Papa mostly works or goes on speaking tours."

"So who is he to judge what kind of marriage we might have? His own sounds rather miserable." Jimmie's tone is judgmental, and his frown is deep.

"Mama takes care of things at home, so that he can devote his life to the movement," I protest, although I'm not quite sure why I'm defending them. "She takes care of me."

"So, you'd want me to leave you at home while I go out touring with the band?"

Now, I'm . . . I don't know. Befuddled, angry, confused. I reach for the ice cream, and Jimmie deftly keeps it out of my grasp.

"No, I don't think I want that," I say. "I am not certain what I want."

Papa and Miss Fauset have made me think of what it might be like if Jimmie's career isn't what he hopes for. Now I cannot commit. Even though I love Jimmie, I want to see something more.

"If we give ourselves time, I think we will come to the right conclusion," I say, starting to get frustrated with this, because it feels like he's not listening. "We don't have to decide right now."

"When you graduate and you're back home in Harlem, then what will you do? I will still be here." There's something else in his voice now, along with the anger.

"That is a long way off, Jimmie. There is no rush."

"I cannot be apart from you an entire summer without knowing that your heart is committed to mine the way mine is committed to yours."

"It sounds like you don't trust me."

"I do trust you, but the last time we were apart, your papa found a suitor for you, and you went along with his plans as if you had no choice in the matter." Jimmie's voice rises with irritation. "I cannot go through that again, Yolande."

Tears spring to my eyes. I can't help it. "You said you'd forgiven me for that, but you haven't forgotten it. You're holding it against me, and that's not fair."

"What wasn't fair was finding out in a letter that the girl I was true to for two years was seriously seeing someone else."

"Miss Fauset told me that I needed to see you angry with me before I agreed to forever, and I thought she was wrong. But maybe she was right."

My words hit him hard, and for a moment, he just sits there. Stunned.

"Miss Fauset is against us too?" he asks, now more subdued. "I thought she was on our side."

"She isn't against us, Jimmie. Not like Papa. But she says that true love endures through time. She said someone in the Bible . . . um . . . was it Joseph? He worked ten years and then got to marry the girl he loved."

"Jacob," he corrects me. "And it was fourteen years. But I don't know if that story applies to us. We were separated for two years, and you nearly slipped away."

Why does he keep talking about George when I just shared my body with him? My innocence. I can never get that back, and now he's making me regret it.

"Did what we shared the other night mean nothing to you, Jimmie?"

"It means everything. In my heart, you are already my wife."

"I thought that when I shared myself with you, like I had with no one else, it would erase what happened when we were apart," I say through sobs. "But it seems that you will never forget that one misstep."

"I have forgiven you."

"But you're making demands based on George, who meant nothing to me—he was Papa's choice."

"You're saying that, but were you planning to break things off with him? If he hadn't embarrassed you by getting engaged to someone else would you be wearing his ring?"

"Jimmie . . ."

"If your papa had gotten him to propose, what would've stopped you from saying yes?" The anger has returned to his voice, and his questions are impatient and demanding. But no matter what I've said, I don't think he'll ever truly believe me.

"That didn't happen, because it wasn't supposed to happen. What was supposed to happen was this. Us. We were meant to find each other again, here at Fisk, and if we're meant to be together forever, nothing will separate us."

"If? That is the problem. You need to weigh your options, and I do not."

"I am not weighing options, Jimmie. I'm just saying that we should be engaged when we are ready to be wed. There is no need to announce it before then, to invite harsh judgements from anyone."

"You don't want your papa to know? How will we court in secret when he has spies that tell him everything you do while you're here?"

I nearly swoon at the thought of going home for the summer and being interrogated by Papa about me and Jimmie. I won't get any rest, and there will be an endless stream of proper suitors being sent my way.

"You're right," I admit. "Papa will be insufferable."

"You were supposed to say that you don't care if your papa knows."

"I didn't know I was being tested," I say, feeling many things but mostly annoyance and hurt. "Perhaps I should take the summer to study, so that I can pass with flying colors."

Jimmie pushes the bowl of now liquid ice cream away and sighs. "I'm tired and must be up early for church tomorrow. I have some repenting to do."

"Repenting?"

"If you don't ask God to forgive you after sinning, He won't answer your prayers," Jimmie says.

He stands and walks over to the counter to pay for our ice cream, leaving me to wonder just what prayers he has to lift before God.

Why should he ever have to repent about loving me?

Chapter Twenty-Five

May 1923
Nashville, Tennessee

I just can't sing in the choir today, not after that conversation with Jimmie. Seeing that I'm in distress, Minnie sits next to me. Not that the choir misses us. They are probably relieved to see me sitting for once.

Chrystal smirks at us from the front row, making me wonder if Jimmie has confided in her. She stands as close to the piano (and Jimmie) as she can muster, probably wearing her cheap perfume and her dress that's too snug for Sunday morning.

While he plays the piano accompaniment to "Great Is Thy Faithfulness," Jimmie looks defeated and emotional. My eyes are locked on to Jimmie as the choir sings the words of the hymn. Maybe the lyrics of the song speak to Jimmie, but I almost can't take it when I see the tears stream down his face, especially since he doesn't attempt to wipe them away.

My anchor here at Fisk, broken and in tears. What am I to do if he cannot hold me up?

Now I'm crying too, at these thoughts. Perhaps everyone thinks we are carried away by the Holy Spirit.

But Jimmie is crying over us. Over my inability to say yes. Over Papa's dismissal.

Then, Chrystal, that demon, steps out of the choir loft. She walks over to Jimmie, with a handkerchief in her hand. I bet she pulled it from her bosom and that it smells of her cheap perfume.

Because Jimmie is playing, she cannot hand him the handkerchief, so she brazenly wipes his tears away. The more he weeps, the more she wipes. I am frozen in place, unable to leave Minnie's side while Chrystal acts like Jimmie's wife in front of an entire congregation of people.

This is too much.

I feel woozy, and my legs feel like rubber.

I—

Chapter Twenty-Six

May 1923
Nashville, Tennessee

My eyes flutter open and I'm in a hospital bed. *Great*, I think to myself. *Hospital Bed Yolande strikes again.*

I squint to try and adjust to the light, but I feel lethargic and groggy like I've been sedated and given pain medication. All from a fainting spell?

"Yolande?"

Mama's here. If she had to travel from New York, I've been here at least a few days.

"Ma—"

Tears form at trying to speak. My throat is raw and scratched. That only happens when they shove the oxygen tube down your throat. During surgery. What has happened?

I try to pull myself to an upright position and pain shoots through my abdomen, almost making me lose the contents of my bladder.

Mama jumps up and rushes over. "Yolande. Let me help you. You've had surgery. You'll rip your stitches."

Mama helps me out of bed and to the toilet, but my mind is spinning. But my throat hurts so badly that I can't pepper her with questions.

Once I'm safely returned to bed, Mama gives me a cup of water. It hurts to swallow, but still refreshes. I'm so parched, this water tastes like it was brought from the Euphrates. I think of Langston's poem and smile, but then, of course, that memory is connected to Jimmie.

I set the cup down and hand it to Mama. "W-where's Jimmie?" I croak.

"He's been here, every day. All the flowers are from him. Cards too."

My room is full of beautiful bouquets. Spring flowers, my favorites. Tulips, peonies, and lilies. The scent of them doesn't quite cover the disinfectant hospital smell, but it helps.

"W-where—"

Mama shakes her head. "Don't you want to know why you're here, Yolande? You can worry about that boy later. He is not important now."

My throat is too inflamed to yell, so my eyes must speak for me. My glare says, *He is important to ME*.

"You had surgery for an abdominal adhesion. It was a complication of your appendix removal surgery last fall. The doctor said you must have had symptoms. Pain, digestive issues, and the like. But you haven't mentioned any of that in your letters." Mama's tone bites and snaps. "Only requests for clothing items, your social calendar, oh, and plenty of talk about that boy."

This is clearly a reprimand, and I am undone. How is it that I am sick? Clearly my body is failing me, and I am being scolded as if I could have done anything to stop this.

"Where is Jimmie now?" I ask, pushing past the pain.

"The term is over, Yolande. You've been here two weeks."

"Two weeks?"

"Jimmie is home with his family or wherever he goes over the summer."

He didn't wait to see if I'd be all right? He didn't stay behind? How does he think he's ready to be a husband and here I am sick, but he's having summer break?

"He wanted to stay," Mama says as she takes her seat by the window and picks up her book. "But I sent him away. He was not needed. I am here."

"I need him."

"Oh, stop it. You don't need him, and he doesn't have a pot to pee in nor window to throw it out. Where was he going to stay while you convalesce? The dormitories are closed for the summer."

Papa has many friends here. Jimmie could have stayed with the Beauregards. They love him so. He's helpful and would have paid his own way. But why didn't he press for this? Why would he let Mama send him away?

As much as I love him, and he loves me, that's not what a man would do. And if Mama could run him off, how does he ever expect to survive Papa?

"Yolande. The doctor mentioned that the adhesion could have been irritated by . . . sexual activity. Jimmie is not a small boy . . ."

"Mama."

"You must be careful. An unexpected pregnancy could kill you."

Lord have mercy. I forgive Jimmie for fleeing. If Mama lit into him about this and made him feel as if he caused my injury, he's probably tearing himself up with guilt.

"We are careful, Mama," I say, searching for the right words, because there is no point in lying when I know Jimmie. If she interrogated him, he folded like a blade of grass. "And I am a grown woman."

"A grown woman?" she scoffs. "You don't even buy your own undergarments. You both are children, existing only by the generosity of your parents."

Mama's harsh words, when she is usually my place of solace, bring forth a gush of tears. I cannot make them stop.

Now Mama seems exasperated as she rushes over with tissues and more water. Forcing me to sip, she wipes my eyes and nose with the firmness she used when I was a toddler.

"Stop this, Yolande. You're going to make yourself sick," Mama fusses, her voice kinder now. "You will see Jimmie after the summer holiday, and all will be well."

I shake my head. She doesn't know where we left things. The uncertainty. That I had rejected his proposal. She hadn't seen his face in church, or Chrystal drying his tears with her breast-kerchief.

"I gave him the address where we'll be staying in Pleasantville," Mama says, smoothing my hair. "He promises to write. That will be enough."

It isn't enough. But it will have to be. I have no other choice in the matter. I have no money of my own.

"And Jimmie came here. He wouldn't leave until I made him go." Mama smiles like she's remembering my Jimmie's determination. "I think he wished he could sleep right here on the floor."

That's my Jimmie. Full to the brim with wishes. His heart is pure in that regard, and surely that counts.

But what does a man do when he wishes for something? Does he believe in magic or create his own?

Chapter Twenty-Seven

Are you going to sit on the porch all summer?"

I look up at the young man speaking to me and one word comes to mind: roly-poly. He has a small head; smooth, but not unpleasant, face; and a round, soft-looking belly. Like he's never played in any kind of ball game ever. Like he reads books and eats sweets all day. But his smile is so friendly and inviting that I can't help but give a tiny grin in return.

"If you keep blocking the tree I'm trying to draw, it might take me all summer holiday to get my picture done."

"Are you an artist?"

He says *artist* like the French pronunciation of the word. *Artiste.* That makes the hair on the back of my neck stand tall.

"I'm just drawing a picture for my scrapbook. A remembrance for myself of how it seems to lean to the right like it's had a rough day."

Roly-Poly laughs, then turns to look at the tree. He's still blocking my view.

"That tree sho' is tired," Roly-Poly says in exaggerated Southern patois. I close my eyes trying not to be amused, but failing. When I open my eyes, he's staring at me.

"Who are you?" I ask. "Now that you've committed yourself to interrupting my afternoon."

"I'm your neighbor. My name is Countee Cullen. My parents, Reverend Frederick Cullen and Mrs. Cullen, own the white house two doors down." Just like he said *artiste*, he says his name like it's a French word and pronounced with a little accent mark.

"Oh. I am Yolande. Are you here all year round?"

"No. My father is a pastor at Salem Chapel AME in Harlem."

My mouth forms an O with surprise. That church is one of the biggest congregations in Harlem. Well, no wonder he looks so pleasant and rotund. He is the reverend's son. I'm sure he gets more than his fair share of sweets from the church ladies.

"My friend over there"—Countee points across two yards to an extremely handsome young man perched on the front stairs of a neat bungalow eating an apple—"Harold, said I should come and introduce myself to Dr. Du Bois's daughter."

Oh, good grief.

"Are you friends of my papa?" I ask, now suspicious of their motives.

"We're friends of a friend. And perhaps I'm almost a friend."

"For heaven's sakes, boy, which is it?" I roll my eyes at his riddle.

"I'll have you know, Miss Lady, I am of age."

My drawing pencil clatters to the ground as I completely fall apart laughing. Roly-Poly seems to think he's done something clever, too, with that too-satisfied grin on his face and his thumbs tucked into the tiny pockets on the sides of his vest. I can barely pull myself together from cackling at the ridiculousness of it all.

Harold, the pretty one, still munching his apple, jogs over to Countee. He probably wants to know what has me over here in stitches.

Seeing him up close, this Harold must be one of the handsomest men I've ever seen. It's too bad Roly-Poly is the one grinning at me. Harold could've been a good distraction from my sadness over Jimmie.

"Countee, you never said which," I say after finally recovering from my laughing fit. "And hello, Mr. . . . . Harold, is it?"

Harold shows me all his pearly whites. "Harold Jackman. Pleased to make your acquaintance, Miss Du Bois. I see Countee has you tickled. I didn't know he was so funny."

"Well, he was just telling me that you are friends of a friend of my papa, but that wasn't the funny part. He called me Miss Lady, and I just fell apart."

Harold looks at Countee and shakes his head. "I knew I should've come with you to supervise. Yes, we are friends of Miss Jessie Fauset. Countee here is a prodigy. A poet, a scribe, a playwright. The whole world is going to know his name."

"Oh, well then if you aren't already Papa's friend, you will be indeed," I say, now understanding. "He just loves poets. Your art is the kind he approves."

"He's already been published several times in *The Crisis* and *The Brownies' Book*," Harold says, "so I am sure your papa approves of Countee."

"Ah, well we were bound to meet at some point then, weren't we?" I ask, truly surprised that we hadn't already been introduced.

Countee walks up the few steps and is now standing on the porch, uninvited. "What kind of art does he not approve?" He looks at my drawing. "Certainly not yours, I hope. Your drawing is coming together rather nicely."

"Oh, never mind that," I say. "You might as well have a seat. You too, Harold, since Countee seems to have invited himself over for tea."

"Is there tea? And sandwiches?" Countee asks gleefully. "I don't mean to impose. I simply wanted to say hello to a young woman I'd like to get better acquainted with this summer."

Countee and Harold both sit on the lovely porch furniture, and I close my sketchpad. It looks like I'm going to be entertaining guests for a time.

"How have we missed each other in Harlem?" I ask, more to Harold than Countee. I can't help it. He's just so handsome.

Probably hearing the chatter, Mama peeks out the front door, but she smiles when she sees Countee and Harold. She seems to approve of these well-dressed young men.

"Well, hello," Mama says as she pushes the door all the way open. "Are you Reverend Cullen's son?"

Both true gentlemen, Harold and Countee scramble to their feet. They both give Mama toothy grins, and she is tickled as can be.

"Yes ma'am, Mrs. Du Bois, I am Countee Cullen, and this is my friend Harold Jackman. We came to introduce ourselves to Yolande. My parents' house is two doors down."

"I am aware. Tell Carolyn I said hello."

"I will."

Mama's eyes rest on Harold for a moment. "Aren't you a handsome devil," she says.

"I like to think I'm an angel," Harold says, "but I'm afraid that the ladies at New York University might say otherwise."

Countee bursts into giggles and Mama joins him. She is charmed to pieces by these two. More charmed than I am, but then she always is, whenever there are young men about. It always seems like she flirts with them, like she's remembering her own youth. Mama is still pretty, too, so sometimes the young men flirt back. The ones that do can forget about getting my attention.

"I, for one, am glad he has graduated," Countee says. "Now maybe some of those young ladies will look my way."

"I am sure you have your fair share," Mama says. "Two handsome, brilliant young colored men can have just about any young lady they choose."

"Is that so?" I ask. "Don't we young ladies have any say in the matter?"

"Well, of course. But the young ladies are much more plentiful, I am afraid," Mama laments. "Unfortunately, some very fine young women look up and find themselves without a partner."

"That is true," Countee says somberly. "Like our dear Miss Fauset."

Mama's mirth fades. "Well, I am not entirely sure Miss Fauset wants a husband of her own. Would you all care for lemonade and cookies? I just made some fresh."

"Yes ma'am. That would be lovely," Harold says. "Thank you."

Mama rushes away from the door almost too quickly. Countee and Harold exchange confused glances, and I must admit I am also perplexed by Mama's strange behavior.

"What do you think she meant about Miss Fauset?" Countee says in a hushed tone. "Are they friends? I think she might indeed like a husband if one presented himself."

"I'm not quite sure," I whisper back. "I don't know that I would call them friends. She works for Papa, so I believe Mama just looks at her as one of the staff. A person in Papa's circle."

"Will your papa be joining you here on holiday?" Harold asks.

"Oh, no. He never vacations with us. This is our girls' time."

Harold gives Countee a sidelong glance. "I see," he says, as if he's understood something I haven't said or implied.

"Well, I hope we can have some fun this summer," Countee says, "in between your girls' time. Harold and I have lots of fun here."

"Sometimes, we must make the fun, though," Harold says with a mischievous gleam in his eyes. "These folk can be quite dull."

Countee laughs. "That is the entire truth. But we'd love for you to join in our summer shenanigans."

"Oh! Well, you should've led with that. There's nothing I love more than shenanigans—"

"And debauchery?" Harold asks.

I let out a loud and very unladylike hoot. These two just might be the cure for my summer blues.

"Yes indeed," I say. "Bring on the debauchery."

Chapter Twenty-Eight

Tell me about the boy you're here pining away after."

I stare at Countee for a moment. He's sitting cross-legged on the edge of our picnic blanket. I wonder if I should tell the truth. His good-naturedness disarms me, so I decide that he's asking for pure reasons.

"What makes you think I'm pining away after a boy?"

"Are you moping over a girl?" Countee asks with wide eyes. "That is an entirely different conversation, one that I'd also be delighted to hear about."

I laugh and shake my head. "How are you this wicked and the son of a reverend?"

"Don't you know? Preachers' kids are the absolute worst."

"Well, I believe it. You and Harold both are just as raunchy as you wanna be."

Countee grabs his chest as if I've stabbed him. "I am not raunchy. I simply am observant. You are pining away, and girls don't swoon this hard unless they've indulged in some raunchiness themselves."

I press my lips together, unable to stop myself from turning beet red at this observation. That, of course, tickles Countee even further.

"I am as pure as the driven snow, I'll have you know," I say with a mostly straight face.

"Oh yes, indeed. The snow after my father's Ford has driven back and forth across it a few times."

My mouth hangs open while Countee howls. I have never seen anyone as amused by their own jokes as Mr. Roly-Poly.

"You are just too tickled, aren't you?"

"I am, but I am only trying to cheer you up, ma chérie. I hope I have succeeded."

The smile that tickles the corners of my mouth is genuine. "You have."

"So, then, will you tell me about him?"

"Do you want me to be sad all over again?"

"If he makes you sad, I think you should let me help you forget him," Countee says, scooting a bit closer on the blanket.

"He doesn't. He's wonderful and sweet," I explain. "But he wants more than I can promise him right now."

"Why can't you promise? Do you have a wandering eye, Yolande?" Countee's questions are somewhat offensive, but they get to the heart of the matter, I suppose. "You strike me as the loyal kind."

"I am very loyal, and I happen to love Jimmie."

"Oh! Le nom de l'homme est Jimmie."

"Yes. His name is Jimmie."

"Well, if you love him, then why can you not make promises?"

I narrow my eyes trying to think of the words. "Mon père ne l'aime pas."

The understanding on Countee's face is immediate. "How unfortunate."

"Yes, it is."

"Is your lover unworthy of you?"

"I am the one who isn't worthy. He is good beyond measure. In fact, I just may end up ruining him."

"Impossible."

I recall the look on Jimmie's face in the church that Sunday. That lost, empty stare. That nowhere, purposeless look. And his tears wiped away by that wench, Chrystal.

That is what had stolen the breath from my lungs. I know that the doctors discovered the adhesion near my appendix, but what had floored me that day was Jimmie's lost look. Because Jimmie always knows where he's going. He is my guide. And I'd broken him.

"I hope we are not irretrievably broken."

"Have you written to him?"

"Yes."

"And he you?"

"Yes, Countee, he's written me back."

"Well, then you are not broken unless you want it to be. He is still open to love."

"You make it sound romantic."

"Isn't it? I am not sure that I know, but I imagine love must be splendid," Countee says, waving his arms with the grandeur of his words. "All the poems I've read about it make love seem like something one shouldn't live without."

"Oh? Recite for me a love poem you know. Help me to know what it should feel like."

Countee grins, as pleased as can be. "I will recite to you one of my favorites. I learned it for classes. It's called 'Annabel Lee' and it was written by Edgar Allan Poe."

Now he jumps to his feet from the blanket. "You don't have to stand," I say. "It's just the two of us."

"Oh, but I do. The poem and the poet both deserve my reverence and respect."

"All right then." I giggle. "You have my full attention."

Countee clears his throat, then takes a deep breath. On his exhale he seems ready. He starts to recite the verses and he's animated with the words, but it's more than that. It's like he cherishes each of them, carefully cradling each syllable like a little girl carrying an egg across the kitchen to her mother when she is first allowed to help with the baking. His eyes light up and his feet shuffle from side to side in an almost rhythmic dance.

I've never seen anyone love a poem this way.

"Countee, that was beautiful," I gasp. "Can you say the line about the angels and demons again?"

And neither the angels in heaven above,
Nor the demons down under the sea,
Can ever dissever my soul from the soul
Of the beautiful Annabel Lee.

I want to remember that line. "Could you write that out for me?"

Countee rolls his eyes. "So you can write it in a letter to this boy?"

"How did you know?"

"Do you know how many times I have shamelessly used this line when the girl's name rhymed with Lee?"

"So, you understand?"

"Well, sure, but it doesn't mean I have to like it."

I stare at Countee for a moment, not quite sure how to respond. He's so quick-witted that he seems to always get the last word when we quip. And his smirk lets me know that he's won.

"I have left you speechless," Countee says. "Again."

"You have. I suppose it's because I cannot determine if you're flirting or not."

"That would be pointless since your heart belongs to someone else. I seek only a sweet, dear friend."

"Well, you already have the sweetest and dearest and handsomest friend in Harold. What on earth do you need me for?"

Countee shakes his head and laughs. "I liked it better when you were speechless."

I join his mirth. I feel light as a feather here with Countee, and the dread of going back to Fisk in the fall with the uncertainty of things with Jimmie feels so far away.

"Your laugh is something else," Countee says. "It makes me want to tell you one million funny stories in rapid succession."

And just like that my spirit sinks like he tossed me a satchel full of bricks.

"He says my laugh sounds like a jazz composition."

Countee ponders for a moment and gives a deep respectful nod.

"Oh, he's good," Countee says. "Perhaps he deserves the poetry."

He deserves more than poetry. He should have it all. Including a girl whose love comes freely and isn't encumbered with doubt.

Chapter Twenty-Nine

July 1923
Pleasantville, New Jersey

We've finally talked Mama into coming out of the house and spending time with some of the other ladies vacationing in Pleasantville. Mostly, it was Countee insisting that his mother was thrilled to have the wife of Dr. Du Bois over for tea. He'd even brought a handwritten invitation from his mother, Carolyn Cullen, so Mama believed she was welcome.

I am not convinced of the welcome part, only that Countee had put up a fuss for me to attend. If Mama knew that she still wasn't truly wanted, she would tell those ladies they could choke on their little old tea.

At any rate, we're here, and Mama has worn a beautiful floral dress and matching hat, perfect for the occasion of a formal tea party. Clearly, Mrs. Cullen's friends are drab in comparison.

"Is this your first time in Pleasantville for summer holiday?" Carolyn Cullen asks Mama as she places another tray of sandwiches on the center of the dining table.

Countee, Harold, and I opted not to sit at the table with the mothers and aunts. We're observing it all from the sofa where we must be careful not to spill or drop any crumbs. Mrs. Cullen seems to be somewhat obsessive with her tidiness, which if she got to know Mama, she would realize is something they have in common. Mama has been terrified of germs since my brother Burghardt died.

"I spent time here years ago," Mama says. "But it is the first time for Yolande. We like to visit different places, you see. Great Barrington and sometimes Europe when we can."

"I heard you spent a good many years in Europe," Mrs. Darcy, a doctor's wife from Washington, D.C., says. "Were you in Paris?"

"Mostly we were in England during the war. Yolande attended school there," Mama says, her tone a tiny bit annoyed.

She does not like to be put on the spot this way. Her friends back home in Brooklyn and Harlem don't do this. I hope she can last the entire tea without excusing herself with a headache.

"And Dr. Du Bois remained behind in New York running *The Crisis*?" Mrs. Cullen asks. "I don't know what my husband would do without me by his side. He doesn't have an independent bone in his body."

"I know what you mean. My husband can't spend more than a few days without me either." Mrs. Darcy gives Mrs. Cullen a knowing glance and they both giggle like much younger women.

All the ladies at the table laugh at this, except Mama. I think it is sometimes an embarrassment for her that Papa has no qualms spending months at a time away from her, and I think these women know it.

"Will has lots of help at the magazine. He was insistent upon Yolande taking some of her education abroad," Mama says, holding her ground.

"Your husband does have a very competent staff," Mrs. Cullen says. "Miss Fauset is a dear friend of our family. To hear her tell it, she is often the brains behind that entire operation."

Mama's eyebrows shoot up, and I get nervous. These ladies are treading into dangerous territory. Mama takes a bite of her cucumber sandwich and chews very slowly, probably deciding how to respond, or not respond at all.

Countee jabs me in the side with his elbow. "My mother loves Miss Fauset," he whispers. "Like she's her own daughter."

I keep my eyes fixed on Mama. If necessary, I will feign illness to rescue her.

"Miss Fauset is a brilliant woman," Mama says at last. "And quite competent. Will has said on many occasions how indispensable she has become to *The Crisis*."

"And she made quite the impression at the Pan African Congress a couple years back," Mrs. Darcy adds. "I am happy to say I was one of the key supporters of bringing her into the sisterhood of Delta Sigma Theta Sorority."

Mama only smiles and sips her tea. She has no interest in sororities of colored women, but I do. Margaret and Anna Welmon are destined to be members of Alpha Kappa Alpha Sorority like their mother, but maybe I'll follow in Miss Fauset's footsteps.

"I'm going to be an Alpha man like your father," Countee whispers. "Can't you just see it?"

Harold shushes Countee. "I'm trying to hear them, and your whispers are loud."

"Well, they aren't very interesting," Countee says. "I'm only here for the food."

Harold shakes his head. "You keep eating," he whispers. "Yolande, do you want to join me outside for a cigarette? Countee does not indulge."

Neither do I, but I am not sure I should decline the invitation. It feels like a friendship overture, and I'd like to be Harold's friend. He has been reserved, unlike Countee, who has gone overboard to make me and Mama feel accepted.

I follow Harold outside to the Cullens' lush and exquisitely manicured back yard. The vegetation is so different from Harlem, but it reminds me of Nashville in the spring. It is a nice enough day that the tea party could have been out here on the patio.

Harold pulls a cigarette case out of his jacket pocket and presses the little button to open it. "I hope you like Benson and Hedges," Harold says.

"I . . . um . . . don't have a preference."

Papa smokes Benson and Hedges, though, so I'm sure that means it is the best cigarette for anyone who might smoke.

"Yolande, have you ever smoked a cigarette before?" Harold asks while teetering on the edge of laughter.

"Well, no," I admit. "But I didn't want to be rude and turn down your invitation. It seems I've gotten to know Countee very well this summer, but you are still an enigma."

"I like to think I'm more esoteric than anything."

"I'm not sure I know what that means."

"That I'm only meant to be known and understood by a select few," Harold says as he lights a cigarette and hands it to me. "Watch. I'll show you how."

Harold holds the cigarette up to his lips and takes a long drag with his eyes closed. Then he holds his breath for a half beat before letting the smoke come out of his nose and mouth. He looks incredibly debonair doing this.

I try to copy Harold's actions, but the smoke burns my throat and nostrils, and I cough and spit instead of letting the smoke ease out.

This is not fun, and I'm sure I look ridiculous.

Harold covers his mouth with the hand not holding a cigarette and his shoulders shake with laughter. "It takes a minute to get the hang of it. Try it again, but don't swallow the smoke."

"I wasn't trying to swallow it the first time. It found its way down my throat all by itself."

Harold closes his eyes and shakes his head. "You are just plain old funny without even trying."

I take another drag from the cigarette, and this time not only does my nose burn, but my eyes water. Harold roars even more.

"Maybe it's not for me," I say, glaring down at the offensive little stick.

"You'll get the hang of it if you keep practicing," he says. "And you don't strike me as one who gives up easily."

"Well, now, that is true," I say. "I usually keep right on going until I have what I want."

Harold lifts an eyebrow. "Mmm-hmm. That's part of the reason I asked you to join me out here."

"I thought you wanted to smoke."

"I do, but I also have a question for you that I hope you won't find too intrusive."

"Intrusive?"

"I'd like to know your intentions with Countee."

I flick the ashes from the cigarette in imitation of Harold. "I don't know that I have any intentions at all. He's a sweet kid. I'm enjoying our summer holiday. Besides, aren't you the one who told him to introduce himself to me?"

"I didn't think he'd be so taken with you, not right away. You aren't the kind of girl he typically loses his marbles over."

"Oh really?"

"He usually chooses more reserved types. Genteel."

"Genteel? I am genteel, aren't I?"

Harold blows out another puff of smoke. "I think you're more rambunctious and opinionated. Countee finds you challenging."

"I am not trying to challenge him. So, if he's feeling that way, he's created the conflict all in his imagination."

"It's a good thing, how he feels. He's written Miss Fauset raving about you. I am just concerned that his feelings are not reciprocated."

I take another drag of the cigarette. This time, I manage to push the smoke out without burning my throat, but it still doesn't feel like much fun yet, and I'm starting to feel lightheaded.

"I've been clear with Countee that I'm only interested in friendship."

"And somehow he's still become enamored with you."

"I can't help it if he doesn't hear my words."

Harold stares at me for a long moment. Long enough to make me uncomfortable, as if he's seeing straight through to my heart where there's only room enough for Jimmie.

"Listen. He's got a tender heart, and I'm asking you not to handle him too roughly."

His ask sounds like a demand. There's no question mark at the end of the statement.

"Will there be trouble with you if I do handle him roughly?"

"I don't want trouble with Dr. Du Bois's daughter. I'm only concerned about my friend."

"Well, maybe you ought to introduce him to a girl or two and not hog them all for yourself."

Harold raises an eyebrow and chuckles. "Does he say I do that?"

"He says it's hell going around town with you, the handsomest man in Harlem."

"That blasted nickname. It's stupid. I don't hog anyone, and Countee has his fair share of attention. Don't let him make you think otherwise. His humor is often self-deprecating."

"I see." I shrug. "Well, you don't need to be concerned about Countee with me. I enjoy his friendship, and I have told him, quite plainly in fact, that I have a young man I'm seeing at Fisk."

"He mentioned that. I find myself concerned nonetheless."

"Like I said, it's for naught."

I hand Harold back the rest of his Benson and Hedges and leave him standing there while I rejoin my mother and Countee. I thought Harold was a friend as well, but now I am not entirely sure.

Chapter Thirty

Miss Fauset seems pleased as punch when she opens her door to me sandwiched between Countee and Harold. I bet she can't wait to tell Papa about my visit. They'll probably both fall to jubilant pieces about me traipsing around Harlem with a poet. It's Papa's dream come true.

"Uh, bonjour Countee, Harold, et Yolande?"

"We hope it's . . ." Countee begins, but Miss Fauset puts up one finger and shakes her head.

"En français, s'il vous plaît."

I squeeze my eyes shut trying to remember as much rudimentary French as I can. If only Papa had sent me to school in Paris instead of England, I'd be fluent by now. Not everyone is like Miss Fauset, who majored in French and Latin at Cornell.

"Nous espérons que tout va bien, nous avons amené Yolande."

I have no idea what Countee just said. This is going to be a long afternoon.

"Bien sûr, j'adore Yolande," Miss Fauset squeals. At least I know part of this one. She loves me.

"C'était l'idée de Countee," Harold says.

Countee's jaw drops in shock, but Miss Fauset only laughs. I am not 100 percent sure of the translation, but I think he just blamed Countee for bringing me along.

"J'ai compris ce que tu as dit, Harold," I fuss, not sure I have the proper tense, but I do want Harold to think I understand him even if I am catching only every other word.

"He's showing off," Countee says, and we all laugh as Miss Fauset hastily ushers us into her parlor with the rest of her guests.

There are a few people I recognize. Miss Rose is a librarian at the 135th Street library, and she knows everything about everyone's business. And she loves to tell it too. Before we get home tonight, all of Black Harlem is going to know I showed up here with Countee and Harold. Nella Larsen is another colored writer who also works at the library.

There's a very dapper young man who waves when we enter the room, so he must be a friend of Countee's and Harold's. We take seats on the couch and armchair next to him, with Harold on the chair looking like a real adult, needing only one of his cigarettes or a pipe to play the part.

I would really like to know how Miss Fauset is in possession of all these attractive young colored men in her friend circle. First Harold, and now this quiet, sophisticated, gentlemanly fellow whose name I don't know. Where is she hiding them? Why will she not share them with single girls looking for husbands, since she does not seem to care about being anyone's wife?

"I'm glad you're here," the young man says, turning on the couch so that he's facing me. "Now maybe they can interrogate *you* on how you spent *your* summer holiday."

Countee laughs. "That will take all of five minutes and then they'll want to return to the excitement of your European adventure."

"Well, I think your summer was quite advantageous and adventurous, Countee," I say. "Yours too, Harold."

"Ah, mais oui," Countee says. "We met Yolande. Have you two been acquainted? Langston Hughes, esteemed poet, meet Yolande Du Bois, artist and daughter of Dr. W.E.B. Du Bois."

Artist? Countee is being entirely too kind with that designation, but since I am in a room with writers, I will allow him to exaggerate. I just hope no one asks where my work is displayed, because then I'll have to admit the only gallery interested in my pictures of trees and bowls of fruit is my papa's scrapbook.

"Bonjour, Miss Du Bois. It is a pleasure to make your acquaintance, though I won't ask how you've come to cast your lot with these ne'er-do-wells."

Langston extends his hand for me to shake. While his palm is cold, the squeeze he gives my hand is warm and friendly.

"The pleasure is all mine," I chirp, wishing I could think of the right words to say in French. "I was feeling blue this summer, but Countee and Harold lifted my spirits. I'm glad they were around."

"You are an angel for saying that," Countee says, "but you were my summer muse."

Harold glances up at me, his left eyebrow rising slowly, calling to mind our conversation and his threat.

"I'd like a summer muse," Langston says. "Alas, I did not find one in Paris. I found mostly grime-encrusted streets. Give me Harlem any day over Paris."

"Harlem over Paris?" Harold's lips curl, and his tone is laced with . . . perhaps incredulity. "I cannot disagree more."

"Those are your British roots showing themselves," Countee quips as he swats Harold's knee. "You would choose a European city over Harlem."

"And here I thought you knew me better than anyone," Harold responds. "My London birthplace has nothing to do with my opinion. The experience of being a colored man in Paris is superior to my experience being the same man in Harlem. I, however, wouldn't live anywhere other than Harlem."

"Boulevardier that you are, I would expect nothing else," Langston says with a wink. "I could write a poem about your exploits. I'd call it 'A Prince in Harlem.'"

This seems to tickle Harold. Warmth exudes from the grin he gives Langston. "If I am the prince, then Yolande here is the princess."

"She certainly is," Countee says while jumping to his feet. "That reminds me, I have a surprise for you, Yolande, but it is also a surprise for Miss Fauset too."

Countee rushes out of the parlor, presumably to go and find Miss Fauset. Langston and Harold exchange a knowing glance that maybe I am not supposed to see. I certainly have no idea what secret thought passes between them, and suddenly I feel like an outsider.

"I wonder what that's all about," I say.

"He mentioned you in one of his letters," Langston says. "That is a rarity, so my assumption is that he's quite taken with you."

"It's rare for Countee to talk about young ladies he fancies?" I ask. "What else do young men write each other about?"

Now both Langston and Harold explode with laughter, but I have no idea what I've said that's amused them so.

Countee reappears with Miss Fauset and Mrs. Larsen in tow. Harold stands to offer his seat, and Mrs. Larsen takes the spot next to me.

"Quelle est votre surprise?" Miss Fauset says.

"Un poème," Countee says, then looks at me. "I wrote for Yolande after we spent one afternoon on a hill in Pleasantville, having a splendid picnic."

"A poem?" Harold's question drips with suspicion.

"I didn't know anything about this," I blurt in defense of myself for whatever reason.

"Oui, oui, ma chérie. C'est une surprise," Countee says cheerily, but Harold's hot gaze is enough to wither.

Countee stands up straight and juts his chin skyward.

As surely as I hold your hand in mine,
As surely as your crinkled hair belies

The enamoured sun pretending that he dies
While still he loiters in its glossy shine,
As surely as I break the slender line
That spider linked us with, in no least wise
Am I uncertain that these alien skies
Do not our whole life measure and confine.
No less, once in a land of scarlet suns
And brooding winds, before the hurricane
Bore down upon us, long before this pain,
We found a place where quiet water runs;
I held your hand this way upon a hill,
And felt my heart forebear, my pulse grow still.

Countee takes a deep bow as everyone gives him applause. My clapping starts a half second after everyone else's. I should be pleased, but this feels like a declaration of sorts. A declaration I do not agree with in front of people who know Papa.

"Magnifique, Countee. Tout simplement magnifique," Miss Fauset gushes.

"Will you help me in perfecting it?" Countee asks. "Your tutelage has brought me closer to being worthy of my pen's ink."

"I wouldn't change one word, cher. It is perfection."

"A muse indeed," Langston says.

I lock gazes with Harold. The lopsided grin on his chiseled face mocks.

"Thank you, Countee. I am honored," I whisper. "It's a beautiful poem."

"Now tell your papa to help me get it published," Countee whispers back, to everyone's delight.

Except Harold's.

Chapter Thirty-One

September 1923
Nashville, Tennessee

It feels peculiar after such an entertaining and eventful summer to be back at Pearly's with Jimmie, in our familiar booth, eating my usual cheeseburger and soda. Jimmie is his usual self, smiling, handsome, and extra buff from football practice. There is comfort in the familiarity of our routine, but something feels strange. Is it me? Am I different?

Certainly, the cigarette dangling daintily from my fingers is new. Jimmie's eyes keep going to the puff of smoke as it flows out through my nostrils, and my slightly parted lips. I must say I've gotten good at it. Très chic, as Countee would say.

"Tell me you didn't work the entire summer," I say to Jimmie as he scarfs down the last of his fried potatoes and pops some of mine in his mouth. "You must have done something fun."

"My work is fun, Yolande," he says with a grin after swallowing his food. "Playing at Mr. Morrison's speakeasy was exciting."

"But when did you rest?"

"I'm a young strapping lad," he says, pounding his fists on his chest. "I don't need rest."

My raspy, throaty chuckle sounds foreign even to me, so I wonder what Jimmie thinks of it. I sound like a lady. *Miss Lady.* Now that I've thought of Countee's joke, I'm reduced to giggles, and I feel a bit like my old self. Not this person who should be in Paris, strolling down the boulevard enjoying her cigarette.

"What's so funny? I am a strapping lad, am I not?" Jimmie asks.

I don't mind him thinking that my laugh is for his antics. I prefer that he thinks that. I don't want to get things off to a dreadful start.

"I had to rest, otherwise I'd never survive this year," I say before taking another puff of my cigarette.

"Should you be smoking?" Jimmie asks, a concerned frown forming on his brow. "Is that good for you?"

I chuckle. "It's only every now and then. Don't worry so much. I'm fine."

Jimmie narrows his eyes and stares at me for a long moment. Like when you see a familiar face and you're trying to place the person. Maybe I *am* different, and he can see it too.

"It is your senior year," he finally says after relaxing some, "you're nearly to the finish line."

"The finish of one thing just seems to lead to the beginning of another thing. Do you know what I mean?"

"I suppose."

"It really does. Finishing here at Fisk just means that I must figure out graduate school and then find a job as a teacher."

"When did you decide to teach?" Jimmie asks. "I've never heard you talk about that before."

I can hear the alarm building in his tone. The argument forming. And dear God, I don't want it. I don't want to go back to where we were before summer break.

"I really enjoyed coordinating the Decagynian spring program, and I think I'd like to do that with students. You still have another year in college, right?"

Hopefully this will hold him off from demanding an answer from me. At least if I'm teaching, I'm not courting anyone, right? So, he should be fine. Everything should be fine. I hate that anxiety has me pulling smoke through this cigarette like nobody's business.

Why am I anxious about this?

"Well, let's just enjoy our time this year," Jimmie says, seeming to pick up on my nervousness. "Our last year together at Fisk."

"I'm glad we're together, especially since I must face Chrystal and her minions without Minnie. She withdrew and is going to Howard this year."

"She withdrew? But why?" Jimmie asks. "You two were as thick as thieves. I thought she'd like to cross the stage with you."

"Well, there was an accusation made by Miss Callinge about a missing five dollars, and Minnie's parents didn't appreciate their virtuous daughter being accused of theft."

She'd written to me all about it, after the fact, and not in enough time for me to try and get anyone's help. I suppose she was embarrassed about it all, but now I'm only missing my friend.

"Now, maybe you can be friends with Chrystal then, since you're all still here together."

I roll my eyes. "Jimmie, please!"

"Chrystal's not so bad."

I take a long drag on my cigarette that's nearly done now. I let one singular plume of smoke come from the corner of my mouth.

"I liked the poetry you sent me, and the drawings," Jimmie says, very wisely changing the subject from his friend.

"Wasn't that a lovely line? The entire poem moved me so."

"Will you share it with the Decagynians?" he asks.

"Yes, of course, but I have plans for us this year. I'd like to leave a legacy with our literary society."

"I love that idea. A Yolande Du Bois legacy here at Fisk."

"When you put it that way it makes me think of my papa."

"He has a legacy here, but yours will be different. It will belong to you and not him."

I shake my head and put the cigarette out in the ashtray. "I belong to Papa, so he will share the glory of anything I do well."

Jimmie seems riveted by my hand pressing on the cigarette butt as the heat dies and gives up its last bit of smoke.

"When did you start smoking cigarettes?" he asks.

"Isn't it chic?"

Jimmie shrugs. "I don't know if I am the authority on what is chic."

"You are not." I agree.

"Well, I think being a jazz musician could be considered chic, right? I am not a complete square," Jimmie retorts.

"You do have potential, my love. And you certainly have the looks. I just need to get you back to Harlem so you can learn what's on the up and up."

"One of your Harlem friends taught you to smoke, then?"

My laughter trails off as I lean forward and rest my elbows on the edge of the table and my chin atop my now clenched fists. I've fallen silent and it feels heavy. It seems I won't be able to escape what happened at the end of last school term, no matter how much I try.

"What is the question you really want to ask, Jimmie?" I say on the heels of a breathless sigh.

"I believe I asked the question that I want answered." His tone has a bite to it, but I am also irritated with him.

"But why does it matter who taught me to smoke? What is the question behind the question?"

"It may not matter at all. I suppose it all depends on the answer to my question."

"If it was Margaret who taught me?"

"Was it Margaret?"

"No."

"Now you're being evasive." He's gone beyond annoyance now, but if we're going to do this, we might as well get it out of the way.

"Only because I know what you're truly asking, and it worries me that nothing has changed over our summer apart."

"What does that mean?"

"If I tell you my new friend Harold Jackman taught me to smoke, what would you say?"

He sits taller in the booth, his chest expanding and contracting with rapid breaths. If he wasn't angry, it would be incredibly sexy. "Is this the truth? Was it a person named Harold Jackman?"

"Yes."

His nostrils flare, but so do mine. He probably wants to ask if Harold is Papa's current matchmaking attempt. If he does, I swear it's going to be over with us. I spent the whole summer pining away after him and dreaming of his touch, and he's still hung up on George W. Cuffee, the husband that never was.

"I'm curious how you met," he says, trying to sound calmer, but failing. "Surely, he is someone you admire."

"How did you come to that conclusion? That I admire him."

"Because you've clearly decided to imitate him. By smoking, I mean. It makes you seem like a different Yolande."

Okay, maybe the smoking is somewhat off-putting. Perhaps that is what makes him so nervous.

"I do admire him, but not for the reasons you might assume. He is a fixture on the scene in Harlem. Everyone knows him, and he manages to move between social circles with no care for what people say about him. He is the most authentic person I have ever met."

"That is high praise. Did your papa introduce you?"

Damn you, Jimmie!

"There it is. There is the question. I didn't think you'd express it. I thought you'd keep pretending."

"You just praised another man for his authenticity, so how could I not be transparent?"

"To answer your real question, no, Papa didn't introduce us. Harold and his friend Countee, who was our neighbor in Pleasantville, spent the entire summer cheering me up as I was distraught over missing you."

He looks away from the tears now freely flowing down my cheeks. I want him to see the pain he's causing with his suspicions. This is not what love should feel like.

"I missed you every moment of every day," he says, with an apologetic tone.

"I missed you as well! But I wonder how long it will take for you to trust me. It never enters my mind that you will betray me when we're apart."

"I would never."

"But you aren't as sure about me, and that breaks my heart. When Countee recited the poem I shared in my letter, my heart was filled with love for *you*. My thoughts were toward *you*."

"And has your papa's opinion of me changed? That is what fills me with uncertainty. If he does not approve of me, I worry about how I will be replaced."

"I have and will continue disobeying my papa for you."

"I don't want you to have to disobey him. I want him to honor your choice."

"We have no control over Papa, Jimmie." I want to touch him, but I resist. He is the one hurting me. He should do the comforting.

But he does not. He sits there stewing about things we cannot control, instead of planning the future. Like tonight. Like how he can sneak me somewhere nice and have his way with me. Like a man who was dreaming about his woman all summer would.

Like my future husband would.

Chapter Thirty-Two

November 1923
Nashville, Tennessee

Jimmie and the rest of the football team have bested our biggest rival—Morehouse—again, and our Piggie even scored the final touchdown. I love it when we are victorious, even though I've never been much for sports myself, except to watch the boys. But if boy watching is a sport, then I have a varsity letter in that.

But today, the only boy I'm watching is Jimmie. I march right next to him in the victory parade.

"Piggie! Piggie!" I chant along with the Decagynian crew, minus Chrystal and Amanda, who never march with us. They go along with the Harmonias and their misspelled signs.

Though things started off rough this year, we've fallen right into our regular groove with our Friday night tradition at the hotel. We spend the night in each other's arms, me binding my heart to Jimmie's, even if things aren't perfect.

As we stroll into Pearly's together, I vaguely notice everyone observing us. Not that we've been private with our relationship, but it still gives me some satisfaction to see Chrystal's envy on public display. She's pretty enough to find a boyfriend, so why doesn't she? Is she just waiting for me to graduate, so she can swoop in like a vulture?

We sit at our booth, which has been left empty for us even though Pearly's is jam-packed. But I'm not surprised at all. We're one of the most popular couples on campus.

"I think I will throw caution to the wind and have a milkshake today," I chirp. "In celebration of you, Jimmie, and the rest of the team."

Jimmie seems concerned. "I don't want you to be sick later."

"Oh, Jimmie. I'm going to sketch a picture of you right now, wearing your worried, fatherly face."

I laugh as I open my sketchbook. Countee sent me this as a gift to encourage my art. Mostly, I make sketches of my favorite places on campus, but occasionally I try to draw a person's face.

I take out my charcoal pencil and squint for a moment to get Jimmie's one especially sour look. Then I take a stab at re-creating it. But while I'm sketching, Jimmie decides to smile and pose.

"No, don't smile," I tell him. "I want you to just keep being a grumpy old man who likes to keep his girlfriend from enjoying a milkshake."

His frown returns. "I am a good boyfriend who wants his girlfriend to be free of a tummy-ache."

"Oh yes. That's the face I want. Good and grumpy."

Jimmie points to an envelope sticking out from the top of the sketchbook. "Someone else likes to draw I see. Or is that a letter you're sending to someone?"

"What?"

"There are flowers drawn on the edge of the envelope," Jimmie says. "Very nice."

I pull the envelope out. "Oh no. This is a letter from my friend."

"Minnie?"

I sit my pencil on the table as my smile fades into a frown. Why does he have to be like this?

"No. Not Minnie."

There is a challenge in my tone, a dare. Because I want him to stop this. I want him to grow up.

"Then who is it from?"

The waitress, Regina, comes to our table before I can reply. "What'll you two be having? Piggie, your meal is on the house for bringing in that win!"

"Thank you." He sure doesn't sound as excited about the free meal as he should, probably because I'm glaring at him. "I'll have a burger with lots of cheese and fries, and a chocolate milkshake."

"And you, Yolande?" Regina asks.

"The same, except my burger can have the regular amount of cheese."

That milk in the cheese and milkshake are going to have me in pain this evening. I can tell Jimmie wants to object to my order, but since I'm already giving him my angriest face, he doesn't say a word. At least he's smart enough to know that much.

"Okay," Regina says. "It'll be right out."

I continue to glare at Jimmie as Regina walks away. I slam my sketchbook closed, but now I don't know how to go back to our conversation without it turning into an argument, because I am livid.

"The letter is from Countee," I finally say. "My friend, the poet."

"Oh, I see."

"Do you have anything else to say?" I ask saucily. "Any other interrogations?"

"No, Yolande. I was only curious." He speaks quietly, in response to my rising voice. Maybe hoping I'll calm down.

"Countee is just a kid, and I only have a friend affection for him. In case you have questions you aren't saying aloud."

"A kid?"

"Yes, he's in his second year at New York University."

"I'm in my second year of college. Am I a kid to you?"

"He's a year younger than you are, Jimmie. You know I don't view you that way, but I admit you are acting childish now."

I am exasperated and tired because this is beyond childish. But I wish I had done a better job of hiding Countee's letter, because I should've known he'd act this way.

"Am I not to have friends then?" I ask.

"You aren't under interrogation, but at least you know Chrystal and I are friends. It isn't a secret."

"And neither is Countee, or any of my other friends. And I will continue to write him, and any other friend."

Now let's see what he says. Let's see how mature he's become. Let us see if there is any trust between us.

"Well, that is fine, since I am not going to stop being friends with Chrystal. We must trust each other, right? I trust you."

"Your lips say those words, but your interrogations say otherwise."

"I am doing the best I can. I apologize, Yolande."

I sigh deeply. "You should try harder, Jimmie. You really should."

I open the sketch pad to my drawing of Jimmie and add his mustache over the grim frown. It's a pretty accurate depiction of what I see in front of me.

I wonder if he is trying at all, because I watch as his eyes go to the envelope once more. He must want to read the letter, but he's just going to have to remain curious about that. I doubt he'd enjoy Countee's sappy sentimentality, and I have no patience for the litany of questions that are sure to follow.

Chapter Thirty-Three

December 1923
Harlem, New York

It isn't a foregone conclusion that I will board a train in Nashville to travel home to New York for Christmas. Sometimes Papa doesn't want to pay for train fare. Other times, I'm struggling in a class or two and must stay behind to finish an extra assignment for an unyielding professor who cares nothing about Papa being an alumnus. If I spend the holiday season in Nashville, it's quite all right because there are plenty of parties and dinners for me to attend.

But this year is our first Christmas at our apartment on St. Nicholas, so Papa thought we should celebrate together, and so I am home. And without Jimmie.

I trace the edge of Mama's new marble dining table that can seat eight people. It seems strange for us to have a table like this since Mama rarely entertains anymore since we moved to Harlem. Such an expensive piece of furniture for just the three of us.

Mama has attempted a beef roast of some sort. The seasoning is good, but it is hard to chew. Papa struggles to gnaw a hunk of it, which gives us a welcome pause in the conversation. If it is even possible, Papa has more suggestions than usual. And soon these will turn into instructions. I am not in the mood.

Papa stops chewing his most recent bite and swallows. Then, his eyebrows lift as if he has just recalled something, and he points his fork in my direction.

Uh-oh.

"Yolande, I received your request for an additional five dollars for Christmas gifts for your acquaintances."

I received your request for . . . Am I simply a debt that he must satisfy? A papa should understand the requests of his daughter should not be handled in the same way he addresses his creditors.

"Yes, Papa. I have simply run out of money. I wasn't aware that I was coming home for Christmas, and I allocated all my funds to gifts for my dear friends at Fisk. I think you would be proud of me for not procrastinating. I was finished shopping by the second week of December, but then Mama wrote that I would be coming home, and I realized then that I would need something for my Harlem friends, besides a card."

"Five dollars is a little steep. Who are you buying for except the Welmon sisters?" Papa interrogates. I am sure tired of being asked questions all the time.

"I have plenty of friends in Harlem. Countee, Harold, oh and Miss Fauset too."

"Miss Fauset rates more than a card?" Mama asks with a chuckle.

"She has been helping me to figure out what I might do next. After graduating from Fisk."

"Is that so?" Papa asks now, peering at me with more interest than he's given to anything else I've said since I've been home. "What does she suggest?"

"She thinks I should come home and work for *The Crisis* as an intern."

"There is much you can learn from Miss Fauset, Yolande. That is a splendid idea," Papa says, clapping with glee.

"I hear Miss Fauset practically runs the entire operation," Mama says. "So, you will learn a lot, Yolande. Your daughter may retire you as the editor one day, Will."

Papa scoffs. And that clipped sound says, *I'd like to see* that *day*.

"Or maybe I'll start my own magazine, with my artwork."

I throw my shoulders back authoritatively then grin at Papa. His face falls into a grimace, like he tried to grin back but didn't quite make it there.

"Have you seen the news about your friend Countee Cullen?" Papa asks. "He is quite the toast of the literary town, beating out all those undergraduates to win the Witter Bynner Poetry Prize."

Now Papa is practically shimmying with excitement. I don't think I've ever heard him be that thrilled about something I've done. I wonder if he'd be so indifferent if someone suggested Countee taking things over at *The Crisis*.

"Yes, Papa. He sent me a clipping from *The New York Times*. I'm proud of him."

"I am glad to hear you're still corresponding with Countee. Miss Fauset and I are proud of him as well," Papa says wistfully. "She practically mothers him . . . along with Mrs. Cullen, of course."

"She does," Mama says, "but he's got a doting father in Reverend Cullen too."

"At any rate, now that I know who all you're planning to buy a gift for, I will approve the five dollars," Papa says. "But we have many improvements and repairs to make to our property, along with your school fees. I am going to request that you not pepper your mother with requests for inconsequential things."

"Yes, Papa. I will take better care of my allowance. Jimmie always teases me about frivolously spending my five dollars on things I don't need. He thinks I'm wasteful, really."

"Now I can agree with his assessment," Papa says. "But he has decided to marry you without understanding the kind of life you are used to living. Your privilege befuddles him, and you would be unequally yoked if you ever agreed to marrying him."

If I didn't need these five dollars I'd roll my eyes. I don't feel like hearing Papa's negative viewpoints on Jimmie for the whole time I'm home. Or ever.

"Papa, you have already made it clear, on several occasions, that you do not approve of Jimmie."

"Well, I feel the need to continue voicing it, because it has fallen upon deaf ears. Your mother says you speak about him a great deal in your letters."

"Jimmie is my closest friend and protector on campus."

The recently installed telephone rings, and Papa's eyes light up. "Will you excuse me? I've been waiting all evening for this call."

Mama nods, as if Papa was truly waiting for our approval and not simply being polite. I push the tough meat on my plate underneath a mound of potatoes. My appetite has left me.

"Mama, why is Papa so cross whenever we start to talk about Jimmie?" I am used to his gruff directness, but he has an extra edge to his tone tonight.

"I don't think he's cross. Only disappointed."

"I know he thinks Jimmie is a distraction, but he isn't. He is a help to me. You've seen it yourself."

"I have."

"I promise to get more Bs than Cs next term. It's just that with everything I do on campus, it's hard for me to manage it all."

"Your father isn't disappointed in your grades."

"He isn't? He's always pushing me to study harder. I fear I'll never be worthy of him. Whenever it seems as if I've pleased him, he raises the mark higher."

Mama puts her fork down and sighs. "Yolande, do you realize that news of your exploits in Nashville quite frequently makes its way here to Harlem?"

"My . . . exploits?"

"Yes. Gallivanting around town with Jimmie. Often at indecent hours . . . in unsavory places."

The Andrew Jackson Hotel isn't unsavory at all. Whoever has

brought gossip back to Harlem has added untruths, but I doubt that Mama will want to hear about me being at any hotel.

"We're of age, Mama."

"You already know how I feel about that argument."

"I *am* of age, Mama," I remind her again. "And Jimmie is wonderful to me and for me."

"You don't know what's good for you. That is why your papa is frustrated with you and your choices."

"But aren't they my choices to make?"

"Of course. As your parents, we want to protect you from harm. Maybe we don't always go about it the right way. But it's because we love you."

"Jimmie isn't going to cause me harm."

"No, but a life of poverty and struggle will be detrimental to you both."

Must they keep repeating the same threat about the poor and penniless life I'll have with Jimmie?

"We'll just learn how to make do with less," I say with defiance. "Lots of people do that, you know?"

Mama's lips curl into a mocking sneer, deflating my spirit and my confidence.

"Make do with less? This from the young lady who just twisted her papa's arm for more money to spend on gifts. You've never had less, and you've never had to make do."

Mama's words feel harsher than Papa's admonishments. She's usually on my side, and in times like this, we stand against Papa together.

Now, I feel alone on an island.

* * *

I escaped Papa's movement planning only because my holiday fun includes Papa's new obsession, Countee Cullen. If I heard his name one more time or another exclamation about that poetry contest, I do believe my head was going to explode.

Miss Fauset's holiday literary tea is a welcome distraction even if the invitation came as a bit of a surprise. I am not exactly in that circle. My close friendship with Countee and mentorship from Miss Fauset put me on the outskirts of it, but I accept any blessing that gets me away from Papa's sermonizing.

Countee hints that this gathering will be special, and I've brought along my gifts for Harold, Countee, and Miss Fauset. I thought it might be in poor taste to come with gifts for some and not all, so I convinced Mama to bake a cake for the tea party. That will be gift enough for the rest of the attendees.

I feel quite chic in my winter coat with a real mink collar attached. Papa did not want to buy it, but when Mama convinced him of how fetching it looked on me, and how much wear I'll get out of it here in New York with our bitter winters, he acquiesced. Maybe he hopes it'll help attract any husband other than Jimmie.

And now as I stand at Miss Fauset's door stroking the soft fur, I remember my mother's words about never having had to make do with less. It's a good thing a mink will last for years, because it might take years for Jimmie to be able to afford to buy me another one.

Miss Fauset opens her door after I knock, but this time she is not surprised at my appearance. I do feel somewhat a part of this scene, even if I am on the fringes and not a real writer like Countee and Langston. Perhaps some of their talent will transfer to me and I'll amaze Papa with a tale in verse about my life at Fisk.

"Bonjour Yolande, comment vas-tu?"

"Je vais bien, merci. I've brought your Christmas gift and a cake from Mama."

"Mrs. Du Bois baked a cake for my party?" Miss Fauset seems quite surprised at Mama's kindness.

"Yes, she sends her regards," I say, abandoning my French, as did Miss Fauset, as I step across the threshold. "For a moment I thought she was going to join me because Papa is being quite insufferable since our dinner last night."

"I hope everything's all right."

"Yes, we're fine. Just the usual, you know. Trying to make sure I don't throw my life away marrying the wrong man."

"Mon dieu!" Miss Fauset says. "Come in and enjoy a few festive moments, then."

"You better enjoy yourself as well. I'm sure you will be called upon to help find me a proper prospect."

"Absolument. Countee, Harold, and Langston are already here, in the parlor."

"Oh good, I haven't seen any of them since I got home."

Miss Fauset leads me to the parlor and before I'm even in the room, Countee is on his feet. He rushes over to hug me. It is a warm and optimistic hug, full of longing. Harold then follows with much less fervor. Langston doesn't rise; he merely touches the tips of my fingers with a warm smile.

"Sit, please," I say as I choose the space next to Harold on the sofa. "Don't make a fuss over little old me."

"I am always befuddled by young ladies," Countee gushes as he eases back down into his seat. "If one isn't chivalrous there are many complaints about the lack of manners, but then when you go out of your way, they tell you not to make a fuss."

"Les femmes sont très . . . déroutantes," Miss Fauset says to Countee while patting his shoulder.

I am not sure what she said. My French is still abysmal, no matter how much time I spend with Miss Fauset.

"C'est vrai," Countee sighs.

Well, whatever Miss Fauset said, Countee believes it. I'll have to remind myself to ask him later.

"Félicitations pour le prix de poésie de Witter Bynner." My French is possibly incorrect, so I hope I didn't say anything vulgar.

"Merci, Yolande."

"May we speak English, s'il vous plaît?" I plead. It takes me too long to try and translate my thoughts to French.

"Yes, yes, but only because I want to hear Countee tell us the story behind his award-winning poem," Miss Fauset says as she perches on the arm of the sofa.

"You'll not want to hear my pontifications on the subject."

"No doubt I'll grow tired of it," Langston says in that devilish way he has of quipping with Countee.

We all laugh at Langston, except Miss Fauset, whose amusement only reaches her eyes.

"Well, just for Langston, I will tell the entire tale behind this poem. Especially because Yolande is here, and she is a part of the story."

"I am?"

Now everyone is on the edge of their seats in suspense. I am not sure I want to know how I inspired another of Countee's poems. I only want to be Jimmie's muse, not Countee's.

"Yes, when you liked 'Annabel Lee' by Edgar Allan Poe, I thought I might like to write a poem that tells an epic story."

Harold cuts his eyes at me, crosses his legs, and leans back in his chair. Every bit of his body language says displeasure.

"I did quite enjoy 'Annabel Lee.' But I think what my friends and I like most about your poem was the care taken to describe the brown girl even though it's so sad. Everyone is dead at the end."

"Poets are always murdering their subjects on the page, and I agree that this poem is one of the epic variety," Langston says with a shrug. "And where are these girlfriends of yours that enjoy poetry? Why did you not bring them today?"

"Oh, I'm referring to the Decagynian Society at Fisk," I answer Langston, and then glance up at Miss Fauset. "We host monthly literary teas, Miss Fauset. You would love it. It's just like what you have here today, except our snacks are nowhere near as sophisticated and special as yours."

"Literary teas? I am impressed," Miss Fauset says. "Why don't you write an article about the Decagynian Society for *The Crisis*?"

"All right, I'll send it next month. At our January tea we're going to discuss Countee's poem."

"That is just splendid." Countee smiles happily. "I am overwhelmed by the support of my friends."

"I hope that I can count on your support as well," Miss Fauset says, "when my first novel, *There Is Confusion*, is published in March."

Everyone ogles Miss Fauset with shock and disbelief as she shares this overwhelming, life-changing news with no warning. Then the room erupts into a cacophony of chatter, congratulations, hugs, and kisses.

"This is a surprise!" Harold exclaims. "When did you find out? We must celebrate."

"Only a few days ago. You are the first among my writing friends that I've told. It is starting to feel real."

"A debut!" Countee sounds delighted. "Tell Dr. Du Bois to prepare your successor, because soon you will be a famous writer!"

I recall Papa's reaction during our conversation about him having a successor. I do believe Papa thinks he will live forever. Or maybe he plans to take *The Crisis* to his grave.

"Oh, I don't know about that," Miss Fauset demurs. "You know most notable authors are not appreciated until after they're long gone."

"It's true," Langston Hughes says. "One hundred years from now we'll be all the rage."

"Such pessimism will not be tolerated," Countee commands. "You will be the toast of the town, and we will certainly be here to celebrate you. You are worthy of enormous success."

Whenever Countee speaks it sounds like he's piecing together stanzas, lines, paragraphs, and verses. Like he wakes every morning with the intention of transforming the day into a literary masterpiece.

"Well, let us eat cake then," Miss Fauset says. "To celebrate Countee's award and my debut."

While everyone has cake, I lightly tug Harold's shirtsleeve to get his attention. When he looks up, I motion with my hand for him to follow me to the other sitting room, since the rest of the tea party ladies have joined us in the parlor for the celebration.

"You'd like to speak to me about something, Yolande?" Harold asks suspiciously.

"I only want to give you the Christmas present I bought for you."

I extend the decorated gift box to Harold, and he gingerly takes it from my hand.

"Oh, but I didn't get anything for you."

"That's all right," I tell him. "I wasn't expecting anything in return."

Harold lifts his eyebrow while pulling loose the shiny bow. "Oh, there's always an expectation of a return on investment."

"It's a gift, not an investment."

Harold chuckles as he turns over the shiny cigarette case I purchased at Blumstein's. "Thank you," he says. "This is so thoughtful of you."

"You're welcome. Isn't it chic?"

"It is indeed."

"It's partially to thank you for making my summer memorable."

"I am too flattered. But why are you flattering me?" Harold asks.

"Because I can't stand the thought of you disliking me. And I don't think we ended things on a high note."

"I don't dislike you, Yolande. You are my favorite socialite on the Harlem scene."

"But you don't trust me regarding Countee, and he's become such a dear friend to me."

"Liking you and trusting you are two different things, Yolande. If you're honest with yourself, you'll realize there are always people you like a good deal that you do not trust."

This is not going the way I thought it would. Harold was supposed to be so pleasantly surprised by my gift that all his doubts about me would disappear.

"I've done nothing to make you distrust me, Harold. I really want us to be good friends."

"And I hope we shall," Harold says as he turns the cigarette case over in his hands. "For Countee's sake at least."

"What's happening for my sake?" Countee asks, having snuck away from the group to join me and Harold.

"Harold and I becoming the best of friends," I say as I hand Countee a small box that also has a bow on top. He happily accepts it and starts to tear off the bow.

Unlike Harold, I am sure Countee is expecting a gift. He mailed me the most beautiful scrapbook that I've already started filling with photos and other notable items.

A broad smile breaks out on Countee's face, as he lifts the black, gold-tipped fountain pen out of the box. "I love this, Yolande," he says. "And I am thrilled about the two of you becoming better friends. I want all my cherished friends to be able to come together under the same roof."

"Well, you've accomplished that. Or Miss Fauset did with her gatherings," Harold reassures him. "I'm here, Yolande, and Langston too."

"I have other friends too," Countee says, "and you will all hold hands together in harmony."

"Speaking of everyone being harmonious, excuse me while I liven things up a bit." Harold slips a flask from his jacket pocket and winks.

Harold slinks off to the punch bowl. Countee and I watch him stealthily slip the top from the flask and dump its contents into the punch. Then, he gives it a swirl with the ladle.

"What was in that flask?" I whisper to Countee.

"Who knows. Whiskey he got from some bootlegger?"

"Oh, then I'll make sure to have some."

"I hope you don't die." Countee laughs.

"I've got a stomach of steel." I pat my midsection and Countee howls.

"You, of all people, should beware that poisonous concoction. If you wind up in the hospital, Dr. Du Bois will blame us all."

"I am tired of everyone trying to keep fun things from me, just because I have had a few bouts with a doctor. Jimmie is always chiding me about the foods I eat." Countee winces at the mention of Jimmie, but I pretend I don't see it. "I like fun and bad foods as much as the next person."

"Jimmie. The infamous Piggie Lunceford."

"How do you know we call him that?"

"Do you think the Harlem biddies don't discuss the exploits of Dr. Du Bois's daughter?"

My eyes widen though I shouldn't be shocked that Countee has heard the same gossip Mama has. "They speak of me and Jimmie?"

"On more than one occasion, I heard it said at my own mother's table, 'Have you heard about Yolande and Piggie?'"

I wonder if Mrs. Cullen is the one receiving the gossip or the one sharing it. If she was sharing it, I wouldn't be surprised if she'd wanted Countee to overhear. Like Harold, she seems to distrust me as well, and her disdain extends to my mother.

"Papa has already heard enough tales about me and Jimmie. I hope he isn't getting them from Miss Fauset too."

"I have heard he's expressed his displeasure on the subject on more than one occasion."

"What *haven't* you heard, Countee?" I snap, feeling quite frustrated that, as usual, I am the subject of everyone's gossip. "Between you and Harold, you must know every dirty little secret in Harlem."

"Harold perhaps, but not me." Countee's mirth fades, and suddenly he seems uncomfortable. "I don't pay attention to tales that have nothing to do with me."

That is very curious. Very curious indeed.

"Well, Jimmie and I have nothing to do with you."

Countee nods slowly. "Jimmie certainly doesn't, but I wish that you did. One day you will look up and wish you hadn't spurned my attentions."

"I do not spurn you, Countee," I protest. "Truly I don't. Perhaps one day I will be able to accept your attentions more unreservedly, but in the meantime, I do not think it's wrong to feel only a friendly affection for you."

"Tread lightly, Yolande. The delicate fabric of my dreams is in your hands."

"You make tragic things sound so beautiful, Countee."

"And yet all my lovely words aren't enough to lure you away from your athletic Adonis."

"Love must run its course. If it shall be forever, I'd like to give it time to take root."

"Now who's the poet?" Countee asks, the disappointment in his voice thick enough for me to clutch in my hands.

"You are quite funny with that. I'd never call myself a poet while standing next to you."

"But your words are enough to spark hope or throw a man like me into despair. That's exactly what poetry does."

I hold out my arms to embrace Countee. He responds by clinging to me until I let him go.

"Countee, you are my cherished confidant. I hope you continue to write me beautiful poetic letters with your new pen."

"Not even your muscular beau can stop me from doing that. Unless he finds me and breaks my fingers."

"And you know that he's muscular too? Good heavens, Countee."

"Do not blame me, blame the biddies."

No wonder Harold doesn't trust me with his best friend's heart. Why would he, when Countee's decided to fall in love with little old unavailable me?

And I simply cannot seem to resist being adored, even if the feelings are not mutual.

Chapter Thirty-Four

February 1924
Nashville, Tennessee

I t isn't quite spring yet here in Nashville, but today the sun shines like it believes it's April, and the warm breeze must think winter has gone to hide. So, when my friends Lydia, Anna, and Frances suggested that we gather our beaus since they're all on the basketball team and fix them a nice Valentine's Day lunch, I thought it was a splendid idea. Especially when Lydia said she'd bring her Brownie camera so that we could capture it all for our scrapbooks.

But, of course, I couldn't let *them* manage the planning. If left to them, the picnic would consist of crackers, cheese, and sliced apples pilfered from the dining hall. We must do better than that for the handsome varsity men we've managed to snag.

So, I've enlisted Jimmie (of *course*) to help me set everything up at the picnic tables at the park near Ebenezer, because heaven forbid there be any fraternizing on campus, even though this gathering will be perfectly virtuous.

I chew my bottom lip as Jimmie hoists the basket heavy-laden with little triangle sandwiches, cookies, and jars filled to the brim with lemonade onto the table, unable to stop my mind from being flooded with memories of how Jimmie's strong arms lift other things. With Jimmie playing every sport there is, his back and arms are always muscled and the shirt he wears today stretches just so across his chest. I could swoon at the sight of him, but I steel myself. Can't go fainting and being put to bed when all the unattached heifers are roaming the campus looking for any old Valentine.

Jimmie rearranges the flowers I've placed in a vase atop one of my freshly laundered sheets, now serving as a tablecloth. Mama would scream if she knew the sheet she bought at Blumstein's, because I'd begged for it, was being used outdoors.

"That looks perfect, Jimmie. I wish I'd been holding Lydia's camera to capture you fixing the flowers. I think I'll try to sketch it from memory tomorrow."

"Nothing looks more perfect than you do," Jimmie says with a mischievous wink. I love it when he's as saccharine and sweet as the tea down at Pearly's.

"Aw, you don't mean that, Jimmie. Say it again," I tease.

"You don't believe me? Maybe if I said it in a rhyme like your poet."

I lift a suspicious eyebrow. "*My* poet?"

"Yes, the one you write weekly letters to."

"Oh." I wave my hands, shutting down this matter altogether. "Countee. He isn't my poet. He's all of Harlem's. Just won a big award for writing."

Jimmie takes slow steps toward me, rocking from side to side as if there's music playing in his head. "I met a girl once and made her all mine. We'll be together forever, for all times."

"I love it. And it does indeed rhyme," I say as Jimmie finally reaches me and scoops me into his arms as I hoped he would.

He nuzzles his face into my neck and inhales with his eyes shut tight. Like he's trying to remember my scent for later when he's alone in his room, maybe to be fodder for his dreams. If that's the case, I hope the dream is naughty. It is Valentine's Day after all. Love should be on his mind, and that means me.

"I can write you more rhymes if you'd like," Jimmie says. "I'll set them to music all for you. We can have the libretto of Yolande."

"Now that you've mentioned the music part of it, you must do it. I'll have my song by Easter please."

He sets me down in the moist, mossy grass and then kisses my cheek. He reaches into his jacket pocket and pulls out the loveliest Valentine's Day card. Jimmie must've spent at least a dollar on this. On the cover of the card is lace cut into the shape of a heart, and in the center of the heart is the front of a tiny blue house. All around the lace are beautifully drawn pink and white lilies, and on the edges is golden scrolling.

I open it to read the message inside.

Inside your heart is the only place I feel at home.

Love,
Jimmie

"Oh, I love you too, Jimmie," I say, reaching out for him, needing to feel his touch again.

"I'm sorry my words in the card didn't rhyme," Jimmie says squeezing me even tighter, "since you've become so fond of poetry."

I pull away to search Jimmie's eyes to see if he's serious or only teasing me. I cannot tell.

"Well, I like it, but the way Countee speaks is sometimes a bit overblown. He doesn't utter a sentence that couldn't be in the middle of a poem."

"I don't think I can compete with that."

"You don't need to. I'm not attracted to him. He's only my friend. Besides, I prefer your velvety musical notes. Now hug me again."

He does, and I snuggle into his warmth as a cool breeze blows through the leaves in the oak tree above our heads.

"Thank you for my Valentine's Day card. I'll give you your card tomorrow night at the Andrew Jackson Hotel."

Instinctively, Jimmie looks around nervously to see if anyone's heard me. He's so worried about getting caught that I'm afraid he doesn't enjoy it as much as I do, and that is a tragedy. Although, after learning that our business is all over the streets of Harlem, I should exercise more caution as well.

"Well, if you give it to me tomorrow," Jimmie whispers, "it's late and then it must be extra sweet."

"It's already as sweet as can be, but I'll put some sugar on top."

I stand on my tiptoes to place a soft kiss on his lips. His arms go limp as our tongues dance. He only ever seems weak when our lips touch, and then it's like we're having our first kiss again and again. He groans as his strength returns and he lifts me off my feet.

"You are mine," he whispers hoarsely in my ears. "I won't share you with a poet or anyone."

"I am yours," I whisper back as the other couples start to arrive.

"Look who started the party without us," Captain Bragg says as he and Lydia sit on one side of the picnic table. "I thought we were having a group picnic."

"We haven't started eating yet," Jimmie protests.

"No, you're just snacking," Lydia says with a giggle, as she cozies up to Captain Bragg. "Parfait de Yolande is on the menu."

"Quick take a photo of us for my scrapbook," I urge Lydia.

"Okay," Lydia says. "Here, Jimmie, hold my umbrella in your arm like a gentleman shielding his lady love from the sun."

Jimmie takes the umbrella and shakes his head. "Why can't we just take the picture?"

"It's called a pose, Jimmie," Lydia explains. "Now, Yolande hook your arm through Jimmie's and look up at him like you love him."

"I do love him," I say loud enough for only Jimmie to hear as I gaze up at him.

His tiny smile seems serene like Mama's, but the peace doesn't reach his eyes. In fact, they look troubled, and I don't know what to do about that.

Lydia snaps the photo, freezing this moment in time for my scrapbook. I'll place it right next to this beautiful card.

So that I'll always remember.

Chapter Thirty-Five

Because I cannot seem to execute a Decagynian Society event without Jimmie's help, I've recruited him for my big senior year finale. Well, I do have an entire club and officers to help, so maybe I don't *need* to enlist Jimmie. Perhaps I just like to flaunt him to Chrystal, who is determined to remain in the club and in my vicinity. A big-haired fly in my ointment.

"I think there should be a table at the front of the room for the guest of honor. Do you agree?" I ask as I stroll through the spaces between the tables Jimmie's already rearranged several times.

"There is a special guest?" Jimmie asks as he trudges over to one of the tables to move it to the front of the room.

I place a pretty spring flower arrangement in the center of the front table. "I didn't tell you? Miss Fauset arrives today on the afternoon train."

"You did not. You just said the party was to celebrate her book release."

"I'm sorry. With all the fretting and planning, I must have forgotten. Do you mind if we go pick her up from the train station in Miss Nellie's car? I've already asked her, and she said she doesn't mind."

"Of course. Is there anything else you need me to do, your royal highness?"

I gawk at my loyal boyfriend with faux outrage. "Have I been demanding too much of you these past few days? I'm sorry, but this literary tea is our spring pageant this year. All the administrators will be here, and it must be grand. It's my last hurrah as president."

As we inch closer and closer to my graduation, I must remember to be more considerate of Jimmie's feelings. He's been anxious, and so have I, about our inevitable separation. I want to be happy about completing my degree, but I don't want to be apart from Jimmie, because when we're apart, he's fretful and jealous and that doesn't bode well for us. I hate it when he's that way. When we're together on campus for long stretches at a time, he's attentive, loving, and caring, and I forget his jealous streak. At present we are the most envied couple on campus, but we're drifting toward a murky and undecided future.

"I cannot imagine the Decagynian Society without you."

"I am sure Chrystal will try to gather enough votes to make herself president next year, and then that will be the end of things."

Jimmie laughs, and I don't like it one bit. Because I mean it. Chrystal will destroy the club with her daft ideas.

"What's so funny?" I ask angrily, making him laugh even harder.

"I think you are the only one who thinks Chrystal is evil," he says with a straight face after pulling himself together and coming to stand next to me.

He plucks a white daisy out of my arrangement and tucks it into my hair.

"That's because she saves her most vicious attacks for me," I say with my signature guilt-inducing pout.

"I know you don't like it when I defend her," Jimmie says, sufficiently guilt riddled. "But sometimes your dislike for her makes you exaggerate things."

"Save your kind words about her for anyone other than me," I snip, realizing I sound about as childish as Jimmie does when he's fussing about Countee, but oh well.

"All right."

"I'll be gone in a few months, so you and your *friend* can have all the fun you want."

"And you'll be in Harlem, where I'd much rather be than Nashville."

And now I feel awful because he truly sounds miserable about this unfortunate truth.

"With all the extra classes you've taken, you only have one more year." I hope this reminder helps ease his nerves some.

"And then we can be in Harlem together."

I nod reassuringly as I smooth the tablecloth on one of the tables. "Everything is perfect now, Jimmie. Thank you for helping me, always."

* * *

WE'RE EARLY PICKING up Miss Fauset because Jimmie has baseball practice later. He's even worn his practice gear, because he'll only have a few moments to drop Miss Fauset off at her lodgings and me at Jubilee Hall before racing back to the baseball field.

"I sure hope they get here on time," Jimmie says. "I don't want to be late for practice. Coach makes us do push-ups if we're late."

"Then you'll just be stronger and hit more home runs, so that's a win for everyone," I reassure him, rubbing his arm.

Jimmie grins at me and shakes his head. "What am I going to do with you?"

"Love me, that's it."

Just as Jimmie's knee starts to bounce, fretting as he always does, the train pulls into the station. Only a few minutes late. He jumps out of the car and runs over to the platform, and I follow him, but not as quickly, because I am not about to work up a sweat in this midday sun.

I see Miss Fauset when she emerges from the train, and luckily, she's holding her bag in her hand. We won't have to wait for the handlers to unload things if this is the entirety of her luggage.

She smiles and waves at us as she approaches. "Bonjour, Yolande! Bonjour, Jimmie!" she says as she gives both of us warm hugs and Jimmie takes the heavy bag from her hand.

"Hello, Miss Fauset. Or bonjour?" Jimmie says. "Did I say it right?"

"You did!" Miss Fauset says, beaming up at him. "Have you grown another inch? I don't remember you towering over me this way the last time I saw you."

"He has," I add, reaching up to rub Jimmie's broad shoulders.

"Well, my mother said she thinks I'm still growing too," Jimmie says bashfully, "and wonders when she'll stop having to let out the hem in my trousers."

I understand Miss Fauset's enchantment with Jimmie. It's hard not to be when he's such a gentleman and so easy on the eyes. He has the same effect on Mama.

"Is this your only bag, Miss Fauset?" Jimmie asks.

"Well, yes, but I am not alone," she says, squinting as she looks off into the distance for her traveling companion, and my mind starts to race. Not alone? I sure hope Papa hasn't surprised us again, because I don't want him bringing a dark cloud to me and Jimmie, not now when we're doing well.

"Oh. Is Dr. Du Bois with you?" Jimmie asks, his voice full of trepidation. "Yolande didn't mention he was coming."

"No, it isn't Dr. Du Bois. It's my friend Countee Cullen. He's just retrieving his bag."

Jimmie spins on one heel and glares at me, as if I had something to do with this. My goodness! This may be even worse than Papa visiting.

"Countee Cullen. The poet, who's been writing to my Yolande," Jimmie says with a smile that shows so many teeth it reminds me of an animal ready to pounce on its weaker prey. "I am dying to meet him."

Miss Fauset glances over at me, and I hope she can read my mind.

What was she thinking, bringing him here? Or was this a plan she and Papa concocted?

Instantly, my head starts to throb. And when Countee emerges from the crowd, making a beeline straight for us, I feel a fainting spell coming on.

"That's Countee walking toward us now," Miss Fauset says. "I hope there's enough room in the car for his things and mine."

As Countee approaches, I watch in horror as Jimmie assesses him like one would size up an opponent. I've assured him Countee is no threat, but he's standing chest out, shoulders squared, and scowling. I gently rub Jimmie's back, hoping that my touch assures him of my affection, while giving Miss Fauset my most judgmental gaze.

"There should be plenty of room for Countee's bag," I say to Miss Fauset. "But if you'd told us he was coming we would've been better prepared for his arrival."

I say this partially to let Jimmie know that I had nothing to do with this chicanery, but also to rebuke Miss Fauset. She's aware of how I feel about Jimmie, and she knows that Countee fancies me, and that Papa fancies *him*.

"Countee thought it would be a nice surprise," she says, grinning like she can't see how unnerved Jimmie and I both are.

Countee's expression is, of course, warm and friendly as he reaches us, and I watch poor Jimmie struggle to reciprocate. Countee sets his bag down and gives me a very chaste hug. Wise of him. Jimmie takes his extended hand and shakes it.

"Yolande, I hope you're happy to see me!" Countee gushes. "And you can only be the jazz musician she raved about all summer, Jimmie Lunceford."

Jimmie narrows his eyes at Countee and bites his bottom lip, disarmed and unsettled. I press my lips together trying not to laugh. Countee is too much!

"I am he," Jimmie says. "You're the poet."

"*The* poet? Well, I'm *a* poet. Miss Fauset tells me I might be a good one someday."

I roll my eyes. "This is false modesty," I say. "Countee knows he's amazing, Jimmie. Just like you know you're a musical prodigy. Miss Fauset, we're surrounded by legendary young men today."

"Mon dieu," she says. "Well, that is wonderful. Since they would need to be legendary to hold a candle to us, ma chère."

"Agreed." I leave Jimmie's side and join Miss Fauset.

As we walk to Miss Nellie's Ford, I whisper, "Whose idea was it for Countee to come? Was it Papa's?"

Miss Fauset smiles. "How did you guess?"

"He's incorrigible."

"Funny, he says the same about you."

Chapter Thirty-Six

March 1924
Nashville, Tennessee

I am so glad Miss Fauset is here for our literary tea a whole day early so that we can have a separate private dinner with only the Decagynians to discuss *There Is Confusion*. The rest of the campus and administration can share her tomorrow.

Dr. and Mrs. Beauregard have agreed to host us, because Miss Fauset and Countee are staying with them in their spare bedrooms. Having Countee here complicated our plans. It was intended to only be us girls, but now we've invited the boys to our private dinner, because since Countee arrived Jimmie has been glued to my side.

When I told Mrs. Beauregard we were all coming, including the young men, she set up extra tables and fried a batch of chicken and pork chops and made dozens of biscuits and a whole mess of potato salad.

Miss Fauset sits at the head of the main dining table in the seat of honor, with Countee at her side, while Jimmie and I, Frances, Anna, and Lydia crowd into the remaining seats at the table. We've all brought our books for Miss Fauset to sign, making this a true literary event.

"Mon dieu!" Miss Fauset exclaims. "I don't know how we will chat about the book after that amazing meal. I'm so full I'm about to pop."

"Oh, but we must," Frances says. "But first may I compliment you on your haircut, Miss Fauset? It's très chic!"

"Merci, Frances," Miss Fauset says as she fluffs her short 'do.

"I'll tell your mother you admired it and maybe she'll take you to my hairdresser over the summer."

I doubt Frances's mother will let her cut her long heavy hair. They both love walking into Harlem's social events tossing their tresses. Mine is nowhere near as long as Frances's and I am sure Mama will be against me cutting mine, but I wouldn't anyway. My face is too round, I believe, for that kind of style, although it is very fetching and sophisticated on Miss Fauset.

"Enough about this," I interject, wanting to get straight to the meat of our discussion. "Can we please talk about Joanna?"

Miss Fauset laughs. "Is she your favorite character, Yolande?"

"Of course she is," Countee says. "I can't see her rooting for Maggie."

"It's not that I didn't want the best for Maggie," I counter. "I just didn't find much in common with her."

"*Common* is the exact word I would use to describe her," Lydia says. "And that must be the reason Yolande favors Joanna."

"Excusez-moi. I will speak for myself," I say. "I admired Joanna because she had a talent, and she was willing to pursue it at all costs."

Miss Fauset nods. "I do see how that would resonate with you, Yolande."

"But I don't like how she tried to keep Maggie from her brother," Jimmie says. "As if the Marshalls were too good for Maggie."

"I don't know if Joanna felt that way," I say, defending my heroine. "But I certainly don't like that Peter entertained both Maggie and Joanna."

"That's typical," Lydia says. "Men can be quite disgusting."

"Well, Joanna wasn't interested in marriage until the very end of the book," Countee says. "What was Peter supposed to do?"

"Why did you decide to have Joanna marry, Miss Fauset?" I ask.

"I do not believe I've had such spirited discourse from any other group of readers," Miss Fauset exclaims, sounding gratified. "But I will say that ultimately, I believe artists, writers, dancers, musicians, and the like are very influential on society. Perhaps I was not brave enough to see Joanna's ambition through to the end as if she were a man. Maybe I thought it was too unrealistic."

"Are you not sure?" Anna asks. "I just love that the romance between Joanna and Peter was brought to a happy end. That is all I really wanted out of the story."

"I think that is what most everyone wanted to see in the end," Miss Fauset agrees politely. "But I am not sure it is a happy ending. Just a realistic one."

"Are you like Joanna, Miss Fauset?" Jimmie asks. "You are pursuing your gifts. Do you see yourself coming to a similar end? With marriage, I mean."

Miss Fauset shifts in her seat, making me wonder if this question is too personal. But I'd like to know the answer as well, since Miss Fauset never has a beau at her side.

"I am not sure what my end will be, Jimmie. I am a working woman with an amazing career that I never thought possible. And now, I've published my first book."

"But do you not yearn for love?" Lydia asks.

"Absolument," Miss Fauset admits. "I am a woman. I have a heart too."

"Hence the title," Countee says. "There is confusion."

Miss Fauset laughs. "Indeed."

I grow quiet and listen to everyone pepper Miss Fauset with questions about Joanna, Peter, Maggie, and Phillip—the characters I've been consumed with since we read this novel.

I wonder what Papa thinks of Joanna. He clearly believes in colored women marrying husbands and creating gifted progeny, but he pushes and pushes me to refine the talents I have. In that way I will be a match for a gifted husband.

But I have spent four years at Fisk and am still unsure if I should write stories, draw pictures, or plan pageants and events. Or marry

Jimmie as soon as I take off my cap and gown. That's what *he* wants, but as much as I love him, I am not sure if that's what I want. Not right away. Not before I prove myself worthy of carrying the Du Bois name.

My whole life is confusion, I'm afraid.

*   *   *

EVERYONE HAS GONE from the Beauregards' house, including Countee, who Jimmie volunteered to take to Pearly's so he could meet more Fisk students. I'm happy that Jimmie is so hospitable to Countee, but I'm also leery. Although I've told Countee that I only want to be his friend, it doesn't change the fact that he feels otherwise.

But I wanted to stay behind and talk to Miss Fauset. I need her advice, especially since it's her book that has me in such a state.

"You didn't want to go with your friends?" Miss Fauset asks as she sips tea from Mrs. Beauregard's fancy china. "I'm fine here by myself."

I'm glad Miss Fauset has not slipped back into French. She does it so effortlessly and I always feel like a dolt when I can only understand bits and pieces of things.

"I've been to Pearly's a million times. They can miss me this one time."

"How are you feeling about graduation? Your parents are so proud of you, and I wish I could be here to cheer for you."

"You're not coming?"

"No, things fall apart at *The Crisis* when your father and I are both away at the same time."

"He's always in a better mood when you're here, and I just want him to be nice to Jimmie."

"Jimmie impresses me. He has not let your father run him off."

"Oh, not for lack of him trying though. Sending Countee here has got to be his worst slight yet."

Miss Fauset pours a second cup of tea and offers it to me. I take it and sigh.

"Your papa just wants you to remember the options you have waiting at home in Harlem. He thinks Jimmie has you under his spell."

"Papa is so determined to marry me off right away. I don't think I'm ready to be a wife, although if I was I'd want Jimmie as a husband." I hate that this sounds like a grievance when I love him so.

"And he doesn't want to wait for you?"

"He will, but he's so insufferably melancholy over it. Like if I leave Fisk without us announcing our engagement, then I'm going to slip through his fingers."

"Does he know how Countee feels about you?"

This question makes me wonder what conversations Countee and Miss Fauset have had. I confide in her a great deal, and she knows some of my secrets. If she's advising Countee based on things that I tell her about me and Jimmie, I don't think that's fair to either of us.

"Do you?" I ask, feeling slightly distrustful of her in this moment.

"He's mentioned a time or two that he can't wait to get you back to Harlem where he can sufficiently woo you," she says with a chuckle, as if it's delightful, but I'm not so sure I'm amused.

"Woo me? Oh, Countee is too incorrigible. And if he says these things to you, he must say even worse to Harold. That's why Harold distrusts me so."

The corners of Miss Fauset's mouth turn downward in a slight frown. She may not agree, but she hasn't seen Harold accost me with his words. "No. Harold is just a protective older brother to Countee."

"Well, Countee doesn't need protection from me."

"You aren't stringing him along just a tiny bit, ma chérie?" she asks with some skepticism in her tone that offends me.

"I've told him how I feel." My response is too short and teeters on disrespectful.

"But you answer all his letters."

"His letters are literature, Miss Fauset! I enjoy them so. I feel smarter and more eloquent after each one."

Miss Fauset hangs her head and chuckles softly. "He is quite charming in print. Your papa thinks he may end up being one of the finest colored writers of our time."

"Only because of your tutelage."

"The gift was there without any intervention from me. I've merely nudged him in the right direction."

"Can you nudge me too? As I read your book, I felt like I was walking with Joanna. I understand her and why she got married."

"Enlighten me. Tell me what you think."

"She just had something to prove to herself and the world. That she could attain her dream. And then once she stood on the stage to dance in front of the audience, she had nothing left to prove to anyone."

I wait to see Miss Fauset's reaction. I hadn't shared my thoughts on her novel with the group. I hadn't wanted anyone to think about me and my papa in the context of the story, so I had planned to share these thoughts privately with Miss Fauset only.

"And she got married because she'd succeeded in that."

"Yes, yes! And she always knew that one day she and Peter would be together."

"Are you sure we're still talking about Joanna?" Miss Fauset smiles, knowing me so well.

It suddenly occurs to me that maybe my life was fodder for some of this tale, and I don't know quite how to feel about that. Will anyone we know in Harlem read it and think of me?

"Oh, Miss Fauset, I get so anxious thinking about being a wife."

Miss Fauset sips her tea slowly, pausing, hopefully to think of a solution.

"Jimmie has another two years of school."

"One year. He's taken extra classes over the summers and breaks so that he can graduate a year early."

Miss Fauset's eyes widen in surprise. "Well, he's determined, isn't he. No matter. Let's go ahead and do what we talked about before and have you intern at *The Crisis* next year."

"Papa wants me to go to Columbia and get another degree."

"You can do both. We can schedule work around your classes once they start."

"I'd like that."

"You're going to pledge Delta, correct? I cannot sponsor you because I am an honorary member, but I believe Eslanda Robeson will."

"Mais, oui!"

Miss Fauset seems tickled by my spontaneous French. "And Countee, I'm sure, will reintroduce you to the Harlem scene."

"Don't forget about Harold. We must include him, lest Countee get the wrong idea."

"Or maybe you need Harold to chaperone. Maybe you're the one who doesn't want to be alone with Countee."

I cannot help but sigh. "Miss Fauset, please."

"Who knows. Maybe you'll see something in Countee that strikes your fancy. Once you're away from Jimmie . . . and his spell."

Miss Fauset is not helping here. She's as bad as Papa about her favorite little poet.

"I thought you liked Jimmie."

"I do, I do. But I love Countee like he's my own son."

Miss Fauset thinks Countee is something special. And I would have to agree.

But so is my Jimmie.

Chapter Thirty-Seven

June 1924
Nashville, Tennessee

The end of our undergraduate matriculation is celebrated with commencement exercises. Because it is the beginning of our adult lives. The dawn of greatness.

It felt like this day would never arrive, but now that it's here, I'm sure the hours will race by in a blur with me struggling to trap each moment and lock it in my memories.

After pinning my hair into a small chignon on the nape of my neck to accommodate my graduation cap, I'm finally ready to walk across the stage and shake Dr. McKenzie's hand. And then put fair Fisk behind me.

Jimmie went to collect Mama and Papa from the train station last night, against my better judgement, but I haven't seen them yet. We had a rehearsal at the chapel that ran late, so I will see them at the ceremony. I hope Jimmie didn't say anything about being their future son-in-law. I asked him to try not to antagonize Papa, but when Jimmie's heart feels something, the words just come bubbling out. He doesn't think about things first, and then I must clean up the aftermath.

I hear Miss Nellie's voice in the hall. "Graduates, please be ready to line up in five minutes, to start our processional over to the chapel."

I step out into the hallway and am grateful to see Frances and Lydia also standing outside their rooms, as fretful and as nervous as I am in their black gowns and black caps.

"You two are as lovely as ever," I say as I walk over to join them near the entrance to the stairwell. "The Decagynian Society's best members off to conquer the world."

"You can conquer the world," Lydia says. "I just want to go to Paris for the summer."

Frances laughs. "Paris? It must be nice. It's right to work for me, helping my mother take care of my younger sisters."

"Is that all? What did they send you to college for?" Lydia asks, although the same question was on the tip of my tongue too.

"They sent me to college to find a husband," Frances says. "And I didn't quite manage that, so my mother will start her own search as soon as I get home."

"What about you, Yolande?" Lydia asks. "I'm sure your parents have a graduation soirée planned, and a summer abroad."

"There will be soirées and summering indeed. But maybe not abroad this year. I'll take a few classes at Columbia University over the summer to prepare for graduate school."

"Graduate school?" Frances asks. "Aren't you even going to take a break?"

A break? Frances must not know anything about Papa. There is no resting with him until greatness is achieved, or until a gifted husband is acquired. Or both.

* * *

MY STOMACH STARTS to churn as I walk into the chapel in the graduation processional when I notice Papa isn't sitting next to Mama. Instead, he's with the special guests, dignitaries, and speakers. I was hoping he wouldn't do anything to draw attention to himself on my graduation day. That he'd just sit with Mama and celebrate like a father should.

But my father is Dr. W.E.B. Du Bois. I should have known better. He cannot be in front of a crowd without somehow reminding them of the struggles of every colored person. Even when I'm supposed to feel joyful, the oppression of my people must be at the front of my mind when Papa is nearby.

I take my seat, with my eyes trained on Papa, to see if he will look my way. Then I see Papa's speaking portfolio in his lap and my stomach flips again.

I swoon and sway during the musical selection by the Harmonias, so much that I hardly even enjoy Jimmie's piano solo. My mind drifts during the greeting from the administrators and the speeches from our class valedictorian and our class president. Beads of sweat form right under the band of my graduation cap and they trickle down the back of my neck from dread at what Papa might do or say.

My ears ring as the head of the alumni association introduces Papa as one of Fisk's most esteemed alumni, and my stomach wraps itself into a series of knots that all twist and squeeze. I feel myself sliding to the right in my seat as Papa walks to the stage.

My neighbor notices my discomfort. "You all right, Yolande?" she whispers.

It's a girl I don't know very well, so I give a tight nod. "Just a little hot, that's all."

"Well, let's hope your father talks fast," she says, fanning herself with her program. "I'm hot too."

I want to tell her that she can stop hoping for that. Papa is worse than the most long-winded church preacher once he gets going. We might as well get ready to soak through the armpits of our dresses and dress shirts.

His speech starts off with a long Latin quote and its English translation, but I know he's only just getting started.

Less than a minute into his speech and Papa has started to talk about all the ways colored people have been mistreated. And it's about to take an even darker turn. How do I know? He just used the word *vituperation*. I have never known the English language to contain such a word.

I squeeze my eyes shut and refuse to let myself faint. If I do, I'll miss the part where I get to cross the stage and receive my diploma. But I can feel dozens of eyes staring at me, maybe wondering if I put Papa up to this. It takes every bit of my resolve to keep from sliding onto the floor.

Oh no, oh no, oh no. Now Papa has given the alumni a call to action. He says it's a day of turning. Why couldn't he start the turn after my graduation? Why does it have to be today?

And now, my fellow graduates have betrayed me. They are cheering Papa on with applause and hoots and hollering. Because he is chastising the administration for all the rules they've heaped upon us. Papa is railing against the rules now that I am leaving, when he's been quite happy to have me under them these past four years. He wants to free everyone else's children, but what about his own? I've been complaining about these rules since my freshman year! Why is he taking such a stand now when he didn't stand up for me?

I look over at Jimmie, hoping for a show of support from my love, but he looks enraptured by Papa too.

After ten minutes, I can tell that he is starting to wind down as the cadence of his speech slows. As well he should. He's called out the administration for their rules, told the alumni they aren't doing their jobs, and invited the students to a protest.

He has turned my graduation into the beginning of an all-out war against Dr. McKenzie.

Typical Papa.

Chapter Thirty-Eight

June 1924
Nashville, Tennessee

As an act of defiance and revenge against Papa for that abysmal speech, I escaped his party with the alumni. I left him and Mama there to hobnob with Papa's friends and plan his crusade against Dr. McKenzie. It's none of my business anyway since I won't be here next year. I'd much rather be with Jimmie at the Andrew Jackson Hotel. I'm truly a grown woman now—a college graduate.

Feeling somewhat relaxed as I puff my post-lovemaking cigarette, I absentmindedly drop ashes into a metal tray every few moments as Jimmie watches. I know he hates when I smoke in bed, but he won't dare complain tonight since we will be leaving each other soon enough.

"You're a Fisk graduate now," Jimmie says as he twirls a strand of my hair between his fingers. "Part of the body of alumni your father spoke about. How do you feel?"

"About graduating or about Papa's grandstanding?" I ask as I take a slow drag of the cigarette.

"You thought he was grandstanding?"

"You didn't?" I chuckle as I put the cigarette out. "Eleven minutes of pontificating. Part of it in Latin for God's sake. All because he has decided that Dr. McKenzie must go."

"But he told no tales about the rules, and how McKenzie has held us under his thumb," Jimmie says, passionately defending Papa. "When he said that white children are told to hitch their wagons to stars, but that colored children must settle for nice honest lampposts, I felt that in my soul."

"That was toward the end of his speech," I say. "By then, my rear end had gone numb, and the heat of all the stares had me sweating like a pig."

"You're just saying that because it's your papa. It was a great speech, Yolande. I feel ready to take over the world, or at least Fisk University."

Completely surprised, I sit up in bed, untangling our limbs so I can look at him to see if he's serious.

"Godspeed on your movement, Jimmie. I'll be in Harlem. I never thought I'd see the day that you became one of Papa's fans."

Jimmie can't meet my gaze. "Well, Dr. Du Bois isn't studying me at all. I may have won your mother's favor, though."

I don't know why, but the silky hair on Jimmie's chiseled chest catches my attention, and I reach over to stroke it. He groans. "Mama has a thing for handsome men, just like I do. You never had to worry about her."

Jimmie smiles and crawls naked out of the bed. "Come back," I say. "I'm not finished with you."

"I've got a surprise for you," he says.

As much as I love surprises, I'd much rather be cuddling next to Jimmie, inhaling his scent, and feasting on his perfection.

"You're a work of art, Jimmie. I will never tire of looking at your body."

"Good," he says, "because you're going to be looking at it for-ever."

"You won't look this way forever, Jimmie. One day you'll be old and wrinkly and have a potbelly."

He dives back onto the bed and laughs. Then, he places a box on the pillow where I have myself propped up by my elbow.

I should've known this was coming.

"Then you'll just have to remember how I am right now," Jimmie says, looking calm and satisfied as I slowly sit up in the dim light and gingerly open the box.

"A ring."

"Yes. My father gave it to my mother when he asked her to marry him."

"S-so . . ."

"I'm asking you, again, to marry me." His tone is even and measured, like he's practiced this, in the mirror, dozens of times, and imagined my response.

"But you've already asked, and I've said yes, eventually."

His jaw tightens. This was not the response he wanted. "With the ring we declare it to the world."

Yes, to the world. And to Papa.

"Jimmie, I—"

As he lies there, with his jaw locked tight, nostrils flaring, chest heaving up and down, I know there is only one acceptable response for Jimmie. I have his heart, and he has mine, but I stare at the box and the ring, not ready to put it on, yet.

The ring means wife and children. It means responsibility. It means no more Yolande.

And I haven't quite figured out who Yolande is yet.

"What if I could be like Joanna?" I ask. "She went after things. She aspired."

Jimmie looks confused for a split second. Then, recognition. "You're unsure about marriage because of a character in a book?"

I'm not going to let him minimize my feelings. This is important. I am important. And I'm not going to disappear because he wants me to put on a ring.

"But in the end, she married," Jimmie says, still disappointed, but his jaw relaxed some.

"By then it was what she'd chosen," I explain, trying to reason with him. "When she was younger, she had no choice."

"Don't you love me? What else is there except spending a lifetime with the one you love?"

How can I make him understand that this has nothing to do with my love for him? Are all men this self-centered?

"What else is there? Jimmie, you have another passion besides me. You have your music. What if I have that same kind of greatness inside me?"

"And when you've found it? Then what?"

"Maybe I'll be somebody important."

"When did you ever care about that?" Jimmie asks, as if he's the only one with aspirations, dreams, and goals.

"Always. You just want me to be your wife more than anything else. If I'm ever to be your wife, it will be *in addition* to all else."

Jimmie rolls over, snatches the ring box from the pillow, and snaps it shut. Then he lies on his back once more, staring at the ceiling.

"Please don't be angry, Jimmie," I beg tearfully. "It breaks my heart when you're cross with me."

"I'm not angry. But you said *if*, Yolande. You are not sure about marriage."

"Of course I'm going to be married one day, Jimmie. I don't have any choice in that. I must have children."

"So, if you know you will be married, but you refuse my ring, it is *me* you are unsure about."

Jimmie's logic is sound, but when he says it this way, aloud, it makes me feel terrible. Because I love him so.

"I simply cannot go from my papa's house to my husband's without seeing what is out in the world for me."

"Or who."

"That is what you seem determined to think, but the only person I'm trying to discover is Yolande."

Jimmie silently ponders my words. The anger has drained from his expression, and it's been replaced with something close to acceptance, but not quite. Our love may be complicated, but this request is not.

I crawl across the bed and snuggle next to him, listening to his steady breathing and the rhythm of his heartbeat. I pull the sheet and blanket over our bodies and wonder if this is the last time I'm going to be with my Jimmie.

And if it is, I'd better etch it onto my soul.

So that I can always remember.

PART III

Chapter Thirty-Nine

October 1924
Hillburn, New York

This weekend is dedicated to the very serious matter of my initiation into Delta Sigma Theta Sorority. Miss Fauset could not be here, because she has run off to Paris to pursue her favorite thing, the French language. But since she is the one who got me interested in Delta in the first place, I figure that she is here in spirit.

Thirty of us, members of the Alpha Beta Chapter, and some men of the Alpha Phi Alpha Fraternity Eta Chapter hiked up the side of Houvenkopf Mountain in Hillburn, New York, to a wonderful picnic area. This is where Marcia Brown and I were initiated with a private ceremony.

Today, on the nineteenth of October, nineteen hundred and twenty-four, I became a woman of Delta Sigma Theta Sorority. A few days before my birthday, I am now reborn into a sisterhood of women.

I don't know if other girls who have an abundance of sisters, cousins, and family members have the same feeling I have when joining organizations like Delta, but I suddenly feel part of something grand. Now, even though I'm an only child, wherever I go, where there are other Deltas, I will be called *soror*. This word, to me, means more than *sister*. It means that we are joined in purpose—something that I am seeking, and that I hope to find as a Delta woman.

As new initiates, Marcia and I sit at a picnic table and are being properly attended to by our Alpha brothers, with lemonade and sandwiches. Several times on the journey up the mountain, which was not too arduous, I thought of Jimmie, and how he would've wanted to hoist me onto his back and carry me when I got too tired. But, of course, the walk was part of my journey, so no help from a generous boyfriend would've been allowed.

Thinking of Jimmie today was a rarity, however. Since I've left Fisk and gone headfirst into my work at *The Crisis* (which has increased since Miss Fauset set sail for Paris) and my classes at Columbia, I have not allowed myself time for sorrow over him.

My new soror, Frances Gunner, sits across the table from me. Frances is no stranger, though; we've known each other all our lives. She's six years my senior, and her plain, studious looks match her personality. Frances is a serious woman, but enthusiastic about writing and education. Our fathers were close associates at one time, but had a falling out some years ago over movement ideas. Still, Papa would be thrilled for me to add Frances to my circle of friends. He's in favor of anyone who has a head on her shoulders and wants to do more than go to parties and Harlem dance clubs.

"How do you feel, Soror Du Bois?" Frances asks. "Are you ready for what comes next?"

"Yes, I am." Although I am not sure what she means.

Her serious expression is interrupted with a tiny smile that reminds me of Mama. "Wonderful. Because we have a lot of work to do. Can I count on your help with the convention in December?"

"Of course!" I say, excited that *this* is what she means.

I am thrilled that the Delta Sigma Theta Sorority convention this year is going to be in Harlem. My first year of membership and my chapter will take center stage. Whatever I am asked to do, I will do. How I will accomplish the work of my sorority, my classes, and get everything done at *The Crisis* too is a mystery. But I will.

"Perfect," Frances says. "We need assistance with hospitality for our visiting chapters, and we are engaged in a last-minute fundraising effort for our scholarship. Soror Brown, I hope to engage you there, as well. I hear you are well connected with some potential wealthy donors."

I glance at Marcia and grin because I am sure Frances is referring to Marcia's beau, Ferdinand Williams. An Alpha man and a dentist. She is a lucky young woman to have landed him. He's handsome, brilliant, and rich. A trifecta of blessings. But she is a beautiful and educated woman herself, having graduated from Atlanta University, so he is equally fortunate to have her.

"I should be able to scare up some donations," Marcia says. "I am eager to be involved as well."

"I just love the enthusiasm of new sorors," Frances says, as Juliette Derricotte sits next to her at the table with her picnic plate.

Juliette is an odd-looking young woman, but I cannot say she's unattractive. Her large piercing eyes devour me, and her smile is too broad. But I don't know if she can help that, because her mouth and nose, though well-shaped, are overwhelming for her narrow face.

Immediately, I find myself on guard and my smile fading. I know that she is now my soror, but Juliette is someone I try to avoid. She hasn't done anything wrong that I can put my finger on, and she is quite brilliant, but there is something about her that gives me pause.

"Are they enthusiastic?" Juliette asks. "I'm sure your father is proud of you, Yolande."

In every conversation I've had with Juliette, she finds a way to include something about Papa. We could be talking about the best products to stop our monthly flow, and she will ask what Dr. Du Bois recommends. It's exhausting to be near her because of this.

"He is very proud," I say. "But Frances, have you written any new plays lately? I'd love to hear about your productions."

I wonder if Frances knows this is an invitation for her to rescue me. "Yes, I have a new play called *The Light of the Women*. It's about Harriet Tubman, Sojourner Truth, and many other great Black women from our history. I am going to perform it with some students at a school in Harlem. You must help me with it."

"Oh, I'd love to. Do you know that was one of my favorite things to do at Fisk? Put on pageants. I'm particularly good at that," I say.

"You'd be a great educator then," Juliette compliments me. "Is that what you're going to do after you complete your studies at Columbia?"

"Soror Du Bois may not make it into the workforce," Marcia tells her, motioning to the Alpha brothers huddled together under the trees and chatting. "Felton Clark has designs on you already. Were you aware, Yolande?"

"He does?" I ask, squinting over at the men and taking a good look at Felton.

He is a handsome devil, that's for sure. Tall, exactly how I prefer them, with that silky creole hair that lays down just right without a lick of pomade.

"We're both pursuing master's degrees in English," I say, trying not to give any opinion that might be shared as gossip. "I've had several classes with him. Very brilliant."

"Is that your honest assessment of him?" Juliette asks with a chuckle. "I bet your father would approve."

I close my eyes and shake my head to keep from laughing at this incorrigible girl. She is correct though. Papa would more than approve of Felton, and since I haven't received a letter from Jimmie since I left Nashville, I am currently unattended.

"Well, he is genuinely nice, and I've enjoyed fellowship with him in classes and now we will have a new bond. He's a fraternity brother now."

"An Alpha man like Dr. Du Bois," Juliette tells me.

I sip my lemonade as Frances's hand goes up to her face to mask her smile. Not that Juliette is the least bit embarrassed or ashamed of her unabashed admiration for Papa. I just hope she doesn't ask for an invitation to dinner because she is now my soror and I may have to oblige. I shudder at the thought.

Chapter Forty

November 1924
Harlem, New York

I've prepared myself for this conversation with Papa, gone over in my mind the many ways that it might go and thought of all his possible objections. I think I'm ready. It's such a small thing that I'm asking. I asked Mama to help by preparing his favorite meal, fried chicken.

After he's helped himself to his third piece of chicken, I take a deep breath. Now is the time.

"Papa, do you think it's possible for me to use Miss Fauset's office at *The Crisis* while she's in Paris?"

Papa's rapid chewing slows until he stops and swallows. At least he is not frowning. He is considering.

"The space you share with Miss Foster is not sufficient?" he asks.

"It would be if she didn't chatter all day. I like her, Papa, but I am trying to concentrate and get things done as quickly as possible. I am only there part-time and must be productive."

Papa smirks, as if he can't help himself. "Your work requires more focus than Miss Foster's?"

"Well, yes. It does. She is simply providing responses to letters where you have told her what to say. I am finding news items, creating narrative works, and drawings. The work is simply not comparable."

"I see."

"And I am sure Miss Fauset won't mind. I will be respectful of her things, and I won't open any of her drawers or touch any of her papers. I simply want a door that I can close."

"For privacy?" Papa asks.

"More quiet than privacy. The art requires that much."

Papa sits back in his chair and wipes his face with a napkin. The smirk hasn't left and is now accompanied by a proud gleam in his eyes. If I was a son, I'm sure I wouldn't have had to ask for this. It would've been offered.

"You may not use Miss Fauset's office."

"Papa . . ."

"But there is another office that is available. It's smaller, but it is private, and you'll be able to get your work done."

I suppose this is a fitting compromise. Miss Fauset *is* the literary editor of *The Crisis*. Her name is at the top of the magazine.

"I appreciate your boldness, Yolande," Papa says. "But how would it look to the rest of the staff if I gave you Miss Fauset's office to use? You work part-time."

"I don't know how it would look."

"Some would claim nepotism, Yolande. Some already say it, because of your employment in the first place, but I don't care about that," Papa says, placing the napkin on the table and brushing the crumbs from his slacks. "If a father cannot employ his daughter, then what is the point of having the authority to hire? You must, however, prove yourself worthy of perks."

"I understand, Papa."

"To that end, you will only use the office I provide when you are working on something that requires privacy. If you are not composing a narrative piece or working on a drawing you will sit with Miss Foster."

This is not the answer I was looking for, but I suppose it is a decent compromise. I don't know how I will prove myself worthy of a private office full-time, but I am determined to do so.

"My hours may be more erratic this month and into December with the Delta Sigma Theta Sorority convention looming. I hope you understand that. I also have exams."

Papa claps his hands gleefully. "Yes, yes, I'm aware. And I love this. I am proud to see you take such a great interest in the work of your sorority. I have a check for you, for the scholarship fund."

"Thank you for not making me have to ask," I say with an easy chuckle. I like this version of Papa. It feels like we could be . . . friends.

"I hear that one of my fraternity brothers has convinced you to allow him to escort you to our annual formal dance."

I glance at Mama, and she quickly looks away, guiltily. "Yes, Felton Clark has asked, and I have graciously accepted his invitation," I admit. "I have several classes with him, and we're getting to know each other."

"He is a strong prospect," Papa says approvingly.

Of course, Papa approves of Felton, which is why I was loathe to mention it to him at all. I don't necessarily want him involved in it, but there was going to be no way around it after the dance. Papa was going to see us together and start to formulate his plans whether I liked it or not.

But Felton and I are keeping things very . . . cordial. Yes, that is the perfect description. I am enjoying his friendship, and I have no expectations of it.

"I like him as a friend, Papa," I say. "That is enough for now."

Papa opens his mouth to say something, and then snaps it shut again. I am glad about that.

"Are you still going out this evening with Margaret?" Mama asks, changing the subject.

"Yes. Some friends are having a gathering at the Walker Studio."

I leave out the fact that we may go dancing at a black-and-tan club after the gathering with Countee, Harold, and our other friend Roberta Bosley. Papa doesn't need this information, and I only share things he *needs* to know.

"Ah, well perhaps you'll run across Felton while you're out and about," he says cheerily. And hopefully.

Or perhaps not, Papa. Perhaps not.

Chapter Forty-One

December 1924
Harlem, New York

There is a current of expectation and excitement as hundreds of my sorors sit shoulder to shoulder in the gymnasium of the Harlem YWCA. They're perched in their finery on hard wooden folding chairs, but unaware of any discomfort. All of us shine in dresses and suits of varying shades of crimson and cream, in anticipation of something. I cannot be sure what. Inspiration perhaps? For me . . . a charge. At any rate, we are perched at the edges of our seats, hanging on every word of our president, Soror Dorothy Pelham.

The Harlem YWCA, down and around the block from the men's facility, is the perfect venue for our convention this year. It's a beautiful building with four floors. The gymnasium, where we usually perform all types of exercise, has been transformed with rows and rows of chairs and a slightly raised area for the speakers. In the basement is a cafeteria that can seat one hundred women at once, and on the fourth floor, an indoor pool.

But Delta Sigma Theta Sorority is a growing organization. We already serve nearly one thousand women in thirty-four chapters as far west as California and as far south as Texas. We will need a larger venue next time we're in Harlem. The sisterhood is enlarging its borders.

I am struck to my core when the importance of education is discussed. Being able to matriculate through undergraduate then postgraduate studies is something I have taken for granted. But the responsibility to reach and teach others has not previously been pressed upon me and I willingly accept.

Then, I am on my feet with all my other sorors as a one-thousand-dollar scholarship is presented to Soror Gwendolyn Bennett to study art in Paris. I cannot contain my joy for Gwendolyn. She is a professor at Howard and her artwork is often featured in *The Crisis*. And now she will study in Paris. What masterpieces await us upon her return?

And speaking of Paris, Miss Fauset sends all the delegates a cablegram.

Soror Frances Gunner reads it aloud. "Greetings, Sorors, from Paris. Congratulations on a successful convention. In sweetness and light, Soror Jessie Redmon Fauset."

This is met with thunderous applause. Everyone loves Miss Fauset. I wish she was here to experience all this with me, so that we could have the memory to share years from now over a cup of tea. It tickles me for a second that I have this thought, like years from now I won't have anything better to do than to sit around lollygagging and drinking tea with Miss Fauset.

I should imagine Miss Fauset giving me notes on my collection of short essays with drawings attached. That seems to be where I've landed with my writing. Poems don't suit me, nor does short fiction, but I love making witty observations about the world. Like what the park looks, smells, and feels like after a warm summer rain. I am a great observer of things. I notice small details that others do not.

I believe what's happening at our convention now may be the highlight of today's opening session. Honorary Soror Alice Dunbar-Nelson has written beautiful lyrics of a song meant to be a Delta Sigma Theta Sorority hymn. She read them aloud and now Honorary Soror Florence Cole-Talbert is singing the words set to a glorious melody.

I am not the only one overcome with emotion. By the time she sings the last words, we're on our feet again, eyes shining with tears of a shared mission, fierce determination, and this sacred expression of sisterhood.

* * *

THE GROUP OF sorors and guests that assembles at the Walker Studio is a very subdued bunch, so A'Lelia Walker, the owner of this fine establishment and hostess of the best parties in Harlem, greets us with the genteel, high society version of herself. Her hair is pulled back into a very sleek bun and her silk gown is adorned with a single string of pearls. She makes sure to greet each woman, who is not only a guest in her studio but a potential customer of her company's hair products.

The food is always outstanding, no matter who is celebrating, because A'Lelia has her own caterer. But our Alpha Phi Alpha Fraternity brothers made sure to procure a menu of comfort foods after our long day. Fried chicken and pork chops, collard greens, potato salad, rice, candied yams, and cornbread washed down with lemonade. And although A'Lelia, according to Harold and Countee, has her own bootlegger, so the whiskey and gin are plentiful, the Delta women will not be partaking tonight. This will be a teetotaler's affair.

I am enjoying Felton Clark's company, but when I see Frances standing with a plate laden with food and nowhere to sit, I wave her over. "You can have Felton's seat, Frances. He won't mind."

His strained smile tells me he does mind, but the Walker Studio isn't really for sitting, it's for mingling. "You don't mind, do you?" I ask Felton. "I need to speak with Frances. You understand?"

He nods and makes a grand gesture of offering Frances his seat, which she accepts graciously. She gives him a strange look as he strides away.

"Is he all right?" Frances asks, chuckling at Felton's antics. "He seems pretty high strung about something."

"High strung. What a perfect description. He has just been waiting all evening to get my attention, and when he finally did, I want to talk to you, after having been with you all day."

"I wouldn't expect him to understand that. He wasn't in the room with us." She bites into a chicken leg, and her eyes light up with pleasure.

"Well, I'm having trouble myself even describing my feelings about it all. I'm overwhelmed, I'm heartened, I'm devastated too." My hands flail about as I try to explain myself while Frances chews. "All these things all at once, and yet I want more!"

"Devastated?" Frances asks, looking confused as she wipes away a few crumbs with her napkin. "Tell me more about that one. I haven't heard anyone else feel devastated."

"No? How can they not be utterly distraught thinking of all the scores of girls who will never receive a college education?"

Frances nods, understanding. "I see. But Yolande, you should know the area that grieves you is your natural area of service."

This makes perfect sense to me. To have that tug at my heart so fervently, surely, I must act.

"So, should I join the scholarship committee? Indeed. What is our next goal? Two one-thousand-dollar scholarships?"

"You are welcome to join that committee, but I was thinking of an even greater service. In the area of education. You are pursuing your master's degree in English, correct?"

"Yes."

"If you teach, you can bring what you learned at Fisk to a young woman or young man who may never see Jubilee Hall. We didn't receive this education just to attract husbands." She glances over at an increasingly impatient Felton, then back at me with raised eyebrows. "No matter what our fathers say."

I chuckle sadly. "Your father can't be as bad as my papa."

"Oh, I'm sure he is."

"Well, are you ever going to marry?"

"Eventually."

I throw my head back and laugh, imagining myself giving that to Papa as my marriage timeline. "That is not an acceptable answer for my papa."

"You are your own woman. While we have obligations to our family and our race, we can decide when we fulfill them," Frances says. "Once you are bogged down with a husband and children, you won't use that advanced degree for anything other than writing exquisite letters to your friends."

Immediately, this calls to mind Mama and her letter writing. Frances is right, of course. When would she have had time to use her education and knowledge outside of our home?

Then I think of Joanna from Miss Fauset's book. This is why that character's journey resonates with me so. She wants greatness, but eventually she's sucked back into what society expects. What everyone expects. The confines of marriage.

"I implore you, Yolande. Delay, if you can, the finality of marriage and family. Even if it's only for a year or two. It can make all the difference."

I desire this—my own legacy. One that has *my* name on it. I want to be remembered as someone other than the vessel for Dr. Du Bois's grandsons.

Chapter Forty-Two

December 1924
Harlem, New York

The theme of my look tonight for the Alpha Phi Alpha Fraternity Annual Formal is "A Dream in Crimson and Cream." Now I'm not sure if anyone else has a theme, but not everyone is a princess of Harlem *and* a neophyte of Delta Sigma Theta Sorority.

Since we're exhilarated from our convention weekend, and every prominent Delta is in attendance, I may as well honor them while dazzling everyone else.

It's a little after ten o'clock and we've just arrived at the new Renaissance Casino ballroom although the festivities started at nine thirty. Papa wanted to be on time because he's old, and he's concerned about things like where to park his Ford and how far he might have to walk in the cold, so Felton and I let him and Mama go ahead without us.

This place is spectacular and the decorating committee spared no expense in transforming the already beautiful room into a lush wonderland of greenery and sparkling lights. There are vines, palm trees in the four corners, and a stunning dance floor in the middle where handsome couples are already taking advantage of the live band.

On entering the ballroom anyone can see that my long, cream, velvet gown is sophisticated and modest with its boatneck collar and long feathered sleeves. But as I pass, an observer will notice a deep plunge, particularly the feather-accented dip, in the small of my back. This is where my ample hips are an added asset. On a slimmer woman, the cut of the dress would hang loose and move dramatically on its way to the floor. But on me, the fabric clings, pausing at my horizontal red sash and bow that sit right under the curve of my hip. A woman's silhouette, on a gentleman's arm.

I opted for no necklace to disturb my collar, and for my bosom to be the only accompaniment to the top half of the gown. And after a lengthy deliberation, I decided on drop pearl earrings. Papa procured my final accessories when he saw my dress hanging in my closet. A custom-made silk and feather handbag, with a pearl clasp, and silk shoes with a pearl bow.

Thank heavens it's a dry winter night because I sat for hours getting this side-swept wavy bob hairstyle. And instead of the lighter, sweeter shades I prefer, tonight called for a crimson lip. After all this work, I ought to be seen.

Tonight, the biddies may collect every morsel about me. I'm feeding them with a spoon.

"I feel like I've died and gone to heaven, you look so good, Yolande," Felton whispers as we cross the ballroom to my parents, who are seated at a large table with the Cullens.

Countee stands and seems happy enough to burst when I choose the seat next to him for Felton to pull out for me. I wave my hands at our polite fathers who try to rise.

Everyone says pleasantries because the Cullens already know Felton from Alpha Phi Alpha Fraternity, but the way Papa makes a fuss over Felton worries me. Felton and I are friends, and I enjoy his company, but that is all. I do not need Papa meddling.

"What's wrong?" Countee whispers.

I look over at Countee, having to pull my attention away from a dialogue Papa and Felton are having about the quality of primary education in the south. "Nothing? Why do you ask?" I whisper back.

"You're frowning. And . . . you look much too beautiful tonight for a frown."

Countee's lyrical timbre disarms me, and my expression softens. "Where is Harold? Who did you escort?"

"Harold is making his way around the ballroom, giving attention to all his admirers. He started at the southern smilax and has worked his way around to the palms."

"And you? Is it Sydonia or Fiona tonight?"

Countee shakes his head. "One is a wish. The other a prayer."

"A lie's still a lie, no matter the sayer."

Countee's eyes widen and his jaw drops. "What? A response in verse? The rhyme perfect. Rhythm as well."

"And truthful, because you are lying," I say with a laugh. "A wish and a prayer. Those girls are smitten with you."

"I wish I knew the sources of your gossip."

"I would never share gossip, Countee. You know this. Especially the slanderous kind."

Countee lifts a hand in agreement. "I apologize. You are a Delta woman. Of the highest moral character."

"And don't forget it."

Felton taps my arm. "Are you my date or his?"

Enjoying his jealousy, I take my good time turning my head. "I was going to ask if you were enjoying Papa's company, because Countee here is a wonderful dancer."

Countee looks nervously at Felton and then away, but then I tap Felton's chin, and he forgets all about Countee, as he should.

"Come on," I say in my most sexy, husky, womanly tone, "let's go sample the finger foods."

Felton stands then helps me from my chair, and we stroll across the ballroom to the buffet. I pause near the seven-member jazz band. Nothing like Mr. Morrison's Jazz Orchestra, but certainly good, and hearing the music makes me long for Jimmie. For the first time in many months, I feel a slight ache for him.

Pride is the only thing that's kept me from writing to him. We were together on his birthday. But for mine, I did not get a note or a card. Then nothing to say how the football season had gone. Or any insider letters with information about the protests on Fisk's campus for *The Crisis*. Then nothing for Thanksgiving.

Now, I do understand correspondence goes both ways and that at any time, I could've been the first to send a note. But it's also telling that neither of us broke down and submitted to being the first to write. Is that a bad omen? Has the magic from the Tree of Hope gone bad? Does the magic only live past West 132nd Street and 7th Avenue and not all the way down in Nashville?

Maybe I'll get him a card for the New Year. He's graduating soon and maybe he could use some encouragement. He no doubt misses my jokes and my flirtations.

But as Felton stands at the edge of the dance floor, beckoning to me to join him, I know deep down, I won't send the card, and I won't receive one either.

Somehow, the magic has faded, and I don't know how or if it will ever return.

Chapter Forty-Three

May 1925
Harlem, New York

I freeze as I hear the front door to our apartment slam and Papa's booming voice. He's not supposed to be home from Africa yet. Mama said tomorrow or maybe even the day after.

"Nina," Papa roars, "please move your books and sewing from my desk. I've asked you not to use my personal space for your frivolities."

He's walked in already angry about something. Anytime he comes in fussing at Mama about absolutely nothing, it means he's had a disagreement outside before getting home. It must be a burden, having a husband and carrying the weight of his misplaced anger. I will not allow it when I become a wife.

"Will, you were on another continent and your desk lamp has the best light. Are you going to storm in here angrily when you haven't seen me in months?"

I ease my bedroom door shut as quietly as I can. Hopefully, he'll think I'm out on the town with Margaret since it's Friday evening, and I'll escape unscathed.

But then I hear Papa's signature loud and intrusive rap on my door. So now it must be my turn.

I try to think of a tiny fib to hide that I'm on my way to *The Opportunity Magazine* award dinner, where Countee is being honored. Papa explicitly wrote to me that I was not to attend because of what Papa claims was underhanded treachery about the magazine's literary prize.

The Crisis had been planning its own award, and Miss Fauset mentioned it in literary circles. But then Charles Johnson, the editor of *Opportunity*, rushed and announced their award first, taking all the attention from *The Crisis*, making Papa seem like a copycat. He was furious, and he and Miss Fauset had a falling-out over it. Rumors say that may have been the reason she ran off to Paris last year.

But I am a free woman, and Countee is one of my dearest friends. How could I not accept his invitation?

When Papa knocks again and louder, I know I cannot stall any longer. So, I swing the door open and rush to hug him. Maybe if I shower him with affection, he won't notice my party dress.

"Welcome home, Papa."

"Where are you going all dressed up?" Papa asks as he holds me at arm's length to examine my outfit. "Have you finally accepted courtship from Felton?"

"Papa, no. Felton and I are great friends. Nothing more will come of it."

He gives me a look of disdain that seems too severe for the infraction of saying no to a date.

"If not Felton, then who are you seeing? And where are you going?"

I cross my arms defiantly and frown. "I do not think I need to divulge every move I make. Mama doesn't demand that."

Papa doesn't reply with words, but his expression threatens.

"I am going out with Margaret," I mumble.

"That is the who. Now the where." His tone is sharp and indignant. I don't appreciate it one bit.

"Oh, I'm sure we'll get up to our normal shenanigans. There's a black-and-tan club she's been wanting to try out. Happy Rhones. Have you heard of it?"

"Yes, I have. Some years ago, I saw Mamie Smith there with a few colleagues."

"Colleagues?" I wonder which ones. "I bet Mama would've enjoyed that. She does like to put on pretty dresses every now and then."

"You are attempting to change the subject."

And it was working for a moment.

"So, you and Margaret are going to Happy Rhones for the evening?" Papa perseveres.

His stare goes right through me, as if he already knows I'm fibbing, so I might as well tell the truth.

"Well, first, we're going to the Fifth Avenue Restaurant for a bit."

His eyes narrow to slits as he shakes his head in disgust. "The Fifth Avenue Restaurant, where they're holding the *Opportunity* dinner?"

I was hoping he wouldn't know the venue. I suppose I must tell him now. He couldn't get more infuriated than he already is.

"Yes, Papa."

"I believe I wrote to you and forbade you from going to this party."

"Yes, but you were being unreasonable. Countee is sure to win an award tonight. Langston too. Aren't you happy for them?"

"That has nothing to do with you disobeying me."

"I'm sorry, Papa. I promised Countee. Miss Fauset is going to be there as well."

"I cannot direct the movements of Miss Fauset, but I cannot have my own daughter at Charles Johnson's affair. I won't hear of it."

How do I explain to Papa that I am not a ten-year-old girl anymore? He glares at me, his snarled lip looking sinister and threatening.

"This isn't a grand scheme against you or *The Crisis*, Papa. We simply are going to support our friends."

"Perhaps you'd like to go and live with Miss Fauset. Since her guidance is more valuable to you than mine."

"Papa, you are not listening. Countee is my dear friend, and I want to see him celebrated. Langston as well. I hope you and Mama have a wonderful evening."

For a moment, I think Papa is not going to move a muscle. That he might be intending to block my path out of the apartment from my bedroom.

Then, finally, he steps aside grudgingly. I rush past him before he changes his mind, pick up my pocketbook from the table, and dash for the door. Normally, I would get some extra money from Papa for any post-party activities but this time I don't think that's a good idea. And Margaret and I don't often need additional funds. There is always someone to pay our way—us being Harlem socialites and all.

"Come home at a decent hour," Papa barks after me.

I know that Papa and I have different definitions of *decent*, but this is not the time to discuss technicalities.

Welcome home, Papa.

* * *

DESPITE THE EARLIER ugliness with Papa, I am feeling quite festive about tonight's affair. Margaret and I both decided on pastel-colored suits with matching fedoras. She's in light pink, and I chose cream. Our sorority colors. Heads turn as we walk through the door, but I'm not sure the reason. It could be how fetching we look, or it could be the fact that no one expected W.E.B. Du Bois's daughter to be here tonight.

"I told you everyone would be looking at us," Margaret whispers. "We look like Easter Sunday."

"No, we don't. We are très chic, Margaret. They're looking because we are the belles of this ball."

I locate our table. Harold is already sitting there, and he stands as we approach.

"*He's* at our table?" Margaret whispers. "Good grief."

"Hush," I whisper back. "He's my friend."

"Not true. You're both Countee's friends."

I hold out my arms to embrace Harold, and he does give me a very polite hug. Not the kind you'd give a friend, but the kind a young man might give his aunt. Margaret sits before he has the chance to hug her. She needn't have worried though; Harold dislikes her as much as she dislikes him.

"Hello, Miss Welmon." Harold's tone is so dry that I must bite my lip to keep from laughing.

"Mr. Jackman."

Harold looks at me and rolls his eyes. I cover my mouth and shake my head, glad to be seated between the two of them to function as referee.

"You ladies are dressed to the nines," Harold says. "Those fedoras are quite fetching."

"Thank you, Harold. I knew I'd run into you here," I reply, "so I had to be mindful of my attire."

As always, Harold's suit fits him like a glove, and his hair is groomed to perfection. His clean-shaven face is as handsome as ever, and his cologne is the most alluring scent. Us girls came to be seen, and apparently, so did Harold.

"What is that cologne you're wearing?" I ask. "I've never smelled anything quite like it."

"And hopefully you never will. It's a custom scent. It was a gift from a friend of mine in the south of France."

"Hmph," Margaret says. "Must be nice having those kinds of friends."

"It is. If you weren't such a stick in the mud, I'd introduce you to some."

Margaret twists her lips to the side and looks Harold up and down. "I don't need to be introduced to anyone by the likes of you."

"Suit yourself," Harold says. "I just heard you're saving yourself for Charles Waters, but he's having a time this spring already."

Margaret huffs and stares straight ahead.

"Is Countee here yet?" I ask. "I'd like to wish him luck before the program starts."

"He and Langston stepped away to meet some very important literary people, and then they're going to be seated here with us."

"Oh, there isn't a table for the guests of honor?" I ask, finding this quite strange. If Papa were doing this event for *The Crisis*, he'd make a big to-do about the finalists for the awards.

"I believe there was supposed to be, but Countee asked to sit with his friends," Harold explains. "He'd probably like to be near us if he doesn't win. His heart is wounded so easily by these things."

"But he will win something tonight. He and Langston are neck and neck in every literary contest these days."

"They are the best of the best," Harold says. "What do you expect?"

A stylish young woman, also wearing a fedora, sits next to Harold. "The best what?" she asks.

He grins widely. "Zora. Hello, my dear. Have you met Yolande Du Bois?"

"Hello, Yolande, I have been meaning to have Harold make the introduction. I am Zora Neale Hurston, and I'm a writer too."

Miss Hurston has the kind of face you don't forget. Once she smiles, and you see those cheekbones and dimpled chin, it's over. I'd love to make a sketch of her in her fedora cocked to the side. And while sketching, I'd want to hear her thoughts about anything and everything. The gleam in her eyes tells me she's got something consequential to say.

"It's a pleasure to meet you," I say, hoping she can tell I mean it. "This is my friend Margaret Welmon."

"Pleased to meet you, Zora. You must join us for tea, even if you are friends with this miscreant." Margaret's greeting for Zora is sincere, not like the snarky ones she saves for Harold.

Harold laughs. "Zora, Margaret and I have been embattled in a war of words since the first time we met. However, we are bound to be in the same rooms due to our love of Countee and Yolande."

"But I will not hold your friendship with Harold against you," Margaret assures Zora.

"I enjoy a good war of words myself," Zora admits. "And Harold is a worthy opponent."

"Zora, your name sounds familiar." I'm trying to place where I may have heard it. "Where did you go to college?"

"Howard University. Is that where you matriculated as well?"

"No, Fisk is my alma mater. But my good friend Minnie Carwin was at Howard for one year. Perhaps I heard your name from her."

"Yes, I remember Minnie. We met only briefly, but she seemed like a load of fun." The skin around Zora's eyes crinkles joyfully, hopefully indicating a pleasant encounter with my friend.

"That is a perfect description of Minnie. I can't wait to write her and tell her we met, and I concur on the tea."

Zora lifts her eyebrows. "Only tea?"

Her expression and what it implies tickle me. "Well, if Harold and his flask appear, who knows what might happen."

We all laugh now, including Margaret.

"Oh look, Miss Fauset has arrived," Harold says while motioning to the door. "I didn't think she'd come. It's a good thing your father's out of the country."

Zora pops up from her seat. "I must meet Miss Fauset."

"Do you need one of us to make the introduction?" Harold asks. "I'd be happy to."

"No, I think a powerful woman like her would prefer me striking up a conversation instead."

Powerful? Is that how the writers view Miss Fauset? If only she didn't allow Papa to rule over her at *The Crisis*. But she also defied him tonight, so maybe she is done being pushed around.

"Coincidentally, Papa came home today," I say to Harold after Zora leaves the table. "And he wasn't too thrilled about me attending tonight."

"Interesting. You've chosen to disobey him? Fisk has done wonders for you, Yolande." Harold strokes his chin as if he has a beard. "I never thought I'd see the day."

"Hush, Harold," Margaret fusses. "You are a mess."

"I am only making an observation," he protests.

Countee rushes over to the table and falls exhausted into the seat on the other side of Harold. Then, I suppose he remembers that he hasn't yet greeted me tonight, and he jumps up to hug me and Margaret. Margaret might not be too fond of Harold, but she likes Countee well enough. She doesn't rebuff his hug or grimace like she does with Harold.

"How is your evening going, Countee? Why are you so tired?" I ask.

He exhales loudly and shakes his head. "Do you know how much it takes out of a person to talk to dozens upon dozens of people? And for them to all remember you and your name and where they met you? Even when you were a small child?"

"I do know what that's like," I say. "It happens every time I have to go to an NAACP event with Papa."

"Then you do understand. I'd just like to crawl into my bed and go to sleep."

"Are your parents here?" I ask, hoping that they're not going to be seated at this table. I don't want to sit here with Mrs. Cullen scowling at me all evening.

"Yes, I gave them my seats at the head table, so that they can gloat properly when I win first prize."

"Someone is sure of himself," Margaret says. "There are a good many talented writers here tonight."

"Indeed," Countee says, "and any of them could best me in this contest. I have read all the entries and they're glorious."

This is a thing I love about Countee. While he is excited about the idea of winning the award himself, he's just as thrilled about the thought of Langston or any of his other peers prevailing as well.

Just as the program is about to begin, I catch Miss Fauset's eye at her table, and she blows me a kiss. I give her an air-kiss in return and a wink. We've both outsmarted Papa tonight, it seems. If there is hell to pay, we can face it together.

Chapter Forty-Four

May 1925
Harlem, New York

I'm late getting into the office this morning because I had to celebrate Countee's and Langston's wins last night. And boy, did we celebrate. A'Lelia brought out her good supply for her literary boys. Thank goodness the shenanigans happened behind the private closed doors of the Walker Studio.

Besides, it's Saturday. Most sane people are off today enjoying their families. But not the staff of *The Crisis*. We have a half day on Saturday. Deadlines to the printer to meet, and letters to answer. Papa says the mail still comes on Saturday and the phone still rings.

I have managed to make myself look presentable, even though I got far too little sleep. But when I woke up and Papa was gone, I knew I needed to shimmy on downtown. He just got home from another continent and is at work and I only bounced and bopped around Harlem.

When I get to the desk area I share with Miss Foster, I can tell that something's wrong by the somber look on her face.

"What's going on?" I ask.

Her eyes cut toward Papa's office door. "I think Miss Fauset just resigned."

"What?" I ease down into my seat, my knees no longer trustworthy. "Why?"

"I don't know, but I think it has something to do with that dinner last night."

"No!" I gasp, wondering if Miss Fauset and Papa had a bigger disagreement than I realized.

We both jump when Papa's office door swings open and Miss Fauset rushes out. She seems unnerved but determined to put space between herself and Papa as quickly as possible.

On her way past, she pauses in front of our desks. "Ladies, it has been a pleasure and honor to see you both mature into fine professional w—" Her voice cracks, but she steels herself. "Women. Please call me whenever you need me. Au revoir, mes chères."

The wetness in her eyes tells me she's on the brink of weeping. She loves this magazine so much. Why would she leave over such a minor disagreement? And why would Papa allow it? He's able to command everyone every other time. Why not now?

The Crisis needs Miss Fauset. Papa might be the visionary, but Miss Fauset is the heart. The writers are here for her. If Papa had seen how they flocked to her side at the *Opportunity* dinner, he would have seen how important she is to the movement.

She composes herself, then glides out of the office, feminine and ethereal. Papa emerges from his office moments later looking like he's seen an apparition.

"Miss Foster, Yolande, you may take the day off," Papa says, a slight tremble in his voice, making him for once sound every bit of his fifty-seven years. "Mr. Dill will be in later to take care of the mail."

Miss Foster hurries to gather her things and fly out of there before Papa has second thoughts, but I hang behind, fretting over Papa. I cannot leave him this way.

"Are you all right, Papa? I don't have anything to do this morning. I don't mind staying."

The left side of Papa's face twitches as if he's trying hard to smile but never quite succeeds.

"Go enjoy your weekend, sweetheart. I am fine."

But he doesn't sound fine. He sounds broken and forlorn.

"She will come back, Papa. Miss Fauset loves *The Crisis* as much as you do."

Papa's empty gaze and fallen expression are unsettling. He is not the kind of man a person offers comfort, but I want to comfort him. I don't know how, though, and that makes me ache for him even more.

"No," he finally says after a too long and tortuous silence. "She is gone. Her love for *The Crisis* is the reason she left."

This makes me think of a story I heard at church one Sunday morning when I was away at Fisk. About King Solomon and two women who brought him a baby. The woman who was truly the mother wouldn't let the baby be divided in half with a sword. I wonder if staying here with Papa and all his demands felt like that sword.

But what on earth will Papa do without Miss Fauset?

Chapter Forty-Five

July 1925
Harlem, New York

Felton is push, push, pushing the boundaries of this friendship and I've reluctantly allowed it because Jimmie has graduated and I still haven't heard from him. And he in turn has not heard from me. The embers of love in my heart for Jimmie remain, but they have cooled from lack of tending.

Besides, having Felton around keeps Countee's pursuit of me in its proper platonic place. In fact, Felton and I are eating lunch right now while I wait for Countee. Then, against Felton's wishes, I will abandon him to attend a literary affair with Countee at the library. And of course, that will turn into an after-soirée at Small's Paradise. Lately, I've been invited to more gatherings in the writing community. And I have even more to do at *The Crisis* since Miss Fauset left.

"Have you heard back from the boys' junior high school?" I ask Felton.

"I have not. Have you heard from the girls' school? Surely with your papa's connections and your soror's too, you'll get a spot."

"I sure hope so."

Since graduation Felton and I have both applied for teaching positions at the Harlem junior high schools along with, it seems, every Negro teacher in America. I can't blame them. Harlem is the place to be and everybody's trying to get here.

"Do you have another plan if you don't get hired?" Felton asks.

The possibility that I might not get hired had not occurred to me. Teaching at a school in Harlem has been my only plan, although I suppose I can always stay on at *The Crisis*.

"If I don't get hired, I'll probably just keep working at the magazine."

"What if you could teach somewhere else?" Felton asks.

There is a smile tickling the sides of his mouth that makes me uneasy. Or maybe it's his questions. It feels like he's building up to something.

"Do you mean Brooklyn?" I ask cautiously. "Most of their teachers are white, Felton. If I really want a shot at reaching Black children, my best bet is right here in Harlem."

He chuckles. "There are Black people all over the country, Yolande. Not just in New York."

"Well, of course, I know that. But why would I leave New York?"

Felton takes a bite of his sandwich and chews very slowly. Grinning as he chews. I don't have a good feeling about this.

"What if you married a man from somewhere else? You wouldn't even leave New York then?"

Felton is from Louisiana. Here it comes.

"I am not thinking about that at all. I don't have marriage prospects. I'm thinking of making an impact."

"What if you could do both? Be married and make an impact?"

These questions feel like a trap. Felton must already have answers, or he's anticipated how I might respond and prepared himself for a debate. I don't appreciate being ambushed.

"Tell me what you mean," I say, done with the charade. "Clearly, you've been thinking on this already."

Felton nods, his smile is gone now as well, replaced with a solemn expression.

"I haven't heard back from the boys' junior high school in Harlem, but I do have an offer to come work on the staff of Wiley College in Marshall, Texas."

"Oh, well congratulations, Felton! We must have a big going-away party. I know your fraternity brothers are going to really make it grand."

"It could be *our* going-away party," Felton says.

His eyebrows are raised, like he's waiting for me to say something positive.

"I have not applied for any jobs in Texas, silly," I say, swatting him on the leg with my napkin. "That's too far and too country for my liking. No thank you."

"But they have plenty of teaching jobs there, junior high school, high school, and even at the collegiate level. You'd be welcome in Marshall. They need Negro teachers."

"There's a reason the jobs are plentiful. Because the hangings are plentiful and the Klan is as well. Give me Harlem any day, Felton."

He clears his throat and sits up straight. "What if you were there as my wife? We'd be together."

"We're not in a courtship, Felton. We're only friends," I remind him.

"But I'm asking now if you might be interested in more than friendship."

I've known this was coming. I'm surprised that it's taken this long.

"I've already talked to your father about it," Felton adds. "And he thinks it's a splendid idea."

"You spoke to my papa about courtship, marriage, and moving me to Texas before you even asked me if I'd be open to it?" I ask hotly, feeling myself getting increasingly disturbed by the moment.

Felton's light complexion cannot hide his embarrassment. Redness creeps from his neck and stains his cheeks.

"I—I thought we enjoyed each other's company," he stammers.

"I do enjoy our friendship," I tell him flatly, each syllable precisely enunciated.

"And you've never thought it should go any further?" he asks, his embarrassment now souring, as it does sometimes with men, and turning to ire. "I am a full-grown man, Yolande. Not a boy."

"But you started a conversation with my father about courting and marrying me, as if I'm a child and not a full-grown woman."

Felton sighs. "I do not think of you as a child. I was simply with your father at a fraternity fellowship, and the conversation drifted in that direction."

Drifted? I'm sure my papa steered it in that direction.

"Felton, I hope me rejecting this offer doesn't tarnish our friendship."

"So, you're rejecting it?"

"Yes. I have no desire to move to Texas. I have decided to teach for a few years, here in Harlem. Then I will see what transpires for me when it comes to marriage."

Felton laughs. "You'd better hope there's someone interested in you when you're almost thirty."

"I will worry about that when the time comes," I snap.

Felton shakes his head and continues to eat his food, letting out a few chuckles between bites as if this will shake my confidence or make me feel desperate enough to take what he's offering.

Who does this man think he is? Felton has chosen the wrong girl to threaten with loneliness.

Perhaps while Papa was advising Felton on our future marriage, he should've told him I'm a woman who likes to feel loved. And who is loved.

Or was once.

Chapter Forty-Six

August 1925
Harlem, New York

Things have gotten much calmer at home for me and Mama since Papa is producing his *Star of Ethiopia* pageant in California. It gets him out of the house and away from us for a few weeks, which is for the best. He's been in a sour mood since Miss Fauset's departure, and I've avoided him as much as possible since that disastrous conversation with Felton.

Since Papa's been out of town, I've spent every night of the week going to speakeasies and shows with Harold and Countee. Sometimes Margaret joins us as well, but mostly she's tied at the hip to Charles.

Tonight, there's a new jazz band playing at Connie's Inn on Seventh Avenue between 131st and 132nd Streets. Harold is fond of Connie's Inn not just because it's a black-and-tan club, but because the owner is a known bootlegger, and his VIPs (of which Harold is one) have access to a secret menu.

Being able to get whiskey isn't a draw for Countee or me; we both are closer to teetotalers than most. We care about the music because it's the dancing we want. Oh, and of course the food. Countee is so fond of Oriental dishes like Chinese chicken fried rice and mushroom and pepper chop suey. I'm fine with just a hamburger and a soda.

Mama looks up from her book when I emerge from my bedroom in my red satin sheath. It comes to my knee, with fringes on the hem and just enough stretch so I can really move on the dance floor.

"Well, look at you," she says. "Going out on the town again?"

Mama knows exactly how to phrase things to make you wonder if she's being sweet or just sounding sweet. Well, I can read between those lines: she's judging me about the amount of time I spend partying in the streets of Harlem.

"Mama, please."

"I'd just noticed that the two of us haven't dined together all week."

I want to mention that she hasn't cooked anything I wanted to eat all week, but that might hurt her feelings, so I bite my tongue.

"How about Sunday dinner, Mama? That will be nice."

"All right. I'll make a nice roast."

Mama's roast is not an incentive to forgo fun, but again, I will keep that comment to myself.

I hold out the double string of pearls that she and Papa bought me for graduation. "Will you put these on, please?"

"That's a lovely perfume," she says as she latches the small clasp that I can never manage on my own.

"Oh, Countee bought it for me. He says it's French."

"Hmmm . . ."

I turn around to face Mama. "What's wrong?"

"A man buys a woman expensive perfume when he'd like to smell it on her."

"Oh, no, Mama. It's nothing like that. Countee knows I enjoy nice-smelling perfumes. Harold is always wearing some European scent or the other, and they smell divine."

"That doesn't change what I said."

"Maybe Papa wants there to be more between me and Countee, but I regret to inform you there is only friendship."

"I am simply observing."

I give a tight smile as I pull on each of my elbow-length gloves.

"Countee and Harold are waiting for me downstairs, Mama. Please try to enjoy your evening."

"I will."

I kiss her on the cheek. "Don't wait up for me. I'll be out late."

"I am aware. You know, one day, Countee's going to get up enough nerve to come call on you without Harold at his side."

When it comes to Mama and her observations, I wish sometimes that she'd put her eyeballs on another subject.

* * *

THE MUSIC IS jumping at Connie's Inn. Countee and I start to toe tapping and shoulder bouncing before we even get inside. But as soon as we enter, Harold disappears, off to find the special secret menu stash.

Countee and I have one destination—the dance floor.

And it is *packed*. Black couples, tan couples, and a mixture of both shimmy, shake, and do the Charleston. There is a tangle of swinging arms, elbows, and stomping feet, but oh boy is it fun. Countee and I laugh and laugh as we try to synchronize our movements, and by the time we finally get it, the song is over.

"Countee, when I kick my left foot up, you are supposed to tap it with your right foot," I say, laughing so hard I must hold my belly as the band takes a break.

"I'm trying, but it's like you're either a half step ahead of me, or I'm a half step behind. I can't tell which."

"And then you keep forgetting to move your arms." Tears are pouring out of my eyes, and Countee laughs too.

"Well, it's all about the fun, right?" Countee says. "As long as we don't stop moving."

"You're right, but we are going to get this Charleston tonight, Countee, if it's the last thing we do."

"I'm not going to make any promises," Countee says, and this starts up a whole new round of laughter. He is unashamed of his two left feet and elbows. "Let's get a cool drink before the dancing starts up again."

We push through the crowd to what would be the bar if they were serving whiskey out in the open. Countee procures two glasses of sweet punch that we polish off in record time because we hear the band starting up again.

"Come on," I say. "I want to get closer to the band. They sound good!"

This time, Countee and I find our rhythm quicker and we're almost coordinated with our Charleston movements. Until I hear something that grabs my attention. The familiar warble of a saxophone.

"You feeling all right?" Countee asks as I stop dancing altogether and turn to face the bandstand.

I raise my hand to let him know I'm fine, but my feet move toward that sound. I know it. My heart knows it. Every riff, run, and note coming from that instrument call to me. I can feel Jimmie's presence here. I'd know his music anywhere.

I get to the edge of the bandstand and stop. It's dark, the band is dressed in black, and they're seated a ways back from the dance floor. But I search their faces until I find the one I'm looking for.

Jimmie.

As our eyes meet, I'm overcome with emotion. I didn't know how I'd feel about seeing him again. If I wouldn't care about having not gotten a letter or card from him in more than a year. Or if I'd just be happy to lay eyes on him. But I feel every emotion all at once— anger, relief, joy, love . . . lust. I just want to feel his arms around me.

Countee is at my side now as I sway in time to the music. His presence feels like an intrusion.

"Yolande?" he whispers.

I don't want to answer him, so I just point up at the bandstand. At Jimmie. Countee tilts his head to one side and stares. He probably wants me to go back to dancing, but I'm not moving until the set is over.

As they play, Jimmie eases out of his chair and plays while he walks over to the edge of the stage. He plays with the band, but for me. And even though there's not enough room in this place to move right or left without bumping into someone, it might as well be empty. All I see is Jimmie.

At the final note of the last song, Jimmie sets his saxophone aside and leaps off the stage, landing between me and Countee. And with one hand he gently grabs me by the waist, wraps his hand in my thick hair, and pulls my face to his.

For a moment, I don't care about virtue as my lips hungrily crash into his. I swoon at the taste of him. Then, when he releases me from his grasp, I rock back on my heels, as intoxicated as if I'd had some of that bootleg whiskey in the back.

"Jimmie, what are you doing here?" I ask breathlessly, when I can finally form words, my hand stroking his chest, not wanting to lose contact with him.

"I have a summer gig, and during the day, I'm going to City College," Jimmie explains.

"Why didn't you tell me you were coming? How long have you been here?" I feel myself panicking. Had he seen me with Felton? Did he think it was anything serious?

"No, no, sweetheart, I just got here this afternoon and had to come straight to the club," Jimmie says, squeezing my shoulders and then kissing the top of my head. "I wouldn't let a whole day go by without coming to you."

Then, I turn to Countee, hoping that it isn't going to be weird with us here together in Harlem. Harold is at his side now, his gaze darting from Jimmie to me and back again. He sips his whiskey from a paper cup and frowns.

"Countee, you remember Jimmie from Fisk?" I ask. "Harold, this is my Jimmie."

"*Your* Jimmie?" Harold's eyebrows shoot up so high they nearly touch his hairline.

Jimmie extends his hand to shake Countee's and then Harold's hand. "Good to see you, Countee. Pleasure to meet you, Harold."

"You made it to Harlem," Countee says. "Welcome."

"Of course I'm here," Jimmie says snarkily. "Yolande is here, so I am here."

"Harold and I will have to show you around to all our regular haunts," Countee says, almost smiling, but not quite.

Jimmie looks down at me and kisses the top of my head again. "Yolande can show me. Right, sweetheart?"

"Of course, I will."

Jimmie looks up at Countee and shrugs. "I guess you're not needed then, Countee."

Countee and Harold stare at me, perhaps waiting for me to correct Jimmie, but I think he's said it all. Now that Jimmie's back in Harlem, I don't need Countee to take me dancing at Connie's Inn, for soirées at the Walker Studio, or to watch the roller-skating servers at Small's Paradise. Even though he's my dear friend, with Jimmie here, I don't need Countee for anything really. Anything at all.

Chapter Forty-Seven

These two weeks I've spent reuniting with Jimmie have been glorious. We just picked up from where we left off like we haven't gone an entire year without corresponding. Neither of us seem to want to bring up the topic of our separation, so it just hovers in the background of things.

At night, we lie together wherever Jimmie can score a private room. Sometimes at Hotel Olga, other times at the apartments of his friends who are away. His hands have not lost their skill, and my body has not forgotten his touch.

By day we eat lunch at the Y and stroll all over Harlem. This is the place where our magic was born, and where we most feel connected.

Papa comes home tomorrow, however, and I fear the light we feel will quickly dim.

"What's bothering you, Yolande? You haven't touched your ham sandwich," Jimmie says as I push the food around on my plate. "It's your favorite."

I don't want to tell Jimmie I'm fretting about Papa. It will just upset him.

"I'm fine. Just brooding, I suppose."

"Well, let's do something to get your mind off whatever's ailing you."

"What are we going to do?"

I can't think of anything we haven't done in Harlem. We've been to every park, club, and speakeasy. We've shopped at Blumstein's

and read books together in the 135th Street library. We've walked by
the river and had ice cream, popcorn, and warm peanuts. None of it
erases Papa's scowl from my thoughts.

"We're going to get to know each other better."

"Jimmie, what are you talking about?" I laugh. "You know me
better than anyone."

"Who is the one person, living or dead, that you would want to
lunch with?" Jimmie asks, just as serious as can be.

"Is this a real question?"

Jimmie chuckles. "Yes, it's real. I'd like to know."

"Well, if I could talk to anyone living or dead, it would be my dog,
Steve. He died when I was fifteen, and I still don't think I've gotten
over it."

"Your dog? All right, but I meant a person."

"Steve was a person. He was my best friend and Mama had him put
to sleep. He was sick, but I blamed her for his death."

"I thought Margaret was your best friend."

"Well, she's my best girlfriend. Steve never judged me, and he was
never jealous of my pretty dresses."

"Would you ever get another dog?"

"I don't know. I loved Steve, but it was such demanding work taking care of him. Maybe if I have children one day."

"When *we* have children one day, I suppose I'll need to build a
doghouse."

This story seems to amuse Jimmie, but I was devastated about losing Steve and thinking of him now makes me sad all over again, even
though it's been many years since he died.

"I wrote a poem about him. Do you want to hear it?" I ask.

"Yes, I would."

I clear my throat and sit up straight, channeling Countee whenever he recites poetry.

"It's called 'Steve.'"

Tender shaggy friend of mine,
With eyes of tragic brown,
When I watch the evening stars,
I seem to see you looking down.
Just a dog!
Dear, kind, understanding eyes
I think God loved you too.
And when at last I cross the bar,
I'll see the eyes of you.
Just a dog!

"That was beautiful," Jimmie says. He reaches across the table and touches my hand, probably because I'm blinking back tears. "I can tell you really loved him."

"I did. I remember why I wrote this poem. Papa had gotten angry at me for still crying about Steve years later. He'd said Steve was just a dog, and that I could have another."

"He didn't care about your feelings. That's hurtful," Jimmie says. "I can understand why that bothered you."

"Yes. Okay, now your turn. Who would you want to talk to, living or dead?"

"I've thought about this, and I think I'd like it to be my great-great-great-great-grandmother or -grandfather, wherever they lived in Africa. I'd want to talk about the music that's in my blood. It had to come from my ancestors."

"My papa would love that response, Jimmie. He wants every colored person to discover their African roots."

"Your papa would love a great deal of things about me if he'd give me the chance. Parents love me."

I lift my eyebrows. "Which parents?"

"Your mother for one. And all the other parents of daughters that want my attention."

"The countless parents of daughters?" I laugh as I ask this, enjoying making Jimmie squirm.

"Not countless, but quite a few. You know those ladies at the church think I'm a good catch."

"You are, and you're going to have dinner with us tomorrow night. At our home."

"Is your papa aware?"

"No, but neither is Mama. It's my home too, so I am going to entertain my love."

Jimmie sighs. "It would be lovely if they'd just invite me."

It would. But that will come in time. The first hurdle will be them accepting this adult, college-educated Jimmie as my grown-up beau. Small steps.

*   *   *

THE FIRST TIME Jimmie came to our home for dinner in Brooklyn, we were children. Tonight, he will dine with us as a graduate of Papa's alma mater, and a graduate student. He is someone who should be taken seriously.

But I cannot let his arrival be a surprise because Papa has been temperamental these last two months with Miss Fauset's departure from *The Crisis*. I don't want to add to his anxiety, or mine, especially during this sweet reunion Jimmie and I are having.

"Jimmie is joining us for dinner," I announce as Papa reads a book at the dining room table.

Mama steps out of the kitchen and into the dining room, perhaps to sweeten any harsh words that may fly, or maybe just to see what unfolds.

"Lunceford?" Papa says as he closes his book. "He's graduated from Fisk, I presume."

"Yes."

"He was very instrumental in our protests against Dr. McKenzie and the administration," Papa says in an unexpectedly positive tone. "We accomplished much."

"I am glad to hear that," I say, not sure if I should trust this demeanor.

Then Papa goes back to reading his book without any further commentary. This is not like him at all, and now I'm going to be worried all evening. But a knock at the door signals Jimmie's arrival, so I don't have any more time to strategize or deliberate.

I open the door. Jimmie stands there with a fresh haircut, a new suit, and bearing gifts. He glances over at Papa and then leans down to give me a very chaste hug.

"Something smells good," Jimmie says with a bright smile. "Is that roasted chicken?"

"Don't get your hopes up about it being good," I whisper. He squeezes his eyes shut and laughs silently as he steps inside.

I watch Jimmie's sweeping gaze assess our living room and dining room from our home's entrance. I wonder what he thinks of Mama's expensive French furniture and Oriental rugs. He tilts his head with interest, taking in the paintings on the walls. Everything here is even more opulent than the Brooklyn apartment that he visited years ago.

"Beautiful home," he remarks as I take the flowers from his hands.

"Thank you. I love these," I say as I rush to deposit the bouquet into the waiting vase on the dining room table.

"Good evening, Dr. Du Bois," Jimmie says to Papa, who has again closed his book and strides into the living room.

"Mr. Lunceford. I haven't heard your name in months. I thought that you had moved on to greener pastures. But a Fisk alumnus is always welcome in my home."

I lock gazes with Jimmie as I rush back in from the flower arranging. I should have known that Papa was too calm at my announcement of Jimmie's arrival.

"I don't know what you mean by greener pastures, Dr. Du Bois," Jimmie says, his warm smile a challenge to Papa's snark.

"Just an expression," Papa says with a matching grin, as he invites Jimmie to sit on our new sofa.

But first Jimmie offers Papa a package wrapped in brown paper and tied with a string.

"Dr. Du Bois, I brought you a gift," Jimmie says.

Papa stares at Jimmie and the package for a long excruciating moment. Why does Papa seem vexed? Who is this disturbed by friendliness and manners? Why would a gift be a reason for contempt?

I watch Papa's expression soften as Mama appears from the kitchen with a huge dose of serenity in tow. She's still wearing her kitchen apron, but Jimmie doesn't seem to notice as he gives her a friendly embrace.

"It is so good to see you, Jimmie," Mama says, blushing at his sudden affection. "Have you gotten taller?"

"Maybe," he says with a chuckle. "My mother says it seems like I'll never stop growing."

"Well, we are short people," Mrs. Du Bois says. "Isn't it interesting how different traits are passed down from generation to generation? We've never had any height in our ranks."

"Perhaps Yolande and I will have tall sons," Jimmie blurts. Papa's nostrils flare, but it's already too late for Jimmie to take back his words.

Quickly, Jimmie gives another wrapped package to Mama. She beams and sits on the sofa already ripping into the paper, unlike Papa who's still just holding his gift and staring at us. Jimmie sits next to Mama, and I sit on the other side of her. I suppose Papa feels strange standing while we huddle on the sofa, so he sits in his armchair.

"Yolande told me some of your likes and dislikes," Jimmie says to Mama, and then looks up at Papa. "So, I hope I did well."

Mama opens her gift box and sighs with pleasure at the personal tea set with a tiny tea pot, cup, and saucer. There's also a tiny silver spoon for stirring.

"This is perfect, Jimmie," she says. "Thank you very much. It was very thoughtful of you to bring us gifts. Open yours, Will."

Unable to stall any longer, Papa removes the paper from his gift. It's fancy stationery and an expensive writing pen.

"It's for your letter writing campaigns, Dr. Du Bois," Jimmie says gleefully. "For the movement."

"Thank you," Papa says. "These days, I often type my letters on the typewriter, but there are times when that is impractical. I will get use from this."

There is no excitement in his voice. Perhaps he only thanked Jimmie so as not to seem rude. But politeness is better than his being rude. That is a step in the right direction.

"Would you like to wash your hands in the bathroom, Jimmie?" Mama asks. "We're just about ready to eat dinner."

Jimmie nods and stands. "Mrs. Du Bois, your home is beautiful," he says as he follows Mama down the hall.

I glare at Papa. "Be nice," I hiss.

Papa just lifts his eyebrows innocently, like he's done nothing. He sits his new writing utensils down on the coffee table and we both go into the dining room. Papa sits and I bring out the platters and bowls of food from the kitchen.

When Jimmie finishes washing his hands, Mama and I point out where he should sit. The other head of the table across from Papa.

"There's nothing like home cooking," Jimmie says as he sits. "With all the restaurant meals I've had of late, I miss my mother's cooking."

"I tried my hand at roasted chicken and vegetables," I say. "I hope you like it. I've been in the kitchen all day."

"I'm sure I will."

Papa reaches for the chicken platter to get things started. But Papa must not have remembered that Jimmie is religious and likes to pray before eating. No matter, Jimmie bows his head, closes his eyes, and says a silent prayer for himself.

"So, James," Papa says when Jimmie is done praying. "What brings you back to Harlem? Besides Yolande, I mean. Clearly, you're enamored with her."

"You are correct about me being enamored, sir, but I am also here to further my education and work."

"Where are you working?" Papa asks, and it dawns on me that this has become an interrogation. I hope Jimmie doesn't notice.

I also notice that Jimmie struggles with swallowing the chicken. It is a bit dry. He takes a huge gulp of water before answering Papa's query.

"I have a gig with a band at Connie's Inn, and I play for various churches on Sundays. On weekdays I will be studying, but I also help coach young athletes at the Renaissance Ballroom."

"With all that, I'm surprised you have time for courting," Mama says.

Papa lifts an eyebrow at Mama. "But they do have time. All of Harlem knows about their courtship."

"That's good," Jimmie says. "It should scare away any cads that might think they had a chance. Yolande is going to teach in Harlem while I work and finish my studies. Soon, we'll be married and have our own home like this one." Then he has the audacity to wink at me as he takes another big bite of his chicken.

Mama and I exchange worried glances as Papa tears into his tough chicken. Then, as he chews, he laughs. An ominous, humorless laugh. But Jimmie joins him, and it is clear he's unaware.

He seems to think he and Papa are two men sharing a joke. Equals. I don't know if I have the heart to tell him he's mistaken.

Chapter Forty-Eight

August 1925
Harlem, New York

Even though I arrived at Hotel Olga to meet Jimmie under the cover of night and used a side door to enter the building, I felt watched. Someone has carried news of our Harlem capers back to Papa. Have they seen us here too? Have my Delta sorors heard? Is that why I haven't been selected yet for the teaching position in Harlem? But when I shared my concerns with Jimmie he simply said, "You're of age."

I absentmindedly take long drags from my cigarette. I've started to do that when I feel anxious, and I don't like it, but for now, the nervousness is getting the best of me.

"Jimmie," I whisper in case he's dozed off. I'm lying across his lap paging through a magazine.

"Yes?" His voice sounds like he was about to fall asleep.

"Did I tell you the job is as an English teacher? I'd be teaching students about literature."

"You'll be good at it. When do you think you'll hear?" he asks, now sounding fully awake.

"I don't know. I hope it will be soon. The school year starts in a few weeks."

"If you really want to teach, you'll get a call back from a school in Harlem."

I reposition my body so that I can see him, and I put out my cigarette, because he hates the smoke blowing in his face.

"Jimmie, you're saying that like you know I will get a teaching position for sure."

"What is for you won't pass you by. Have faith."

I don't quite understand how Jimmie's faith works. Are we still in God's good graces when we're doing all the sinful things we've been warned about our entire lives?

"I hope you're right."

"I am," Jimmie says, stroking my inner thigh. He's starting a fire and making me forget my troubles. "Dinner with your parents went well, don't you think?"

I laugh. "I don't know about that. Papa was being strange."

"You think so? It seemed to me that he's finally accepted us."

"I'm not sure about that. He can be hard to read," I say with a sigh. "But at least he wasn't disrespectful."

"What are you unsure about?" Jimmie asks. "Has he been up to his matchmaking again?"

"He hasn't been matchmaking."

"Someone sent me a newspaper clipping," Jimmie says, still stroking my thigh. "It was a photo from a formal dinner—"

"Jimmie."

He sits up in bed, his back against the headboard now. "You looked beautiful."

"I know the photo you're speaking about. It was in the *Inter-State Tattler*. The Alpha Phi Alpha Fraternity holiday formal."

"You had an escort," Jimmie says. "And it was *not* your little pot-bellied friend."

My jaw drops for a second. "Don't poke fun at Countee. He's not an athlete."

"Well, I'm not concerned about him. I did worry about the guy in the photo, however."

"You don't need to worry about anyone," I explain, feeling annoyed, but hoping it isn't apparent in my voice. "That man is a classmate and friend. He's also an Alpha fraternity brother, so he escorted me to the dance."

Of course, Felton's invitation to join him in Texas pops into my mind, but because I didn't take that seriously, I'm not going to mention it. Surely there are things Jimmie isn't mentioning to me, so I'm not going to allow him to interrogate me.

"Jimmie, we didn't write each other for a year, and now we are reunited. Can we not do the questions?"

"You can ask me anything," Jimmie says confidently. "I didn't write because you said you wanted time to discover yourself. I didn't know if you wanted to hear from me. And then when I didn't hear from you, I thought I was right."

"Then why did you come to New York after you graduated?" I ask.

"I am here for you, my love," Jimmie answers, "but I am also here for my music. Jazz is king in Harlem. I hoped you'd want me back, but I wanted Harlem even if you didn't love me anymore."

I don't know why, but this makes me feel relieved. "I'm glad you're here. And I'm happy to share Harlem with you."

"I'm ready to share something else," Jimmie says in a low husky voice.

I would be frightened by the hungry growl that comes from Jimmie if I didn't feel the same hunger myself. Our bodies collide and then fall back into the bed linens.

And then we make love until we're breathless.

* * *

I EASE OUT of bed, slowly untangling my limbs from Jimmie's. I need water, a snack, and maybe a few drags from my Benson and Hedges. I stumble to the dining table that holds the remnants of our dinner, my legs still rubbery from our lovemaking.

I pour a glass of water and take a pinch of the cake slice Jimmie had waiting for me when I arrived. He knows how much I love sweets and how they make me plump, but he doesn't care. He squeezes and caresses every one of my extra inches of flesh. I am warm clay in his hands.

His tenor saxophone sits on the chair, in front of his music stand. There is a music book, and loose sheets of music stacked on the stand. On the small table next to the chair, there is a machine that clicks, helping Jimmie keep time with the music.

Peeking over at Jimmie to make sure he's still asleep, I lift the saxophone's strap over my body, positioning it between my breasts. It feels heavy and cold against my skin. I hold the mouthpiece to my lips and pretend, wishing I'd learned to play an instrument.

I examine the instrument and press the buttons, dancing and swaying like Jimmie does when he's at Connie's Inn on the stage.

But I guess I'm swaying a bit too much, because I bump the music stand by accident and all the music falls to the floor. I glance over at Jimmie, hoping he hasn't awakened. He hasn't, so I lift the instrument over my head and gently set it on the chair, making sure not to bump the mouthpiece and crack the wooden reed.

Then, I kneel to gather the sheets of music to place them back on the stand. From between the pages of the music book, a postcard and photograph tumble out.

The postcard is a photo of Jubilee Hall, and on the back there's a note scrawled.

Happy graduation, Jimmie.
Fly high and reach your dreams.

—CRT

Those initials. Chrystal Rose Tulli.

But the photograph is like a punch to my gut. It's Jimmie and Chrystal, in the same pose that we took at the Valentine's Day picnic one year. Jimmie holds an umbrella, and she clutches his arm, gazing up at him—as if they're a couple. I don't know if it's meant to poke fun at our photo, or if it is truly a romantic pose. Either way, it makes my stomach lurch and my head spin.

The picture falls from my hands and floats to the floor as I let out a bloodcurdling scream. Jimmie immediately jumps out of bed in only his underwear, but he rushes to me just as I start to swoon.

"Darling, what's wrong?" Jimmie asks with what seems like true concern on his face.

He guides me into the chair and kneels beside me, rubbing my back the way he always does when trying to calm me down. I cannot form words yet, so I point to the photograph on the floor. Jimmie looks at the photo, and then back at me. The panic in his eyes proves his guilt.

"That is not what you think it is," he says.

"What do I think, Jimmie?" I ask, finding my words. "Are you reading my mind?"

"No, but it's Chrystal—"

"Yes. It is you and Chrystal, posed like a couple." My voice rises, and I don't care who can hear us in other rooms or in the hall. "When you claim to love only me!"

"Claim? Yolande. The past five years of my life I have been consumed with my love for you."

"But not consumed enough to stay away from the girl who hates me and would have you for herself if she could."

"She can't," Jimmie says, taking my left hand that would be wearing his engagement ring if I'd accepted it. "You are who I love, and who I plan to spend the rest of my life with."

"But what were you doing the entire year with her? Did John

sneak her into the Andrew Jackson Hotel for you? She's grinning hard in the photograph. Did you touch her the way you touched me?"

Jimmie drops my hand and stands, his concern turning to anger. Fine. I don't care about him being indignant when I have proof of his treachery in photographic form.

"I have never betrayed you, Yolande. Even when you weren't true."

Now my fury drives me, holds me up and keeps me from fainting at the stress of this. He always goes back to George Cuffee. Always. He's never let that go.

"Is this revenge for what you think happened with George?"

"What I *think* happened? The man wanted to marry you, Yolande. Am I to believe that it was only your place in society that he wanted? Only favor with your papa? Let's not start talking about who was touching who, because I know what you like to do."

"Are you calling me a whore?"

"No, Yolande."

My blood simmers from rage. I cannot believe this. I may have allowed a chaste kiss on the cheek and he held my hand from time to time, but George was a gentleman. He wouldn't have tried anything, and I wouldn't have let him.

"You are the one I love, Yolande." Jimmie comes close again and runs his fingers down my spine. I close my eyes and ignore the tingling. "I offered you an engagement ring, not her. You refused it."

"So, I was the champion then?" My voice is quiet now and unsure.

"What do you mean? There was never a competition."

"There must've been a contest of which I was unaware. It's the only way I can explain how the man who says he loves me could be taking a couple's photograph with someone who hates me."

"You're not innocent in the conflict. You hate her too!"

"Which is exactly why my boyfriend shouldn't be on outings with her."

"Only while my future wife is being photographed for the *Inter-*

State Tattler on *her* outings. How many potential sons-in-law have you been photographed with?"

I am quite tired of having my loyalty questioned by Jimmie. I know that he loves me, and I love him too, but it means nothing if he cannot find a way to trust me. Will wearing a ring magically make me more trustworthy? I should think not.

"I'm going home, Jimmie."

"And then what?"

"I don't know. I need to process how I feel about you and Chrystal, away from you."

"There is no me and Chrystal," Jimmie roars. "Stop saying that!"

"You saved the picture! And the postcard. They mean something to you."

Jimmie crosses his arms and tightens his jaw. He's breathing heavy like he's just run a race and lost. My stomach lurches looking at him, thinking this could be the end.

"I'm done chasing you," he says. "I came all the way here, with no money, living in a tiny room at the Y, because I love you."

I start tearing around the hotel room, pulling on my clothing and gathering my things into my arms.

"I might not be waiting for you the next time you change your mind," he threatens.

"I'm sure you'll find someone else to keep you company."

Tears escape my eyes and trickle slowly down my face. I feel so foolish. But strangely enough I understand now how maddening it must have been for Jimmie to wonder what had happened with me and George. Because I am infuriated at the thought of Chrystal's lips on Jimmie's, and her lying in his arms.

I don't mind sharing Jimmie with Harlem, but I damn sure am not sharing him with Chrystal Tulli.

Chapter Forty-Nine

August 1925
Harlem, New York

*W*e *regret to inform you . . .*

Any letter that starts with these words comes to steal a wish, and this one is no different. I am being told there are no available teacher positions anywhere in Harlem, but they will keep my information for future openings.

My stellar recommendations, Papa's influence, even my sorority ties were not enough to convince a school board to hire the daughter of an agitator. Especially when my college grades were mediocre. Other candidates surely shined brighter.

Or perhaps no one wanted to hire Hospital Bed Yolande, since every one of my illnesses makes the *Amsterdam News*. Maybe they thought I'd be more trouble than I'm worth.

Besides, why should a princess of Harlem work anyway? Surely, they expect that my wealthy papa will keep me in furs and pretty dresses until some dashing gentleman sweeps me off my feet and down the aisle to the promised land of holy matrimony.

No one sees that Papa's funds dwindle from time to time when his book royalties and speaking engagements go from feast to famine. No one has to hear his complaints about how he needs money to keep up with the expectations *he* created with his larger-than-life persona. Heaven forbid I wear the same dress at two social engagements in a month. Folks might start to think Dr. Du Bois's wealth isn't secure.

If I had any tears left, I'd weep. But I've spent them all on another stolen wish.

I fold the letter and put it back in the envelope, and then I set the offensive thing on the dining table.

Papa emerges from his study with a cloud of cigarette smoke following behind him. He's reading a letter on his way to the kitchen but pauses when he sees me sitting at the table.

"Has today's mail come?" he asks.

I nod.

"Did I receive anything?"

My eyelids flutter shut as I shake my head. I am afraid to say anything. If I open my mouth, I may cry to heaven and scream until my throat is raw and sore. Silence is best for now.

"Well, what came then?" Now Papa sounds annoyed with me, but what do I care? What other wishes do I have for him to trample upon?

I point at the letter, and Papa snatches it right up. He quickly reads it then sighs.

"Yes, I was informed you wouldn't be hired," Papa says wearily.

My eyes begin to twitch nervously. Why would someone inform him before I knew?

"You should've accepted Felton's proposal," Papa says, with a surprising amount of compassion in his tone. "This wouldn't be a concern if you had."

"I don't love him," I say, finding a hoarse and wounded version of my voice. "And I don't want to live in Texas or Louisiana."

"None of that matters when it comes to marriage." Papa sits next to me and when he puts the letter down it slides across the shiny waxed wood, coming to a complete stop in front of me, almost daring me to hurl it into the fireplace.

"What I feel doesn't matter?" I ask Papa. "Love doesn't matter?"

"Marriage is a necessity, as is family. Having offspring, raising them well, helping them discover their gifts so that they may be a credit to their race. These things matter."

"Are they the only things that matter?"

"No, the movement matters. Lifting our people out of oppression is the thing that drives me," Papa explains. "It is my life's work."

"I want to teach children who may never get to a university," I say, feeling surer of myself. "I want to create my life's work as well."

"You're seeking a teaching career instead of marriage to an impressive man. You could help with the movement and get married. Your love and consideration of a brilliant man like Felton *is* life's work. Do you think your mother contributes nothing? Do you think her life means nothing?"

I have interrogated these thoughts and ideas within myself. I see and appreciate what Mama does in support of Papa and in raising me. But it is not wrong to want more.

"Mama's life is the one she chose. Can I not choose differently? Miss Fauset—"

Papa's hand goes wearily to his forehead as he shakes his head and sighs again. "I should not have allowed her to influence you so much. Miss Fauset's thoughts on marriage are unconventional, but she cannot even take a definite stand on the subject. The characters in her books can't even decide."

"It's not just Miss Fauset. My soror, Frances Gunner, is an educator," I object. "Women can do something besides marry and have offspring, Papa."

"Frances Gunner is almost thirty," Papa scoffs. "She may never marry. Is that what you want?"

I stare at Papa, unfazed and unblinking. Disparaging the women I hold in high regard is not helping his case at all.

"Very well, then. My friend has offered you a position at Dunbar High School in Baltimore," Papa says. "It is with the colored-only part of their district. You know how I feel about the color line, but it is heavily enforced there."

Baltimore. Away from here for a while. Away from Jimmie. I don't want to see him all over town. I don't want him trying to convince me that the photo with Chrystal was nothing. It was something. But I also don't want to see him in Harlem with another woman. I could not survive that.

"Splendid. Let them know I accept."

"The pay is only eleven hundred dollars a year, but that should be enough for you to get home a few times a year and to afford your lodging."

"What else do you think I might need?"

Papa's eyebrows furrow. "Yolande, you are old enough to understand that my finances are not currently as abundant as they have been in the past."

Yes, I've noticed that Mama's travel has become more infrequent, and that Papa's new business ideas have come at a near fever pitch and have not always been successful. I did not think we were in trouble, just that the coffers needed replenishing. But if Papa admits that money is an issue, his finances are surely worse than I can imagine.

"Papa, is this the real reason you want me to marry Felton?"

Papa shakes his head. "I want grandchildren, and your health has never been hearty. The older you get, the more I worry about your ability to have children."

"But there is more?"

"Yes," Papa admits. "A husband taking on the financial burden of your needs would be a help to me and to your mother."

"I do not mean to be a burden, Papa," I protest.

"I know you love Jimmie, but I do not want to be left caring for both of you when his musical career fizzles."

The photo of Jimmie and Chrystal flashes before my mind, but so do Jimmie's apologies. My feelings about him are a confusing mess, so it is easy to accept Papa's assessment now.

"I suppose that means summer at the Sorbonne is out of the question."

Papa gives me a sad smile. "Perhaps you could plan for next summer and Felton could come along. My finances should be recovered enough that I would be able to help."

There must be another solution to our family's financial woes other than marrying me off to the most attractive and wealthy option. It feels like enslavement all prettied up with a French bow on top.

"I will save money and not ask for things I don't need." I say this not truly knowing what that means. I *need* everything I ask for.

"We can start with you surviving without an allowance. You'll earn a teacher's salary that will cover your rent and other pittances. For major purchases like clothing and medical bills, I will be there to assist."

"All right."

"But, Yolande, your teaching career must be a temporary venture." Papa does not sound furious like he usually does when I don't immediately agree to his terms, just direct. "If not Felton, then you should find another suitable husband soon. Childbearing is best accomplished by young women."

"Yes, Papa."

Papa squeezes my hand lovingly. "I am sharing these things because you are old enough now. I am proud of what you've accomplished in your education and your desire to impact the movement. But you must understand the obligations of adulthood."

As if the burden of Papa's legacy wasn't already heavy enough to carry, now I must also be concerned with the family's financial status and well-being. Baltimore feels like an escape . . . or at least delaying the inevitable. Perhaps with time away this horrible fog of uncertainty will lift, and my choices will become clear.

Hopefully when I must fulfill the obligations Papa speaks about, it will be with a man who makes my heart sing like Jimmie does.

Maybe I'll find him in Baltimore.

PART IV

Chapter Fifty

May 1926
Baltimore, Maryland

To my surprise, the guiding light in the fog of my harrowing first year as a high school teacher in Baltimore was my rock-solid friendship with Countee. His letters, his poetry, and his sporadic visits kept me tethered to sanity.

It is not the children making me feel undone. It is the lack of freedom caused by my sudden poverty. My salary is eleven hundred a year, divided into the nine months I am here in Baltimore. With taxes and my rent deducted, I have less than twenty dollars a week for food, groceries, a trip to the beauty shop, and whatever else I might need. Thank goodness Papa has sent me periodical subscriptions, because I can't afford a book, a magazine, or even an ice cream cone. I have, on more than one occasion, simply run out of funds and had to borrow money from one of the other teachers who lives here. If Papa knew this his head would explode. The idea of his daughter out begging (because that's what he would consider it) would not sit well with him. He'd rather me haggle and postpone paying a debt before asking someone for a nickel.

The children are a joy. We're doing a spring revue with short skits, songs, dances, and poems. I had wanted to do Frances's play, but they told me they'd had enough of Harriet Tubman and Sojourner Truth at church. I was sure they weren't telling a lie about that, although one could never hear about those women too many times.

It was Countee who truly helped me to survive. I look forward to seeing him and hearing from him. Today he's coming to help me with the revue.

I tidy the boardinghouse's shared entertainment space, where we usually just sit around and talk after dinner, chatting about the school administration or giving advice about some girl's relationship woes. If anyone is entertaining a guest, the rest of us clear out after dinner to give the girl receiving company some privacy. Tonight, it's my turn.

Since Countee will be hungry after traveling, I've prepared sandwiches, cake slices, and cola. An indoor picnic for us, like the kind we used to have in Pleasantville.

A short while after I've set everything up, Miss Parker, the landlady, brings Countee into the room. His round, friendly face is a familiar and welcome sight.

"Hello there," he says. "You didn't have to go through all this fuss for me."

"Yes, I did. Please do come sit down."

Countee sets his bag down by the door and comes to join me on the sofa. Face as sweet and kind as ever, he doesn't look a day over sixteen, but he's twenty-four.

He quickly gobbles one cucumber sandwich and then another before gulping down the soda.

"Thank you for having these. I ate my train snacks so early in the ride that by the time I got here I was famished," he says.

I laugh at how bright his eyes are as he speaks. There really is a boyish innocence there that brings joy to every space Countee happens to be in. It just radiates from him.

"I figured as much. Have another."

"I will, but first, tell me how you've been. You sound so dismal in half your letters that I had to see about you."

"Oh, things aren't too bad, I suppose. The year will be over soon, and I'll have the summer."

"Yes. I wish you were going to Paris with us."

"Don't remind me," I say with a dejected pout.

I foolishly thought I'd be able to save enough to pay for part of the trip, dazzle Papa with how responsible I am, and he'd send me to the Sorbonne at the last minute. That did not happen. I haven't saved a dime, and I fear Papa's financial difficulties are worse than he's letting on.

Countee goes to Paris with Reverend Cullen every summer, and sometimes Harold travels with them. It is in vogue for the cultured and talented crowd to go to Europe in the summers, especially Paris. The men don't mind going even if they can only scrounge up enough funds for the ship fare. Langston once told us he voyaged to France and arrived with two dollars in his pocket and had to lodge in a room with no heat in the dead of winter. He claims he would've starved to death if it hadn't been for a dancer he gave a place to sleep. She shared her food, and he shared his room.

I am not up for that kind of adventure. I need a comfortable bed with a reliable dinner. So, I will not be traveling over the ocean this summer.

"I'll be trolling the streets of Harlem when I come home," I add glumly. "I don't even know if I'll get to Great Barrington for a holiday."

"Well, since you'll be stuck at home, you'll be happy to know that your Jimmie has left the Harlem scene."

"He has?"

I don't know if I'm happy about that. I may be relieved that I don't have to revisit the angst of last summer, but I don't feel joy at learning he's gone.

"Yes. I heard he's gone back to Tennessee."

"Perhaps Harlem was too much for him." I try to sound like I don't care.

"Harlem has eaten a good many country boy alive," Countee agrees. "The parties, the women . . . although Jimmie was never seen with another woman on his arm."

"Why are you telling me this, Countee? I do not care who Jimmie is seen about town with."

Countee laughs. "You most certainly do. Your mind and body have moved on from him, but your heart has not."

"Who are you seen about town with Countee?" I ask, to change the subject. "Tell me about your exploits."

"I am waiting for you to come to your senses, Yolande. Can't you see I'm courting you?"

"The letters, poetry, and visits? This is courtship?" I tease him. "You're sneakily courting me?"

"I am. Have been since I met you in Pleasantville."

"Why, if you think my heart belongs to Jimmie?" I can't quite tell if he's serious.

Countee smiles. "Because, we humans have giant hearts, with the capacity for so much love. I only need a tiny piece of your heart to bring me joy. With him gone, there may be a sliver of your heart that's untended. I could clear away the thorns, water it, and love could bloom."

"That was lovely." I applaud.

Countee grins, but his eyes are sad. "And still you have not melted into a puddle. That should have worked."

"Has it worked on other women?" I ask, knowing of Countee's many loves.

"They all pale in comparison to you."

I kiss Countee's cheek, thinking he at least deserves some affection, even if it feels a bit sisterly.

"One day there will be passion when your lips touch me," Countee says ruefully. "Until then, I accept this sweet substitute."

"Or maybe I'll realize too late that I should have fallen for you sooner. Once Fiona accepts your marriage proposal."

"I hear you're closer to receiving a proposal than I am," Countee scoffs. "Dr. Du Bois has been calling Felton your fiancé."

"He has? Oh, my goodness. That is both old news and dreaming on his part."

"And Felton's?"

"Felton knows better. He made one romantic overture and told me it required me to move to Texas."

"Texas? Oh my." Countee's eyebrows shoot up.

"See? Can you blame me for saying no? Texas?"

Countee shakes his head. "No thank you."

I burst into laughter at Countee's disdain. He's even more offended than I am at the thought of being anywhere other than Harlem.

"Well, I really do wish you were going to Paris with us this summer. You, Harold, and I could paint Montmartre red."

"You and Harold don't need me to have fun."

"We don't, but I enjoy it when you're there. I always end up being a third wheel at some point. I'd like, for once, to be the one sneaking off to do raunchy things in dark corners."

I laugh. "I'm sure you do plenty of that."

"We've never done it. You and I." He stares at me.

"You're flirting with me? You are, aren't you?" I can't help but be surprised.

"Is it working?" Countee asks. "Would you mind if I kissed you?"

"I wouldn't mind."

I instantly regret granting this permission. The awkward, fumbling kiss that smashes into my lips is a waste of rule breaking (we're not allowed to kiss men on the lips under this roof). It isn't exciting. It doesn't make me feel weak in my knees. It surely doesn't make me feel like I'm in any danger of being ravished by Countee. Sadly, the secret place between my thighs is as dry as Mama's Sunday roast.

"That was nice," Countee says.

Was it? Who has he been kissing for him to think that was good? Or is he just trying to make me feel better?

Since I can't be sure, I smile as if I agree.

I wonder if what Countee says is true. Is there a sliver of my heart that he could water to make love grow? Or is attraction an instant thing? I've only ever had it hit me like a speeding locomotive train, so if there's another, slow burning kind, I have not yet known that experience.

But Countee's friendship is true, at least, and dear to me. I know there is a place in my heart for that.

Chapter Fifty-One

July 1927
Paris, France

We should get married."

I shake a scolding finger at Countee and laugh, because how can I truly be cross with him when we're having lunch at the most romantic little outdoor Parisian café? Especially while he has that wry grin on his face.

"Stop it, Countee. I can never take you seriously."

"Well, your papa must agree. He sent you to Paris this summer, didn't he?" Countee's eyes shine as he says this, as if he's in on some big secret. He isn't. Everyone in Harlem knows I'm here. It was in our favorite column of the *Inter-State Tattler*.

"He sent me to study art at the University of Grenoble. With Margaret no less."

This big adventure is Papa's apology, I think, for not being able to send me to Paris last summer when I wanted to study at Sorbonne, and his finances wouldn't support it. He created a grand itinerary for me and Margaret that started in Canada and took us to London, Paris, Grenoble, and then back to Paris, where we are now for our final two weeks.

It has been glorious, and probably is my last hurrah on Papa's dime. I will be twenty-seven, after all. Any future trip like this will be funded by a husband . . . if I ever have one.

"Yes, yes, your studies. I forgot about that," Countee says. "But who says I'm not serious about us?"

He thinks he's so fashionable with his little black beret tilted atop his head. Countee and Harold have a matching set, and we've traipsed all over Paris taking photographs of them looking like little brown Frenchmen.

"Umm . . . let me think . . . Fiona Braithwaite and Sydonia Byrd."

Countee shakes his head and sighs as if he was waiting for me to mention two of the countless girls he's pursued.

"Things never really launched with Sydonia, not for lack of trying," Countee explains. "And you must know about Fiona."

I'd heard about the canceled engagement. Margaret implied that there was something salacious about it, but then she always finds the most heinous gossip tidbits. I refuse to engage in such things.

"You seem to be as unlucky in love as I am."

"You don't know the half."

Now I'm curious. By anyone's measure, Countee should be a good catch. He's educated and, while not wealthy, he's certainly not poor. His name carries weight in Harlem, as does his father's. The only thing he lacks is the stunning good looks of his best friend, but often women are not concerned with that as much as men. Surely, he must be able to find someone to take him up on his offer of poetry-filled courtship.

"Then tell me. What do you think happens with them, Countee? What drives them away?"

"I am not sure with Sydonia, but Fiona accused me of being in love with someone else."

"That's simple to rectify. Tell her she's wrong."

"She's not wrong."

A heavy silence hangs between us. I should not have gone down this path. I don't want to hear the rest.

"Je t'aime, Yolande," Countee says as he takes my hand across the table and caresses it too intimately.

"Countee, you know you are my dear friend, and I love you as well, but we've never even been on a real date, just the two of us. How can we even think about marriage?"

"We're on a date now. We've had picnics, been dancing, and have had trips to the beach."

"No. This is two friends having lunch. And those were friend outings."

"So then let's go on one here, in Paris. No one to report back to your papa if things don't go well."

"Where will we go?" I ask, feeling like we've been all over Paris and seen about all there is to see.

"I know the perfect place. A little dive Langston told me about. I'll let it be a surprise."

"And no Harold? No Margaret?" I ask, wondering what Countee and I will do without the two of them. Harold is the bringer of all things fun, and with Margaret around, we never have to worry about a bottle of wine. Men are always sending things for us to eat and drink when she and I are together. Even when the boys are there, these men don't care. Margaret is too ripe a piece of fruit for them not to try their hand at getting her attention.

"No. Just the two of us. Like it was the first summer we met and enjoyed each other's company."

I narrow my eyes suspiciously. Although I know that Countee has been "courting" me in his mind for years, this feels different. More urgent. The stakes feel higher.

"How do I know you aren't just asking for my hand because you need Papa's recommendation for that Guggenheim Fellowship you keep talking about?"

Countee grins. "Because I've already asked him to do that, and he's agreed."

"I see."

Of course he would. Countee is almost as dear to Papa as I am. Another candidate for the son he wishes he had, or the son-in-law he's determined to gain.

"I just happen to think that I've been going about this search for a wife all wrong," Countee says. "So, this will be an experiment of sorts."

"Please enlighten me."

"I've been trying to woo these women with poetry and gifts. Soon I'll be out of sonnets and money."

This tickles me and draws out a laugh. "You'll never be out of words, Countee. Have you heard yourself?"

"That's true, but no one wants a poverty-stricken poet."

"Agreed, but poverty goes along with that line of work. Thank goodness you have your father who will leave you with an inheritance."

"See! You understand. That is why I am starting to think that it might be better to marry a dear friend who accepts and loves me as a person, not just as a potential suitor."

I wonder for a moment about my parents. Were they ever friends? Are they now? They are partners in some ways, but I wonder about friendship.

"There is something to be said for our connection," I concede.

Countee's friendship has gotten me through many tough times. Countee is also firmly a member of the Harlem elite. There would be no objections from anyone at our pairing.

"Dr. Du Bois would want us to try our hand at this, I believe," Countee says.

"What Papa wants is not important."

"Ce n'est pas vrai, Yolande. C'est très important."

"Oh non, monsieur. Parlez anglais s'il vous plaît."

"Well, it's not like you have any prospects . . . at the moment," Countee says, "not that you aren't worthy of an ocean of suitors."

"You don't have any prospects either, although you've sent poetry to half the eligible ladies in Harlem."

Countee shrugs and bites a hunk of cheese. "A man must use the thing that makes him attractive. Poetry verses are my peacock's feathers."

I descend into laughter, completely unable to hold it in. "I cannot take that sentence seriously with the word *cock* at the end of it."

"Yolande, stop for a moment. If we're going to take this any further, I must be transparent about something. Your papa did approach me with the idea of us marrying."

I knew it. Papa just cannot help himself.

"You wooed Papa," I say with a weary sigh. "Like every other man whom he's approved of."

This wounds Countee. He doesn't want to be counted with the others, I'm sure. "But am I not your dearest friend? What keeps it from being more?"

"Countee, you don't want me to answer that. I don't even know if I can."

"Well, Yolande Nina Du Bois, beautiful brown girl who stole my heart upon a hill, I absolutely want to know why you haven't been swept off your feet at the very thought of me."

"Oh, my goodness."

"Will you do me the honor . . ."

"You are insane."

"Of being my bride?"

I have imagined, I suppose, that a man might propose to me in Paris. But I thought that man would be playing the saxophone in a jazz club. Not sounding poetic while eating sausages and bread at a table in a café.

"You don't love me," I say even though I know this is a lie. Countee may love me as much as Jimmie did. It just *feels* different in a way I can't put my finger on.

"Lies. You don't love me, but I would drink your bathwater, Miss Du Bois."

"Is that love? Is it? It is disgusting. Ce n'est pas de l'amour."

"Oh! Je t'aime. We would make a great pair. We'd be in the *Inter-State Tattler* Society section every week."

I chuckle as I imagine this. "This is true. Can you imagine the wedding? Between your father's church and my father's movement friends there'll be hundreds of people there."

"I'm thinking of how stylish we'll all look. Me and Harold wearing sashes and Langston too."

"Won't you care what I'll have on?"

"I know what you'll be wearing. It'll be big, frilly, and untouched, good girl, virginal white."

I know good and well Countee doesn't think of me as untouched or virginal. He's teasing me again, and he proves it by winking at me. And I toss a hunk of cheese at him.

"Am I wrong?"

"No, you are not. I will certainly be wearing white and there will be frills, and I'll have at least eight bridesmaids."

"Your Delta Sigma Theta Sorority chapter sisters."

"Yes, except Margaret and Anna are Alpha Kappa Alpha Sorority."

"That's right," Countee says. "There will be plenty Alphas, Deltas, AKAs, and maybe an Omega or two as well. Are we planning a wedding, then?"

"No, not yet," I say. "You must still take me on this date, remember? Now I'm looking forward to my surprise."

"There are a lot of things about me that would surprise you, Yolande," Countee says with a flirtatious wink. "I am happy to show you all of them. One at a time."

Is this a raunchy version of Countee? I have never looked at him that way. Never felt my pulse quicken regarding him. Is it possible? Am I open to it?

"It feels like you and Papa have conspired against me," I admit. "I can never trust fully a man in league with him. Papa's only motive is heirs, and I am the only vessel for them. I wish my brother had lived. Then he could be the prince of the Talented Tenth and I could be free."

"What would you have done with that freedom?"

This question makes my heart heavy. The dark cloud of Papa's legacy hovered over me and Jimmie from the start. It tainted something pure. I can't be sure of it, but if not for Papa's legacy perhaps I would've believed in our wish the way Jimmie had from the very beginning. Maybe we'd be married right now, and I'd be drawing pictures of him playing his saxophone before he went out on the stage.

"It doesn't make sense to think on such things," I say sadly. "I am who I am, and Papa is who he is. You are Countee Cullen, Papa's co-conspirator."

Countee squeezes my hand again as if he understands the source of my sudden sadness. "Well, even though he has suggested many times that I ask you out on dates," he says, "I have hesitated to go along with his plans. I know you are your own woman. I have been friends with you long enough to understand that."

This is surprising, especially since he, by his own admission, has been wooing me for years.

"Why are you no longer hesitating, then?"

"I never thought you'd stay in Baltimore. I thought you'd find an excuse to go running back to Jimmie. But you didn't."

He doesn't know how many times I wanted to do just that. But the image in my head of that photograph, and the letters from friends who told me they had seen Jimmie and Chrystal on campus together after I graduated. Never the way we were, and never at the Andrew Jackson Hotel, but Chrystal certainly wasted no time pursuing him, and Jimmie *had* entertained her, as much as he liked to claim otherwise. Even if he was just passing the time until he came back to me, it was with *her*.

But I don't think I can ever rid myself completely of Jimmie. Our time has passed, but the mark is there for eternity.

I cannot, however, allow myself to go on this way. While I enjoy instructing my students, I am not getting any younger. I don't want to be labeled as Dr. Du Bois's spinster daughter, nor do I want a life of struggle. I like the idea of being a pillar in the community with Countee. He's already revered and celebrated, and with Papa pushing him into the spotlight, he will only shine brighter. This will be a fruitful union, and our friendship could become more. He, at least, is dedicated to that notion.

"I think I can be content as your wife," I say. "And Papa would love to somehow score a coup with your gift passed on to a child in his lineage."

"Our gifts together."

"Countee, you always said that I would fall for you when it was too late."

"C'est vrai."

"Ce n'est pas vrai," I respond, finally squeezing his hand back. "Je t'aime."

I do love Countee. The fire does not burn feverishly as it does for Jimmie, but it is a flame that comforts, like the one in a hearth. The fire between me and Jimmie consumes us until there is no logic or reason.

Perhaps it is time for me to accept that logic and reason are better for me than consuming passion.

Chapter Fifty-Two

July 1927
Paris, France

In our Paris apartment, Margaret only partially pays attention to my scurrying about trying to get ready for my official date with Countee. It really was a coup that one of Miss Fauset's friends was out of the country and allowed us to stay here for free. We overspent at the beginning of the summer on sightseeing tours in Grenoble, exactly what Papa instructed me not to do, since I was on a strict budget of four hundred dollars for the entire summer. But we do have beautiful photos to show for it, so there is at least that. Margaret's parents gave her more money to spend than I had, so she was not worried, but I dreaded the idea of writing home to Papa for more funds. Of course, I was going to if I needed to. I wasn't going to be poor in Paris.

I hold up a black beaded gown on its hanger for Margaret to see. I need her to help me decide what to wear. She is indifferent to my dress selections and the date, so she glances up, gives a tight headshake, and returns to the book she's reading.

"Margaret, I need you to pay attention. I can't decide between this one and the yellow one."

"Are you trying to look like a vixen or are you going to high tea? The yellow reminds me of a tea party."

"You would know about tea parties, wouldn't you?" I chuckle at my own joke at the expense of Margaret and her Alpha Kappa Alpha Sorority sisters. Of course, they do a great deal more than drink tea, so I'm only teasing.

"Oh, yes, that's right," Margaret says. "Wear something crimson. Isn't that supposed to stand for courage with you Deltas? You'll need courage to enter a courtship with Harold Jackman's best friend."

"You like Countee. Stop it. We've had a lovely time."

Margaret closes her book and sighs. "Yes, we friends have gotten on famously these two weeks. And I am happy to have them here, since their French is so much better than ours."

"I'm afraid Papa's grand idea to finally make me fluent in the language has failed."

I could barely understand the French instructor at the University of Grenoble, where Papa had arranged for me and Margaret to take classes for a month. My drawing class went well, though, and was quite enjoyable, but I was so happy for that month to be over so that we could come to this little apartment in Paris.

"Were we supposed to be taking those classes seriously?" Margaret asks. "I thought it was merely a way to secure affordable room and board during our summer adventures. That's what my father told me."

"He did?"

"Yes, he says your papa is very skilled at getting things for free or at a discount. He throws his name around to see what his influence will get."

My jaw drops, but then I can only laugh. I didn't realize people knew these things about Papa. I thought it was a secret that sometimes he relies on his notoriety when it comes to acquiring things outside of his means. I'm shocked that Mr. Welmon knows. I wonder who else does.

"But we've got lovely photos of us in the mountains. I can't wait to get home and put them in my scrapbook."

"We have not and will not photograph our shenanigans with Countee and Harold," Margaret says. "There needs to be no evidence for the Harlem biddies."

There is no Prohibition here. Alcohol and good times flow freely. In the two weeks we've been staying near them, we have had shenanigans that should never become exposed.

"We hope there's no evidence. Countee loves to write everyone about everything," I say. "He's probably told Langston and Miss Fauset all the things we've been up to."

"And his father too."

"Oh, my goodness! Yes, the good Reverend Cullen is Countee's other best friend. Could you imagine me telling Papa about us being drunk from French whiskey and walking the streets arm in arm?"

"No," Margaret laughs. "His mustache would curl even tighter, and his head might just explode. But Countee's probably written a poem about it. He's called it 'Brown Girls in Paris.'"

I laugh so hard my stomach hurts. When Countee gets it in his mind to write a poem, you have no choice about being the subject.

"Please explain again why you are agreeing to court him," Margaret says. "I haven't heard that Felton is engaged yet. He's handsome, with money!"

"Felton wanted me to move to Texas and have a bunch of babies. Can you imagine me living in the south?"

Margaret scrunches her nose and shakes her head. Everyone can see how distasteful that idea is—except Felton. "So far away from your parents? No, I can't imagine that. You're their only daughter."

"And he was never going to budge on that, so I didn't take him seriously."

"Well, there are other options besides Countee. In all of Harlem, there must be a better beau."

How can I explain that there is no one who can hold a candle to Jimmie? So, why not Countee?

"There is no one else I'm interested in, and I'm almost thirty, Margaret. Soon, I'll look up and I'll be just like Miss Fauset."

"But don't you admire her?"

"Yes, but she just seems lonely. She has only her work, and the writers she mentors. Where is her passion? It's like she isn't even a woman."

Margaret shakes her head. "Yolande, you can never make your mind up on anything. You ran away from Jimmie, trying to be like that character in Miss Fauset's book."

"Joanna. And that's not the reason I ran from Jimmie. Besides, if you'd finished the book, you'd know Joanna married in the end."

"Well, now you're casting your pearls before swine. Countee might be one of the best poets in Harlem, but he and Harold may have too much fun here in Paris *and* in Harlem." Margaret lifts her eyebrows and purses her lips like she knows more than she's saying. "That's probably why Fiona called off their engagement."

I was wondering when she was going to bring this up. She loves to refer to things she's heard about Harold and extend those things to Countee. Meanwhile, none of these things have been proven, and she's never seen anything with her own eyes.

"We've been with Countee and Harold here in Paris, and what have you seen?" I ask.

"Dancing, partying, drinking of whiskey," Margaret says. "But of course they aren't going to allow *us* to see them with their pants around their ankles."

"Margaret!"

"I'm just saying, I wouldn't pick up what Fiona cast off."

"That's fine because you aren't courting him. I am."

"All right, then, wear the black dress," Margaret says, throwing her hands into the air dismissively. "It's your funeral. Might as well get the mourning started."

I roll my eyes at Margaret and hang the black dress back in the closet. I'll wear the sparkly yellow one.

It feels perfect for the occasion. Bright, like our future.

* * *

"WE'RE HERE," COUNTEE says. "Le Grand Duc. The hippest place in Montmartre."

My gaze travels around the tiny place, only needing a few moments to take it all in. There are folk crammed onto the little dance floor. The dancing spills over to the handful of tables where black and tan enjoy heaping plates of chicken and dumplings and smothered pork chops that smell amazing. Black men with white women. Black women with white men. Everyone laughing and free in a way we don't have back home, not even in Harlem.

But the music is jazz, and it reminds me of Jimmie.

A pretty, high-yellow woman with a head full of shocking red hair rushes over to us, a wide and brimming smile on her face.

"Countee!" she squeals as she wraps him in the warmest of embraces. "Why didn't you tell me you were coming? I would have saved a table for you."

"Brick, my dear, it was a surprise," Countee says. "Have you met Yolande Du Bois?"

The woman squints to get a better look at me, then she smiles and nearly knocks me off my feet with her hug. She smells divine, like sweet perfume and liberty.

"We've never had the pleasure of meeting," Brick says, "but any friend of Countee's is a friend of mine."

"She's a friend of Langston's too," Countee adds.

Brick throws her head back and laughs. Her joy is the catching kind, and it gets all over me. She must be the life of every party with a laugh like that.

"Well, this is double the honor then," Brick says. "My name's Ada Smith, but everybody calls me Bricktop on account of my red hair."

"It's a pleasure, Miss Bricktop," I say with a giggle, slowly letting myself enjoy this night.

"Come on, there's a table in back. I'll have the kitchen get you something good to eat."

"While we're waiting on the food, I sure would like to stomp," Countee says. "Will you sing us something we can dance to?"

"Absolument!"

Miss Bricktop says something to the band, and they start playing a lively number. Countee starts bouncing his shoulders before the song can even get going good.

"Can you do the Lindy Hop?" Countee asks over the loud drums.

"I can do the Charleston. What is the Lindy Hop?"

"It's new. Watch me!"

Countee spreads his legs and starts stomping and swinging his arms in time to the music.

"We're playing this song for my friend Mr. Countee Cullen, y'all," Bricktop says from her tiny stage in front of the band. Her booming voice carries over the music and fills the place. "He's a poet from Harlem, so he's good with words, but baby, I heard from a little birdie that he also likes to swing!"

The band kicks up and so does Countee. I just bounce from side to side trying to keep up.

"My name is Bricktop, I was born in the lion's den," Bricktop belts. "And my nightly occupation is stealing other women's men!"

The laughter bubbles out of me, from the song to Countee's feverish dancing.

"Come on," Countee says, taking my hand. "Let's swing!"

I copy Countee's feet and swing my free arm. He leans back and I do too, stomping, swinging, and laughing. We move in a circle and other dancers start to cheer us on. We go and go until the song is through and we're breathless.

"Everybody clap for my Harlem friends," Bricktop says as the music dies. "They got two left feet, but they sure are pretty!"

I laugh until my sides hurt as Countee leads me to a table in the back. We pass a beautiful woman who looks familiar, sitting alone at a table. I want to wave because I'm sure I've seen her before, but it seems like everybody here is from Harlem or has been there. Even the white people.

We squeeze into the tiny space, side by side, with very little room to move. Our bodies touch, arms and thighs, and I wait to see if I'll start to tingle. Am I thinking about it too much and trying to force things? It would help if my thoughts didn't keep drifting back to Jimmie. But it's the jazz that keeps taking me there.

The food comes out and from the very first bite, I know someone from down south back home put these recipes together. I haven't tasted chicken this good since we got off the ship in Europe.

"This is delicious, Countee! Why are you just bringing me here? We must come back with Harold and Margaret."

"If I had known it would make you this giddy, I would have brought you the first night and every night until it's time to go home."

"Am I giddy?"

"You are. Eyes shining and skin sparkling. Montmartre looks good on you."

"We should stay."

Countee laughs and the beautiful woman at the other table winks at us. I don't think Countee sees on account of his laughing, but I wink back. She's wearing a black and gold flapper gown, and her short haircut is in that hip new wave style that looks glued down to the head with some sort of gel. It doesn't move or puff out when a girl dances, and it holds up all night. She's got so much makeup on— lipstick, rouge, and eye paint—that I wonder how she looks under it all. Then she sticks out her tongue and crosses her eyes, and I laugh.

"Is that Josephine Baker?" I whisper to Countee. He nods and waves in her direction.

"Oh yes. She and Bricktop are close friends."

"You just know everyone and everything, don't you?"

"I suppose. It's Harold and Langston really. I ride their society coattails."

"I disagree. You ride no one's coattails. If I am a princess of Harlem, you, my dear Countee, are a prince."

"It takes royalty to know royalty I suppose."

Then he kisses me. I jump from the unexpected but not unwelcome contact.

"I'm sorry," I say, trying not to laugh. "I wasn't ready. Try again."

This time he tilts my chin and plants a warm kiss on my lips. It's pleasant, I suppose, but nothing shivers or trembles.

I'd like to shiver and tremble.

I pull Countee closer and return his kiss. Deeper, with tongue, and a great deal of longing. It's been a long time since I had a man's touch. And I'm in Paris, where there are no biddies of Harlem to run back to Papa.

This is an invitation.

"Yolande, my love," Countee says breathlessly as we separate. "Is it suddenly too warm in here?"

"Yes, but we're wearing too many clothes now. We should go back to your apartment and take some of them off."

The shock on Countee's face makes him look so young. Like a little boy caught swiping cookies before dinner.

"Shouldn't we save that very special moment for our wedding night, ma chère?" he asks, looking away and blushing.

"Well, make me feel like a proper whore, why don't you!" I shove Countee playfully.

"No, no, no, my love. I just want everything to be perfect with you. I've been dreaming of you, of us, since I saw you drawing on that porch in Pleasantville," Countee says, planting sweet kisses on my cheeks and fingers and forehead. "I don't want anything to spoil that dream, you see."

"All right, then. The wedding night," I concede. "But kiss me again, so I can dream too. Of what's to come."

Countee kisses me again, and I concentrate, waiting to feel a spark. There was a small something peeking out the corner. A tickle of desire. Hopefully, Countee can coax it out and make it grow into a flame. It's going to take more than these butterfly kisses and sonnets, though, that's for sure.

Perhaps, these things take time.

Chapter Fifty-Three

September 1927
Harlem, New York

Although I am weary from our voyage back from Europe and I really do feel this could wait a few days, Countee is eager to tell Papa the news of our engagement. Perhaps he thought once I got home and breathed the Harlem air, I'd gather my wits and tell him to find another muse for his sonnets. But he was safe. The Harlem breeze held no such magic. In fact, the humid September weather just reminded me it was nearly time to begin the second year of my teaching contract in Baltimore and my pauper's life there.

Countee is coming over for an impromptu tea. Since we only got back home yesterday, I am groggy and tired. It's the middle of the day and I'd like to be winding down for bed.

I plop down on the couch and let Mama answer the door when he arrives. When they come into the living room, I perk up at Countee in his perfectly pressed suit and vest. He looks ready to go to Sunday morning service.

Mama motions for Countee to have a seat next to Papa. But Countee smiles. "Is it all right if I sit next to Yolande?"

Papa, who was only curious before, now scoots to the edge of the couch, his eyes glistening with excitement.

"Yes, Countee, that'll be all right," Mama says and then takes the seat next to Papa while Countee sits next to me.

"Do you two have news for us?" Papa asks. "A courtship?"

"Will," Mama chides. "Give him a chance to get it out."

"I gather you enjoyed your time in Paris," Papa continues, ignoring Mama in a way that lightly scolds her for trying to rebuke him.

"Dr. Du Bois," Countee says in a confident-sounding, grown-up voice, "as you know, Yolande and I have shared a dear, close friendship for many years. Well, we have decided to commune with each other in cherished friendship and love until death do us part. In holy matrimony. If we might have your permission and blessing?"

I didn't know so many words were required to tell Papa we're getting married, but it sounds so eloquent when he says it this way, I'm glad for the extra words.

"I don't think you need my permission," Papa says with a hearty laugh. "You're of age."

I can't help the loud choking sound that escapes me. Papa is hilarious for that bit. Truly. But Countee stares at me uncomfortably until I calm down.

"Sorry. There was something caught in my throat."

I glance at Countee from the corner of my eye and he's struggling to maintain his composure. Mama too. She covers her mouth to keep from laughing. But Papa misses the joke entirely. Surely, he must know that even if we don't need his permission, we sure desire it, else we suffer for not having it later.

"But you certainly have my blessing," Papa says. "I will craft engagement notices for the *Amsterdam News* and the *Baltimore Afro-American*."

"Wait, Papa!" I hold up a hand. "I'd like to tell our friends first. I don't want them to find out from the newspaper."

Papa considers this and then claps. "I know! We'll have a welcome home dinner. Right here. For you and Margaret. And you can announce your engagement there. It will be a surprise."

"What do you think, Countee?" Is this a first request of my fiancé? Oh, it feels strange thinking of Countee this way. He will soon be my husband, and that feels even more foreign.

Countee wraps his arm around me, pulls me close, and kisses my forehead. It leaves a moist spot. I have the sudden, visceral urge to wipe it away, but I force a smile instead.

"I think that sounds wonderful, Papa Du Bois. Is it all right if I call you that?"

"Why, certainly," Papa says lovingly.

Oh, he is completely smitten. Countee had already won him over, but I am quite certain that Papa just fell in love.

* * *

I DON'T KNOW if I can recall a time when Papa was ever this thrilled. I thought this dinner party was for me and Margaret, but it feels like Papa's coming-out soirée.

"Yolande, look at this!" Papa comes racing toward me from his office waving a sheet of paper from his typewriter. "Tell me what you think."

Papa is asking for my opinion on something? It might just be the end of the world. At the top of the sheet of paper it says *Bill of Fare*.

I look up curiously at Papa as he sits next to me on the sofa. "Is this for the party?"

"Yes. Isn't it funny?"

I suppose *Cocktails: As harmless as the hostesses* might be construed as funny by someone. Someone old. Not me. But Papa is so pleased with himself that I refuse to tell him I'm not all that amused.

"Papa, it's so funny. Fried chicken à la Marguerite? Margaret doesn't know the difference between frying and boiling, so I hope Mama is helping."

"Of course she is, but I expect you and Margaret to be in the kitchen. It is your party after all."

I raise my eyebrows until I'm sure they're half off my face. "Papa, it's *your* party."

"This party is to celebrate what I'm sure is to be a successful union between you and Countee."

"I'm going back to Baltimore in a couple weeks to start the new term, so we won't get to spend very much time together."

"That's fine. Countee and I will start the plans for the wedding."

He says that like it's the most normal thing ever for the bride not to be included in her own wedding planning.

"Papa, don't you think I'd like to be a part of that as well?"

"Of course, but since we'll be here together, we can oversee some of the more mundane things you won't care about, like the venue, guest list, invitations, catering, announcements, and the like."

"Ummmm, I'd like to be involved in all those things," I say with a chuckle.

"Ah, well, I'll be sure to include you then," Papa concedes, although I don't know if I believe him.

"Do you think Margaret is interested in Countee's friend Harold?" Papa asks, changing the subject. "I can assist if she'd like me to put in a word for her."

I laugh out loud. "Papa . . . no."

"I don't see why not. A helping hand is a good thing. I want the best for you young people. Those among us who are gifted have a responsibility to our race to produce heirs."

Except that Harold and Margaret can't stand the sight of each other, and Margaret doesn't think Harold is interested in producing heirs or even being with women.

"Yes, I know. You've told me this before."

"Well, it bears another telling. Sometimes I don't think you're listening to me. The years you spent on that musician were priceless. Once time is wasted it cannot be recovered."

How did this turn into a speech? I thought this was a fun conversation where Papa was sharing the silly bill of fare he made for the party. Now, I'm being lectured about my responsibility to the colored race.

And I hate it when Papa mentions Jimmie, even if he doesn't say his name. It's like calling forth a ghost. Nothing good can come of it.

* * *

SINCE THIS IS our engagement party, even though no one knows except the four of us, Papa is dressed for the occasion. We couldn't leave Reverend and Mrs. Cullen out, even though Mama objected. She still hasn't forgiven Mrs. Cullen for treating us poorly all those years ago in Pleasantville.

Countee and I both agreed to surprise Harold and Margaret with the engagement. We insist it's just because we want to see their reactions at the same time. But I think we're both secretly hoping that they won't talk us out of it.

Not that I don't want to marry Countee. While I may not burn for him the way I do Jimmie, the love we feel for each other is familiar and safe.

These are the things I've been telling myself. Again and again. To convince myself that this isn't the silliest idea ever.

Margaret gets here early, since we're supposed to be preparing this dinner with Mama. But she doesn't look like she plans to cook anything. She's already wearing her dress and red lipstick.

Mama steps out of the kitchen and shakes her head. "Do you need an apron, Margaret?"

"We were really cooking? I thought it was part of Dr. Du Bois's joke. I didn't think I was actually going to fry chicken. My mother has a lady for that."

"A lady to fry chicken?" Mama seems appalled by this, but I wish we could hire the cook they use. Her pork chops are mouthwatering.

"Yes, Mrs. Du Bois. My mother is not a particularly good cook. We'd all be skin and bones if we had to eat her food."

"I see," Mama says. "Well, you might as well sit down in the living room. Yolande can help me. We wouldn't want you to ruin your dress."

"Thank you, Mrs. Du Bois. I will make it up to you in some way. I promise."

Mama doesn't look like she's going to wait too long for Margaret to make good on this.

I follow Mama into the kitchen where most everything is already half-prepared or almost done. The only thing left is frying the chicken so that it can be hot when our guests arrive in an hour or so.

"Yolande, reach up and crack the window. I don't want my entire apartment to smell like a greasy spoon. Why would your papa choose fried chicken for a dinner party?"

"It's his favorite, and your fried chicken is quite tasty."

"Just like a man. Because it's *his* favorite, he plows forward not asking or caring what all goes into its preparation."

Mama has been more vocal with her complaints about Papa since I told her I was marrying Countee. I don't know if this is an initiation into the sisterhood of wives, or if she wants to scare me half to death.

"I think Countee would much prefer to eat at restaurants every night. He's not much of a homebody at all."

"Well, that can get quite expensive. His mother, I'm sure, prepares his meals some nights of the week."

"The nights we don't dine out, I'll make us sandwiches. We can have picnics in our dining room."

Mama chuckles. "Picnics? Is that something you like to do together?"

"Yes, that's our favorite thing. The first summer we met, Countee says he tried to woo me with picnics."

"I see." Mama rinses and dries her hands, then drops the pre-seasoned and pre-floured chicken into the hot grease with a long pair of tongs. A cloud of fragrant smoke rises from the skillet. "I wondered if you two had anything at all in common."

"Mama. Countee and I have been the best of friends for years. We have lots of things in common."

"But do you love him?" Mama's eyes search my face.

"Of course, I care for him."

"Do you love him like you loved your Jimmie?"

I swallow a hard lump in my throat. "Why would you bring him up tonight? I've moved on from him."

"I know. And I am aware of your reasons. I just want you to be sure before you make this commitment to Countee."

"Mama, you know I'm hardly ever sure of anything."

She narrows her eyes at me. "Listen here. Now is the time for womanhood. These times of you getting sick at the first sign of scrutiny are over. You will throw that indecision away and have regard for others' feelings."

"Mama, where is this coming from?" I'm startled to hear her tone.

"You don't know how broken that boy was when he came here looking for you."

"What boy? Jimmie?"

"Yes. After you gave him only what he should've received on your wedding night and had his nose wide open, you toyed with his feelings."

"He took a photo—"

"I already know your flimsy reason, Yolande."

Flimsy?

"Even if he'd had a dalliance or two with some girl on campus. He came to his senses and chose correctly."

Jimmie must have come looking for me. He'd come to beg for my forgiveness and hadn't wanted it to be over. And she'd said nothing.

"Mama, why are you only telling me this now?" Not that it would have changed my decision. I'm just shocked that she's been holding all this back.

"Because I don't want you to trifle with *this* boy's heart. Jimmie is not part of Harlem society, but Countee is. His mother will never let us hear the end of it if this romance unravels."

Oh, I see. This is about her place in Harlem society. But if anything, I have more to lose there than she does. I am the one on the social scene. If things go sour between me and Countee, I'll have to move to another city for good.

"Well, I'm hoping that Miss Fauset helps me form a tighter bond with Mrs. Cullen. I am surprised Papa didn't add Miss Fauset to the guest list for this party."

"I am not," Mama says shortly, and turns back to the frying pan.

* * *

DINNER WENT SWIMMINGLY, mostly because Mama cooked her best dishes and Margaret and I stayed out of her way. We entertained the guests as they arrived with the hors d'oeuvres and Prohibition-safe cocktails.

Now with bellies full of fried chicken that needs to settle before we have dessert, we all gather in the living room. Papa has borrowed chairs from a neighbor so that we can all sit comfortably.

Reverend and Mrs. Cullen are the only ones who look like they'd rather be anywhere but here. Mrs. Cullen's had a sour expression on her face since she walked in the door, and I saw her grimace after taking one bite of Mama's fried chicken. Reverend Cullen just looks stressed, like he's in a hurry all the time, but at least he has kind eyes.

Margaret and Charles are close these days. Since we got back from Europe, they've been inseparable. She snuggles next to him on the loveseat, and since we're all friends he feels free to throw his arm around her shoulder.

"Before we hear all about Yolande and Margaret's adventures in France, which we will gladly consume over coffee and my wife's butter cake," Papa announces, "Yolande and Countee have something exciting they'd like to share with everyone."

Papa nods at Countee and he stands. We hadn't discussed how this was going to go, and now I wish we had. Countee looks prepared to speak at length, and I can't string two words together about this.

"I met this beautiful brown girl on summer holiday in nineteen twenty-three, and she captivated my heart from the first glance," Countee says. "I have been blessed these short years to enjoy the closeness of her friendship. Now, we aspire to an even deeper, more holy bond. That of holy matrimony. I have asked for Yolande's hand, she has said yes, and Dr. Du Bois has blessed the union."

Mrs. Cullen makes a gurgling sound as she clutches the pearls around her throat. Reverend Cullen rubs her back with a solemn and resigned expression on his face. He does not, however, look surprised, so I suspect that Countee broke it to him early. Judging by his mother's reaction, that is probably for the best.

I wonder if Mrs. Cullen was still holding out hope that Countee would marry Fiona Braithwaite. Oh well. I suppose she'll have to be content with little ole me.

Harold and Margaret both sit frozen in shock. I have never seen either of them with nothing to say, but today they are dumbstruck. Thanks to Countee, I don't have anything to say either. He's said every necessary thing.

He pulls a small box from his pocket and opens it. I forgot about this part. The ring! How could I forget he was going to give me a ring?

Countee kneels in front of me. "When my mother gave me this ring, she said to give it to a young woman worthy of wearing it. And you are. Will you marry me?"

"Yes, of course I will. But I don't have anything poetic to say."

"Your *yes* is a song in my favorite key," Countee says with a smile. His words match the love in his eyes.

I beam at Countee as he places the ring on my finger, a pretty, twisted silver band with a sparkling round-cut solitaire diamond. It must be almost one carat. I am impressed and proud to wear this ring, though I truly hope I'm worthy of it and Countee's love. I'm tired of everyone thinking I'm fickle.

Harold slowly rises as he claps. "Congratulations, brother."

Once the ring is on, I wave my hand so everyone can see. Mrs. Cullen looks away with tears in her eyes. How dare she cry during our happy moment?

Papa glares at her. "This is the time when our children enter adulthood, and we should usher them into this reality with well-wishes."

"Agreed," says Reverend Cullen in the tone he usually reserves for his sermons. "This is a good and beneficial union."

Still standing, Papa strides over to me and Countee. He kisses my forehead and gives Countee a warm bear hug. My heart swells at Papa's joyousness and knowing that my actions have caused the feeling.

"The wedding will be in April," Papa announces.

It will? I prefer summer to spring. April showers could ruin my hairstyle.

"It's the only month I'm not bogged down with travel," Papa continues. "Reverend Cullen, you and I will discuss a date, since I'm sure you want the ceremony to take place in your sanctuary."

"It seems you've got things all settled," Mrs. Cullen spits angrily, her tears being replaced by fire. "This is *your* wedding, Dr. Du Bois."

Though she clearly meant these words as an attack, Papa responds with the most gracious smile.

"You will be happy you left the planning to me," Papa says. "All of Harlem is going to want to honor this couple, so we must find a way to accommodate them."

I haven't left the planning to him. Has Countee? Mama's serenity is gone, and worry is what I see etched into the lines of her forehead.

Should I be worried too?

Chapter Fifty-Four

February 1928
Baltimore, Maryland

Countee has taken a short trip down from Harlem to visit me, but instead of us sharing a sweet date and talking about the delightful and naughty things we're going to do on our honeymoon, we're going to have our first disagreement. He and Papa have been up to wedding planning mischief, and if we do not get on the same page, there may not be a wedding.

"Papa has written to me about the wedding," I snap, the letter in my outstretched hand. "He says you all had lunch and put your heads together on a few things."

"I wouldn't say quite that." Countee takes the letter and reads it. "He gave so many suggestions that it made my head spin. I merely listened."

"Do you see where he's called me ostentatious?"

Countee narrows his eyes as he scans the page. "He doesn't call *you* ostentatious. He said that about the number of bridesmaids you want."

"I don't care what he thinks. I will not exclude any of my dear friends here or in Harlem."

"Well, I don't have sixteen close friends to escort sixteen brides-maids."

Countee pats the seat on the couch next to him, so I sit. I know he wants me to not be angry, but he hasn't had to deal with Papa his entire life. He doesn't know what this is like.

"This is why you and Papa don't need to have any unsupervised meetings. Anyway, two of the girls are junior bridesmaids, and they don't require an escort."

"So then, can we exclude the junior bridesmaids?" he asks tentatively as if he doesn't want to risk making me angrier.

"We cannot."

"Yolande, love, please be reasonable. Your papa is thinking of the expense."

"All right. There's one bridesmaid we can remove from the list," I snip. "*Your* good friend, whom I love, Roberta."

Countee's tiny mouth forms an O as he shakes his head. "She'd be crushed. Rob is looking forward to standing up with us."

"Well, it's sixteen, then. Anyway, Papa should've been saving my whole life for this moment. He wants the wedding more than I do."

My knee trembles. I feel completely alone in this battle against Papa's wishes.

"You don't believe that. You're just feeling cross right now. Might we compromise? He's provided fifty dollars for your dress, so he clearly wants you to be happy."

"How much compromising must I be subject to? He's already forcing my ceremony to begin when it's almost nighttime. We'll be exhausted in the beautiful wedding suite Papa procured for us."

Here is a chance for Countee to tell me how much he wants to ravish me all night long—that it doesn't matter how late the wedding festivities end, he's going to have his way with me.

"The time of the wedding couldn't be helped," he says instead. "I think your father tried his best to make it earlier."

He simply ignored my comment about the honeymoon suite. I'd just like to hear, one time, how he can't wait to touch me, because his kisses haven't stoked a fire in me, even though I hoped they might.

"Papa just hopes people eat before they come."

"No matter when a colored man eats, he can always find space in his belly for a meal paid for by someone else." Countee chuckles as if he's said something amusing.

"That may be true, but Papa intends on feeding people chicken salad sandwiches no matter what time the ceremony begins. So, why not earlier?"

"A'Lelia may give us a pre-wedding tea or luncheon at the Walker Studio since your papa canceled the reception there."

I did not know Papa had canceled a reception at the Walker Studio, because I had no knowledge of the reception to begin with. He and Countee keep arranging things without my knowledge, and Mama's because she would have mentioned this in her letters. Papa has turned my wedding into a movement fiasco, and as always, Mama and I are the last ones he asks for suggestions about his plans.

Papa must have bitten off more than he could chew with his planning if he's now trying to limit my number of bridesmaids and canceling reception spaces. I bet he tried to convince A'Lelia to give him a cut rate because of her closeness to Countee. Knowing her, she would've balked at his audacity. And it's also just like her to now host her own party in our honor instead. It will annoy Papa, but we would never turn down her generous offer.

"He's got some nerve anyway," I rattle on, ignoring Countee's attempt to interject. "He's the one who invited more than one thousand people. These are his friends and associates, not mine."

"When parents pay for the wedding, they like to think they're in control of things. My parents have only submitted a few names to the guest list."

"That's not fair!" I exclaim, a bit surprised to be advocating for the Cullens.

Countee gives a helpless shrug. "They have agreed that this is Dr. Du Bois's affair, not theirs."

"But surely there are members of the church that your mother would like to have there."

"If there are she has not said so."

I cannot believe I care what Mrs. Cullen wants, since she hates me so. Margaret told me she heard that Mrs. Cullen wept for days when Fiona Braithwaite called off the engagement, because that's who she wanted as a daughter-in-law.

Papa is out of control, and there is no one to rein him in. Mama has washed her hands of it, and clearly so have the Cullens. Countee only wants to please Papa, so that leaves me to put my foot down.

"Well, I am the bride, and it is *my* wedding," I say with a frustrated pout. I need my fiancé on my side.

"Our wedding," Countee reminds me.

"So, you stand up to me and not Papa?"

"I would stand up to your father if I disagreed with him. It just so happens that I have no preference in the matters he's decided."

"I do have a preference, and you should stand with me. I will have all sixteen of my bridesmaids, no matter the cost. They've already been asked, and I will not un-ask them. If Papa wants to save money, he can uninvite a hundred of his NAACP cronies."

"All right, ma chérie. Whatever you want."

"I mean it, Countee. And you can tell Papa that, since you continue to have secret meetings with him."

"The meetings aren't secret. It's just that you're here in Baltimore, and I'm in Harlem. It is not an effort to exclude you."

"Soon, we'll all be in Harlem together." I try to improve my mood. "Won't that be grand? We'll go to the Savoy as husband and wife."

Countee cocks his head to one side as if he's trying to imagine this. "Does anyone we know stay on the scene after they get married? It's like they marry and float right away."

"There are some, but they do more society things, you know? Harold may have to raise hell without you."

The blank expression on Countee's face makes me uncomfortable. Has he not considered what married life is like? Or did he think we would continue as we always have, three good friends roaming about Harlem getting up to mischief? Or maybe he's thinking of the fun he has when I'm not there. The fun Margaret keeps trying to tell me about.

"Just remember you're marrying me and not Papa and you'll make the right decisions in those meetings," I say to close this argument.

Countee gives my hand a chaste tug. Too chaste. "I know who I'm marrying, and I cannot wait to spend the rest of my days with you, my love."

I squeeze Countee's hand back even though his declaration feels empty. What will we spend the rest of our days doing? Will I listen to Countee recite poetry until death do us part? He will have to touch me at some point if we will have these hordes of babies that Papa demands we produce.

The quiet whispers of doubt that previously lurked at the edge of my thoughts push their way to the front of my mind. And now doubt no longer whispers.

It screams.

Chapter Fifty-Five

I don't know why we thought it was a clever idea to allow A'Lelia Walker to host a pre-wedding tea at the Walker Studio on our wedding day. The logic had seemed sound. Our special out-of-town guests might get hungry with the wedding starting at six o'clock in the evening. And Harold hosted Countee's stag party on the third floor at The Dark Tower last night, so it was convenient. But I do not think we accounted for how hectic this day would become.

This morning, all sixteen bridesmaids' bouquets were delivered to our apartment instead of the suite at the Walker Studio, where we're getting dressed. Then, the delivery driver would not carry them to the suite because he had other stops, so Papa had to do it because Mama and I were at Walker Beauty Salon getting our hair done.

Then, Mrs. Cullen had another fit and had to be prescribed a nerve pill to get through the day. I wish she weren't going to be in a haze when we exchange vows, but I suppose it's better than her hollering in the church.

Luckily, A'Lelia has provided two large suites for me and the bridesmaids to get ready. The groom and groomsmen will get dressed at the church's parsonage. And we've rented two automobiles to transport us to the church.

This tea party is much more elegant than our reception is going to be. And I am happy Papa said he was too busy to attend, because if he saw this spread of hors d'oeuvres, meat carving stations, fine china, and desserts, he'd think A'Lelia was trying to upstage him.

But I am grateful for A'Lelia's generosity. I know she and Countee are quite close. She even named her club on the third floor The Dark Tower after one of his poems.

From my seat on an ornate white sofa, I observe my groom in his natural habitat, with his friends. He moves through the throng of guests with ease, chatting and drinking whiskey, hugging, laughing, and reciting poetry. Most of these people are from his tribe of writers, poets, and artists. As much as Papa wants me to be a part of this world, I am only connected through Countee. My Delta sorors aren't here today, except the ones in my bridal party, and they have chosen to remain in the bridal suite and away from the main action of the party.

Not even Margaret, my maid of honor, has joined me. She says these are not *her* kind of people. Whatever that means.

Folk walk by and congratulate me, but no one remains seated on the couch next to me, making me feel lonely when there must be two hundred people here. What would they have to talk to me about? My latest drawing of a bowl of fruit? My cherished high school students?

These are Countee's kindred spirits. The artistic toast of Harlem. Every young writer, singer, and musician of note is here with Harlem's favorite photographer James Van Der Zee documenting it on film.

Finally, Harold plops down next to me, already several tumblers of whiskey in. At least he doesn't reek of it. He can thank his expensive French cologne for that. He could drink an entire bottle and still smell divine.

"Your teacup is empty, bride-to-be."

I glance down at the pretty blue and white cup that was recently filled with a cinnamon-flavored whiskey masquerading as tea.

"Yes, but Countee has had enough for both of us."

"He'll be fine," Harold says cheerily. "I've seen him drink much more and recite an entire poem from memory."

I laugh at the idea of this. "As long as he's able to say his vows, I don't think anyone will mind him being sloshed."

"Papa Du Bois would have a fit if he couldn't say I do."

"My papa might just love Countee more than he loves me," I say, now wishing I did have more whiskey to chase that sobering thought.

"Even more now that Countee's won the Guggenheim Fellowship."

"Papa is excited about that. He's been bragging on Countee nonstop."

"Although you must not feel excited about your new husband leaving you behind right after the wedding." Harold makes a sad face and consoles me with a pat on the back, but I have no idea what he's talking about.

"Leaving me behind?"

"To go to Paris for the fellowship. His father and I are traveling with him for the summer to help him get settled in. And to enjoy Paris on someone else's dime." Harold bursts into laughter, but I cannot gather words to form a reply.

Fortunately, Harold sees Langston across the room and rushes over to decide some last-minute groomsmen detail. I search the room for Countee. He's having a spirited discussion with Nella Larsen and Zora Neale Hurston, so I dare not interrupt now.

We had not decided anything about the Guggenheim Fellowship, although I assumed that we would go to Paris together. Why would I think otherwise? There was certainly no discussion of Harold and Reverend Cullen accompanying him. Does Countee think even after getting married that he will still be able to move about like a single man?

* * *

IN THE MASSIVE suite A'Lelia has provided for me to get dressed, I try to push away negative thoughts. I would simply like to get to the end of this exhausting day and on with the rest of my life with Countee.

A'Lelia checks in on me before going over to the church. She looks radiant in her pink chiffon dress and diamond necklace. She wears a pink headband across her forehead that holds her perfectly sculpted curls in place and the pink flower behind her ear.

I must seem out of sorts, because instead of just peeking in and being on her way, she sits like she has time for a visit.

"It's almost time for your ceremony," A'Lelia says. "Are you excited?"

I open my mouth to say the proper, polite response. "I don't even know what I'm supposed to feel." And the truth came out instead.

"Hmmm," A'Lelia says, sounding empathetic.

"How do you know if you're making the right choice?" I ask. "It feels so monumental. Bigger than anything I've ever done."

"Well, I'm not sure I am the right person to ask that question," A'Lelia says with a hearty chuckle. "I'm on my third husband, honey. Picking a husband is a weighty choice that can have a consequence or two. But it can be undone."

"Hmmm." Now my thoughts are spiraling. She's right. Maybe I shouldn't have asked her.

She touches my arm lovingly. "I hope there's at least a little joy in there. Somewhere."

"Oh, there is. And I love Countee," I quickly add, knowing he is her dear friend.

She nods as she stands to leave. "Countee is a kind man. You could do worse. I will be clapping loudly from the pews."

This is true. I could do worse. But that isn't what concerns me.

Mama appears from the hallway and thank goodness, she is her usual serene self. Her rose Georgette gown is stunningly demure, and her youthful face needs no cosmetic enhancements. And with all these bridesmaids milling about, I am glad to have her calming presence.

"Do you think I should have gotten a floor-length gown?" I ask, examining my knee-length cream satin dress hanging from a hook on the back of the dressing room door. "Even with the lace, now I feel like it's not enough."

"Don't fret, Yolande. It's perfect. The train will give the illusion of length, and you won't have to worry about tripping over the hem."

That is the reasoning we used when selecting this design, and I remember all that. It's just that suddenly this day has become so much grander than I expected.

"I hear the guests have already started to arrive at the church," Mama says. "And that there's hardly any available seats."

"Already? The wedding isn't for another two hours."

"Well, Reverend Cullen warned his congregation in advance yesterday during service that all of New York City would be in the gallery."

"Oh, my goodness."

Mama shakes her head. "The Cullens' church has never seen a crowd like it will this evening."

"Have you seen Mrs. Cullen's gown? Did it look nice?"

"I'm not a fan of the color," Mama says, "but she does look nice in yellow. It would help her a great deal if she smiled. She looks like she's on her way to a funeral."

"I think her yellow will fit right in with the bridesmaids' rainbow-colored taffeta. They're going to look like Easter morning, so the people who didn't make it out to church yesterday can pretend they had Easter service."

"I suppose. But everyone looks so pretty, and the weather is just gorgeous. I was worried it might be too hot since the past few days have felt like summer. Thank goodness the temperature dropped quite a bit. You may need your mink stole after the ceremony on your way to the honeymoon."

I keep putting off thoughts of the honeymoon and our wedding night.

Mama brings over a small box. It's Countee's wedding gift to me—a platinum and diamond bracelet set.

"This was such an appropriate and thoughtful gift," Mama says. "Along with your pearls, you will make a most elegant bride."

Margaret bursts into the room without knocking.

"Did someone say the Queen of England was getting dressed for her wedding in here?" Margaret says with a laugh. She's still tipsy from all the Prohibition tea we had a while ago.

"Close the door behind you," I say. "I don't want the chaos to come in here."

She smiles. "There isn't very much chaos. Unless you mean the sixteen girls looking like an Easter basket and trying to figure out whose bouquet is whose."

Mama's eyes widen with alarm. "Oh, good heavens. Let me go and help them before things get more confused."

Mama rushes out and Margaret giggles as she sits next to me on a gorgeous European settee. "Now that we're rid of her, how are you really feeling? Are you ready for this? The first of us to cross over into holy matrimony."

"I am feeling everything all at once, I think."

"Do you doubt Countee's affection for you?"

"No, that's not it. It just feels like things are being discussed and planned without my knowledge. I'm used to that with Papa, but I never expected Countee to be the same way."

"He's a man, Yolande," Margaret says gently. "They all move about the world not caring about what we want."

"Well, I certainly want to be with my husband when he travels to

Paris for this fellowship. He's lost his mind if he thinks he's just going to leave me here and go with his father and Harold."

"What are you talking about?" Margaret's eyes widen.

"Harold told me that during the tea party."

"He said that he and Reverend Cullen are going to Paris with Countee?" Margaret looks as incredulous as I probably did when Harold uttered the words.

"Yes, and that they're leaving me behind. Is that how marriage works?"

Margaret considers this for a moment. "Your mother doesn't travel with your father, does she? Maybe they think it's something that goes without saying."

"But I don't think my mother wants to travel. I am quite fond of Paris, especially after our last adventure."

"Countee should just make this an extended honeymoon. The two of you enjoying each other in Paris, without having to worry about someone reporting back to your parents. You can be as wild and free as you want."

"That's exactly what I was hoping for. I'd like to cozy up in Le Grand Duc and do raunchy things in dark corners. That's what Countee said we'd do!"

Margaret bursts into laughter and I join her, even though I am halfway serious. There is nothing naughty to speak of with me and Countee, and I don't quite know what to do with that. Or about it.

"Well, after tonight, when you and Countee finally go all the way, he won't want to leave you behind," Margaret says. "You'll be doing all the naughty things you want, all over Paris."

"I'll be popping out babies like a hen laying eggs. Papa will be so pleased."

Margaret howls with laughter. "We may never get you home from Europe."

"Countee is crazy about Paris."

Margaret does a naughty shimmy. "Aren't you at least excited for tonight? You know, not having to worry about prophylactics and all that?"

"Oh, yes, I guess so."

"You guess? Well, even if you aren't, I'm sure Countee is."

"I think he is, but it's just so different with him."

"Than with Jimmie?"

I squeeze my eyes shut, having not wanted to utter his name today, for fear of bad luck. "Yes, but I'm not thinking about him right now. Help me put on this diamond bracelet."

"It's gorgeous. Ji—" I glare at Margaret, and she swallows the last syllable of his name. "I mean he-who-shall-not-be-named could never afford something like this."

"No matter. Countee and I are being married today, so I don't care what someone else can or cannot afford."

A light knock on the door thankfully ends this dialogue with Margaret. My maid of honor should help ease my nerves, not rattle them.

"Come in," I say.

Papa opens the door wearing a huge smile on his face. He looks so handsome and chic in his suit and sash. Just like Countee wanted.

"May I speak with Yolande a moment, Margaret?"

"Yes, Dr. Du Bois. You're looking dapper, sir."

"Why, thank you, and you and the rest of the bridesmaids look beautiful." Papa beams.

"Don't go far," I tell Margaret. "I need you to help me in a few minutes. Mama too."

"Okay, I'll find her."

Margaret glides out of the room, and I get nervous all over again thinking about walking down the aisle.

"How are you feeling?" Papa asks.

I can't divulge my nerves and uncertainty to Papa. This is the happiest day of his life.

"Excited to get this evening started." I'm not looking him in the eye. "Mama says the church is nearly full."

"Nearly? The church is full to capacity and is standing room only at this point. Everyone who's anyone in Harlem is there along with dignitaries from all over the country."

"Oh, my goodness. Countee said it would be like a royal wedding."

"It is royal. Any white person who might want to describe colored people as uncouth or uncultured will only have to look at the newspapers tomorrow. They will see the Talented Tenth reign supreme."

I do not comment on this. I shouldn't be surprised that Papa would turn this into a day for the movement. There will probably be a four-page spread in *The Crisis*.

"I just wanted to give you a few words of advice before the ceremony."

At least this feels normal. It wouldn't be Papa without lectures, instructions, and admonishments.

"Yes, of course, Papa."

"Don't go into marriage nervous about living with your husband and building a foundation. Remember that your job as a wife is to use your gifts to help lift your husband to the peak of his own giftedness. That will ensure that your children will want for nothing when they come into the world."

"It would help any nervousness that I might have if my husband wasn't leaving me behind as he begins the Guggenheim Fellowship."

"Yes, Countee and I discussed this. I agree it's for the best."

"What?" I hear my voice rise with my anger, and my heart races.

"Countee believes it will be good for you to stay on a while at the high school. That way he can be at the height of his creativity without having to fret over your needs."

"Fret!"

"Yes, and your pay should take care of your needs in Baltimore while Countee and I pay off the bills from this extravagant wedding."

So, I must continue to work even as a wife? That is unheard of in our social circles, and not how I imagined things at all. I had already mentally composed a gracious letter of resignation.

"A husband should make provision." My lips form a pout.

"But this is a special circumstance. What Countee can achieve during this fellowship can change the course of history. You are a blessed woman indeed to be a part of it."

I want to scream at the top of my lungs, but I know if I do, I will completely unravel.

"Maybe you'll even have my first grandchild during his time there if things go well during the honeymoon. You all can name him Countee William Guggenheim Du Bois Cullen."

Papa has a hearty laugh while I stare at him in horror.

"I'll leave you now so you can be dressed on time. Your transportation will be here at half past five. We will go on time. This affair is starting late enough."

Papa lets himself out without even seeming to notice that his advice has left me in shambles. He even hums some tune to himself, just as pleased as can be.

Perhaps I can have someone trouble A'Lelia's bartender for one more cup of tea. Or three.

Chapter Fifty-Six

April 9, 1928
Harlem, New York

There is sheer pandemonium at Salem Methodist Episcopal Church when I arrive. I didn't envision wedding guests pouring out of the building onto the sidewalk, or that the streets would be so congested that our cars would have to inch down the road.

"This is madness," I whisper to Margaret, as our car finally pulls up in front of the church.

"I hope there'll be lots of gifts," Margaret replies with a laugh. "Don't worry. It'll all go by in a heartbeat."

There are ushers to help us inside, and to keep the crowd from pressing in on us, but as we get out of the car, cameras flash from every side and journalists scream questions at me. This is my wedding day, for heaven's sake. I don't have any time for questions. I just smile and wave because I don't want any bad photos to be taken of me, but I sure can't think of two words to say to anyone.

"Here, let me fix your train," Margaret says as she unravels it so it can float out behind me as we enter the church's vestibule.

It's quieter here, without the reporters yelling, but there are still folk flashing photos with their own personal Brownie cameras, so my plastered-on smile remains. This is really happening.

"Are you all right?" Margaret whispers.

I nod, feeling very thankful for my best friend's calming presence. I keep my eyes on Papa and his extended hand. He's going to walk me to the altar. Only a few more steps, and I'll have his help holding me up.

"Yolande! Yolande!"

My feet stop moving, because I know the voice. Of course he's here. He went to my home to win me back, but no one told me. Margaret had spoken his name and conjured the Wishing Tree magic.

Jimmie is here. And calling out to me.

Margaret strategically places her tall frame between me and the voice because she must have heard him too.

"Keep going, Yolande. Your papa's just ahead."

But I must get a glimpse of him, even as Margaret hustles me forward. I turn my head to the sound of his voice, and our eyes meet.

My Jimmie is sandwiched between two men with cameras. His hand stretches forward, like if he could only reach me, he might snatch me away from all this. From the church, from Countee, from Papa. To what, I don't know. I am not sure that I care. I just know that he's here, and when I think of what that could mean, I am overwhelmed.

I don't know how long my gaze is locked in his direction. It feels like an eternity before my knees start to buckle and I feel consciousness leaving me.

But magically, out of nowhere, Papa appears at my side. He wraps one strong arm around my back, steadying me.

Papa glares over at Jimmie as a tear races down my face. Then Papa gently wipes away the tear, turns me to the front of the church, and guides me inside.

And away from my Jimmie.

I cannot feel the ground beneath my feet or even see a few paces in front of me as my eyes fill with tears. If it weren't for Papa, I wouldn't be able to move.

There is music playing. I don't know which song it is. I did not select this music. I hear the click of cameras, and as I slowly blink my tears away, I see nothing but unfamiliar faces.

Thousands of onlookers gawk at me, proud smiles on their faces as if they knew me when I was a baby. Some of them have watched me grow up on the pages of *The Crisis*.

Papa has shared me with the world, and now my collective aunts and uncles are here with good wishes. Some have traveled far, at great expense, to see me marry Countee and to eat chicken salad and a slice of cake in the church basement. To witness a union that will create another generation of their Talented Tenth.

And Jimmie is HERE.

At the altar Papa hands me over to Countee while Margaret steps forward to spread my train behind me and take my bouquet.

I do not think Countee will be able to catch me if my legs give way. Hopefully the horde of groomsmen will be able to soften my fall.

Photos of me collapsed at the altar will be in tomorrow's news. At least my train will look good. Hospital Bed Yolande will spend her wedding night in a hospital bed.

JIMMIE IS HERE.

I hear Reverend Cullen speaking, but his words sound garbled. He must've made a joke or two because everyone laughs. Expressing their collective joy, because Papa has turned it into a movement moment. They might as well be laughing at my expense. For a moment I wish I had gotten a longer dress in case my knees start to knock.

Then we're kneeling at the altar, and Margaret Pennybacker is singing. This I did ask for, because the song would move me more than Reverend Cullen's prayer, but it's too loud—distorted even. Thank goodness we're kneeling. Now if I faint, I won't have too far to roll.

Jimmie came for me.

I am afraid to turn my head lest I see him again, so I stare straight ahead until I feel a hand turning my face. It's Countee.

It must be time to recite our vows, so I force myself to focus.

"I, Yolande Nina Du Bois, take you—"

My voice has gone. I cannot continue. I feel myself wobble and Countee wraps an arm around me.

"I'm here, ma chérie," Countee whispers. "We are here together. We can make it through this. Je t'aime."

I swallow and start again. It is like another person is speaking these promises and vows. Not me. It feels like my soul has left my body in search of the one it truly loves.

He said he wouldn't chase me again.

But he did.

And despite that, I floated right down the aisle to Countee. For the advancement of colored people. For a legacy.

For Papa.

Chapter Fifty-Seven

April 9, 1928
Harlem, New York

I cannot erase the image of Jimmie's face in the horde of wedding guests. His forlorn and desperate expression will haunt me until the end of my days.

I don't know if I wanted him to interrupt the wedding and sweep me away, or if I wished I'd run into his arms. Something should've happened. The sky ought to have cracked and the ground under our feet should've rumbled.

I defied the Wishing Tree's magic. Shouldn't there have been hell to pay?

But nothing transpired and Jimmie's face disappeared into the sea of faces so quickly and without a trace that I think maybe he was a mirage.

Now I am in the honeymoon suite with Countee wondering when we're going to get on with things. We're both still fully dressed and neither one of us seems to be in much of a hurry.

"Ji—"

Oh my God. I almost called him Jimmie.

"What were you about to say?" Countee asks.

"Um, just give me a moment to freshen up."

"Didn't you freshen up when you got into your nightgown?"

"Well, tonight is extra special, so I have an extra special surprise."

Countee looks confused as I rush away and into the adjoining bathroom to gather my thoughts.

Once I close the door I shudder. Who almost calls her husband by another man's name right when they're about to consummate their union?

Damn that Wishing Tree and its magic.

The reflection that looks back at me from the bathroom mirror is frightened and unsure.

I don't truly know how this mating ritual is supposed to go. With Jimmie there never seemed to be a commencing. We would be kissing and then our bodies would find themselves entangled.

The wetness that forms on the pretty panties I am wearing for my new husband belongs to Jimmie's memory. I will never be free of him, and I don't think I want to be.

If only Countee could scoop me into his arms and kiss me until our tongues find their rhythm. His eyes don't linger on my breasts and hips like he's trying to memorize every curve. His eyes stay, respectfully, at the level of my eyes.

But tonight, on my wedding night, I don't want respect. I want passion and to feel my body sing. His touches would be no match for Jimmie's, but they'd be touches. And my body starves for it.

But perhaps it isn't respect that holds Countee back. Maybe he believes himself to be too inexperienced to bring me pleasure. Maybe I will have to lead the charge.

I squeeze my eyes shut and take a long empowering breath. We can do this, Countee and I. Men and women all over the world have survived countless nervous wedding nights.

I exit the bathroom, wearing a seductive smile, ready to lead the mating dance. Countee doesn't smile back, but his eyebrows lift with surprise.

"Are you trying to woo me, Yolande?"

I bite my lip to keep the laughter from spilling over. A man does not want to be laughed at in the bedroom, of this I am certain, but since I cannot trust myself to reply, I simply nod.

I glide across the room and stop in front of Countee's chair. I'd like to straddle him, but I'm not sure if he can hold all my weight on his lap.

Instead, I stand between his legs and open my nightgown slightly, hoping to entice him with the twin mounds of flesh that drove Jimmie wild.

But with my breasts at his eye level Countee only gazes upon them as if he doesn't quite know what to do with what's being offered.

"Yolande, I do apologize. I don't know . . . well, I have never . . ."

Oh my. With all Countee's travels abroad and with the romances he's bragged about, I would never have thought that I would be the one to take him across manhood's threshold.

On my wedding night, must I guide my husband? Where is the passion in this?

I take his clumsy hands and place one on each of my breasts. He clamps down hard and I yelp.

"They're not balloons to pop, Countee. Be gentle," I say, "until I ask you to not be so gentle."

"What?" Countee asks, confusion on his face.

The moisture that had accumulated at the thought of Jimmie dries up like a shriveled raisin on the sidewalk on a sunny day. This cannot be my wedding night.

It cannot!

I pull Countee's face to mine, squeeze my eyes shut, and attempt a kiss. It is as disastrous as Countee's fondling. He continues to manhandle my breasts as he puts little dry pecks on my lips as if this is what a kiss is supposed to feel like.

I slightly part my lips to try and coax him into a more passionate kiss, but he seems confused again, not knowing what his tongue is supposed to do or his teeth. Saliva pools in the corner of his mouth, disgusting me to no end.

"Countee."

His arms drop to his sides in defeat. "I am sorry, Yolande. I don't know what's come over me."

I try to reassure him. "You're just nervous."

"I think the long day has taken a toll," he sighs. "Perhaps we can just go to sleep tonight and try again fresh tomorrow."

The long day? We are not old people. This shouldn't be happening.

My wedding night ruined, I step slowly away from Countee. I pull my nightgown closed, now feeling foolish for trying to seduce him. I retreat again to the bathroom and this time to allow myself to fall to pieces.

On the cold, marble floor of the bathroom of my honeymoon suite I realize I have made a grave error marrying Countee.

Chapter Fifty-Eight

Papa is enraged by the article he just read in the *Baltimore Afro-American*'s society column. Everyone is talking about Countee and Harold in Paris while I'm still home in Harlem, having signed a contract to go back to Baltimore in the fall.

After our horrible honeymoon, I went back to Baltimore to finish the school year. We never managed to consummate anything. Countee's apologies were profuse and plentiful. Papa, of course, blames me and my inexperience. I have enough experience to know that I am not the problem, but there is no use trying to explain this to Papa.

"You must try, Yolande, to understand the base nature of a man," Papa had explained. "Everything will not be sugared candies and flowers. Some things your husband desires may seem distasteful and perhaps unusual, but that is only due to your innocence."

I always thought he knew about me sneaking into bed with Jimmie. Did he think we only cuddled?

But now that I'm home for the summer, Papa has forgotten all about lecturing me on how to be a good wife. Much more urgent are the weekly news stories in the *Tattler* and the *Baltimore Afro-American* penned by Geraldyn Dismond.

"It's like she's obsessed with Yolande and Countee," Papa says to Mama, who is only half-listening to his tirade.

He throws the newspaper onto the table and slumps into his chair. He pushes away his slice of apple pie, no longer interested in dessert.

I've finished one slice and half of a second. This gossip makes me nervous and when my nerves are bad I crave sweets.

"The wedding was a big spectacle, Will," Mama says. "People are interested in it."

"Well everyone knows Countee is going to work with the Guggenheim Fellowship. Why would anyone imply anything untoward about it?"

"Because it makes absolutely no sense that his best man is at his side instead of his wife, Papa," I fuss. "If I was writing a salacious gossip column, I'd think that was notable too."

"The article conveniently leaves out the fact that Reverend Cullen went along, and that Countee and Harold have been the best of friends for years. Or that you all spent time together in Paris last summer," Papa raves. "The writers want people to come to the worst possible conclusion without actually saying it themselves. It's a nasty, nasty business."

"They say it's journalism," Mama says.

"Whether it is or isn't, I must join Countee. I cannot go back to teach in September."

"You must go back. You signed a contract and now they're expecting you," Papa says, much too forcefully for someone who got me into this pickle in the first place. "You cannot go back on your word."

"But Papa, I wouldn't have signed the contract for next year had you and Countee not decided that I should stay behind while he goes ahead to Europe."

"That was a purely financial decision meant to help you both be on solid footing after the fellowship ends," Papa explains.

"And now look what's happened. I'm being ridiculed, once again, in the newspapers. I would love, for once, to not have to worry about that."

The corners of Papa's mouth twitch. "You don't know what you're asking for. You should feel privileged that every Negro in America knows your name."

I wish they'd forget it.

"Your contact got me the job," I say, changing the subject and my tone to a much calmer one. "Perhaps they can help me get a leave of absence."

"I will write a few letters. If I'm successful, I will help you get to Paris. But if you and Countee run into financial difficulties while abroad, I will not be able to supplement his stipend," Papa says. "You will need to request help from Reverend Cullen. I am still recovering from the expense of your wedding."

If we have financial difficulties, Countee and I will figure them out together. Papa's meddling has done enough. If we are to survive this, we must start behaving like a married couple . . . in every way.

Chapter Fifty-Nine

September 1928
Paris, France

The Paris apartment is pleasant enough. Countee has taken great care to fill it with all the things I like. Fresh flowers, paintings, bowls with sweet smelling herbs and spices. He even placed a pretty ashtray next to my side of the bed along with a platter of lovely Parisian baked goods. But there is a heaviness in this space.

Maybe it's because when I wrote to Countee that I had obtained a leave of absence from teaching and was coming to stay in Paris with him, he did not seem excited about it. He even asked me if I could change my mind and stay in Baltimore.

He says he doesn't care about the gossip, but he wasn't in Harlem, enduring the whispers and stares. That was my burden. Countee, like Papa, only seems to be worried about bills, ledgers, and bank statements.

Or perhaps, Countee is simply worried about our unfinished business. The inevitable joining of husband and wife that has yet to happen. I hope that happens now that we're in a place that brings us joy.

"Are you tired, ma chérie? You have been traveling all day," Countee says after placing my bags in the bedroom.

"I am, but I'd like to go somewhere nice for dinner. To set the mood."

"Of course. Would you like to go to our favorite café?"

"Now, that might be romantic. Since that is where you informed me of you and Papa's plans."

Countee chuckles. "You make it sound like a business arrangement."

"Is it?" I do wonder.

"Absolutely not," he insists. "There is no other woman I'd rather spend my life with."

And yet he hasn't seen me in months. His new bride. Shouldn't he be champing at the bit to tear my clothes off?

"Yes, Countee," I say. "Dinner at our café will be splendid. Maybe we can go dancing too."

Countee's eyes light up with what seems like hope. "I think that would be wonderful."

* * *

AFTER DINNER AND prolonged dancing, we returned to our apartment. Again, I changed into a pretty nightgown and made myself smell like cherry blossoms.

At least this time, Countee kisses me with what feels like passion. His lips seem to find their intended target, and I feel something stirring in me. But it doesn't matter really, if I am aroused. I can fake my way through, I just need us to get to the intended destination.

Margaret gave me some things to try to entice Countee. Things I never had to try with Jimmie, because I only had to look at him and he was ready to pounce.

I join Countee in bed. He has a nervous expression on his face.

"Should I turn off the lamp?" he asks.

"If you want to that's fine."

He does and then pulls me close to him under the blanket. It isn't completely dark, because our bedroom is flooded with moonlight. He smells like fresh cologne and the soap he used to wash himself when we got back from dinner.

I squeeze my eyes shut and reach down to touch Countee through his underwear. I press my lips to his, trying to find our rhythm, whatever it may be.

Countee shifts under the blanket, but even with my kissing and fondling I don't feel even a hint of an erection. Is there something physically wrong? Is he unable? Is that why Fiona Braithwaite called off the engagement? Is that why Sydonia Byrd shunned him?

How in hell can I give Papa progeny if I cannot bring my husband to arousal? And Papa will blame me, of course.

"Countee, what is it?"

He has a sick expression on his face as he swings his legs off the bed. He begins weeping, his face in his hands. I feel terror.

"Tell me? Are you impotent? If you are, we can figure something out," I say searching for the right words, any words that will stop his crying. "There are doctors. African herbs. Perhaps we can go for prayer."

"Prayer?" Countee asks incredulously. "There is no prayer that can fix my depraved brokenness."

Depraved?

"Countee, please. I cannot help if I don't know what's going on."

"When you do know, you still won't be able to help."

I get quiet now and join Countee on his side of the bed. My legs dangle next to his and I put my arm around his shoulders.

"Yolande, I believed that you and our marriage would be the solution to my problem. That I might be able to simply pretend my way into being a good husband and maybe even father."

What problem? I need him to speak plainly and not in code. I want to scream, but his weeping has stopped, and his talking is much better than the sound of those choked sobs.

"But it is readily apparent that I am not cured even at the sight of your naked flesh. I had thought it was because I had never been with a woman that I did not have the same uncontrollable urges my other male companions seem to experience."

So, he is impotent. God in heaven, what a catastrophe.

"Did something happen to you when you were a child? An accident perhaps?"

Countee looks at me and exhales heavily. "Yolande. I am not impotent."

"Then what . . ." My voice trails off as my mind connects the pieces.

"For reasons unknown to me . . . perhaps God placed it in me before I left the womb . . . but while I find women alluring and beautiful, I prefer, it seems . . . the sexual touch of a man."

I leap up and stumble away from Countee. Not wanting to touch him or the bed. Wondering if he has had a man here in our temporary marital home.

"Yolande, I am so sorry. If I had known I'd be unable to perform I would not have dragged you into this ruse."

"H-how do you know you p-prefer men?" I stutter, grasping at straws, hoping there's a way through this. I didn't leave Jimmie standing in the church foyer for this. "H-have you been w-with—"

"Yes. Here and at home, but I had been told it was quite possible, and it may be possible still for me to have attraction to both sexes."

Here and at home?

"Harold?" I ask, not wanting the answer.

"What? No. No, no, no. Not Harold. He is like my brother. There is no sex attraction between us."

If he says *sex attraction* one more time, I swear I'm going to faint dead away.

"I don't believe you."

"I am not supposed to tell you this, but Harold has an illegitimate daughter here with a Parisian woman named Sophia."

After he just told me a man can want and desire both, I'm supposed to believe anything that comes out of his mouth?

"You do know I cannot stay married to you." My voice trembles with sadness. Countee is sharing his truth, but what is going to happen to my life now?

"I was hoping you wouldn't say that," Countee says in a panic.

I pace the room in front of the bed, weeping and reeling. "Papa has made it clear that my one job is to give him gifted grandchildren. We won't be able to do that, will we?"

"There are ways. I have heard one can inject—"

"Have you lost your mind?" I shriek. "I want to be married to a man!"

"I AM a man!" Countee roars as fresh tears wet his cheeks.

But I cannot see him broken this way. My friend. My confidant.

I run to embrace him as he collapses into my arms, somehow finding the strength to hold us both up.

"I'm sorry, Countee. I did not mean that. You are every bit a man, but we must divorce. This isn't just about Papa. I have needs of my own. I can't live like this."

"We can stay here in Paris, and both do as we please. You can take a lover if you wish. I will still take care of you."

"I don't want a lover. I want a husband."

I want the one I can never have now. I want my Jimmie.

"Please, when you file the divorce papers, you must file it here in Paris, so that we can simply say that we're incompatible," Countee begs. "No one needs to know the reason."

"I must tell Papa, or he will put this entirely on my shoulders. He may even still do that."

"Fine," he says reluctantly. "I know Dr. Du Bois will keep my secret."

Indeed, he will. After he stood up grinning at my wedding, with his chest stuck out to the entire collection of colored people, he will never utter a word of this.

Chapter Sixty

Countee is already seated at our table at our favorite Parisian café, taking slow drags from a cigarette when I arrive. The tension that draws lines on his forehead ages him. But this is a different Countee. Not disheveled, but not pristine. Shirt unbuttoned at the top, sleeves rolled to the elbow. Light stubble on his chin. Skin dry and ashen, when he is typically glistening.

He puts the cigarette out as I approach, and he stands. Still a gentleman. That hasn't changed.

We pause for a moment. How do we greet each other now? Then, I lunge forward to hug him. The embrace is desperate on both our parts, full of the love and friendship that we share. I lightly brush his cheek with a kiss before we separate.

As we sit, Countee gives me a strange look that's a combination of thanks and hope. But I can't think of anything to say.

"Were you all right in the apartment last night?" Countee asks. "I was worried about you being there alone. I know how you sometimes fall ill when under stress."

"I didn't like it very much. Please come back."

Countee nods. "I will, only until we can have your mother come out to stay with you. I'm going to London for a while."

"London?" I can't keep the surprise out of my voice.

"Yes, I need a moment of reflection and to be able to channel everything I feel onto the page. I can afford a small apartment there."

"How can you afford an apartment?" He can barely afford the one we're meant to share in Paris.

Countee clears his throat and averts his gaze. "I have a friend in London."

I can't do anything except stare at him because I do not want the details.

"And what am I supposed to do while you're there?"

"You can do whatever you'd like to do. Take an art class if you want," Countee says as if we're just shooting the breeze, planning a vacation and not the deconstructing of our lives. "I know you have an interest there. Explore Paris. I know we don't have a lot of money, but there is plenty to see without spending very much. You could pass weeks in the museums alone."

"Are we going to talk about what happened?" I ask, wondering if there is anything he might like to add or correct now that we've had time to sleep on things.

Countee lights another cigarette. It is so strange seeing him smoke. He's never done it around me, but then he clearly has a life that's remained unseen to me.

"Yolande. Did you truly have no idea? I thought you might suspect . . . most girls I've courted . . ." His voice trails off, and I think of Fiona and their broken engagement.

"Why would I assume such a heinous thing about you?"

He winces. "Can we not use words like *heinous*? Please."

I reach across the table and grab the hand that isn't holding the cigarette. Both of his hands are shaking with either nerves or rage. I don't know which. "I am sorry. I am trying to understand."

"All right. I'll forgive you that time, but if you're my friend—"

"I am, Countee. I love you even with all this."

"Well, if you love me . . . this is me. I cannot separate this nature from who I am."

"Is this why Fiona Braithwaite suddenly broke your engagement?" I ask, remembering how hush-hush that was.

"Yes. She confronted me with rumors. Some were true, some were not."

"You told her the truth, beforehand?"

This fact irritates me, and I'm sure he can see that on my face. Am I set to be embarrassed again? In all the Negro newspapers from New York to Baltimore to Washington, D.C., to Chicago? Anywhere they covered the wedding of the Negro prince and princess of Harlem, they're going to lap this gossip up with a spoon and wash it down with whiskey.

"I did. I had no choice. She had . . . proof."

I don't want to know what the proof was. "But you did not afford me the same courtesy? Despite our friendship?"

Countee's tough mask crumbles, and the tender man I've known and cherished as a true friend for years returns. His eyes say it all. The sadness there is undeniable.

"Never question our friendship, Yolande."

"All those letters we shared. For years!" I shake my head. "I must say, you know more of my secrets than Margaret. But I knew nothing of yours."

"Well, Harold knows most of mine. But not all."

We share a laugh, because this is who we are always. Friends. We've never been lovers, but now we're impossibly married.

"And you've never been with Harold? I mean he's so handsome!"

Countee shakes his head. "We're only going to talk about me, Yolande, and what I do. If you want to know about Harold, you'll need to talk to him. But I'm not sure we're ready to speak candidly about this."

"Would you have fancied him?"

Countee closes his eyes. I'm prodding, and he's not ready to share this part of his life. All right.

"Okay, well, explain how . . . I know you like girls. I've seen you ogle them at parties. You've gotten all flustered and written poems."

"You know how you find a muscled arm in a dress shirt sexually appealing?"

"Yes?"

"So do I. But I also find the smooth flesh that bubbles over the top of your brassiere exciting. It's just that when I get in the bedroom, that particular imagery is not quite enough to . . . stoke the flames of desire."

"I see," I say carefully, although I'm not sure I really do.

"Perhaps, if there was a man present . . ."

My eyes bulge, and my mouth goes dry. "What do you mean?"

"If you are open to it, there are many configurations of carnality we might try."

"Countee, this is . . . I just . . ." Did he say this to Fiona? No wonder she broke things off expeditiously. My God, this can't be happening to me.

"Eh . . . never mind. I um . . . this is perhaps too much too soon," Countee says apologetically.

I love Countee, but I don't even want to imagine what he might be suggesting. I can only think of how things were with Jimmie. I always imagined a certain freedom to explore even more with my husband without fear of an unwanted pregnancy. But these alternative explorations that Countee offers are not for me.

"Divorce is inevitable, but it is too soon," I say, trying to ground myself in something that feels like reality. "Especially with what's already been printed in the gossip pages. That you went on a honeymoon with Harold. I need to at least be married a year so it doesn't seem like I'm at fault or defective in some way."

"You must've told someone about our disastrous wedding night."

"Margaret," I admit, "and she maybe told Anna or her mother."

Margaret has always been suspicious of Harold and by extension

Countee, but she would never start a nasty rumor about us. She'd protect my reputation at all costs.

"All it takes is one person to start a rumor. But I agree, we should take our time divorcing here. Mama Du Bois can come and stay with you so you're not too lonely."

"I'm sure she won't want to do that, but she will. Just so I can try to escape this mess unscathed."

Countee seems distressed now. I don't think he intended to hurt me in this, but I don't know how he thought I wouldn't be destroyed.

"Come out with me, Yolande. Come dancing. Come see another side of Paris."

I give Countee a sad and tearful smile. "I want to preserve the memories of my sweet friend. The boy on the hill who made me picnic lunches and wrote poems about me."

"He's still here," Countee touches his hand to his heart. "But there exists a much more complex man too, Yolande. I'd love for you to meet him as well."

"I love you, but I cannot."

Countee's smile is as sad as mine but understanding. "My mother has chosen the same path."

"But not Reverend Cullen?" I ask, surprised since he is a preacher.

"No. My father accepts me in all my humanity. He is a hero of a man. Nothing less."

Oh, to have that same unconditional acceptance from one's father! It must be a joy.

The thought of revealing these new developments about my marriage to Papa gives me an anxious knot in the pit of my stomach. Somehow, I will be blamed for Countee's humanity. For not possessing enough femininity and its associated wiles to procure at least one gifted offspring from this gifted vessel.

Chapter Sixty-One

July 1929
Harlem, New York

I'm not sure if this is the right thing to do, but I must get ahead of the speculation that's to come. I am home from Paris, and I can only imagine the news headlines. *Mrs. Cullen Returns Home from Abroad, Estranged Husband Abandoned with Lovers.* Whether anyone has seen a lover or not is of no consequence. Whether or not Countee was abandoned also does not matter. The headline is to make people read the article, and the truth is supposed to lie within.

To that end, I am giving an exclusive story to Geraldyn Dismond. Our booth at Small's is mostly secluded. Besides it's morning, so this place is abandoned.

"I must say, Yolande, I was surprised to get your call," Geraldyn begins. "I thought you'd surely avoid me once you got home."

"Why? Because of all the nasty things you've been saying about me in your society column?"

She recoils. "I've not said anything nasty."

"Maybe not nasty, but not all true either."

"I stand by my reporting," she says staunchly, although I'm not sure she totally believes that.

I clear my throat and pull out a cigarette. "Do you want the story or not?"

"Only if it's going to be the truth."

"It will be, but I think you'll be surprised about how dull it all is."

"Dull?" she scoffs. "What is mundane about having the most extravagant, extraordinary wedding the Negro elite of Harlem have ever seen, only to have the groom escape to Europe on a steamer, then after the abandoned wife gives chase, she winds up heartbroken and home with her aging parents? That sounds very exciting to me."

"The way you've crafted it makes it sound like a novel. But the truth is much plainer than that."

"What would you like to tell me, Yolande?"

Geraldyn sits back in the booth with her arms folded across her chest like she's ready to hear a tall tale. I light my cigarette and take a long drag. I ask myself one more time if I really want to do this.

"Aren't you going to get your pencil out? You're going to want to have notes, aren't you?"

"I'll start writing when you say something newsworthy," Geraldyn replies evenly. "Tell me about Countee."

Oh, she's going to make this hard. "It's not like you don't know him. But Countee Cullen is a nice man. He is one of the very best friends I ever had, and I hope he'll always be my friend."

Geraldyn stands. I take another drag of my cigarette and blow the smoke in Geraldyn's direction.

"Look, you called me, Yolande. You know I'm going to write whatever I want about you being back."

"Don't you want to be able to say your story is a firsthand account?" I ask. "Or does that even matter anymore? Do you only deal in rumors?"

Geraldyn deliberates for a moment, long enough for me to lose my taste for nicotine. By the time I've put out my cigarette, she's sitting down again. This time with her notebook and pencil ready.

"Can I ask that you not run this article until I'm back in Baltimore?" I ask. "My father is going to be livid about me talking to you."

"I understand. I don't want to get on Dr. Du Bois's bad side," Geraldyn says, and looks down at her empty notepad. "I have a favor to ask of him very soon."

I want to laugh in her face, but I don't. If she thinks Papa will ever do her any favors after she's dragged my name through her column, she is insane. This will have to be one outstanding piece of journalistic magic for her to erase the damage she's done.

"I'm ready. What do you want to know?"

"You're here, in Harlem. Is Countee still in Europe?" She's tuned in now, paying attention.

"He is still there. He extended his fellowship, and I was only on a leave of absence from Baltimore schools," I explain. "I need to fulfill my contract."

Geraldyn writes and nods. "I see. Now I did say earlier, I only write the truth. I did have confirmed reports that you were living in Paris and Countee was in London. That was very early on. Were things rocky from the start?"

"You must understand, the logistics of the European stay were in no way indicative of any problems. I went to high school in England and have seen all of London I need to see in a lifetime." I punctuate this with a rippling laugh that sounds like it came from another person, because I don't recognize it. "I enjoy Paris, and my mother joined me there."

"Countee had a visit from his father, you had a visit from your mother. How many parental visits can newlyweds tolerate?" Geraldyn looks up and asks before scribbling something else down. "Do you think that's part of the problem? Are both of you maybe too spoiled for marriage?"

"Well, we both are only children, so perhaps we are spoiled," I answer nervously, wondering if this is a trick question. "I hadn't thought of that."

Geraldyn's eyes rest on my hands folded and resting on the table. "Your ring is beautiful."

"It is, isn't it? I haven't taken it off as yet."

Geraldyn bites her bottom lip and scribbles down a few more words. "Were the two of you separate the entire time you were in Paris? Did you spend any time together as husband and wife?"

"Of course we did. We were in a hotel together right up until my mother arrived, and when I fell sick and was hospitalized in Paris, Countee came to see me every time he was in town."

"There was some talk," Geraldyn says, "unverified, so I made sure to characterize it as a rumor, that Countee was in love with another American girl, and that's why your marriage is on the rocks."

I laugh at this. If she only knew the truth about where my and Countee's affections lie. "I asked Countee about the other girl, and we both had a good laugh about that. We don't know who she could be."

"And is Countee going to get a divorce?" Geraldyn asks bluntly.

This is one fact that I want everyone to know. This is the reason I'm doing this, so that everyone can understand, no matter what Papa might infer, or Harold, since I hear he's been taking my name in vain lately, or Mrs. Cullen—

"He's not getting anything. If there is any divorce gotten, we've agreed that I will be the one to get it. I am thinking about it, but I'm not in any rush, just like I haven't taken off my ring."

This is not my fault. I am not the one to blame here. I went into this marriage without all the facts, and I am leaving it fully aware and free. No one else is entitled to the whole truth about Countee and who he loves. I don't know if this is the story Geraldyn wants, but this is the only one she's ever going to pry from me.

Anything else she writes she'll pull from her own twisted imagination, the whispers of Harlem's biddies, and the sordid letters penned by my nemesis, Harold Jackman.

Chapter Sixty-Two

July 1929
Harlem, New York

Knowing that I have given my account to Geraldyn Dismond, I feel more anchored in my new reality, even if I am stuck for a moment back in Papa's home. The divorce was filed in Paris, not just so we could keep the news out of the society columns as long as possible, but so that the reason for our divorce could remain a secret.

But being back here, under Papa's rule, is maddening. I never thought I'd be rushing back to Baltimore to teach, but I cannot wait until it is time for school to begin.

"This can still be salvaged," Papa proclaims as he paces. Mama and I are trapped on the sofa, a captive audience. "You will go back to Columbia and take classes again. Get a second degree. This time in art perhaps."

"I don't want to go to Columbia. I'm going back to teach in the fall."

"And what about until then?" Papa asks. "You need to go back out on the social scene and hold your head high."

The social scene? There is no social scene for me. I am a laughingstock. There isn't a man in Harlem who would touch me with a ten-foot pole. Hold my head high for what? So I can look at people's faces while they gossip about me?

Countee doesn't have to suffer any of this. He's still in Paris hiding from everyone's scorn, probably checking in with Harold to see when things have died down and it's safe to return.

"Will, this is impossible," Mama says as I burst into tears. "You cannot fix this situation with a letter writing campaign or an article in *The Crisis*. The marriage is over."

"It is not over, Nina!" Papa's voice sounds like thunder. "She needs to get back out there, before she's too old to bear children. If Yolande never marries, we will never have grandchildren. Our legacy will die with her."

Mama stands and closes the space between her and Papa. Their noses nearly touch, but Papa does not retreat.

"Your legacy is all you care about." Mama's usual calm voice is suddenly sharp and enraged. "Your daughter is sitting here broken and all you can think of is what history will write about you!"

"Mind your tone, Nina," he snarls.

"Or what, Will? What can you do to me that you haven't already done?" Papa looks away from her fiery gaze.

Suddenly, I get the feeling this conversation is about something entirely different. Because never have I seen Papa shrink before Mama or anyone else. And I doubt that I'll ever see it again.

* * *

I MANAGED TO escape the beauty parlor without answering too many questions from the curious Harlem ladies who wanted to know all about my marital woes. It helps that I haven't removed my ring, because I can say *My husband is still in Paris*, since our divorce hasn't been finalized.

I don't want to say anything else or breathe life into any of the rumors. Perhaps I should just let Geraldyn publish her story and get it over with, but I know these women well enough to know that the article will just cause more curiosity, speculation, and of course pity. The pity is the worst part of it. The part I truly hate. Because most of the time, the pity just means they're glad to hear someone else is worse off than they are.

As I rush up Lenox Avenue from the beauty parlor to our new place at the Paul Laurence Dunbar Apartments, I remind myself to hold my head high and meet people's gaze with a smile and hello. It's hard because I'd rather not speak, and I want to keep my eyes trained on the ground. But that will only make people think poorly of me or that I've done something to be ashamed of, and I haven't.

And then, right outside the Cotton Club, looking fresh as a shiny new penny, is my Jimmie. As if he stepped right out of my dreams. For the time it takes for my heart to beat a few times, I am frozen in place. But then, the blood makes it to my limbs, and I quickly attempt an escape before he sees me. He is the last person on earth I want to run in to today or ever.

But it's too late. He's seen me, and now he's running toward me like he doesn't care that he's wearing a fancy suit and dress shoes.

So, I wait and try to catch my breath.

"Yolande, it's you," Jimmie says, staring at me like I'm an apparition. "I thought . . . I mean, I read you were in Paris. I didn't know you were in Harlem."

"It is me." His face looks the same. I want to touch it, like I wanted to touch it on my wedding day when he appeared at the church, and Papa pulled me away.

"Why are you in Harlem?" he asks.

I laugh. "I live here. Well, for the summer I do. Why are *you* in Harlem? Didn't you move to Memphis?"

I wonder if he wants to hug me. I want to hug him so badly, but it wouldn't be proper for a married woman to be seen hugging her former lover in the middle of Lenox Avenue. But I want to feel his arms around me. I am starving for his touch. My body remembers him.

"I am here because I have my own band called the Harlem Express," Jimmie says proudly, "and we just got a gig at the Cotton Club."

Jimmie's going to be in Harlem, playing a few steps down from

our apartment? Is the Wishing Tree magic just punishing me now?
"For how long?"

"For six months to start. Maybe longer."

"That's real nice, Jimmie. I'm so proud of you," I say. "If I wasn't a married woman, I'd give you a big hug to congratulate you."

Jimmie blushes and grins. "Thank you. How's that going anyway? Married life."

My smile fades. I wasn't going to tell him if he didn't ask.

"It's not going well at all. We're getting a divorce. It's already been filed."

He looks down at my finger, still adorned with my wedding ring. "But you're still wearing his ring."

"So that everyone in Harlem doesn't ask about it."

Jimmie stares at the ground for what feels like a long time. Like he's pondering his next move. Deliberating.

"I'm staying at the Hotel Olga," he says.

"Is that an invitation?"

"I'd just like to spend time with you. Talk, you know? Share a meal. It's not like we can do that in public with you still wearing that ring."

He's got to know like I know, if I come to his hotel room, we're going to do more than talk. But I'll let him fool himself into thinking he's got honorable intent.

"I'll consider it."

"All right. Friday night, if you can come. It'll be like old times."

Old times. I don't know if it's old times that I need. Perhaps that is the reason my first instinct on seeing my Jimmie was to flee.

Chapter Sixty-Three

July 1929
Harlem, New York

This morning, Mama's usually pleasant, smiling face is replaced by a grim frown, thin lips pressed tightly showing her displeasure. With me, I'm sure. But I am also sure I don't care.

I am not hungry for breakfast, so it's a cup of coffee and a Benson and Hedges while I read the newspaper at the kitchen table. Papa would be annoyed at the latter, but I picked up the habit of smoking and reading from him, so he's to blame for it.

There's a loud knock at the door and I look up at Mama. "Are you expecting anyone?"

If she is, I will remove myself to my bedroom. Not in the mood to answer any questions about the divorce. Or Countee. Or his affairs and salacious activities with other men. I am done talking about all of it, and that's all anyone wants to talk about.

"I am not entertaining today, Yolande," Mama says. "Perhaps you have a caller."

Mama looks down at her book as if she has no intention of moving, meaning she wants me to see about the visitor. Suddenly, I feel thirteen years old again and commanded about by Mama.

I stand and walk over to the door as the impatient knocker continues to pound on the door. Whoever it is, is quite rude.

My jaw drops when I see who it is through the peeping window, but I swing the full door open before she gets the opportunity to knock again.

"Chrystal Tulli. Why are you here? How do you even know where I live?"

"Is that any way to treat a fellow Fisk alumna? I'm surprised at you, Yolande."

"Did I hear someone say Fisk alumna? Is that one of your friends from Fisk?" Mama asks as she appears in the room. "Invite her in. I'll make some tea."

I want to yell that Chrystal is not my friend. She is the one who ruined my relationship with Jimmie. Why would she be here in Harlem at the same time as Jimmie? Why would she be in Harlem at all?

"Well, isn't your mother a dear. Thank you, Mrs. Du Bois. I brought Danish pastry."

Since I don't step aside to allow Chrystal entry into our apartment, she pushes past me and lets herself in. But since Mama stands there welcoming her and reaching for her box of pastries, there is nothing I can do.

"Mama, this is Chrystal Tulli. Do you remember me talking about her in my letters?"

Mama smiles with no recognition on her face, so if she does remember, she is not letting on. "The name doesn't ring a bell. Did she live in Jubilee Hall?"

"I did indeed, Mrs. Du Bois. Yolande and I were in the Decagynian Society together."

"I see," Mama says, beaming. "Well, a Fisk alumna is always welcome."

Chrystal looks all around the apartment, assessing, before handing Mama the box of pastries and then perching daintily on the edge of the couch. I put out my cigarette and sit in the armchair wondering about the reason for her visit.

"So, what brings you to Harlem?" I ask, softening my tone, because Mama is glaring at me, as if I'm the one being rude.

"I travel with the Harlem Express. Jimmie didn't tell you?" Chrystal sneers as she lets this information sink in, but I don't give her the reaction she seeks.

Inside though, I am reeling. Why wouldn't he mention that? He tells me about his engagement with the Cotton Club that's mere blocks away from our apartment. He invites me to his hotel, but fails to mention Chrystal travels with him?

Was the invitation a spur-of-the-moment decision? That must be it. Had he tried to move on since I married Countee? I expected that he would. But then he saw me on the street and our love came rushing back to his heart. Our relationship is an angry ghost. Intent on destroying any happiness we might try to create elsewhere. But doesn't magic always come with a price?

"He didn't mention you, Chrystal. What do you do?" I ask calmly, like I'm truly interested in the answer. "Sing with the band?"

Chrystal laughs. "Oh no. Jimmie would never have his lady doing that. I take care of his business affairs."

I swallow the taste of copper pennies and bile that rises from my throat. I will not fall apart in front of this demon. Not at all. Besides, she's sitting here out of sorts, making declarations about being Jimmie's "lady" when he's invited me to spend time with him in his hotel room. If I was her, I'd hold my tongue on declaring things.

I force a fake and bright smile. "I see. Well, I'm sure you're a hard worker."

"The Harlem Express is going to be world famous soon," she brags. "They should be taken very seriously."

I hate that I put my cigarette out because I could sure use another drag. Jimmie told her what Papa said? She's throwing my papa's words in my face?

"Out of all the people in Harlem you could've visited, you came to see me," I say, finally done with this preposterous dialogue. "Why is that, when we are not friends?"

"I'd like you to leave Jimmie alone. My friend saw you talking to him on Lenox Avenue."

Finally, she's gotten to the point of why she's come in the first place. She could've led with that and said this at the door. Didn't need to waste my time or her money on Danish pastry.

I close my eyes, chuckle, and shake my head. "Jimmie is a grown man. Is he not allowed to say hello to an old friend?"

"Jimmie and I are engaged." She thrusts her hand toward me. I recognize his mother's ring. The one I didn't accept senior year at Fisk.

That copper penny taste comes rushing to my mouth again. Again, I swallow it down. Why would Jimmie invite me to his hotel if he's engaged to be married? Is he not sure about his choice? Does he want to see if there's still a chance for us?

"Well, it seems to me, then, that you ought to be having a conversation with your intended."

Chrystal opens her purse, reaches inside, and pulls out a tissue. She begins to dab at the corners of her eyes, but I don't feel sorry for her. I only look at Chrystal and see the treacherous heffa who tried to make my life hell.

"You don't know what it was like for him when he came to Memphis after your wedding," she says between soft sobs.

"You're right. I don't." I see Mama frown at me from the corner of my eye, as she goes to sit next to Chrystal and offers her another tissue.

"Thank you, Mrs. Du Bois," Chrystal says, looking up at Mama for sympathy. "I almost don't want to tell you, because I think you'd like to hear how broken he was over you. You never cared about how you broke him."

Now I feel my anger rise. The copper penny taste is gone and replaced with fury. "That's not true."

"It is. He was infatuated with you when he first got to Fisk, and you held his nose open until the day you married that poet."

Apparently, his nose is still open, whether he's engaged to this heffa or not. But that's neither here nor there. She's interpreting the story the way she wants to see things, but I don't care to correct her narrative.

"I'm sorry you see it that way," I snap, then stand and walk to the door because I'm ready for her to leave.

"I don't know what he ever saw in you anyway," she snaps back.

"*Sees* in me."

Chrystal's nostrils flare as she dabs her eyes again. "And you're proud of that. Fooling around with another woman's fiancé."

"If I was going to fool around with anyone, it would be because they didn't mention being engaged," I say this calmly, so she can understand that this is between her and Jimmie. I have nothing to do with any deception now.

Finally, Chrystal stands, understanding that she's overstayed her welcome. Well, she was never welcome to begin with.

"I don't want to have to put him back together again," she says, striding to the door. "Leave him alone. You had your time, let him move on. Stop breaking him because you're broken."

Then she turns to my mother.

"I'm sorry, Mrs. Du Bois, I'm going to have to cut my visit short. It was lovely meeting you," Chrystal says, putting on a fake smile.

"Likewise." Mama sounds sad and looks disappointed, but I am glad she doesn't say more and doesn't invite Chrystal back again.

Chrystal walks out of the apartment with her nose pointed to the sky and her big hair blossoming out like a huge afro flower. If she wasn't my sworn enemy, she might be beautiful, but I don't feel bad about the tears streaking down her face. If that makes me a horrible person, then so be it. Why should I be in pain all by myself?

I close the door behind Chrystal and turn to face Mama, who has a deep frown on her face. I sit next to her on the couch, dreading what she's going to say, but knowing I can't avoid the conversation.

"Are you sneaking around Harlem with Jimmie again, Yolande? You aren't even divorced yet," Mama hisses.

"I am not doing anything . . . yet."

Mama closes her eyes and shakes her head angrily. "My God, Yolande. Aren't you tired of being the subject of scorn? Between you and your father, I cannot rest from gossip."

"Papa encouraged me to marry a man who prefers men, Mama. That is not my fault," I argue. "I have always loved Jimmie. I would have married him eventually if Papa had only approved of him and not made me doubt myself, and not made Jimmie feel like a fool."

"You cannot change what has already happened. Those mistakes have been made," Mama says. "Move on with your life."

"Mama, you do not understand the way it is between me and Jimmie. Our love for each other never waned."

"He has a fiancée, Yolande." I can hear the exasperation in her voice, but can she hear the desperation in mine?

"Yes. Chrystal plotted on him from day one at Fisk. She always coveted him, Mama. She could never understand why a man who looked like him had chosen me over her."

"Is that why you always choose the handsome ones, Yolande? I wondered about that. Perfectly respectable young men, tripping over themselves to be with you, and you always want the men all the women want."

"Well, the one I married was funny-looking and portly around the middle, and you see where that got me." I let out a scorned chuckle. None of this is funny.

"That was your father's doing. He encouraged and persuaded you there. Gently nudged you away from the men who were like him."

"*Gently* should never be used to describe Papa. And Jimmie is nothing like him."

Mama scoffs and shakes her head. "Isn't he? A Fisk man, trained in sociology."

"That is where the similarities end."

Mama shakes her head. "No, there is another similarity. He's running behind you while another woman has his ring on her finger."

Mama stares at me, allowing the words to sink in. I had, of course, heard the rumors. Harold had made more than one off-color insinuation, but then he was always sharing gossip. Often he was the source of it. Countee had even commented twice about Papa's "indiscretions," as if it was common knowledge, but I had not-so-politely corrected him both times.

"Mama, what are you saying?" I ask, wanting to hear it from her. Tired of people talking in code. Wanting everyone to just be direct for once.

"I think you know what I'm saying. I have lost count of the women over the years."

I squeeze my eyes shut and feel myself swoon.

"No, Yolande!" Mama snaps. "Open your eyes. You will not faint your way out of this like a little girl. You have chosen to play a grown woman's game, so you will be an adult. You will hear this."

Slowly, I open my eyes. The hard and unforgiving cushion underneath my backside adds to my discomfort as Mama's fury bears into me.

"Your papa was always a handsome man, but his power and his notoriety is what draws them. And probably why he seeks them out!"

"Mama . . ." I beg.

"Some of them, I've befriended," she continues, ignoring my pleas for mercy. "Because I wanted to see what there was that I was missing. They were rarely prettier than I am, though most were younger."

Younger? I can't imagine Papa's stern and domineering persona being exciting or attractive to a young woman.

"Miss Fauset, now Mrs. Harris, since she's finally found her own husband, warmed your father's bedside for years. While you were away at Fisk and before."

Her words just set my blood to boiling. The entire time Papa's been railing against Jimmie and his character, he's been cheating on Mama. But I cannot believe this about Miss Fauset.

"Mama . . . this cannot be true," I protest, shaking my head in disbelief, thinking of all the advice I've received from Miss Fauset. The times she visited me with Papa.

Were they sleeping together then? In Nashville? Then I recall the time Papa read a note from Miss Fauset and put it in his jacket pocket. He'd smiled. What had that note said? Was it a lover's note? Had she invited him to her hotel room later that evening?

My mind is spiraling. The woman who quoted Bible stories to me when I asked for advice? *That* Miss Fauset?

Mama inhales a heavy breath that she laboriously exhales. "It is true, but things between me and your papa are complicated. I . . . hate what he does, but I would never leave my marriage over it."

"You must be mistaken about Miss Fauset," I repeat, because I need Mama to correct this.

"I went to see her once," Mama says, staring off into the distance, as if she's remembering the day. "I had never quite decided on what I was going to say before I arrived. Maybe I intended to ask her to leave my husband alone, like Chrystal just did with you. Or maybe I wanted her to know I wasn't a fool."

"For staying with Papa?" I ask.

"Not even that. No woman, as well cared for as I am, would leave a respected husband over dalliances."

"I would. I did," I scoff, because here I sit in my parents' living room while my husband is in Paris having his share of dalliances with whomever he pleases.

"That is quite different, Yolande."

It's funny how Countee hadn't seen it as different at all. But at least Countee had confessed his sins.

"I wanted her to know that they weren't fooling me. The trips abroad and all over the country. I knew all about her. And the others."

Mama narrows her eyes to angry little slits, probably thinking about what they were doing together that Papa should've only been doing with her.

My nostrils flare with my own disdain, because how dare Miss Fauset sit in our house? Smile in Mama's face? Call herself my mentor and then share Papa's bed? It's too much.

"What did she say when you told her what you knew?"

"She stood there looking like a dumb bunny," Mama scoffs. "Just like you will if you keep carrying on with Jimmie."

I shake my head. Jimmie and I are not the same. "Mama . . ."

"No, you listen to me. I fully and wholly blame your father for continuing to break his marital vows," Mama says, grabbing my arm and digging into my flesh with her fingertips. "But he could not do so without the willing consent of some woman. It does not go against a man's nature to be unfaithful, but it is unnatural for a woman to give herself over to such treachery."

I cannot recall ever hearing Mama speak with this amount of conviction or passion about anything. So, I choose not to debate with her or try to convince her of all the ways where Jimmie and I are different.

Besides, my mind keeps traveling back to Papa, conniving ways to make me cross paths with Countee. That initial summer vacation to Pleasantville, when Mama and I stayed two doors down from the Cullens. We'd never even vacationed in Pleasantville. Always in Great Barrington. But Papa thought it would be nice for us to try somewhere different.

Then, he suggested that Countee visit Fisk with Miss Fauset for my Decagynian affair. I wonder who put the bug in Countee's ear to come see about me in Baltimore when I was all alone and trying to make my mark in the world as a teacher. Was that Papa too? And then sending me to Europe for the summer when we couldn't even truly afford the expense. But when he found out that Countee would be in Paris, with a broken engagement from Fiona Braithwaite, he suddenly came up with the money to send me.

Papa kept pushing me toward Countee when he knew I loved Jimmie. Even if I *did* want to discover my gifts and make a difference as a Delta woman, I was always planning to go back to Jimmie. Always.

"Mama, you never told me Jimmie came looking for me." My accusation is quiet and mournful. If she had told me, it would've changed everything. I think I only needed reassurance that he loved me. "After he and I argued, and I went to Baltimore. He came for me, and you didn't tell me until it was too late."

Mama sighs as her hand falls from my arm and into her lap. "After everything that's happened, I regret that now. But those mistakes are made, and you must move on with your life, Yolande. There is someone else for you out there, I am sure of it."

But I am not sure of it. I am not sure at all.

And now, I don't know whose betrayal was worse. Mama's, Papa's, or Miss Fauset's.

Chapter Sixty-Four

July 1929
Harlem, New York

Did you know?"

The question rolls off my lips before *bonjour* or *comment allez-vous*. I have no capacity for pleasantries, not knowing what I know. That Miss Fauset shared more than *The Crisis* and the movement with Papa.

That Mama had unwittingly then unwillingly shared Papa with Miss Fauset.

And Miss Fauset is married now. To some insurance broker named Herbert Harris, but she's never left Harlem. She's still here, allowing herself to be seen by Mama at social events and restaurants, when she ought to hide her face.

I may have no right to judge her since I was going to meet Jimmie at Hotel Olga if Chrystal hadn't come to our home. But I *am* judging her because they are my parents.

Besides, I couldn't go to Jimmie after all that. Chrystal's revelation plus Papa and Miss Fauset's treachery had soured our sweet reunion. Chrystal had won and I'd lost once again.

"Did I know what?" Miss Fauset asks as if she hasn't already pried the reason for my separation from Countee out of Papa.

Don't lovers share secrets across the pillow? I am sure Papa shared mine with Miss Fauset. Although I hope since she's now married, they're not still lovers. But since she stayed in Harlem, I have no idea whether they are or not.

"That Countee has affection for men." I punctuate each syllable with anger, because she *had* to know. "That he prefers them, if what happened in our bedroom is any indication."

The color drains from Miss Fauset's face. "You mustn't believe what they say in the papers about Countee. You know he traveled to Europe for his fellowship, not to honeymoon with Harold."

"I am not talking about the papers," I respond incredulously. "I'm referring to what Countee said to me out of his own mouth."

Miss Fauset blinks rapidly and takes a few steps backward. She stumbles and sits on her sofa, but I continue to stand. I am not here for a social visit.

"I—I have just known Countee to be a t-tender young man," she stammers. "I had h-heard things, but I never believed them."

"So, you heard these things, but still told me I should marry him?" I advance toward her.

"I was not the one telling you to marry him!" she objects, head shaking and eyes wide. "I only know how much Countee fancied you from the very start, and I don't believe in listening to rumors."

I'm in front of her now, my index finger pointed directly at her face. "You never told me not to marry him, Jessie. And *you'd heard rumors.*"

She stands now and knocks my hand away. "*Jessie?*"

"Yes, you have contributed to the current demise of my happiness." She wants respect, but I have none for her—not anymore. We stand very close, chest to chest, nearly nose to nose. "So, it's Jessie. The pain I feel is too intimate to be calling you *Mrs.* after what you've done."

"All right, then, Yolande," Miss Fauset says, her voice cold. "What could I have done to prevent any of this?"

"You could've told me the truth," I yell angrily.

Miss Fauset turns away from me, takes a few steps across the room, but I am still furious. She looks out her front window at the busy Harlem street, leaving me to wonder what she's thinking.

"I told you the truth I knew," she explains with her back to me. "The rest were only rumors."

"Should I believe the rumors about you and my father? What about those?"

Miss Fauset turns around with an expression that has turned darker. "You wouldn't be asking me this if you didn't think you already knew something. So, ask me what you really want to ask."

I close the space between us. "How could you advise me not to follow my passions for Jimmie when you were following yours?"

"You see where following passions got me," Miss Fauset says with a sad chuckle. "I gave you sound advice. Hearts *are* treacherous."

"No. You and Papa are treacherous! Selfish and heartless! Did you never think of my mother?" I stare at her, truly looking for contrition. I need to see that she's sorry about hurting Mama.

Miss Fauset pushes past me, unable to meet my searching eyes. "Were you heartless when you were talking to Jimmie even after he was engaged? Did you think of his fiancée?"

"I thought you didn't listen to rumors."

She spins on one heel and shakes her head. "I don't. I saw you outside the beauty salon with my own eyes. You've never been one for discretion, Yolande."

"Why do I need to be discreet now?" I shriek in utter disbelief at her audacity. "My entire life has been laid bare and put in newspapers and magazines. Why should I be discreet?"

"Because your father is a very important man to every colored person in this country. You cannot tarnish his good name."

"Really? You and Papa snuck around for years, and you tell me to worry about his good name?"

Miss Fauset closes her eyes and lets out a deep, regretful sigh. "If we were anything, it was discreet."

"And still, Mama knew," I spit, my words full of fire. "Knew and kept quiet about it! Just like you and Papa knew about Countee and pushed me into his arms."

"Your papa had no idea about Countee! You must know that. He would never put you in such a position."

"I don't know what to believe. I only know that the one man I've always loved is lost to me forever. The one man who loved me, despite Papa disrespecting him and trying to drive him away." My tears start now, and I don't know how I'll be able to stop them from falling, but I don't care. "He never cared about Papa's status or who Papa was. He only cared about me. And I know now that no one will ever love me completely and purely as Jimmie did."

Miss Fauset rushes over and reaches for me. Tries to hug me, but I push her away. I don't want her affection.

"I'm so sorry, Yolande," she says. "We all thought we were doing what was best, steering you away from Jimmie."

"If you weren't so busy trying to please my father by delivering a Talented Tenth husband to his unremarkable daughter, maybe you would have seen what was right under your nose."

"But you were so busy trying to please your father that you married Countee anyway." She shakes her head at me.

"I guess we both had the same goal."

"And we both failed!" Miss Fauset says. "Say whatever you like, Yolande, and feel however you want to feel about me. You made a woman's decision when you married Countee. No matter what pressure your father put on you, it was still your choice."

"Jimmie still loves me. He always will."

"Sometimes love is not enough, Yolande. But here you are in my home making accusations, still sounding very much like a child."

She sounds like Mama, wanting me to believe that my love for Jimmie would not sustain us. I imagine Jimmie waiting at the Hotel Olga for me. Hoping that I'd appear, and me letting him down again.

It was a foolish plan he had anyway, since he'd been sharing that bed with Chrystal. But Jimmie had never been much for nefarious deeds. Maybe if I'd shown up, he would have broken things off with her immediately. I suppose I'll never know now.

"Is that what happened with you and Papa? Was your love not enough? Maybe you didn't love him at all. Were you just using him for your literary career?"

Miss Fauset scowls. But will she answer me?

"I'm going to have to ask you to leave, Yolande. I don't speak of those things anymore. It is all in the past."

I stride over to the door, not feeling any vindication. I can only think of how Jimmie must have felt when I didn't arrive at the Hotel Olga last Friday night. Chrystal will never tell him that she came to my parents' home begging me to stay away. He will only know that he tried to salvage our love once more, and I let him down. Again.

But it's only Tuesday. Maybe he's still at the hotel. Maybe there's still time.

Chapter Sixty-Five

July 1929
Harlem, New York

It's too late.

When I walk up to the Hotel Olga and see the Ford outfitted with the Just Married sign, streamers, and cans tied to the bumper, I feel dread in the pit of my stomach. Of course, it can be for any couple. There are weddings every weekend in Harlem, and honeymoons all the time at the Hotel Olga, truly the only hotel in Harlem where Negroes feel welcome.

But deep down I know the car is there for Jimmie and Chrystal. Without proof, I can feel it in my soul.

Because Chrystal has a reason to rush things. Even if she wants to get married in a Memphis church with all her family and friends present, she has a very pressing reason to rush Jimmie to any old courthouse to close the deal. To finish things.

She has no reason to trust that I will stay away from him. Jimmie is a flight risk. She knows him well.

She knows *us* well.

Jimmie asking me to see him was his last-ditch effort to see if we can have our forever. Chrystal is his consolation prize. And she knows it.

If he can have me, he'll take me in a heartbeat. No matter what piece of jewelry she wears on her finger.

I go up to the bellman at the hotel's entrance and ask, "Who is the happy couple?"

He grins and says, "Oh, it's a jazz musician with a gig down at the Cotton Club. Jimmie Lunceford. Got a band called Harlem Express. I hear they're really good."

"They are good," I say, while blinking back my tears. "I've heard them play. They're the cat's meow."

"Well maybe I'll go check them out when I get off work," he says. "You need a room, miss?"

"No, I was just passing by and saw the car. I'm meeting a friend for dinner down the street."

The bellman glances down at my ring and winks. "I'd ask you out myself if you weren't married."

I smile at him through blurred vision. My tears are winning the battle as I fight to keep them in check. "You have a good evening," I say. "I must go."

I hurry away, just before the first one falls, because it is over now. The magic, our love story, the dream of our forever. It is done.

I can continue pursuing Jimmie and probably have clandestine meetings with him at the Hotel Olga, or some other hotel in some other city. We can lie in each other's arms and reminisce about the past after making love. I'll smoke a cigarette, and he will go home to his wife.

And Chrystal, like Mama, will never leave her husband or be able to make him stop his cheating ways. She'll suffer in silence, but feel like she's won, because he comes home to her. She has the title of wife, and what will I have? His heart, perhaps, but Jimmie is honorable, so he won't leave Chrystal either. So, I'll never have what I want. I'll never have a husband and family of my own.

I walk away from the Hotel Olga with a heavy heart. The spell of the Wishing Tree is finally broken. In time the magic will fade, and one day Jimmie and I will both be free. To heal and to love again.

But there is another stranglehold I need to break. A blood tie that is even more powerful than wishing magic.

Chapter Sixty-Six

July 1929
Harlem, New York

Papa comes storming into the apartment. I am sitting on the living room sofa waiting for him. Waiting for this moment. I am glad that Mama has gone to visit friends in Philadelphia. She does not need to be here for this. I don't want her serenity or mediation.

"Hello, Papa," I say. "I hope you ate before you got home because I didn't cook anything. I had a late lunch with friends. If you didn't eat, there's tuna salad for sandwiches."

He sets his briefcase onto the floor and stands across the room from me with his arms folded across his chest, glaring angrily at me.

"Yolande, what is the meaning of this?" he roars. "I pulled strings to get you back into Columbia University. Exhausted favors."

"Did you?" I ask flippantly, knowing that's going to make him angrier.

Papa's mouth closes before he can launch again. He tilts his head to one side. Is he wondering why I'm not quaking in fear?

"You're going back to Baltimore," he says, calmer now and more measured.

"Yes. We discussed this. I was on a leave of absence, and I must fulfill my contract. Isn't that what you said? I must keep my word?"

Papa twitches with frustration. "I did say that, but extenuating circumstances . . ."

"These are *my* circumstances, Papa, and they are not extenuating. I can go back to Baltimore. I've made my own living arrangements this time. I don't need your help with that."

I am renting an apartment with two other teachers. We're going to split the expenses three ways. I may not be able to afford any new dresses, but if I watch what I eat, I'll be able to fit the ones I have for a good while.

"We discussed the fact that you need to stay here," Papa says, sounding very impatient, "where there is more opportunity for you to find a husband."

"There are men in Baltimore," I reply, matching his irritation. "I will do as I please."

He begins to pace. I don't care. He can wear a hole in the floor pacing if he wants. "So, you're just going to throw your youth away? Accept spinsterhood?"

I shrug off his insults. "Perhaps. I heard it preserves a woman's youth and sanity to forgo marriage and children."

"A tale probably told by a lonely old childless woman," Papa scoffs.

I throw my head back and let my maniacal cackle fill the room. "Maybe it was told by a woman whose husband was a philanderer like you, Papa."

He steps backward as if I accosted him. "What?"

"Papa, I have heard about your exploits. I'm not here to judge you for it. That's between you and Mama."

"You have no room to judge anyone on morals or fidelity," Papa says angrily, pacing again.

I shake my head and laugh again. "I just don't know how you found time to meddle in my affairs while you were climbing in and out of bed with Miss Fauset."

He moves toward me like he's going to strike me. I don't move. I squeeze my eyes and wait for the sting of a slap.

It doesn't come.

Slowly I open my eyes to see that Papa has collapsed into his recliner.

"Yolande, I have only ever wanted the best for you," he says, sounding weary, like the older man that he is.

"Jimmie was the best for me." My voice trembles with emotion. "He loved me more than anything, and I love him still."

"You think I'm wrong just because he's playing at the Cotton Club?" Papa asks as he juts his chin forward obstinately.

"You're not a prophet, even if you think you are."

Although I am so tired of weeping, and my eyes are red and dry, here I am starting again. I thought I was out of tears, but my body keeps finding a way to replenish them. They never run dry. I drop my head into my hands and will this pain to end, because how can I survive if I keep hurting this way?

"What I am is a father determined to keep his daughter from going into the pit no matter how desperately she wants to fall in," Papa says, somewhat softer now. Perhaps my tears have pricked his heart.

I look up at Papa with pleading eyes. "How? By dooming me to a loveless marriage like the one you and Mama have?"

Papa sits up straight and peers at me like he's trying to determine where this conversation is headed. He's looking in the wrong place, because I'm not quite sure. I just know that whatever unfolds, it's past time for it.

"You can't think I knew about Countee's proclivities. It's downright shameful and an offense against all the gods for someone as gifted as Countee to not give back to his people with progeny."

"I won't have you disparage Countee," I tell him, my voice rising. "He was trying to make you happy, like everyone else."

"Lies. He wants to hide his perversion in plain sight by appearing normal and marrying a woman!" Papa shakes a finger at me.

"Leave him alone!" I shout. "He is still my friend."

"You'll never find anyone to marry in Baltimore, Yolande." Papa is almost pleading now. "Let me send you to Washington, D.C., or Philadelphia. I have colleagues and friends there who can help."

I cannot believe he thinks I would trust him with my future husband. He chased Jimmie away and thought Countee the pick of the litter. No thank you. I will trust my own instincts from now on.

"I don't want your help." I hold up a hand and shake my head at him. "I don't need it. One day I may give you a grandchild. Or I may not."

"I had always hoped for more out of you, Yolande. You had a firm foundation. Alas, it is struggle that brings about greatness. I should not have spoiled you. You may have turned out differently."

I've spent my entire life trying to please him. Everything I've done, every choice I've made has been with the goal of somehow trying to get his approval. And still, it hasn't been enough! Why did I even try? I could have had the man I love—the man who loved me back—if I hadn't been so desperate for Papa's approval.

"Maybe if you hadn't made greatness a condition of your love," I say quietly, "I would have chosen to love myself sooner." As soon as the words leave my lips, peace envelops me like a warm blanket on a frigid Harlem winter night.

Because I can start now.

I stare at Papa, seeing him for the first time through adult eyes. He's aging even more rapidly these past few years. I wonder if losing Miss Fauset took a toll, or if that was even love at all on his part.

Finally, and for the first time ever, I stride out of the living room and leave Papa sitting in his armchair. I've finished our conversation because I am done. Behind my bedroom door, I realize this is a child's room, with furniture for a much younger girl. I suppose in my parents' eyes I am still their precious little girl.

My father, my hero. Everything I've done to make him proud of me and to deem me worthy. When I've been enough the entire time. More than enough.

But now that I know everything—his treachery and flaws—I can never again submit to his will for my life. I will only be concerned with the advancement of one colored person.

Me.

Chapter Sixty-Seven

January 1931
Baltimore, Maryland

Tonight is the first session of the adult education class I signed up to teach. Not because I don't work hard enough. I am not a glutton for punishment. But it is hard living on a teacher's salary. I can barely make ends meet, much less have a nice dinner out or night at the theatre. These things are quite expensive when paying for them yourself. It makes me appreciate the lengths poor men go through in courting some of us. The spoiled ones of us.

At any rate, hell will feel like January in Massachusetts before I call my papa and ask him for money. It will come with demands, strings, and potential husbands. None of which I am interested in.

He's gotten quite desperate, I hear, interviewing widowers and divorcés, hoping someone will take care of his plump, spinster daughter. But when I am home for the holidays, I do not submit to any of his matchmaking attempts. I refuse them all.

So, I'm here in the evening to teach poor unfortunate souls to read. It's giving back to the community—even if I am getting paid—because they can never find enough teachers to cover all the classes.

I sit at my desk in the front of the room. Even though it's the same classroom I have during the day for my high schoolers, it feels different with older men and women trudging in after a hard day's work, hoping to make a better life for themselves.

Then, when class is about to start, a tall man in a fedora and overcoat rushes in and takes a seat in the back row. As he peels off his coat and I take in his smooth, clean-shaven face and well-fitting suit, I am wondering what kind of lucky mistake this might be.

"Ahem, sir, in the back row, are you sure you're in the right place?"

"This is the adult reading class, correct?"

I nod.

"I'm Arnett Williams and I'm a ballplayer," he explains with a wink. "I'm going to the Negro league soon, and I gotta be able to read the contracts."

His smile gleams brightly like a lantern on a dark night. I feel myself smiling back.

"I don't know if I'm going to be able to learn from a pretty lady like you," Arnett says. "I was thinking it was going to be some old battle-axe."

"Knock it off," says a tired-looking woman in the front. "Let her teach the lesson so we can get home. Maybe she'll be interested in you if you learn to read."

Maybe? If he keeps smiling like that and if his hands can do half of what I think they can (what they *look* like they can), I'm more than interested.

After all, a man I can teach to read after he's grown must be gifted and talented. A ballplayer too?

Sounds like Dr. Du Bois's perfect son-in-law.

Epilogue

July 1942
Baltimore, Maryland

I feel foolish doing this. Standing backstage at the Royal Theater with my daughter, Du Bois, hoping for a glimpse of the band. It's really the bandleader I want to see—Jimmie—although I don't know if he'd care to see me. I am only hoping and perhaps wishing. Therein lies the foolishness. My last wish was the one I shared with Jimmie at the Wishing Tree in Harlem.

"Mama, it's hot and stuffy back here," Du Bois fusses as she tugs at the starched collar of her new dress. "The show is over, so can't we go home?"

"I thought you wanted to meet my friend." I stroke her thick pony-tail, a soothing motion I can remember my own mama doing when I was being a handful.

"Well, I changed my mind now. My tummy changed its mind. It's ravenous."

"*Ravenous!*" I can't help but smile. "That is a very ambitious word choice."

"Papa taught it to me. He says it's when I have a gargantuan hunger."

"Oh my. Well, we must get you sustenance, then."

"We must, Mama. We don't want my constitution getting low."

I stifle a giggle at Du Bois's theatrics. She has learned well from Papa's tutelage. At first, I was concerned that he might not embrace his only grandchild because of who I selected as her father. And he did try to remain stoic toward her in the beginning. It did not last, however. Du Bois is too charming, and Papa is too obsessed with his offspring.

And she is brilliant. Smarter than I was at her age. She would do well at Bedales School. Unfortunately, I cannot afford to send her, and though her father makes decent money playing ball he has abandoned us.

Papa was, of course, livid when I said yes to Arnett's proposal after a whirlwind romance. He refused to help us at all unless Arnett agreed to go to college. Arnett had no desire to go to college, but he wanted me, so he agreed to Papa's demands—if Papa paid the tuition. Turns out, Papa was so worried what people would think if his daughter was married to some uneducated brute that he *did* pay for it. More than six hundred dollars to send Arnett to Lincoln University.

Then when Arnett struggled in school, Papa hounded him and harassed him until he graduated, but he still had trouble finding work. Meanwhile, I'd given birth to little Du Bois and stayed with Mama in Atlanta for a while, since Papa had split with the NAACP and gone to Atlanta University to be the chair of the sociology department.

I even left the baby with her when I moved back to Baltimore to teach, because Arnett's unsavory family of gamblers was there and he wanted to live near them. I'm just glad Arnett didn't object to me leaving Du Bois with my parents. She was spoiled and reared well with them, and Arnett didn't like her whining and crying anyway.

It was not an ideal situation, and it was worsened by the fact that I'd gained weight and was not used to struggling. I hated it really, and so did Arnett. He felt there was nothing he could do to be good enough in my eyes, and to tell the truth, he was probably right because I had married the wrong man—again.

But this time, he wasn't sweet and kindhearted like Countee. He was mean and belligerent and liked to hit when he felt angry. I couldn't deal with being abused, so I found myself divorced a second time.

That was six years ago, and we haven't heard from Arnett since the divorce. It's funny how men just seem to move on from me without a care and I am forced to put the remnants of myself back together.

Even Countee has remarried—a beautiful woman named Ida. I wonder if she accepts his different nature and participates in the alternative activities he offered me? Maybe she's happy with it? I hope so. My tenderhearted friend deserves the kind of love that doesn't judge his humanity.

Papa will always be obsessed with Countee's gift. Even now, he gushes over his former son-in-law, and they still correspond on various matters. Countee is well respected and teaches in Harlem, as does Harold, who is content to be a bachelor and still wears the crown of handsomest man in town.

I don't spend much time in Harlem anymore. My world is in Baltimore with Du Bois. Harlem holds too many ghosts, too many sad memories for me. In Baltimore I have my students and my daughter—the joys of my life.

"Just a little while longer, and I promise you can get a hamburger and a malted. How's that sound?" I ask Du Bois when she won't stop fidgeting.

"Well, that sounds divine."

Then Du Bois's endless stream of demands fades from importance because I hear his voice. His laughter. My heart seizes, weakening my knees and my resolve. But my feet move me in the direction of the sound. Du Bois must scramble to keep up.

He bursts into the backstage area first, with his band members in tow. The only one I recognize is Andy, his old friend.

Jimmie doesn't see me, giving me time to take him in. His saxophone is slung casually across his chest while he talks about the high points of the show, waving his arms passionately. That part about him has not changed, even if he's aged some. But his mature look and slightly receding hairline have only made him more handsome and desirable.

My hand goes to my tummy where the leftover weight from my pregnancy still sits. I wonder what he'll think of my maturation. I am not sure if my changes are marked improvements.

It was a mistake coming here.

Then, Du Bois races past me and right up to the band. She stops in front of Jimmie, and he nearly trips over her as she stands legs akimbo, glaring up at him.

"Are you my mama's friend?" she demands to know. "We've been waiting forever for you to show up."

Jimmie stares down at her with an amused grin on his face.

"Who is your mama?" he asks.

She turns to point at me, and I feel exposed. There's no turning back now.

Jimmie's gaze follows Du Bois's chubby hand as she raises it to point in my direction. When Jimmie's eyes rest on me, he takes in a deep breath that his entire body seems to exhale. His arms drop to his sides, leaving the saxophone hanging only by the strap around his neck.

"Yolande."

He only utters one word, yet I tremble at the sound of his voice. My Jimmie. He is mine still, no matter how many years have passed, no matter who we belong to in court documents.

Nothing can keep my Jimmie from closing the space between us. In four steps we are standing face-to-face, both of us unsure of what comes next.

I see the wedding band on his finger and wonder if he notices the lack of one on mine. Words escape me, but I am determined not to lose this moment.

In one swift motion, Jimmie lifts the saxophone over his head and gently sets it on a table, then not-so-gently pulls me into his arms. His embrace feels desperate and urgent. I'm sure mine is the same. Our bodies meld close enough for me to feel the rhythm of his heart beating. It's racing like the drums in one of Jimmie's upbeat swing compositions.

Or like the pace of our love. Fast, fleeting, yet unforgettable.

When he releases me, both our eyes are moist, though he's only said one word. And my voice has left me for the moment. It takes everything I have to hold my knees in place and not faint. There isn't anything left for speaking.

Jimmie's hand traces the circle of my face, like he's seeing me for the first time and trying to remember my features.

"You're here," Jimmie says. "In Baltimore."

I wonder if he's looked for me elsewhere. Wonder if he's looked for me at all, thought of me. Dreamed of me.

Du Bois's short strides allow her to finally reach us a moment later, and she wedges herself in the small space left between us after our hug.

"So, you are my mama's friend," Du Bois says, her voice breaking the moment's spell. "How does she know a famous jazzman?"

Jimmie beams down at Du Bois. "Why, your mama is one of my dearest friends. She's the reason I'm a famous jazzman."

"That's not true," I say, finally finding words. "Mr. Lunceford was already a gifted jazz player when I met him in Harlem."

Jimmie picks up his saxophone and kneels to bring himself to Du Bois's height. Her chubby hands greedily finger the keys. I gasp and reach out to stop her from touching the instrument, but Jimmie smiles and shakes his head.

"I was playing already," Jimmie says. "But your mama took me to a famous Wishing Tree in Harlem. It helps make people famous."

"And you made a wish there?" Du Bois asks.

"We did."

"And it worked!" Du Bois exclaims. "You have a whole band. That tree is magical. Mama, take me to the magic tree."

"The magic is for entertainers, Du Bois. It doesn't seem to work for other things," I say, blinking rapidly to keep from bursting into tears at my loss.

"It works for other things too," Jimmie says, his eyes fixed on Du Bois. "The tree has forever magic."

Jimmie looks up at me, a tear rolling down one cheek.

"She should be mine," he says.

Even if I wanted to seem unaffected, my own rushing tears tell a different story. I smile sadly as Jimmie stands and takes my hand.

"She should be mine," he repeats, perhaps to let me know the sentiment is real.

But then Chrystal, no longer just Tulli, but now Lunceford, rushes backstage. I quickly wipe my tears with the back of my hand. I cannot let her see me broken. It would give her too much pleasure. She already has my Jimmie, why should she have my dignity?

Jimmie does not wipe his tear, however.

"Jimmie, we must hurry," she says in a flurry of words. "Geraldyn Dismond is going to interview you for a special article, and then we're special guests at a late-night Hattie's throwing at a private club in downtown Baltimore. You know how she is about her par—"

Chrystal's demeanor abruptly changes when she sees me and Du Bois. She narrows her eyes, balls her hands into fists, and glares. First at my baby, then at me, and finally at Jimmie.

"Look. Yolande has come to visit," Jimmie says, oblivious to Chrystal's fury. "Isn't it good to see her?"

"I read in the newspaper that you had remarried," Chrystal says without a greeting. Without friendliness.

"I did remarry," I say, leaving out that I am now divorced from Du Bois's father. That fact had not made the newspaper columns.

"Remarried and with a child. She's precious." Chrystal's sharp tone does not match her compliment.

"Isn't she?" Jimmie says. "She looks just like you, Yolande. And she is spirited like you as well."

"What do you mean by *spirited*?" Du Bois asks, probably not too keen on an unfamiliar word being used to describe her.

"Oh, I just mean you're curious and you like to get right to the point," Jimmie says as he tilts Du Bois's face upward as if to get another look.

Chrystal snatches Jimmie's hand, the one touching Du Bois, and clasps it tightly. "We must be going," she chides. "Yolande, it was good seeing you."

"Don't be a stranger," Jimmie says. "We live in Harlem now. Right on Edgecombe near where you used to live with your parents."

Jimmie and Chrystal live at 409 Edgecombe—the most chic address in Harlem. Margaret told me, a year ago, when she and Charles moved into the apartment upstairs from them. She says they throw some wild parties, with loud music, plenty of liquor, and loose women. And Jimmie is the life of the parties. That doesn't sound very much like the Jimmie I know, but I'll have to take Margaret's word for it, because like I said, I stay away from Harlem these days.

If Papa knows, he must be seething to see Jimmie doing so well for himself. But I am proud of him. Even if Chrystal has the life that should be mine.

If Papa doesn't know, one day I'll have to remember to tell him all about it.

"Don't be a stranger," Chrystal says, repeating Jimmie's words as she pulls him farther from me and Du Bois.

Her eyes say the opposite.

I know that I will comply with her wishes, though I wish I had hugged Jimmie longer, and inhaled his familiar scent a few seconds more.

I will be a stranger, and I won't seek him out. Maybe he'll find joy without me. I whisper a wish into the air that he does just that, if he hasn't already.

But if upon searching, he does not find happiness and comes looking for me, I will never turn him away. I could never turn him away.

I watch Jimmie, his wife, and the band members leave, feeling frozen in time. Until Du Bois taps my arm.

"He seems nice, Mama," she says.

"He is."

"Can we get the hamburger and malted now? I was good, wasn't I? And patient?"

"Yes, my dear, you were both," I say with a smile. "Let's go have your treat now."

Du Bois chooses this moment to hug me tightly around my waist. Her chubby arms enrapture and strengthen me. Her touch keeps me upright when my knees want to give way.

She is the joy I have left. Her brilliance is evidence that I have some talent inside me. Perhaps now Papa believes that too.

Even though Miss Fauset once told me to never trust my heart, I trust it now. And I trust wishes made under wishing trees in the most magical place in the world.

Harlem.

Author's Note

I cannot believe I am at the end of this story! It has been a wonderful ride!

I started the research for this book in the spring of 2023, when I stayed in Harlem for three weeks. I went to the Schomburg Center every day it was open, squinting to read Countee Cullen's letters on microfiche. On the days the center wasn't open, I walked all over Harlem taking photos of landmarks. That was the foundation of my research.

There were other huge treasure troves of letters and documents too. The two biggest finds were the online W.E.B. Du Bois Papers with the University of Massachusetts and the online Countee Cullen Collection from the Beinecke Rare Book and Manuscript Library at Yale. These letters helped me piece together timelines of relationships and really get into the speech cadences of my characters.

The story I thought I was writing was a simple one. A very domineering father, W.E.B. Du Bois, orchestrates the marriage of his daughter, Yolande, to Harlem Renaissance poetry prodigy Countee Cullen. Yolande finds out on the honeymoon he's attracted to men, they divorce, the end. Of course, I would give lots of history, good juicy Harlem flair, and we'd have a great story about a lesser-known historical figure.

But then along came James Melvin Lunceford. Jimmie, aka Piggie. The love of Yolande's life. He nearly jumped out of Yolande's letters to her father, waiting to be a part of this story. From W.E.B.'s comment about Jimmie in a letter, "I am not taking him too seriously," I knew I should be taking him seriously!

According to W.E.B. Du Bois's biographer David Levering Lewis, Jimmie was Yolande's "enduring passion, the man about whom she would spend much of her life dreaming, wondering how different things could have been if they had married." He even speculates that the two continued meeting up for trysts until Jimmie's untimely death in 1947 at the age of forty-five.

But once I discovered Jimmie, I knew he had to be in the novel. The conundrum I faced is the one that I think comes with every historical fiction novel—where does it begin? Since I knew I wanted to center the book around Yolande and Jimmie's star-crossed love, I chose to begin with their origin story. And at first, I thought they met at Fisk.

But then I found an image online from one of Yolande's scrapbooks, and there was a birthday note from Jimmie that was dated a year before he arrived at Fisk. It made me wonder if they could have met before or if my research was wrong. Because they were teenagers. Jimmie lived in Denver, Colorado, and Yolande was in Brooklyn, New York. How would their paths have crossed?

I discovered that Jimmie was in Harlem with Mr. Morrison's Jazz Orchestra in April 1920 for a jazz recording and a six-week engagement at the Carlton Terrace. It was the same spring Yolande was graduating from the Brooklyn Girls' High School. Meet-cute, anyone?

So, this is how I figured out where to start it.

I enjoyed having Yolande and Jimmie fall in love against the backdrop of 1920s Harlem. The Tree of Hope (Wishing Tree) was their North Star when things went awry and the symbol of the magic of youth and innocence that fades sometimes when we're older.

Then, I also had a blast with them at Fisk University. My editor, Rachel, thinks it feels like *A Different World*, 1920s style. I like that. So are Yolande and Jimmie, Whitley and Dwayne? Ha! Speaking of drama, Miss Chrystal Rose Tulli did attend Fisk with Yolande and Jimmie and eventually became Jimmie's wife. There was a funny line about Chrystal in Yolande's diary that made me create their entire conflict. Yolande commented on Chrystal's hair, and that was before Jimmie made it to Fisk. I thought . . . oh boy . . . this is going to be juicy.

The biggest conflict of the novel is between Yolande and her father—Papa, as she called him. W.E.B. Du Bois was both doting and controlling. Yolande was both spoiled and sheltered, being the rainbow child after her parents lost their first baby, a son named Burghardt. Her mother, Nina, was overly concerned with every detail of Yolande's care.

The letters between father and daughter were enlightening as to their relationship dynamic and the choices Yolande made. She spent her entire life trying to please her father, and often not feeling good enough. There is a photo in one of her scrapbooks of her father, with a doodle next to it that says, "To be worthy."

But there was also much love and encouragement between father and daughter as well. Sweet words sent on holidays and birthdays. Excited recollections of parties and events. There is a fun letter from W.E.B. to Yolande recalling an anniversary party given for him and his wife, Nina, by the literary editor of *The Crisis* and rumored mistress Jessie Redmon Fauset that I found fascinating.

It made me wonder if Yolande had heard rumors of the affair and if she'd asked her papa about them, and if he was trying to do damage control. But it also made me think that Miss Fauset was a fixture in their lives, because I also had letters from Miss Fauset to Yolande at Fisk. Since Yolande interned at *The Crisis* and had many pieces in *The Brownies' Book* as well, I thought it made sense for Miss Fauset to be a mentor for her, someone she might admire. A young woman like Yolande would look at a chic, single career woman like Jessie Redmon Fauset as someone she'd like to emulate. Especially as opposed to her mother, Nina, who stayed around the home and took care of her.

But we also had to get to Countee and the wedding, which is the second half of the book.

I got the idea of friend-zoning Countee from reading scores of letters from Yolande to Countee from 1923 to 1929. They're online, so have fun trying to read Yolande's terrible cursive. Your eyes will adjust. But from the moment they met, they had a friendship and what seemed like a one-sided attraction. Yolande constantly apologized for not reciprocating Countee's affections or believing she'd realize too late that he was the right man.

I did not have Countee's letters to Yolande, but I did have his letters to other people about Yolande. He told Miss Jessie Redmon Fauset that he was happy to meet her. He told his best friend, Harold Jackman, that she was the solution to his problem. He also disparaged Yolande's looks to Harold, which I found hilarious, because it wasn't like Countee was a fashion model himself.

But there was certainly a friendship and at times a flirtatious vibe between the two of them, so when people say they had an arranged marriage, I don't think it was that simple. W.E.B. Du Bois certainly was in full support of his daughter marrying Countee and was against her marrying Jimmie. But Countee may not have been W.E.B.'s first choice for his daughter, either. A few months before the engagement between Yolande and Countee was announced, there is a letter from W.E.B. to a friend of his, bragging about another young man who Yolande was briefly engaged to, Felton Clark.

Yolande met and dated Felton while she attended Columbia University for her postgraduate studies. I almost left Felton out of the book entirely because there were just too many boys in Yolande's life. But I found a way to include him without going too deep into their relationship, which was short-lived.

One rumor I frequently saw online initially when googling this subject matter was that Countee and his best man, Harold Jackman, were lovers. This was the "tea" of the day; a story in the *Baltimore*

Afro-American reported that Countee went to Paris with Harold after the wedding, as if they were going on a honeymoon. I couldn't find concrete evidence of a sexual relationship between them during the time period I researched (1920–1932). I only saw evidence in their letters of friendship and brotherhood. Of course, they could've burned the steamy letters, and the curator of one set of letters I reviewed was Harold Jackman himself, so if he wanted to weed out the letters with evidence of a sexual relationship, he had the opportunity to do so.

That being said, I was not looking to erase a love story between Countee and Harold, if there was one. On the contrary, I was looking for evidence to confirm it. But even though the letters I read from Harold to Countee didn't necessarily say "lovers," they certainly gave me a feel of the queer side of Harlem. There is one letter from Harold to Countee, who was in Paris, that describes a Hamilton Drag Ball in Harlem. The descriptions are so vivid and colorful, and I really need to read a novel about the exploits of Harold Jackman, the handsomest man in Harlem.

Yolande, though, was truly the "it" girl of the Harlem Renaissance. If there was a Lori Harvey of the day, it would've been Yolande. Her comings and goings were constant fodder for the newspapers in Harlem, Baltimore, Pittsburgh, Washington, D.C., and Chicago. Even the day she crossed over into Delta Sigma Theta Sorority was mentioned in the newspaper. Anywhere there were significant numbers of Black folks, talk about Yolande's dating habits and the parties she was going to surfaced. So, when she finally got married at the age of twenty-seven it was a big to-do and an even bigger deal when she divorced.

The details of Yolande and Countee's wedding were publicized everywhere, including a four-page spread that W.E.B. Du Bois ran in *The Crisis* magazine.

I used one article in the *Baltimore Afro-American* about Yolande and Countee's divorce to construct the chapter that was a sit-down interview with the society columnist of the day, Geraldyn Dismond. I'm not sure if the interview was given to Geraldyn, but she ran the society pages of all the Black newspapers in the 1920s, so in this book, it made sense to say that the interview was with Geraldyn herself.

In the epilogue, I caught up with our characters about six years after the events in the meat of the novel. Jimmie Lunceford became one of the great jazz musicians of his time. Countee did remarry, to a woman named Ida, and also dies very young, at the age of forty-two.

Our fair protagonist, Yolande, went on to have a long teaching career in Baltimore Public Schools. About midway through my research, I discovered evidence of eight scrapbooks of Yolande's, found in a storage unit on the Gulf Coast. I happened to see photos of one of them on Reddit, because the person who had them was trying to sell them. Well, I wanted those scrapbooks. To at least see them. I reached out to the Reddit poster, but they never responded.

However, the photos were enough to excite me. That's where I saw the note from Jimmie that preceded his time at Fisk! Anyway, those scrapbooks were acquired last year by the University of Massachusetts, and I was able to go and look at them in person. Seeing Yolande's doodles, thoughts, and dreams for the future made me feel like we were old friends. It really helped shape the narrative that I crafted in this novel, and although it is fiction, I hope that she would love it and be proud of the choices I made for her in the story.

These characters are going to stick with me for a long time. I hope they stay with you too.

Acknowledgments

There are so many people to thank for helping to get this novel across the finish line. But I think it all started with FOCAS/SCOPE Elementary School in East Cleveland, Ohio, when I was in maybe third or fourth grade and learned a poem called "Booker T. and W.E.B." by Dudley Randall for Black History Month. I had to learn the part of W.E.B. Du Bois, and we recited the parts as if we were debating.

Learning that poem planted the seed that made Dr. Du Bois's life, and, by extension, Yolande's life, intriguing to me. Hearing about an arranged marriage added fuel to the flame.

So, first, I'd like to thank my wonderful educators at FOCAS/SCOPE Elementary School.

Brent, thank you for your patience, as always. And for letting me sneak away to Harlem not once but twice for weeks at a time to sit in the Schomburg Center. And for finding your own dinner.

I have one of the best editors in the business. Rachel Kahan, thank you for your wisdom and your scalpel. And a huge thanks goes to the entire team at William Morrow. From marketing and publicity, to editorial, to contracts. Everyone! You're appreciated.

Booksellers (especially my ride-or-die indie booksellers) and librarians, how could I do this without you? I can't do it without you. And I thank you for every invite, every program planned, every event. Let's find some readers and put books in their hands!

Thank you to the author community for telling everyone way in advance about my book. No one has to share my social media posts or tell their readers about my release. I promise to pay it forward. I count every repost and every share as a blessing.

Speaking of reposts and shares: to the readers, book clubs, content creators, and influencers—you all rock. Keep amplifying Black books.

If you keep reading, we'll keep writing.

Until next time,
Tiffany

About the Author

TIFFANY L. WARREN is a novelist and screenwriter who has published more than thirty novels. In addition to writing books, Tiffany has written and produced multiple musicals for the stage, as well as several book-to-film collaborations with BET.

Read more from
TIFFANY WARREN

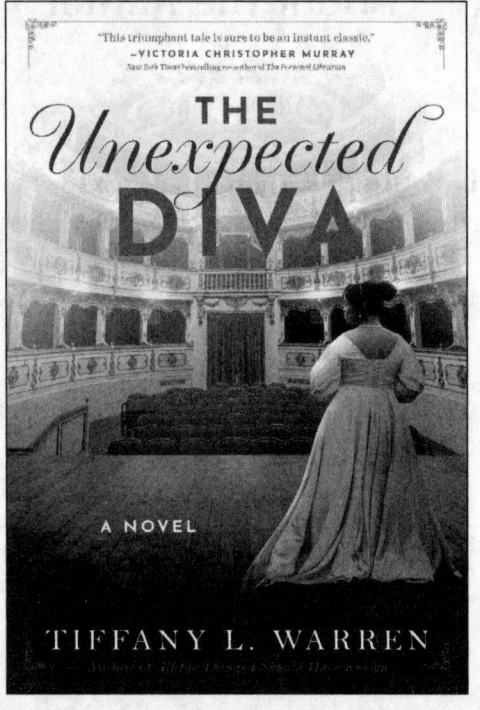

Before the Civil War, Black opera singer Elizabeth Taylor Greenfield reigned supreme on Northern stages—even performing at Buckingham Palace. Novelist Tiffany L. Warren brings this remarkable but forgotten diva's story to life for modern readers.

"How do we not all know the name of Elizabeth Taylor Greenfield? The story of this brilliant, three-octave-range singer—a Black woman born a slave who performed for queens and the luminaries of her day on both sides of the Atlantic in the years before and during the Civil War—is finally given its just due. The fact that Greenfield used her singular platform to take a stand against racism makes her tale all the more remarkable, especially in Warren's talented hands."

—Marie Bendict,
New York Times bestselling author of *The First Ladies*